GRILLING A SUSPECT

"Listen, ah . . . Tom. There's something I'd like to ask you."

He grinned and tossed the paper towel on the counter. "Bet I can guess what it is."

"You can?"

"Sure. And the answer is yes. I'd love to go to bed with you."

"I beg your pardon?"

"That's okay, Ellie." The grin widened. "You don't have to beg. I find you very attractive. You're a terrific looking woman for your age."

I didn't know whether to laugh or slap the young whippersnapper. Even if my ruse had been rather weak, surely, he didn't think my cordial, almost motherly interest in him all this time had been a come-on. Thank you, *bubbe*. That was not the inspiration I had in mind. The Mata Hari approach to worming confessions from men might be more successful with Tom than it had been with the D.A., but I wasn't prepared to make that big a sacrifice.

Checking to be sure the top button of my housecoat was securely fastened, I attempted to clear up Tom's misunderstanding. Only my vanity suffered when he showed just moderate disappointment . . .

Also by Karin Berne

Bare Acquaintances

Published by
POPULAR LIBRARY

ATTENTION: SCHOOLS AND CORPORATIONS

POPULAR LIBRARY books are available at quantity discounts with bulk purchase for educational, business, or sales promotional use. For information, please write to SPECIAL SALES DEPARTMENT, POPULAR LIBRARY, 666 FIFTH AVENUE, NEW YORK, N Y 10103

**ARE THERE POPULAR LIBRARY BOOKS
YOU WANT BUT CANNOT FIND IN YOUR LOCAL STORES?**

You can get any POPULAR LIBRARY title in print. Simply send title and retail price, plus 50¢ per order and 50¢ per copy to cover mailing and handling costs for each book desired. New York State and California residents add applicable sales tax. Enclose check or money order only, no cash please, to POPULAR LIBRARY, P. O. BOX 690, NEW YORK, N Y 10019

SHOCK VALUE

A MYSTERY BY

KARIN BERNE

POPULAR LIBRARY

An Imprint of Warner Books, Inc.

A Warner Communications Company

The characters and events described in this book are entirely fictitious. Any resemblance to any actual person or event is pure coincidence.

POPULAR LIBRARY EDITION

Popular Library® is a registered trademark of Warner Books, Inc.

Popular Library books are published by
Warner Books, Inc.
666 Fifth Avenue
New York, N.Y. 10103

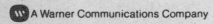 A Warner Communications Company

Printed in the United States of America

First Printing: October, 1985

10 9 8 7 6 5 4 3 2 1

To Shlomo

Acknowledgments

Our special thanks to Shlomo Karni, Gordon Bernell, David Rusk, Michael Hanrahan, Diane Chodorow, Marcia Cohen, Roberta Espinosa, Joseph Gutierrez, Mary Virginia Jones, and John Shaver.

Chapter One

"I say aerobics was invented by an ex-Nazi SS officer turned health freak."

"And I say if you moved your body as much as your mouth, that five pounds you're trying to shed would come off in two days."

In the process of tugging leotards over hips that were still two inches from ideal, even after months of working out, I threw my pal Betsy a dirty look. "It's easy for you to say. Women who are seven feet tall never have enough meat to cover their bones. It's indecent."

"I'll try to blush."

"Don't force yourself for my sake," I grumbled. "But if I were as tall as you, I'd be perfectly proportioned, and you'd look like a scarecrow next to me."

Dressed in my designer-label exercise outfit, as if *haute couture* were any help in fighting a rear-guard action against the effects of time and gravity, I was about to go sweat off some cellulite when another latecomer came bursting through the door.

"I'm going to kill my boss."

Having delivered that threat, Lois McCoin stalked through the pink and white dressing room of Casa Grande's most exclusive health club and slammed her gym bag on an innocent, vinyl-covered bench. "You've heard of justifiable homicide," she snorted, kicking off her black leather pumps. "Well, this would be it. He's a lying son of bitch and I'm so furious I can't see straight."

Apparently not. She pulled off her seventy-five-dollar silk blouse, tossed it on the floor, then proceeded to step on it. I waited until she moved her foot, then picked up the blouse and hung it in her locker. "Mad at Prescott again, are you?"

"Not just mad, Ellie; boiling, raging. When you hear what that fucking bastard has done to me now, you won't believe it."

Oh, yes, I would. For the dignified Lois to resort to the F-word, as she called it, there must be plenty of static at the electric company.

From the other corner of the room, Betsy offered a sympathetic ear. "You don't have to spare our sensitivities. What did the Drake Prescott do now? Take credit for another one of your good ideas?"

"I'm used to that kind of crap. This time he's undermined me completely." Grimly and methodically, she rolled her tights into a neat square before slipping the two ends over her clenched toes. But then she started yanking furiously, as if the varicose vein on the back of her left leg were no more important than a silk blouse. "Before I left the office just now, Drake's secretary showed me the memo he wrote to the powers that be, supposedly recommending me for the promotion I told you about. But that two-faced bastard gave me a no-vote after swearing he'd praise me to the skies. I'm perfectly capable for some department in Public Service of Southern California, but he doesn't feel a woman would 'interface effectively with the hard hats who work in the actual operations area of energy production,' quote unquote," she finished bitterly.

I opened my mouth to make a pithy comment on the small minds of small men, but decided not to add any fire to her rage. There was no love lost between Lois and her thorn-in-the-side supervisor anyway. She'd been complaining about him for months, ever since he was named the head of public relations. Given the state of their internal relations, why he promised to recommend her for anything was almost as surprising as why she believed him. But when PSSC opened their new nuclear power plant, Lois wanted to be communications coordinator. Expecting a pat on the head from Prescott might be wishful thinking, or maybe hope really does spring eternal.

"You know why he wants me to stay where I am," Lois went on in a tight voice. "So I can continue to be his errand girl while he continues to get the title, salary, and kudos. Forget that I'm one of the top contenders for the job at Canyon Escondido. Forget that after twenty-five years with the company, I'm overqualified to take it. Thanks to Drake Prescott, the only move I'll ever make again is out the door when I retire."

"Are you sure the company will place so much importance on his recommendation?" Betsy asked.

"He's my department head. Who else should they check with, my mother?"

"Look here, Lois. If you really think Prescott can cost you that job, do something about him. Go back to his secretary, get a copy of that memo, then march yourself to Equal Employment Opportunity Commission. In case you haven't heard, it's illegal to insult women in writing nowadays."

"I know you work for a law firm, Ellie, but I work in pr and I can guarantee you the power company wouldn't appreciate the publicity of my hauling one of their executives in front of the EEOC."

"They can't fire you for doing it."

"No, but they can play freeze-out. 'Oh, Lois,'" she mimicked harshly, "'so sorry you didn't get the notice about this morning's meeting. We missed you.' And if I complained that information was purposely being withheld, they'd say I was a vindictive old biddy trying to cover my own incompetence by blaming everyone else."

"So quit. Get another job."

"And miss the grand opening of Canyon Escondido," she said with a bitter smile. "Remember, I'm in charge of serving guacamole dip and California champagne to the press at tomorrow's reception."

Though Lois rejected all my advice, I refrained from suggesting what she could do with the dip. Still, it was unfair that the woman who wrote the glossy brochure touting the state's newest and safest nuclear power plant should have been sentenced to KP duty during the great unveiling. Even if Drake Prescott thought females belonged under apron and mobcap, surely some of the company bigwigs knew better. All she had to do was bring it to their attention.

"Why don't you talk to Helen?" I pressed.

Lois thought about that for a moment. "Is she here?"

Regretfully, I had to tell her that the fantastically busy, fantastically efficient Helen Ramirez was up to her lovely ears preparing for a pretrial hearing and couldn't manage an hour off to exercise her fantastic body. I offered to speak to her this afternoon when I got back to the office, but Lois put up her defenses again. No lawyers, no suits.

"Let's go work out, shall we? Just talking to both of you has made me feel human again." She thumped me on the rear. "You still trying to trim those hips, Ellie? Then get moving. If no one wants you when you're old and gray"— she patted the carefully coiffed bleached blond curls she'd worn for donkey's years—"it goes double for fat and sloppy."

To avoid that fate, the three of us ran downstairs to the aerobics class before the last beat of New Wave rock crashed into silence. We caught the final fifteen minutes, then went our own ways to sauna, weight machines, and flotation tank. Membership in the Sports and Sorts Spa entitled everyone to wait in line for the exercise equipment of her choice; and since half the working population of downtown Casa Grande made it a daily ritual to spend their lunch hours getting slimmer, trimmer, fitter, and firmer, the conga line could wind around the building.

They had smiles on their faces. I didn't. To me, the joy of achieving physical fitness was as pleasurable as swallowing live toads. What brought me to the spa three times a week were the dire consequences of not coming. Everybody has to look like a model these days. Embonpoint is admired only on a Reuben's painting, not on you, even if you could have posed for it. So I joined the crowd and took a dose of bitter medicine. And bitter it was. After a half-hour on the Nautilus machines, my abused body could have been measured on a scale that went from I'D RATHER EAT CAKE to LET ME DIE IN PEACE. But underneath all my protests about acrobatic storm troopers making me stretch my sinews to a disco beat, I didn't want to be fat. I was fat once and not at all jolly. In the gruesome months following my divorce, I wallowed in food and self-pity, making Big Macs and a double order of fries my answer to every unfair evil in an unfair world. It was Betsy who beat me over the head with a frozen pizza until I came to my senses. Even so, transforming a pigged-out, displaced homemaker into a slender career woman was no easy task. Converting a Jewish princess into a Trappist monk would have taken less remodeling; a flowing robe was all that fit me anyway. But after months of effort and the wonders wrought by diet, Clairol, and renewed self-confidence, what emerged from the corpulent cocoon was a bouncing baby butterfly, with wash-and-wear brown curls and a size-eight-petite wardrobe. Sure, the new Ellie Gordon was a vast improvement over the old, unmodified munchkin. That still didn't mean I enjoyed fighting a crusade against calories, but like a brave soldier, I kept my *kvetching* down to a dull whine.

Much refreshed after two laps across the pool, I got

dressed and met Betsy in the spa's tastefully decorated cafe for a quick and not-so-tasty lunch of bean sprout salad and carrot juice. To con the members into eating this rabbit food, the snack bar was designed to overlook the three glass-enclosed raquet ball courts so patrons dining *de rigueur* could see the slenderizing effects of healthy living.

I stared down at my unappetizing lunch and thought wistfully about sneaking away for a hot fudge sundae. "Depressing, isn't it?"

"What's depressing, the slop on your plate or Lois's problem?"

I threw Betsy a reproachful glance. "You're the one who recommended this salad."

"You're the one on a diet."

Since I couldn't deny the simple truth, I sank to self-pity. "Do you realize that the starving would be grateful for the 'too, too solid flesh' I'm trying to melt off?"

"So donate your excess to the Poverty Relief Agency. Maybe they'll let you claim the loss as a tax deduction."

"I tried that last year but it didn't work. And speaking of work, what do you think Lois will do about Drake Prescott? You know how much she wants that job. Yet she's afraid to make waves. When I saw her in the sauna just now, she was lying there like a limp dishrag."

"Dry heat is known to produce that effect."

"Scoff all you want, but I think she's going to let Prescott get away with his trick."

"If he gets away with it, Ellie," my friend remarked perceptively, "it will only be because those on the receiving end of that memo think in the same manner."

"I can't believe the whole company discriminates against women, but if it turns out they do, we'll just get Fifth and Shoreside to raise the roof. It's a women's support network, and for Lois's sake, I'm sure we can get them to show disapproval *en masse*."

"How?"

"I don't know." I waved my hand airily. "Maybe get all

our members to shut off their electricity for twenty-four hours in protest."

"And survive without blow-dryers for a day?" Betsy raised a brow at me. "Forget it. Besides, no utility company cares if people decide to live in the dark. They'd just raise their rates to cover the loss."

"Then I'd really picket."

"Did I her the word 'picket'?" Jessica Tobler slid into the seat next to me. "I can't believe you two nonpartisan types would do such a radical thing. Who's the enemy?"

"The public service company," I informed her.

"Count me in," Jessica offered promptly. "And if we rally enough people, we can have that nuke plant closed before it ever opens."

"You're way off base, Jess," Betsy said tartly. "We are not planning an antinuke protest, much as that might disappoint you. Ellie is just speculating about a war that hasn't even been declared yet. The power company's one and only nuclear reactor is not our concern."

"Well, it should be," Jessica flashed at her. "PSSC doesn't need an alternate energy source. They've got enough coal to keep California smoggy for the next hundred years."

This was a longstanding argument between them and one from which I steered clear. First of all, these two articulate spokeswomen never let me get a word in edgewise; and secondly, they would have hooted me down if I dared express an opinion anyway. What did an office manager know in comparison to two scientific geniuses who could hardly agree on a single issue? Naturally enough, since Betsy Hanson was a consulting engineer at the Canyon Escondido plant, she didn't see anything wrong with nuclear energy. But Jessica, who taught physics in one of the smaller colleges nearby, directed an antinuke group called ANSWER. This clever acronym stood for Adequate Nuclear Safety Will Eliminate Risk. Of course, in Jessica's considered opinion, the risk would be adequately eliminated when every nuclear reactor in the country was shut down until all the waste disposal problems were solved. Betsy accused her of suffering the I Don't Want It Buried In My Backyard Syndrome, to which Jess countered, "How about burying it in yours?"

When I finally got to explain the hypothetical battle lines I'd drawn to combat hypothetical labor practices at PSSC, Jess complimented my instincts.

"Why, Ellie Gordon, I didn't know you were such a rabble-rouser." She tucked a strand of shoulder-length auburn hair behind one ear and shook her head at me. "When you went to Stanford in the sixties, were you one of the student insurgents who tried to burn down the administration building?"

"That happened at Berkeley."

"So why didn't you transfer?"

To the twenty-eight-year-old Jessica Tobler, who came along after all dissident fires were banked, those embers of past flames shone like a beacon of light. Public protest got us out of Viet Nam, didn't it? Then wouldn't stirring things up with mass arrests and screaming headlines halt nuclear development? A feature story in *Time* magazine was her aim, and I thought she'd look great on the cover. Not many activist college professors were so fetching in tweed jacket and faded jeans.

"Ellie's not serious about staging a protest," Betsy advised her. "The only demonstration she ever saw was at the shopping center when they showed how to chop cabbage with a food processor. With that limited experience, I promise she's not going to march on PSSC headquarters. Unless, the company's handing out free samples of coleslaw."

"I'd walk a mile for a decent meal."

Betsy smiled. "Have some more sprouts."

I offered them to Jess instead, but she was busy planning how to turn our single professional women's club into an army of feminist foot soldiers. Not that she really could.

When it came time to vote, twenty percent of the members would be gung-ho for Jess's wildest schemes. Twenty percent would cautiously endorse anything else, while the rest would clamor for a party. After all, that was our *raison d'etre*. Besides giving each other TLC and good advice, our greatest joint effort was what I fondly called The Nice But Horny Woman's Haven After She's Had It With The Mad World of Singles' Bars.

On the third Thursday of each month, the Fifth and Shoreside Club held a cocktail party in the quietly elegant dining room of Campi's Neptune Inn. The restaurant was located on the corner of Fifth Street and Shoreside, the inspiration for the club's dignified and understated name. Attendance was by invitation only, and the gilded card only went to eligible males who were personally known by one of the members. This kept it clean, and neat, and informal. The men loved it. So did the women. Not trying to catch an eye across a crowded barroom and no adult versions of that teenage torture, the blind date. Here people met socially for a couple of hours, arriving alone and leaving alone. They could meet outside and exchange business cards, which apparently happened often. In the past year the success rate of our parties included three weddings and discreetly untold meaningful relationships.

Not that everyone wanted meaning. For some people an occasional dinner out was commitment enough.

Those looking for permanence usually were the women who had spent the swiftly passing decades getting an education and advancing their fabulous careers. Now, when they finally took the time to look around for a compatible male to brighten their lives, they also found that time had taken its toll on the quota of single men of the appropriate age or status. Of course, if these dynamic damsels had studied something as impractical as English Lit as I had, they wouldn't have been suffering the lonely rigors of a successful, all-consuming vocation.

If that sounded slightly envious, then I understated my

feelings. What I really felt was a wild jealousy that these pragmatic ladies had the foresight to plan ahead. I, on the other hand, went to college just so that I could hold an intelligent conversation after I was married. Does that seem the brilliant thinking of a Shakespearean scholar? Certainly. We all have "that glib and oily art to speak and purpose not." My first rude awakening was the discovery that I was not usually called upon to sound terribly intellectual while scrubbing the toilet bowl. But even more disappointing, at the dinner parties where I planned to wax poetic for my guests' edification and entertainment, that particular accomplishment was about as much in demand as an impromptu thesis on iambic pentameter. Eighteen years later, I learned another sad truth: getting married did not guarantee staying married. Only herpes is forever, as my son tells me.

So the middle age of my life, a terribly young thirty-eight, found me busy working at a job that had nothing to do with Shakespeare but had the merit of paying the rent. In addition, I'd even joined a singles sorority that played matchmaker for fifty-two women who were all searching for a right-around-the-corner, just-over-the-rainbow Mr. Wonderful. If being an office manager in the prestigious law firm of Abbotts, Devlin, and Devlin barely qualified me as a professional woman in an august assemblage of lady doctors, accountants, and engineers, I did share with them a hopeful belief in fairy-tale endings. My standards weren't so exacting either. All I asked was that a man be reasonably healthy, passably nice looking, and have the brains of a Rhodes scholar. How else was I going to use all my brilliant conversation?

When I brought my wandering mind back to the discussion at hand, Betsy was giving Jessica a little helpful advice.

"Harangues on feminism and politics are not appropriate at our Thursday night cocktail parties."

Jessica lifted one eyebrow. "Who said I harangued?

Look, I'm as interested in meeting men as you are, but anyone who goes out with me had better know how I stand on the issues. It's only fair. A dyed-in-the-wool John Bircher is likely to have a heart attack if I spring my views on him in bed."

"Is that what you call having scruples?"

"No, that's what I call having sex."

When they grinned at each other, it signaled the end of hostilities and the conclusion of our lunch break. Jessica stood up and slung her battered purse over her shoulder. "Time to get back to the classroom, but as long as your consciousness has been raised, Ellie, why don't you join ANSWER's protest at Canyon Escondido tomorrow? It'll make up for your going to the wrong college. I won't bother to ask you," she said, jerking her head in Betsy's direction.

"A mass protest during the grand-opening celebration?" I asked with something less than surprise. "I should have known. But what happened to lobbying in the state legislature with a million signatures on a petition?"

"That's not nearly as effective as waving flags and chaining people to fences," Betsy said dryly.

"What a great idea," Jessica smiled. "Sorry I didn't think of it myself. But I'm just glad we're going. My fatheaded second-in-command got cold feet. Would you believe Tom Grabowski says making a public display of ourselves would be undignified. But I got up on my soapbox and made an emphatic plea that good sense prevail over good taste. PSSC's reception is a heaven-sent opportunity to put on the pressure. Want to come, Ellie?"

"No thanks," I demurred. "Congressman Phillip Abbotts will be cutting the ribbon tomorrow and I don't think he'd be happy to see me carrying a sign that says, 'NOT OVER MY DEAD BODY.' He is still one of my bosses, you know. Besides, Saturday is my day to loll on the beach, paint my toenails, and go out with handsome men."

"Mark Devlin?" Jess teased.

"That's an old story," Betsy informed her. "The *meshugge* Eleanor Gordon claims he's too good a friend to be a boyfriend anymore."

"You Swedes do a lousy Yiddish accent," Jessica remarked, "but I catch the drift. She's crazy all right, except that opens the field for me now."

"On second thought"—Betsy watched me closely—"if you do make a play for the estimable counselor, she might just scratch your eyes out."

"Only the left one," I amended with more truth than humor.

When Jess dashed off with a laugh, Betsy probed my comment. "I wondered if you were still carrying a torch under the publicly banked fires."

"I'm not. The flame has dwindled to a fond flicker, don't worry. But it's time for me to get moving too." I pushed my plate away. "First to the county clerk's office to file a motion, then to pick up an interrogatory for the much-sought-after Mr. Devlin. There may be no romance left between us, but we have a wonderful working relationship. He's the boss and I'm the go-fer."

Betsy put a restraining hand on my wrist. "You aren't going anywhere until you tell me who's the handsome date for Saturday night."

My answer was short and smug. "The Fifth and Shore-side Club has done it again."

"Not the D.A.? Joe Corelli?" She was delighted. "I saw the two of you with your heads together last night, but I thought you were talking shop. Torts, felonies, murders, and the like."

"What a nasty mind you have. The besotted look on our faces was because we discovered a kindred fascination for foreign movies, grand opera, and walking barefoot on the beach. Our eyes are even the same shade of brown." I winked one of mine.

"No matching of astrological signs? Of course, you

didn't forget to tell him that you're available whenever he and the police are stumped in their never-ending fight against crime."

I was used to being teased about my role in solving the sad and frightening business of Katherine Busch's murder, though there was nothing remotely amusing in finding someone strangled or suspecting that you might be the next victim. "Will you forget that episode? It was just a fluke," I scoffed, "and certainly no way to impress the D.A. with my intellect and *je ne sais quoi*."

"Hmm," Betsy murmured thoughtfully. "You're a pretty devious character. Somehow I find it slightly unbelievable that you'd cultivate the interest of Joe Corelli without using him as a source to practice your rare talent."

"You can't possibly think I want to make a habit of catching killers."

"It's instinct, Ellie, my friend. You'll never be able to keep your nose out of things if a suitable mystery presents itself."

"So you're calling me a busybody. All right, I'll prove you wrong. If you promise never to recommend another health food salad to me again as long as you live, I will refrain from solving the next murder that comes my way. A deal?"

"You're on, but I predict you'll be eating bean sprouts within a month."

Chapter Two

Contrary to Betsy's expectations, I did not ask Joe Corelli to let me browse through his unsolved case files so I could exercise my bent for smelling out a mystery. First of all, by the time a case got to the district attorney's office, it was fairly well resolved and on its way to court. Secondly, the only criminal offense committed at Antonio's on Saturday night was my wicked indulgence in a dinner that started with shrimp Mario and ended with torta di Ricotta.

When I joyfully proclaimed that Joe and I had so many interests in common, I never dreamt they would include a mutual passion for food. In fact, I came close to falling in love with him on our first date out of sheer gluttony. Still, that auspicious beginning was only the appetizer in a menu that included enjoying the same books, hating the same music, and being baffled by 28 Down in last Sunday's crossword puzzle.

"Would you call a 'facetious flatfoot' a 'punstable'?" I asked with a shudder.

"No, I'd call him a 'defective' if he stooped to anything so unsporting."

"Ouch," I winced. "I think you just stepped out of bounds yourself with that one."

"Would a little more Chianti help to wash it down?"

I held out my glass, but truthfully, Joe Corelli couldn't have improved my opinion of him if he leaped tall buildings in a single bound. He had a great sense of humor, and his well-rounded education on the streets of New York had given him an intimate knowledge of art galleries, the offest of off-Broadway plays, and of course, the innest of in-restaurants.

He was also extremely attractive. Not in the classic sense of a Latin lover, but I thought he had the rugged appeal of a Venetian gondolier. Since I'd never seen a real gondolier, my comparison was might have been a little fanciful, but Joe had great shoulder muscles and he owned a boat. The rest was easy to see. His curly black hair was slightly laced with gray, and the dimple in his Dick Tracy chin was perfectly aligned with the tiny dent on the tip of his nose. Joe too seemed to like what he saw across the candlelit table. I could tell by the way he kept feeding me compliments and cannelloni, an irresistible bill of fare for someone with my appetites. He seemed particularly impressed when I claimed to have recovered from my rather recent divorce.

"Only nine months," he commented in surprise. "You certainly did recuperate quickly." As if that achievement called for a tangible sign of his admiration, he poured a large dollop of cream into my espresso before I could tell him I was on a diet. "The reason I'm surprised," he added more praise, "is because you're amazingly self-confident. Most people take a lot longer to get back to feeling secure about themselves."

I could have confessed that half my so-called assurance was mere bluff and bluster, but how much should a woman expose on a first date? If not her body, certainly not her soul. I gave him an expurgated version of my trials and tribulations, admitting that I had hidden in the house and gnashed my teeth in despair for three months but editing out the twenty pounds I'd gained in the process.

"Then Mr. Abbotts gave me a job in his law office and here I am."

"What you really mean," Joe shook his head, "is when your ex-husband traded you in for a younger woman, you turned it into the nicest rotten thing he ever did to you."

"That's an interesting analysis, but don't endow me with more strength of character than I have. What got me off my butt was desperation, not daring. 'Some are born great, some achieve greatness, and some have greatness thrust upon them,'" I quipped.

"I'd say you're all three," was his flattering response.

A lesser woman would have batted her lashes in fake modesty. I merely took it in stride. "May I have your autograph?"

Then Joe explained that as a result of his divorce, he traded his New York license for California plates. New coast, new setting, new life. The only thing he had brought with him was his boat, when had been a pain in the neck to tow overland and pointless really, since he had sold it a month later and bought a new one.

"Funny"—he gave a little laugh—"that I made the grand exodus when it was my ex-wife who wanted out so she could find herself."

"And did she?"

His smile broadened. "Yes, married to another lawyer and living in another split-level in Scarsdale."

"It would seem," I said carefully, "that the lady discovered the wisdom of Oz."

Joe looked at me blankly for a moment, then nodded in understanding. "Happiness can be found in your own backyard, you mean."

"Coincidentally, Dan has come to the same conclusion. He wants to return to the old homestead so I can wash his socks and cook him brisket every Friday night just like the good old days. I had to remind him that Ellie doesn't live there anymore. What about your Oz?" I asked. It was an important question. If Joe were still hooked on his ex-wife, I wanted to know before I started liking him too much.

The D.A. was a very perceptive man. He leaned back in his chair and said with just the assurance I wanted to hear, "I'm very happy in my new backyard. It's tough to go from family life to being single, and maybe at forty-three, I'm too old fashioned. A *patron* by instinct and training. Yet here you are, adjusting very well to life without father."

"That doesn't make you unnecessary. Far from it. How old are your children?"

"Twenty-two, twenty-one, twenty, and nineteen." He fished out his wallet and showed me their photos. "Do you have a picture of your son?"

"Will a thousand words do instead? I didn't bring my billfold. No," I held up my hand. "No more espresso. I'll cut it down to a half dozen adjectives. Michael is bright, ambitious, has brown hair, blue funks, and considers his freshman year at U.C.L.A. a good excuse to forget his mother is alive except when he needs money."

"He sounds well adjusted."

"Terribly."

Joe smiled and looked at his watch. "By the way, could we go over to your house in a little while and catch the eleven o'clock news?"

If this were his wily stratagem for worming his way into my bed, at least he was original enough to come up with a new line. "You want to watch television?" I asked suspiciously.

My face must have mirrored my doubts because Joe presented a case that would win in any court of appeals. "No, this is not a dishonorable proposal," he swore. "My hands will stay strictly on the dial that turns to Channel twelve. They filmed some of the speech I gave last night to the Civitan Club, and I want to see what didn't get edited out."

How could I deny such a respectable request? "Sure," I

agreed. "What pearls of wisdom did you lay on the Civitans?"

"I told them about the Crimewatchers program Chief Steunkle and I are promoting."

"Oh, yes. Those neighborhood associations sound like a good way to combat the public's incurable look-the-other-way-itis, but do you really think people will call in if they do happen to spot a suspicious character crawling up their next-door neighbor's drainpipe?"

"We can't put a policeman on every corner, and there is such a thing as citizen responsibility."

"True, but you can't pass a law against apathy, and there is such a thing as nobody caring if you did. Besides, if you get this program off the ground and into action, what are you going to do with all the criminals apprehended? The courts are barely keeping up with the police arrest rate now, not to mention an already overcrowded prison system."

Joe rubbed the dent in his nose. "How about if we send you to Sacramento to lobby for bigger appropriations? You're eloquent enough to convince our esteemed legislators that we need money for more prosecutors, judges, and jails."

"No thanks. I'll help with Crimewatchers instead."

"My first recruit! According to Matt Steunkle, though, you're a certified crime-solver already."

"Was the chief of police bragging about me again? Ignore him. He just likes me because I read the same mysteries he does."

"Nancy Drew?"

I hoped that in the discreet darkness of the restaurant my blush wasn't visible. "Oh, he just calls me that for fun."

"Maybe so, but I'm sure it wasn't much fun for you to be confronted by a murderer," Joe said seriously.

"Don't worry. As I just assured a friend, it will probably

never happen to me again. I'm really a craven coward at heart."

"I find that hard to believe"—he smiled—"but chasing criminals is risky business, and I'd hate to lose such a charming dinner companion after only one meal."

With the promise of further epicurean ventures as incentive, I finished every morsel on my plate to show Joe I was amenable, and the subject of my brief crime-solving career was dropped. When the last of the cognac was consumed, Joe got to his feet. "Shall we?"

On the trail of some after-dinner mints, we took a detour through the Roman villa they call a bar at Antonio's. Sitting under an arch of palm trees was Mark Devlin's nephew, Dennis. He was the youngest member of the law firm, but there was nothing juvenile about the sultry creature with him. Dennis's taste ran to extravagant brunettes with extravagant equipage, but this girl was even better endowed than I had been at my biggest, which mammarily speaking was really saying something.

"Hello, Dennis," I greeted him as he stood up politely. "You know Joe Corelli."

Dennis smiled affably and introduced us to April Evans, explaining that she was a client in need of cheering as well as legal advice.

"I hope it's nothing too serious," Joe said sympathetically.

"No, not serious, just recurring; a custody suit over my children." Then she asked if I were the same Ellie Gordon she'd heard about from Lois McCoin. "We both work in the pr Department at the power company."

"Then you must know Drake Prescott too," I couldn't resist saying.

Looking markedly less enthusiastic, she nodded and took a sip of her drink, somehow managing to spill a few drops on the front of her dress.

"Actually," Dennis amplified, watching her dab at her bosom, "April is his private secretary."

I examined her with sharpened interest. Yesterday Lois had said that it was Drake's secretary who had passed on his disparaging memo. That hardly seemed the action of a loyal girl Friday, but apparently April felt she owed no loyalty to a card-carrying MCP. Good for her. I smiled warmly and wished her luck with the custody suit.

As we wound our way through the bar and out to the parking lot, Joe murmured in my ear, "Do you think Dennis minds that you're out with me?"

"Because you're the D.A.?"

"Because you used to date his Uncle Mark."

"What a hotbed of intrigue downtown Casa Grande is. When all you lawyers aren't in court, what do you do, sit out in the hallway and gossip?"

"We call it a legal probe."

Well, I was pleading the Fifth, and if Joe thought I were the kind of woman who could breezily dance from one partner to the next without a backward glance, so much the better. How could I seem suavely sophisticated if I admitted the end of my affair with Mark Devlin had brought on sheer terror at the prospect of flying solo once again? When Mark told me it was time to spread my wings a little and date other men, I pretended to be brave, agreed that the idea had merit, then discovered to my own surprise that it did. Mark was still part of my life, but not my lifeline anymore. And a good thing too. We really had no interests in common. I was pretty sure that Joe Corelli would never ignore my presence to watch a rerun of the NFL game of the week as Mark had, though to be fair, Mark did like me better than baseball. Still, being with a man who was gallant, attentive, and enjoyed the same things I did would be a novel experience, and that included my eighteen years of marriage.

At the end of the dark, winding road that led to the ocean-front condo I had hocked my soul to buy, the girders of the still-uncompleted townhouses stood like tall, spooky shadows behind the two finished units. As Joe pulled his sporty Fiat X-19 into my minuscule driveway, he asked how a self-confessed coward like me could bear to come home here alone every night.

"No choice," I said, digging for my keys. "The couple who bought my house wanted to move in by the first of the year, so I had to get out or blow the deal. Anyway, there'll be next-door neighbors here soon, a nice retired couple who will keep the bogeyman at bay. In the meantime, I'll just have to live with my fears, especially since I've already made an astronomical down payment for the pleasure of seeing the ocean when I wake up in the morning. There really is a great view from these cliffs."

Those were brave words from someone who had had an automatic garage-door opener installed because she was nervous about scooting from car to house after dark. Not tonight though, with Joe beside me . . . not until a shadow moved in one of the half-framed townhouses.

Clutching Joe's arm for moral support, I called assertively, "Who's there?"

When a figure stepped into the light, my held breath escaped in a sigh of relief. "Tom! What are you doing here?"

"There was a message on my answering machine when I got home tonight. A leak in the toilet at the Talbot place. So I came over and fixed it, but not before water soaked the rug. Hope it dries before they move in."

"Poor man. You must be exhausted after carrying around a sign at Canyon Escondido all day, or is banner waving too extreme for a born-again pacifist?" I teased. Tom Grabowski's attitude about the demonstration might have irked Jessica, but I liked the guy.

"I did more than wave a sign today," he said complacently. "I went all out and got myself arrested. I'm sure it'll be covered on the eleven o'clock news."

Under normal circumstances, I would have invited Tom in to watch himself on TV and gotten all the gory details, but no amount of curiosity was going to make me sabotage my own date. Discreetly reticent, I merely opened the front door for Joe and left Tom standing in the yard.

"Who was that?" Joe asked after we were in the house.

"Sorry I didn't introduce you," I said, offering no explanation for keeping Tom at arm's length. "He's the builder of these little castles in the sun and a real angel. Every time something goes wrong, he's over here in a flash to fix it himself. I have a sneaking suspicion he doesn't have the money to pay his workmen time and a half to work at night."

"That certainly can't be why he was arrested."

"Obviously you need to watch more than yourself on the news if you don't know that ANSWER took their call to arms out to the nuke plant today. Tom was probably lying in the street blocking traffic." I led the way into the living room, flipping on lights and television as I went. Luckily I had done some dusting this afternoon, in between polishing my nails and shampooing my hair, so my old furniture looked as good as my new house. "Here you go. Sit down and relax. I'll be back in a minute."

"Are you going to slip on something a little more comfortable?" Joe kidded.

"No way, so you can stick your tongue back inside your face," I said, crushing his hopes. "After that dinner you fed me, I'll never fit into my black satin negligée."

The bathroom mirror showed a woman who was going on a three-day fast immediately. I didn't look as if I'd gained ten pounds in the last two hours, but I felt like an overstuffed manicotti. Wishing I could escape from the confining elegance of my blue silk suit and tummy-control pantyhose, I settled for brushing my teeth and hair, then added a dab of lipstick. When I returned to the living room, Joe had made himself comfortable, coat removed, tie loosened, and feet propped on the ottoman.

"Have I missed your television debut?" I asked, sitting down beside him.

"Not yet. They're still reporting the international bad news. Come one, snuggle up a little closer."

"What about your hands-off policy?"

"Don't worry. I never renege on a campaign promise."

The D.A. was as good as his word. He put his arm around my shoulders, and there it stayed while we watched the summing up of the day's dramas. Even though Joe's hand never wandered toward more erogenous zones, I was too conscious of that friendly masculine embrace to listen with real attention. Not until Channel Twelve started talking about a local drama, anyway.

"And now . . . a report on ANSWER's demonstration at the Canyon Escondido nuclear power plant.

"A human chain of chanting, sign-waving protestors tried to block the path of arriving guests, here to celebrate the opening of CASA GRANDE's long-awaited nuclear power plant. Along with PSSC officials, Congressman Phillip Abbotts was in one of the several limousines held up by demonstrators outside the fence surrounding the plant. It looks as though some of his constituents will do anything to get the congressman's attention."

I bolted out of the blissful circle of Joe's arms and pointed an outraged finger at the television. "Do you see that idiot jumping up and down in front of Mr. Abbotts' car? That's my son."

Joe only smiled benevolently. "I like his sign. ONE LITTLE MELTDOWN COULD RUIN YOUR WHOLE DAY. Has a nice ring to it."

"It's Jessica's fault," I mourned, falling back on the couch. "She's filled his head with all kinds of nonsense. Michael is supposed to be at U.C.L.A., studying for a physics exam, or so he told me when I asked if he were coming home this weekend to visit his poor, lonely mother. The wretch. 'How sharper than a serpent's tooth it is to have a thankless child.' "

Joe wasn't so quick to agree. "Aren't you overreacting?

King Lear had reason to complain, but Michael just wants to make Casa Grande safe for dear, sweet Mom."

"I think you missed your calling, counselor. You should have been a public defender instead of a prosecutor. Oh, my gosh." I leaned forward. "Look at that."

A film clip of a handcuffed Tom Grabowski being man-handled into a police van was accompanied by a voice-over that claimed one of ANSWER's top organizers had been caught trespassing inside the building. A serious-faced reporter then asked if such an entry hadn't proved the antinuke group's contention that the plant was an unacceptable danger to the community, indeed to Southern California, despite PSSC's elaborate safety procedures. After all, if an unauthorized individual could get past the periphery while the building was filled with people and guards, real terrorists might be able to infiltrate with the intention of destroying the reactor itself.

"I doubt if Jessica would go *that* far," I commented dryly, "though I know she's thrilled about Tom's daring exposé of the plant's lax security. Of course, with you prosecuting, the judge may toss him into jail and throw away the key."

"You think I'm that good, huh?"

"I voted for you, didn't I?"

"I have no idea. Did you?"

"Yes. And with my luck Tom will be sentenced, go bankrupt, and never be able to finish these condos. I'll have these half-built monstrosities surrounding me forever."

Joe laughed and shook his head. "There won't be any grand trial with Tom getting the perfect chance to indict the nuclear industry for gross negligence. Your buddy will receive a slap on the wrist and a fine. You won't even hear any more about it once the media gets tired of beating a dead horse. PSSC will want everyone to forget about their little oversight as quickly as possible." As if to prove Joe's contention, the camera switched to a sportscaster who began enthusiastically enumerating today's NFL scores.

"Somehow that doesn't make me feel one bit better," I said.

Joe pulled me back into his arms.

"Then make your own protest," he urged. "You can stage a sit-in right here on my lap."

That teased a smile from me. "Now I know why you're such a successful politician. I'll bet you kiss babies too."

"When they let me."

I let him. But just as Joe began to inaugurate more interesting methods of nonpolitical persuasion, the anchorman came back on the air. He said the special feature scheduled for tonight's news was being postponed so the station could bring a live report from the Canyon Escondido nuclear power plant.

Joe sat up in a hurry. "I think I've just been preempted."

"Don't worry. You're the D.A. You can always prosecute," I consoled him as the picture switched to a wind-battered reporter at the scene.

"Only hours after the gala reception heralding the inauguration of Casa Grande's new and safety-conscious nuclear power plant . . . and only hours after plant security was breached . . . an accident on the premises has claimed the life of one of the company's executives. In a bizarre mishap, unrelated to and not endangering the soon-to-be-activated nuclear reactor, a simple electrical malfunction in a faulty transformer has caused the death of Drake Prescott . . . PSSC's public relations director. From the sketchy information we have so far, Prescott had apparently left the reception this afternoon to inspect the defective unit, which was delivered only yesterday and placed in this building behind me . . . The electrical testing facility . . . where equipment is always examined for flaws before being put into use. It seems no one noticed Prescott's prolonged absence from the crowd at today's ribbon-cutting ceremony. His body was not discovered until approximately an hour ago, during a routine check

of the premises by night watchmen. It is still uncertain if Prescott's death was due to human error or an engineering failure, but a spokesman for PSSC assures us that the accident has absolutely no connection with the nuclear reactor. A faulty transformer, even at a nuclear power plant, can only cause death one way . . . by electrocution.

Chapter Three

There was an interesting irony about someone getting electrocuted at a nuclear power plant. The danger was supposed to be a radioactive spill, not a short circuit. What ammunition for ANSWER. Now they'd have a double-barreled shotgun to aim at the enemy. Unsafe and unsafe again. But why was the head of public relations playing around with a broken transformer when he should have been wooing the press? If Drake Prescott had been trying to pull a publicity stunt, it sure backfired on him. Being charged to death was no way to promote the electric company. Poor Lois. She was going to have a tough time beautifying PSSC's image after this second blow . . .

I tried reaching her on Sunday morning but she wasn't home. Probably out soft-soaping the media. After supper I gave her one more try, but when all I got was the ringing of an unanswered phone, I went to another source of information.

Naturally, Betsy accused me of being compulsively curious and asked if I had a yen for bean sprouts. Since she'd been called in to consult with company engineers at Canyon Escondido today, I said she was closer to solving anything than I was. All I wanted to know was why the accident happened. How Drake Prescott got into a technical area. Was security so bad at the plant that they couldn't even keep a watchful eye on their own employees?

Betsy had no idea what the snafu was yesterday. She said the reception went off without a hitch despite the demonstrators, and Congressman Abbotts sent me his warmest regards despite my son's antics. But she knew nothing about the transformer, although she described a few things that could go wrong with one. What really went wrong wasn't explained until Monday morning when the newspaper headline blared that Prescott's death wasn't an accident, but murder.

"You mean someone actually plugged him in?" This came from Kimberly Nichols, the new receptionist at our office.

"That's not so strange," Barbara Beauchamp told her. "We once had a client who dosed his wife with insecticide and buried her in the vegetable garden."

"Did it work?" asked Kimberly, all of nineteen and still wide-eyed.

"No. He got ten-to-life and his carrots curled."

"And you," I pointed a finger at Barbara, "are going to get no donuts with your coffee for telling shaggy dog stories."

When the third member of the office staff arrived at work late and with a newspaper tucked under her arm, she too was eager to discuss the tragedy. "I feel sorry for the guy." Diane Romero slid into place behind her desk. "But you know PSSC is going to use his death as an excuse to raise their rates again. Somebody's gotta pay one way or another, and it's usually the consumer."

"Well, I sure don't want to foot the bill for someone else's electrical consumption," Barb said, offering Diane the dregs from the coffeepot before flashing me a glance. You have anything to say about it, Ellie?"

I didn't, but our two part-time law clerks had theories. Robert figured the murderer was an irate shareholder in the company who saw his investment going down the Dow Jones and ending up buried in the nuke plant's waste disposal site. Rosalie thought the crime was committed by a mad scientist from Los Alamos who now regretted his research on nuclear energy. After a while, I gave up trying to keep them quiet, because every client who came in wanted to chew over the possibilities. In a town the size of Casa Grande, a suburban pit stop between the San Diego Zoo and Disneyland, murder was a nine-days wonder, I wondered about it as much as anyone else, but an opportunity to call Lois at work never materialized. I was kept fully occupied all morning just minding my own business, office and otherwise.

The rush started when Dennis Devlin dropped a fat legal pad covered with his scrawled handwriting on my desk and requested a draft of his notes to be typed forthwith.

I picked it up and leafed through. "Dennis, this brief isn't done. Some sections aren't even written yet. 'Whereas the party of the second part et cetera,' " I read aloud in a pained voice.

"You can fill in the blanks with the appropriate jargon. Feel free to smooth out my syntax and correct the spelling. I trust you, Ellie. Your English is impeccable. Just don't give the job to any of the other girls."

"I wouldn't dare. They'd go on strike. And may I remind you, Mr. Devlin, that I did not hire on as a technical editor either."

I handed the pad back, but he wouldn't take it. Instead, he perched himself on the corner of my desk and put a wheedle in his voice. "Why should I bother sweating over the brief when you can finish it faster and better than I can? The last one you typed for me was miraculously improved by your magic touch. The legal stuff is all there, solid as the Rock of Gibraltar. All you have to do is weave the words around it. Tell you what, you do this for me, I'll buy you lunch at Barney's."

The boyish grin plus the compliments did me in. I've always been a sucker for anyone who'd lay his hand on his heart and swear I was a talented so-and-so.

"Forget the lunch. I'm on a diet. All right, but it won't be done today. Tomorrow . . . at five, maybe."

"You're an angel." He slid off the desk. "I owe you a barbecue beef on a bun and a two-olive martini any time you want."

"Don't tempt me," I said crossly, waving him away.

Then Kimberly buzzed me. "One ex-husband on the line."

"Yes? What is it, Dan? I'm up to my ears . . . you're joking. You think Michael has fallen in with bad company? Well, of course he made the news, but . . . Dan, don't be silly." I flopped down in my chair and listened while my former husband voiced his concerns about impressionable children being led astray by revolutionaries. "Jessica isn't exactly a Communist agitator. She's a college professor. . . . Yes," I sighed, "I know all about Timothy Leary. No, Dan. I do not think it would be a good idea to get together and discuss Michael's problems. . . . Okay, I'll admit it. I do not wish to get together and discuss anything at all. . . . No, I don't hate you." I rolled my eyes heavenward. "Very well, I'll call you later in the week when I have some time. . . . Thank you, Dan . . . yes, that's very sweet of you, I do realize it. Oops, my other line is ringing . . . got to run . . . goodbye." I hung up, then leaned on my desk and placed my weary head on folded arms.

"No grand reconciliation?" Barbara asked.

"Not even tea for two."

"You might consider sharing that new condo of yours with him; he pays half, no strings."

"Please. I'm not that hard-pressed for funds."

Actually, Barb was just recommending what had

worked out well for her, though cohabiting with an ex-husband seemed an inconvenient way to avoid a property settlement. The free-wheeling Barbara never let it cramp her style, but I'd find it inhibiting to go on a double date with Dan. Still, Barbara was just trying to be helpful. As the only other unmarried member of the office staff, she felt a kinship with me that transcended her irregular life-style and my conventional habits.

It transcended everyone else's too. Diane was a working mother who went straight home at night to feed, bathe, and tuck in three kiddies and husband. Ordinary. The new-wedded Kimberly was still on her honeymoon. Semi-ordinary. But Barb, bless her irrepressible heart, made *True Confessions* seem tame. When she reported her sexy set-tos, which she did often, the others hung on every word with bated breath. "In a backyard hammock?" they'd chorus in awe. "That's really swinging."

I thought so too, but I was getting used to Barbara. Not the swinging. Or the way the three of them speculated about me. I tried to keep my private affairs private, which wasn't hard since I didn't have much to reveal. But the titty-tats, as I fondly dubbed the titillated trio, made gossip their coffee break. Normally, I didn't give them food for thought . . . that was, until Joe Corelli said it all with his gourmet pizza.

Saturday night had ended on a promising note. After we kissed goodbye at the door, Joe murmured that he'd call me. Since he had shown a marked appreciation for my scintilating wit and my person, not to mention my prowess with a knife and fork, I fully expected to hear from him. What I didn't expect was a twenty-inch-round herald, announcing his intentions to the world.

The delivery boy brought it up on the private elevator that discreetly bypassed the first three floors of the building, but he carried the clearly labeled box through the loungeful of waiting clients. I directed him into the storage room where he set it on the Xerox machine, but it was too late for secrecy. All three titty-tats had come to take a look at the proof I hadn't spent my weekend alone and unloved.

"That is the biggest pizza I've ever seen," Diane said in awe as I opened the lid to reveal my ten-pound epicurean delight. "Look . . . caviar . . . and shrimp . . . Good Lord, Ellie. Are you going to be able to eat all of it yourself?"

"Able to, yes," I answered. "But going to, no. My body is being purged by a two-day diet of celery stalks and vitamin B complex to combat what I consumed Saturday night at Antonio's. Be my guests, ladies."

"No wonder you don't give a hoot about Dan," Barbara said with a knowing wink. "The guy who sent this must really be hot stuff. Let me see the card."

"No way." I hid it behind my back only to have it plucked deftly from my grasp by Kimberly.

"It just says, 'Love, Joe,'" she reported.

Silently I held out a hand for my pilfered property.

"Well, well," Diane smirked. "All my weekend earned me was Sunday breakfast in bed. I'll have to talk to my husband about proper gratitude."

"And how did you earn your just reward, Ellie?" Barb teased.

"I only give age, rank, and serial number, and I lie about my age. So you peeping tomasinas will have to get your vicarious turn-ons from someone else. Let Barb do the honors. I'm taking a piece of this to Mr. Devlin. Oh, and save some for Helen and Dennis, please."

Ignoring their moans of protest, I carried a good quarter of the pizza to Mark's office. His drapes were wide open to let in a heartening stream of winter sunshine, and from behind the wide mahogany desk, he turned in his wheelchair to look at the paper plate in my hand.

"I know. It's dietetic pizza." His green eyes lit in amusement as I placed it in front of him.

"Very funny. Just be careful not to spill any sauce on your tie," I warned.

"Then this isn't a vitamin supplement to your celery regimen? How disappointing."

"This, you sarcastic fiend, is a highly caloric *billet doux* from Joe Corelli, and I'm not having even a bite of it."

"That's very unromantic of you, Ellie. What's the saying? 'The way to a woman's heart is through her stomach'?"

"Well, that tunnel of love has been disconnected, thank you."

"Oh, come on," he coaxed. "Cheat a little. Show that you return Joe's affection by appreciating his inventiveness."

"Oh, I appreciate it, all right. Our D.A.'s quite a clever fellow."

Mark smiled. "Then he has found the way to your heart. When did the two of you get together?"

"Saturday night."

"And you obviously hit it off."

"Off and running. I just want to stay in shape for the chase."

It was unusual to be discussing a new flame with an old one, but Mark was the one who wanted me to test my wings, and he still had a proprietary interest in how I was faring on the singles circuit. It was surprisingly easy to maintain a friendship on those terms, though he deserved the major credit for our smooth transition from passionate to platonic. Mark claimed to have no special insight, but I maintained that the car crash ten years ago that had left him partially paralyzed also gave him a greater understanding of human foibles. At least, he understood mine and liked me anyway. Liked, not loved, as he intimated fairly clearly when we broke up. Oh, well, I'd learned to be grateful for small favors.

"One other thing." I paused at the door. "Have you heard anything about the murder at Canyon Escondido?"

"I only know what I read in the papers, but based on this

pizza, I'd say you should have great luck checking with your inside source."

"Ask Joe?"

"Or call Chief Steunkle. He loves you too."

"Bean sprouts," I said under my breath.

Still, I did end up questioning Joe when he called to find out how I enjoyed lunch. It was late afternoon by then, and luckily, two of the three titty-tats were on a coffee break so I could speak to him in relative privacy.

"Yes, it was delicious," I said warmly. "Quite a treat."

"I hope there was enough for everyone to have a taste."

"Of course. I left some drib-drabs for them."

"Ellie, are you busy tomorrow night? I thought . . . hold on a minute. Frank, get me that police report. It's with the Hopkins file. Okay, Ellie, I'm back. So what about Tuesday evening? Are you in the mood for . . . not that one, Frank. I want the results of the investigative report."

"You sound busy."

"I am. This place is a madhouse today."

"Working on the Prescott murder, huh?" I said casually.

"Prescott? Who's. . . . Oh. No, the police haven't finished with that one yet. I've got two preliminary hearings on Wednesday to finish up and umpteen arraignments in Superior Court for tomorrow."

"Poor baby," I commiserated. "Do the police have any suspects yet?"

"Everybody's a suspect at this stage of the investigation."

"Then they're still checking fingerprints and taking statements," I probed lightly.

"Now I know why Matt Steunkle calls you Nancy Drew. Okay, back to Tuesday night. What would you like? A movie? The theater? Dinner?"

"Not dinner," I objected. Who could afford another five thousand calories? "But anything else you'd like sounds fine."

"Fair enough. I'll choose one of the other options and come by for you at eight."

I hung up the phone feeling exhilarated. Most men would have pounced on my carelessly worded "anything" and suggested the obvious. Not Joe. He wasn't the type to assume he could show up at my door, pajamas packed and toothbrush in hand. The D.A. had sensitivity, an Old World courtliness. He'd appeal to a woman's mind before appealing for anything else. No doubt tomorrow evening would find us exploring the dimensions of our mutual attraction at the Bergman film festival or delighting in each other at the new exhibit at the museum.

"Ellie, did you hear me? I asked if Diane has finished typing the Tyler deposition."

"Oh, Helen. Sorry. Yes, she has; it should be on her desk. I guess I was daydreaming."

"Understandable," she smiled. "I tasted some of that fantastic pizza Joe Corelli sent you. Thanks for saving me a slice."

"How do you know who sent it?" I asked. Surely Mark hadn't ratted on me.

"Some truths are self-evident," Helen laughed. "Kimberly said the enclosed card was signed by a Joe . . ."

"And you saw Joe Corelli talking to me at Fifth and Shoreside," I finished with a sigh of resignation. Try keeping a secret in a small town.

"You're very lucky, Ellie. The D.A. is a terrific guy."

"He seems to be," I said with pretended detachment. If everyone were going to comment on my love life, I'd better learn to be sophisticated about it.

"Before you go off into another reverie of remembered bliss, where is our bookkeeper today? It's almost the end of February, and I want to go over some accounts with her."

"I let Nancy Weaver switch her three days this week to Wednesday, Thursday, and Friday so she could baby-sit with her grandchildren while her daughter job-hunts. Is that going to be a problem? I can call and tell her to come in tomorrow, if you like."

"No, don't change anything. This can wait another couple of days. By the way, do you know anything about the murder at Canyon Escondido?"

"How would I know anything? No, don't tell me. The pizza. Actually, all Joe said was that the police are still investigating. Nothing's come to the D.A.'s office yet."

"Keep me posted," she said, stuffing her Gucci briefcase under her arm and dashing off for a three-thirty court hearing.

And there went the Honorable Helen Ramirez. Ninety percent all business and one hundred percent dressed for it. She was an interesting combination, our sole female attorney. When she joined the law firm as an associate member last summer, I didn't think I'd like her. But in a short time, the ravishing Helen proved she wasn't just a face that could launch a thousand ships. She was also hardworking, pragmatic to a fault, and harbored very little conceit about her good looks. Naturally, since I'm a broad-minded person, I eventually forgave her for being beautiful and smart and chic, though I never quite overcame the feeling that if I ever needed a sympathetic attorney, either of the Devlins would be a better choice. Not that Helen lacked the milk of human kindness; it just ran through her veins with a healthy dash of reserved judgment. She was quick not to jump to a conclusion, swift to believe only half of what she heard, and the first one to stick to procedure. None of the above were indictments of her integrity; quite the contrary. But if I wanted a crying towel to take to court with me, "the fair, chaste, and unexpressive" Helen Ramirez would supply cold comfort.

I finally started Dennis's almost-illegible brief, but when I saw it involved an electrical contractor suing for nonpayment, that reminded me of PSSC and the fact that I still hadn't spoken to Lois. How was she taking the news of Drake Prescott's death? I doubted if she'd be grieving much since he had scarcely been a favorite of hers, to put it mildly. But she was much too kindhearted to rejoice, even if there were a chance this highly unexpected development might mean a step up for her at the company. It seemed inevitable that the management would ask her to fill his shoes, at least temporarily. And if she did her usual job, they might easily make it a permanent arrangement. " 'Tis an ill wind that blows nobody good."

Taking advantage of an almost empty office, I asked Kimberly for an outside line, then swiveled around in my chair so she couldn't hear me. "Extension seven-eight-oh, please." I tapped my fingers on the padded armrest and waited for the operator to put me through. What an adjunct to my life the telephone was today. The reach-out-and-touch technique of communication had brought Dan, Joe Corelli, and my insurance agent, who wanted to sell me another life/term policy. Unfortunately it didn't bring me Lois. She was at a meeting, her secretary informed me.

"You mean, it's business as usual over there?" I asked in surprise.

"Are you kidding? The place is swarming with police," the ever-talkative Jane Chestnut informed me.

"Have they found any clues yet?"

"Maybe. They tore apart Prescott's office and got statements from everyone in this department. I even had my fingerprints taken. Can you imagine? Just because I went to that silly reception."

"The police have to follow a certain procedure, and in a murder case, everyone is suspect at this stage of the investigation," I quoted Joe Corelli.

"Well, you would know, Ms. Gordon, but I don't like it one bit. Not one bit. I didn't kill the man."

"Certainly not," I agreed politely. "Just tell Lois I called, will you? Thanks, Jane."

That evening I finally made contact with Lois as I was getting out of the shower. Dripping on my new wall-to-wall carpeting, I clutched a towel around my shivering body and answered the phone.

"Sorry it took so long for me to return your call," Lois said.

"Oh, that's all right. I know you were busy today. I tried reaching you on Sunday too."

"I didn't get home until late. My monthly trip to San Jose. I did tell you my mother's in a nursing home there?"

"Yes. How is she?"

"Physically, she's fine, but her mind is going. This visit, she didn't even recognize me. When I reminded her who I was, she told me firmly that her daughter was a much younger woman."

"That's terrible!" I said, thinking of my own lively parent who was currently on a cruise to the Galapagos.

By now I was dry enough to perch on the edge of my bed without making a wet circle on my brand-new spread. However, I couldn't very well announce that I was panting to hear the sordid details of the Prescott murder so would she please fire away. Instead, I came in by the back door.

"How are you holding up under the strain of a murder investigation right in your own office? Drake's death must have come as a shocking surprise."

"Not you too, Ellie. People have been making that pitiful pun all day."

"Sorry. I wasn't thinking. But are you all right?"

"Oh, yes. I'm as 'shocked' as everyone else, but truth-fully, I haven't quite taken it in yet. I didn't even know about it until this morning when Jane Chestnut floored me with the news."

"What was Prescott doing in the testing facility anyway?"

Lois was silent for a moment. "Everyone seems to think he'd arranged to meet someone there for a private talk. His murderer, as it turned out."

I pulled the damp towel more securely around me. "He didn't go to look at the transformer?"

Lois sighed. "I'll tell you what I told the police. There was no reason for Drake to inspect the transformer. He wasn't an engineer, and our department has nothing to do with maintenance or repairs."

"Then apparently, he did leave the reception to have a tête à tête with someone. Any idea who?"

"None at all. But I presume when the police finish taking statements from everyone, they'll be able to figure out who was missing at the crucial time."

"They've already ruled out the possibility that one of the demonstrators might have gotten carried away?" I asked.

"The only one we know who got in was that Grabowski fellow, and the security guards caught him almost immediately. Besides, why would Drake want to have a private meeting with a protestor? We already know what they want."

"Then the police have limited the suspects to invited guests only?"

"Not so 'only.' There were about two hundred guests, plus PSSC employees, plus the press. A sufficient number of possible murderers," Lois said in her inimitably cynical way.

"Matt Steunkle will tear out the rest of his hair over this one," I commented, wondering if the chief of police would use the case as an excuse to postpone his retirement for another six months.

I wished Lois well with her mother, then hung up and dove into a nice, warm nightgown. Snuggling under the covers, I never did pick up the whodunnit on my night table that I had planned to finish reading this evening. The Prescott mystery was much more absorbing.

Chapter Four

Tuesday evening wasn't as highbrow as I predicted, but it wasn't unimaginative either. Joe didn't want to see the undubbed Bergman film at the Guild, and the museum closed at seven. So instead, we went to K-Mart. I browsed through the book section while he bought some things in auto supplies. From there we drove to the soda shop for hot fudge sundaes, then came back to my house for a stroll along the beach.

"Boring, wasn't it?"

"Not at all," I protested. "Going shopping together was homey. I had fun." I looked up at the stars. "Do you recognize the different constellations?"

"Uh-uh. But you should by now. I thought you did nothing but walk the terrain and count the stars in your backyard."

"Sometimes I just count the number of yards in my backyard."

"Then we'll just have to hope you don't lose your back-yard in a mudslide," he teased.

"No chance. I've got special insurance."

"A preventive maintenance policy?"

"Renewable every year," I boasted. "For an annual cost of twenty dollars, I've planted wildflower seeds all along this cliff. And when they bloom in the spring, I won't have to worry about soil erosion or drainage problems. All those daisies, lupin, and poppies will hold onto the earth and keep it right where it is."

"You're sure about that?" he asked skeptically.

"No. But if it doesn't work, I'll have the most colorful spill on the whole West Coast."

Laughing, he pulled me close, and we ambled arm in arm toward the zigzag of wooden stairs built onto the face of the cliff. When we reached them, I broke away and called over my shoulder, "Race you to the top."

Joe bolted in front of me, but at the first landing, when he slowed down and let me pass him, I began to suspect the race wasn't quite on the up and up. I knew it for certain when I arrived at the top, still four steps ahead of him, and panted breathlessly, "Winner gets the spoils."

"Okay," he agreed and kissed me.

"Did you lose on purpose?" I asked when I finally was able to speak.

"Sure. The view from the rear was much more scenic." He grinned.

I hesitated. Was Joe hinting for even a closer view? No, thank goodness. He left shortly after that, leaving my virtue and my shaky principles intact, bless his chivalrous heart. He must have sensed from the way I almost tripped over my feet backing away from him that I wasn't quite ready to invite him into my bed. Hell, he hadn't even seen me without eye liner yet.

I suppose most women approaching the end of their fourth decade wonder how an attractive man will react to the great unveiling. Exercise notwithstanding, some parts of my body were beginning to take on a Dow Jones downward curve. And if that weren't enough to dampen my enthusiasm, I had been thrust into the brave new world of singles with no previous training. Let's face it, I grew up in the days when going all the way meant all the way to the altar. Feeling comfortable with contemporary mores was a trick I hadn't quite mastered yet. My initial foray into the sexual revolution was under Mark's influence; not that he had to beg for my favors. I simply decided that saving myself for a second and speculative Mr. Right was more a ritual of ceremonial celibacy than a rational reason to abstain. But along with the joyful discovery that sleeping with a man didn't make him lose respect for you in the morning, I also learned that intimacy with no commitment has its own umbilical cord.

Fortunately, Joe Corelli also considered two dates insufficient foreplay to hopping in the sack. He thought even ten was premature. In the next two weeks, we met for lunch, played tennis, watched sunsets, ate our way through practically every restaurant in town, but still didn't reach the culmination so devoutly desired by ninety-nine percent of all consenting adults. By then I was infatuated enough to consent, but Joe didn't ask. In fact, he was so civilized about suggesting that final step that I began to wonder if he were waiting for an engraved invitation. Then I started brooding about how to word it. I even made a rough draft. Finally I decided only a subpoena would work. Either the D.A. didn't know how to make a case outside of court, or he had fattened me up for the kill, then planned to dump me because I was overweight.

But if preoccupation with Joe's lack of passion filled half my waking hours, I still found a moment or two to speculate about Drake Prescott's murder. Our local paper ran an article a day on the not-so-safe nuke plant, raising questions on the seismic strength of the nuclear reactor should an earthquake strike and the emergency evacuation plan should the reactor malfunction without benefit of a quake. But daily bulletins on the progress of the murder investigation were not reported. That inside story, or part of it, I tried to pry from Joe the night he finally swept me off my anxious feet.

The D.A. was almost as game-crazy as I was, and he bought me a new backgammon set because the toy store still hadn't gotten in a replacement supply of *Trivial Pursuit*. While we played, I probed.

"Do the police have any suspects yet?" I rolled the dice. "Doublets. Four and four. I just made the point."

"Probably," he shrugged, taking his turn. "Okay. Three's are up, and I just moved my fourteenth player to the inner table."

Hardly paying attention, I continued questioning him. "Can you tell me how well Steunkle's investigation is going?" Taking the roll of dice, I lost both sets of numbers because two of Joe's men were blocking my points.

"I don't have anything to do with the police," was his disappointing answer. "But I did read some of the technical reports, and they show that PSSC followed all the proper safety procedures. The transformer that electrocuted Prescott was clearly marked as malfunctioning." He picked up the dice.

"Maybe someone turned it on by mistake," I suggested.

"And instead of running for help, he just quietly disappeared into the crowd?" Joe asked skeptically. "I guess that's possible, but the crime is still murder. Even if Prescott's death was an unintentional error, manslaughter was committed, not to mention a half dozen or so accompanying charges . . . lying on a police statement, concealing a crime . . . leaving the scene . . ."

"You sneak," I interrupted, pointing at the board. "You're beating me."

"It's not my fault if you were busy playing *amicus curiae* while I applied myself to backgammon," he smiled.

"It's not fair," I grumbled mildly. "You bore off almost all your men while I wasn't looking."

Joe reached across the kitchen table and took my hand. "Would you like to concede the game now?"

"No. I'm going to make a grand comeback."

He began rubbing his thumb over my index finger. "Don't you think we've been playing long enough?" he asked quietly.

Well, here was the big moment. Joe was ready to make a dishonest woman of me, and for all my eagerness to let him, I began thinking of reasons why I shouldn't. It was too soon. My thighs were too fat. I still had more questions about the Prescott case. The phone might ring any minute.

Taking my silence for assent, or maybe the way I was clutching his fingers, he stood up and came around behind me. Without a word of protest, I let him lean over and put his hands on my tingling breasts. Of course, I could hardly breathe, much less talk. But when his strong arms raised me to my shaking feet, I didn't have to utter a syllable. The expression on my face must have said it all.

To the victor goes the spoils. Joe might have won the ever-vacillating Ellie Gordon with his play strategy, but I overcame all my misgivings on a Serta Perfect Sleeper. Joe was tender, considerate, indefatigable, and evidently thought I had the body of a Venus de Milo with arms. So much for worrying about the dimples on the backs of my thighs. I didn't even bother with eye liner the next morning. But if entering into an intimate relationship with the D.A. provided ego gratification and emotional satisfaction, it did not give me an inside track with the law. I didn't learn another thing about the events at Canyon Escondido until the following Saturday afternoon. Of course, Joe had been keeping me occupied all week with other considerations, though it was the remains of last night's after-sex sybaritic feast that brought my mind back to the subject.

I was hurriedly stuffing the gunk down the garbage disposal when the blasted contraption started spitting back at me. I called Tom Grabowski to come to the rescue, apologizing that he had to fix the thing now. "There's a water aerobics class at the spa, and I'm supposed to be there in twenty minutes. Oh, and by the way," I added for further inducement, "you did a great job on that TV interview."

"Thanks. I didn't want to come across sounding like an extremist, but Jess thinks I sold out. She says I let the group down."

There was a note of belligerence in his voice, as if he expected me to criticize his performance too, but I just tactfully agreed that he'd handled himself with admirable restraint, though I knew why Jessica was annoyed with him. During the interview, when Tom was asked how close he got to the reactor containment area after crashing the party at Canyon Escondido, he had denied being anywhere near it. Since no one would have known otherwise, he could have claimed leaving his initials etched on the door or at least made a grandstand speech on how easy it was for him to enter the facility undetected. But the closest he had come to expounding upon ANSWER's safety concerns was a mild comment about its not being possible to calculate normal human error in the strictest of precautions. Maybe he just developed stage fright at finding himself on camera, I suggested when Jessica complained to me about it. But she had insisted he had no balls. I thought otherwise but had given up trying to defend him.

"About your garbage disposal," Tom went on prosaically, "I can't get over there for at least an hour, but don't worry, I have a passkey. Just go ahead and enjoy yourself. It'll be fixed by the time you get home."

"You living doll. As a reward, please help yourself to a beer. There are a couple on the top shelf of the refrigerator."

He deserved no less for being such a good sport, though usually I offered him a sandwich for his troubles. Tom had a "lean and hungry look" that aroused my motherly instincts. Sometimes I thought he'd starve without me. Not that a thirty-two-year-old bachelor was incapable of fixing himself three square meals a day, but this one was just too busy trying to put up condos and tear down nuke plants to think about eating. I should be so distracted from food, though if I had Tom's worries, I might lose my appetite too.

Sales were a little slow at Vista del Mar. I'd been here almost six weeks and my first neighbors had just moved in. The Talbots were charming, but seventy-plus; and while Tom would have liked to surround me with more people, none of the other condos were anywhere near ready for occupancy. Cost overruns and factory delays probably. I hoped he wasn't in a contractor's Catch 22: needing the money from sales to complete the project but unable to sell anything until he got money to finish building it.

But now was not the time to contemplate financial recourses for him. I was already behind schedule, and predictably, Betsy was standing at the curb waiting for my Datsun to round the corner.

"You're late." She climbed into the front seat. "Did you oversleep or wouldn't Joe let you out of his arms?"

"Neither," I answered, merging into traffic. "I had garbage disposal problems and called Tom. He's such a nice guy."

"Too nice, according to Jess."

"I know, but if she could see him without the red mist of anger clouding her view, she might find him rather attractive. I think they'd make a great twosome."

"Only if they can stop arguing about ANSWER."

"But that gives them something in common."

"My, my. You're quite the little romantic this morning. What happened, the joyful discovery that you and Joe share the same blood type?"

"So what's wrong with O-positive?"

"Nothing, my infatuated friend, but the ties that bind can also be the chain that chokes. Jessica and Tom are united only against the power company, whereas you and the dynamic D.A. are joined in everything from soup to nuts."

"Must you be so literal?" I patted my expanding waistline. "Joe thinks a small token of his regard is a five-pound cheesecake."

"And you love it. But between bites I'll bet you glean plenty of information."

"About Prescott's murder? No way. I don't have a sprout's worth of a clue on who did it."

"So Joe's not the type to kiss and tell." Betsy smiled perceptively. "I'd have thought while you were sneaking into his heart, you'd be worming your way into his confidence too."

"You should have been a spy for the KGB," I said with virtuous disdain. "But if it's any consolation to you," I admitted, "Joe did tell me what's in the police reports—a big fat zero at the moment."

What I didn't admit to Betsy was my intention of getting a more up-to-date report today. By virtue of her key position at PSSC, Lois should have some idea in what direction the police were going. However, when we arrived at the spa, Lois had other things on her mind. It seemed that some of ANSWER's more dedicated enthusiasts had caused a small confrontation at the entrance to the nuke plant on Friday morning. Lois had been caught in the thick of it, and twenty-four hours later, she was still fuming.

"You and your group are a real menace," she told Jessica. "I had to go out to Canyon Escondido yesterday, and I almost ran over a girl with a baby strapped to her back. The idiot stepped right in the path of my car."

"Good for her," Jess said.

Always having been on the listening end of Jessica's protests rather than the receiving end, Lois hardly knew how to react to this adverse response. "You think it's good?" Her face turned red under the thick coating of makeup. "Well, I think you're all a bunch of lunatics."

"But you believe that building a nuclear power plant on this particular stretch of coastline is sane."

"You know perfectly well that the Nuclear Regulatory Commission requires strict geological testing first," Lois spouted. "Any fissure in a five-mile radius of our plant has been certified as inactive for half a million years."

"That's the party line," Jess retorted, unabashedly peeling off bra and panties before bending over to find her bathing suit in the locker. "You've just been brainwashed by company pr."

"And you live in an ivory tower," Lois said, looking away until Jess was decently clad in a bikini. "Every building on that site has been seismically engineered to withstand tremors from the largest possible earthquake. Did you ever consider that?"

"Those statistics are based on past recorded activity. There is no accurate scientific gauge that can predict the future. What your experts claim is the largest possible earthquake is no more than an educated guess, no matter how many times they make the tests. A mathematical chart is not a crystal ball."

At that point, Betsy and I left them for the relative peace of the noisy indoor swimming pool. "Jess might have gotten the best of Lois in that argument," I commented as we padded down the tiled hallway.

"Professor Tobler is a proficient debater, but she's wasting a lot of time at Canyon Escondido," was Betsy's analysis. "ANSWER doesn't need to combat nuclear power on grounds of safety. The biggest Achilles' heel in the industry is economic these days. That plant has cost PSSC almost ten times the initial estimate; and barring any more delays, it will still be years before the company can turn a profit on Unit One alone. With investors already sorry they got sucked into such a morass, ANSWER would be better off distributing financial reports than BAN THE NUKE buttons."

"I thought nuclear power was such a cheap source of energy."

"Theoretically, it is. A generating station like the one at Canyon Escondido can produce a quarter of the state's electrical resources and be close to forty percent less expensive than a fossil-fueled electric plant."

"It sounds very impressive," I answered vaguely. "But isn't uranium more expensive than coal or oil?"

"I have a feeling," Betsy said with a wry look at me, "that you haven't the slightest idea how nuclear power works."

"Slight is about it," I admitted. "Can you explain without sounding like Einstein?"

"It was James Watt who perfected the steam engine, and basically, that's the procedure. Once heat is created by splitting uranium atoms, it turns the water to steam, which drives a turbine, which turns a generator, which produces electricity. Simple enough for you?"

"Not really, but I gather it's just the splitting of atoms that's causing so much splitting of hairs."

"You got it, though when the reprocessing of nuclear fuel is allowed, there won't be any waste problem because there won't be any waste left over. Then we'll still be stuck with the same old argument about how safe is a three-foot-thick containment wall that houses a nuclear reactor core."

"So Jessica won't be out of business for a long time."

"Neither will Canyon Escondido."

It might become the Hundred Years War of the twenty-first century if both sides held tight, and I could see Lois holding on until the musket fell from her aging hands. No matter what her former boss didn't recommend, and no matter if PSSC refused to come through with the oak-leaf cluster she wanted, under the company line and company propaganda beat the heart of a company woman.

"What would you expect?" Betsy shrugged before sliding open the plate-glass door to the pool area. "Work is Lois's life. She's widowed, her two kids are married and gone. . . . What else has she got besides a senile mother in a nursing home?"

It was just as well that question required no answer,

because the moment we crossed the threshold for our lesson on sleekness through swimming, the melodic strains of "Anchors Aweigh" came blaring out of the PA system.

"Don't forget to salute before you submerge," I said to Betsy with a grin, which was soon wiped off my face when I discovered that pool gymnastics was not an exercise in fluid mobility.

My initial immersion was cocky enough, a dazzling somersault I'd perfected at age ten. But when the young man with big muscles and big teeth started the "legs back, arms forward" routine, I started by swallowing a mouthful of overchlorinated water. Enthusiasm undampened, I bravely attempted the next four drills with equally saturating results, so when Betsy proclaimed that she found the exercises disappointingly easy, I splashed the smart aleck in retaliation.

Imitating a mermaid palled quickly on a few other bathing beauties too, and there were several mutinous naiads sitting on the sidelines when I swam over to take a breather. One of the dropouts was Lois.

"I thought you liked calisthenics."

"Not today," she sighed. "I have a headache."

"Too bad, but the niacin dose we get later ought to fix you up. It's supposed to purge the system of all kinds of noxious things, including flushing cholesterol out of the bloodstream."

Lois was not impressed. "You can have my share. I'll stick to aspirin."

"Speaking of cure-alls, I hear you're doing a super job filling Drake's shoes. That ought to put you in line for a promotion."

"Thanks, Ellie, but you just made that up. With the police nosing around all day, we aren't getting anything done." She gave a bitter little laugh. "The way my luck's been going, they'll probably blame me for that."

"Why so pessimistic? Get back in the swim," I admonished. "Come on, chest out, legs up, and kick."

"Go for it, tiger. I've barely enough energy to watch."

At the end of an hour, everyone else felt exactly the same way, and it would take more than a couple of vitamins to restore life in limbs again. Nevertheless, some gluttons for punishment actually signed up for more of the same. I merely swallowed the niacin tablets and thanked the instructor for a watery workout.

"Anybody for a cup of caffeine-loaded coffee?" I asked as we were getting dressed. "How about it, Lois? Want to stop off at the Espresso Haven for some poisonous substances?"

"And a little chat about a certain police investigation," Betsy added under her breath.

"No thanks," Lois begged off. "What I need more than anything right now is a nice, long nap. We'll get together another time, Ellie, okay?"

"Sure."

Unfortunately, neither the friendly cup of coffee nor the little chat ever materialized. The next time I got together with Lois McCoin was at the county jail after she was arrested for the murder of Drake Prescott.

Chapter Five

My first reaction on hearing the news about Lois's arrest was total disbelief. People we know aren't murderers, or at least people we like couldn't be. Besides, I prided myself on being a good judge of character, and I never once suspected Lois McCoin. Of course, my perception had been known to err on occasion, but the culprit just didn't fit the crime by my estimation. Not that Lois didn't have a motive of sorts, but would a woman who thought filing a sexual discrimination charge was too extreme an action opt for murder as a more temperate solution? So she had once declared that killing Prescott would be justifiable homicide. I discounted what she said as justifiable bombast. After all, people don't usually announce to the world at large that they're planning a crime unless they want to be held accountable for their intentions. But my dear Holmes, I argued with myself, you have overlooked an elementary consideration. If Lois were furious enough to lose her hitherto well-preserved cool because of what Drake Prescott had done, maybe she was mad enough to make him pay for it. Electrocuting a boss for unfair labor practices was certainly one form of employee compensation.

Guilty or not, the idea of Lois McCoin in jail bothered the hell out of me. The county's four-year-old model facility was euphemistically labeled a detention center; but "a rose is a rose is a rose," and no alias could make an arrest procedure smell sweet. Lois had been visited by two plainclothesmen at PSSC and asked to come downtown to answer a few additional questions. Unfortunately, when she answered them, she was booked, photographed facefront and profile, assigned a number for the benefit of corrections officers, and given the blue unisex jumpsuits issued all inmates. Her rings, gold watch, clothing, and other personal effects were locked up for safe keeping, just the way Lois was going to be. Before that final blow, she was permitted three phone calls. In that position, I would have called for a razor blade to slit my wrists. Lois had greater presence of mind, if a bit less exposure to these matters, and she dialed Helen Ramirez with the naive assumption that an attorney could straighten out this absurd mistake without the needless fuss of going to court.

I heard the story secondhand after Helen returned from the detention center. She shook her sleek head. "That's one frightened lady. It was hard work convincing her there's no way I can get her out until the arraignment this afternoon."

"How did Lois take the news?" I asked anxiously.

"She wasn't happy, but she thanked me."

"Then maybe she is innocent."

"Or just polite."

On learning that both our law clerks were tied up for the morning, Helen sent me over to the D.A.'s office to make a copy of everything in the discovery file. This included the pathologist's report, scene-of-the-crime pictures, statements by witnesses, and a complete record of the police investigation. I intended to read it right away; but after paying twenty-five cents a page for the inches-thick dossier, I learned that none other than Joe would be prosecuting. Naturally, finding out why the top man in the office was taking the case demanded some research, but when I went to see him, Joe was busy. No problem. I'd just go back to Abbotts, Devlin, and Devlin, sit at my own desk, and examine the contents of the police file myself. However, the moment I stepped off the elevator, Helen grabbed the manila envelope out of my hand and stuffed it in her Gucci briefcase.

"Can't you wait a second?" I asked her retreating back.

"No. The arraignment is scheduled for three-thirty, and I have a luncheon appointment before tackling all this homework."

"I'll help you cram."

"No thanks." She smiled as the elevator doors started to close.

"Well, study diligently. Your adversary in court is going to be the D.A. himself."

She pushed the hold button. "Not today?"

"Claudette's handling the arraignment, but Joe's scheduled for the preliminary hearing."

Helen looked at me soberly. "The big gun himself, huh? That doesn't look too good for Lois."

"Are you saying Joe only takes airtight cases?"

"When they present themselves, but it's silly to speculate before I've read through all the evidence." She glanced at her watch. "Do me a favor, will you? Meet me in court later. I've got two civil suits in Small Claims after getting Lois's bond set, and it would be nice if you drove her home. Make sure she's all right. Feed her dinner. Tuck her down for the night."

"Play major domo, you mean."

"No, Jewish mother." She released the hold button. "You're a natural for the part."

I didn't protest such blatant typecasting, but the length of the run was longer than I had anticipated. Using her pull with Jack Harrigan, the chief administrator of the detention center, Helen wangled me the extra job of tag-along escort for Lois during the three-minute walk from jail to courthouse via the connecting underground tunnel.

For purposes of security, passage between hoosegow and officialdom was a subterranean, limited-access causeway that had all the charm of a tumbril ride to the guillotine. Feeling ill at ease, I stood by the door and hoped everyone could see the visitor's badge clipped to my lapel. The uniformed woman behind the desk informed me that Lois would be among the next group, but I didn't mind waiting. What did one say to a person who's been accused of murder? Cheer up, maybe you'll get off on a technicality?

A couple of guards came out of a specially marked elevator looking obscenely jolly. Just another routine day in the dungeon for them. Holding the door open, one guard gestured a straggle of prisoners through, five men and two women, all wearing handcuffs, while two more guards brought up the rear. Lois seemed extraordinarily pale but under control; and though some of the prisoners were dressed in the jailhouse jumpsuits, she'd been spared that humiliation.

"Lois," I said, falling into step beside her as the procession started down the ramp to the tunnel. "How're you holding up?"

She'd been staring straight ahead, being brave, I guessed, and hadn't noticed me. Now she looked around. "Ellie? What are you doing here? Where's Helen?"

"She'll meet us in court," I said, obeying the guard's instruction to keep my distance.

"Is everything all right?"

"No change in plan." I smiled encouragingly. "You'll be out of here in a jiffy after the arraignment. Did you eat lunch?"

"I wasn't hungry."

"No matter," I prated on. "You're going to have a wonderful dinner. I'm your date."

By then we had reached the holding cell where prisoners

were kept until someone signaled they could take the elevator up to the third floor. We were forced to part there; and though Lois looked composed entering the courtroom fifteen minutes later, I felt an empathetic stab of pain for her. Flanked by a guard on one side and a gum-chewing whore on the other, Lois seemed incongruously out of place as she sat down, back straight, feet crossed properly at the ankles. When Helen, looking all business and gorgeous to boot, sailed in moments later and flashed her a winning smile, I let out a sigh of relief as if the cavalry had just arrived.

At an arraignment, the presiding judge was limited to acting as a magistrate, imposing bonds and scheduling dates for future appellate actions. For those whose entire defense was established during a five-minute consultation with a public defender outside the courtroom, there was little likelihood of a prolonged debate. But the fee-charging lawyers always had something to say. It generally concerned the amount of bail their clients were obliged to stand and often resulted in some long-winded elocution. As soon as Lois's plea of not guilty was entered, the heavy-duty dickering began.

One would never have guessed, listening to the exchange between the two opposing lawyers, that they were chums in their off hours, members of Fifth and Shoreside. But Claudette Washington, the young, black assistant D.A., and Helen Ramirez took pride in conducting themselves "as adversaries do in law; strive mightily, but eat and drink as friends." This was proven when the judge, after listening to both give their presentations, set bond at twenty thousand dollars and scheduled the preliminary for some ten days hence. The two women nodded at each other, thanked His Honor, then huddled together for a moment, probably deciding where to go to the movies tonight.

Afterward, Helen paused to offer a few words of comfort. "It's all over for now"—she patted Lois's hand—"and Ellie knows just what to do next. She'll deal with the bail-bondsman, then see you home. I know you're exhausted, so let's wait until tomorrow before having a meeting to plan our strategy. Eleven at my office? And don't worry."

Then she was gone, and it was up to me to shepherd her bewildered client through the rigmarole of forms and releases back at the detention center.

An hour later, after skin-crawling delays, the red tape that bound her was peeled off inch by painful inch, permitting Lois a limited sort of freedom. She was ordered to stay in the county and advised to keep in touch with her lawyer.

"Let's get out of here," she said under her breath. "God, I hope there aren't any reporters outside."

"Come on, we'll take the back exit." I peeked out the door to make sure there were no newshounds lurking about, then we dashed across the street to my car.

Wearing dark glasses and a scarf to hide her identity, Lois jumped inside and pulled the visor down. "Hurry, Ellie."

I hurried; and once we left the crowded downtown area for the less traveled side streets, Lois seemed to relax a little, though her voice wasn't quite steady.

"What a godawful experience," she said, slipping off the scarf. "They'll never get me back in that place again."

"Of course not." I agreed.

"Helen is a good attorney, isn't she?"

"One of the best."

"Damn, I wish I had a Valium."

"Take a deep breath and think positive," I directed.

"No, no, it's not that," she waved her hand impatiently. "I want to stop by the office and let them know I'm still alive."

"Can't you just call and break the news?"

"I could, but a picture is worth a thousand words, and that nameplate on my desk is worth twenty years of effort."

"They wouldn't replace you in one day," I protested.

"How long do you think it took them to replace Drake with me?"

I didn't remind her that was a temporary arrangement. Lois was paranoid about her job already; she didn't need any additional comments on the jeopardy of her position. "Do you really feel up to facing that right now?" I demurred tactfully. "Why don't we just go straight to your house, and I'll fix you an omelet. You must be starving; I know I am."

"There's no need for you to drive me, Ellie. When we get to PSSC, I'll just pick up my car and you can go on." Then she sighed. "But if you don't mind waiting and following me home, I could do with some company."

So I sat in the employee parking lot while Lois ran the gauntlet of sideways glances and suddenly hushed conversations in the steel and glass skyscraper that housed PSSC's main offices. I knew it would be a baptism of fire, but when she came out, I could see it had been even worse than I imagined.

She opened the car door and climbed in, then leaned her head against the back of the seat and closed her eyes. "My secretary dropped my car off at the house last night. Wasn't that nice of her? And the bosses have given me a leave of absence. I'm not to bother my head about work for now."

"That's very considerate."

"Considerate?" She opened one baleful eye. "It's an indictment."

I turned on the engine and pulled out of the lot. "You're overreacting, Lois. The company simply wants to protect you."

She snorted. "Come down to earth, Ellie. It's not my welfare that concerns them, but their own. Until this mess is settled, I'm a liability they can't afford."

"Is your nameplate still on the desk?"

"Yes."

"Then quit worrying. Tell the truth, won't it be easier to

deal with this crisis without having to cope with work as well?"

"Frankly, it'll just give me more time to worry, although I can see their side of it. This way, the company won't have to cope with having an accused murderess running one of their departments. After all," she said brittlely, "maybe I really did it. Maybe I've flipped out and I'll start bumping off the rest of them, also. Aren't you frightened to be alone with me, Ellie?"

"Stop that," I ordered. "You can't fall apart now. We haven't eaten yet."

For a minute I though Lois was going to burst into tears. Then she bit her lip and said in a choked voice, "I didn't kill him, you know."

"I know."

Chapter Six

My vote of confidence might have cheered Lois, but it was going to take more than wishful thinking to get her off the hook. Putting somebody else on it was the best way of achieving that end, but those with the power to do such a thing weren't interested in making the effort. With my vast insight into police procedure, culled from years of reading a wide array of murder mysteries, I knew that no one was looking for Prescott's killer as of yesterday. Both the D.A.'s office and the homicide boys were sure they'd found her already. Unless someone obligingly had an attack of conscience and turned himself in, Lois would need a lot more than my faith and good will to win a dismissal of the charges against her at the preliminary hearing.

Still, there was no need to worry. Helen was a top-notch attorney, and Lois was going to provide the hard facts to challenge whatever evidence the D.A. presented. I didn't ask what those hard facts might be. I just assumed they existed just as I assumed that a toy as ugly as a Cabbage Patch doll would never make it as a national obsession. My latest error in judgment came to light the very next morning after Lois emerged, red-eyed and limp, from the initial conference with her lawyer.

Additional evidence that all was not well came when Helen snapped off Kimberly's head for not putting through a call fast enough. Cornering the bad-tempered attorney in the ladies' room a few minutes later, I pulled the story out of her bit by bit.

It seemed Lois had told the police that she hadn't spoken to Drake Prescott on the day of the reception, while conflicting affidavits from several witnesses asserted just the opposite. Six people had seen her approach him. No less than three described her demeanor as aggressive, and as many as five attested that when the public relations director disappeared down a hallway to another part of the building, Lois was at his heels. If these disparate accounts weren't damning enough, Lois's fingerprints on the door and wall of the testing facility made her version of events seem even more unlikely. Assuming there was an innocent, if unfathomable, explanation for these discrepancies, Helen presented her client with the accumulated evidence, only to discover there was no extenuating truth to be revealed. In fact, the truth lay in everybody's story but Lois's.

Under a stiff interrogation by Helen, Lois confessed to omitting a few details from her police statement, such as her confronting Drake Prescott with her knowledge of his perfidious memo and demanding a retraction. But Lois swore she followed him only to the end of the hall where they were able to speak in relative privacy. They did not go into the testing lab, she insisted tearfully, and her fingerprints were there by mere chance. She'd wandered in there earlier looking for an extension cord for the coffeepots, but she'd scarcely set foot inside when a janitor offered her a cord from his storage closet.

Of course, few things are "more tedious than a twice-told tale," but Lois's editorial changes on the second go-round added a certain dramatic value lacking in the first.

Her only excuse for deleting these trifles from her certified narrative to the law was that she didn't want to be tagged as the last person to see Prescott alive . . . apart from the murderer, that is. It would have raised a lot of unnecessary questions, Lois thought. Which was precisely what she had done, Helen charged.

While I agreed that Lois had shown a deplorable lack of common sense in imagining that she could hide from the police what a roomful of people had observed, I believed version two of her chronicle. Here was a chance for her to patch up all the inconsistencies between her statement and everyone else's, yet she still left herself open to doubt. To me, that meant this story, with all its warts, was the whole truth and nothing but the truth. I'd been around Lois long enough to know she was a compulsive neatnik, with never a wrinkle in her skirt, a run in her hose, nor a month's supply of crumpled Kleenex and grocery receipts in her purse. If she had killed Prescott, she would have covered her tracks with a whitewash of lies that couldn't be disputed. Her few words with him would have been an apology for spilling guacamole on his tie. Her chasing after him then could have been with a wet napkin in hand to wipe the offending spot. And while she was at it, the meticulous Lois wouldn't have just sprinkled both her boss and her story with disinfectant, but scrubbed her fingerprints off every inch of the testing facility. But since she had overlooked all these opportunities to clean up her act, the very evidence of her guilt became a demonstration of her innocence, to me anyway.

Unfortunately, Helen did not concur with my psychologically valid analysis. "That is the most convoluted thinking I've ever heard. You and Lois are a perfect match."

"There's no need to get hostile."

"Hostile, hell. I'm downright incensed with that woman, and you're defending her idiocy with the ridiculous argument that she's too smart to be dumb. Well, let me tell you something, Ellie Gordon, only a moron commits the crime of omission on a police statement. No wonder they arrested her. I'd like to wring her neck."

"Let's not compound the felony." I tried for a soothing note. "Obviously, Lois was too frightened to mention her tiff with Drake. You know how things can be misinterpreted."

"Tell me about it." Helen ran a distracted hand through her perfect curls and somehow made them even more attractive. "Wait till the judge hears Corelli's interpretation. It will sound as if Lois had good reason to be scared. I'll never be able to show lack of probable cause, and we are supposed to be seeking a dismissal, remember?"

"I remember, all right. But you can keep in mind that talk is cheap. People who threaten to kill other people seldom act out their fantasies."

"I'm almost afraid to ask," Helen said in a suddenly quiet voice, "but are you saying that Lois openly expressed some sort of malice aforethought?"

"It wasn't *that* open," I said, trying to remove my foot from Lois's mouth, as she evidently had remained mum about a few other tidbits. "Only Betsy and I heard her, and I doubt if we'll be subpoenaed since we never told anyone. Besides, our testimony would just be hearsay."

"Which doesn't make it inadmissible. For your information, if you can quote directly from the person in question, that hearsay could be considered first-hand evidence."

"So? Are you going to call me as a witness?"

"No," she said grimly. "And nobody else better call you either."

"I resent that."

"Resent it all you want. Just don't repeat it."

Sometimes I felt like plucking out Helen's long, mascaraed eyelashes one by one. Exhibiting admirable self-control, I ventured a retort that was merely snide. "Then I'd advise you to pass on a word of warning to Betsy

Hanson as well. Or are you only worried about people who date the D.A.?"

Helen had the grace to flush. "Sorry," she said stiffly. "I trust your discretion. It's Lois's tendency to talk to the wrong people at the wrong time that concerns me. Maybe she threatened Drake's life in front of other witnesses. I'll have to check into it, but that idiot better not have any other surprises in store for me, or I'll quit the case and let her hire F. Lee Bailey . . . for all the good it will do her."

"Helen, you wouldn't."

"Damn right, I would. Lois not only lied to the police, she didn't want to come clean with me just now. I had to pry every word out of her, and apparently she still held some things back."

"Maybe she forgot," I suggested.

"Forgot to inform her lawyer that she threatened to kill the man she's accused of electrocuting?" Helen asked incredulously. "That's not amnesia; that's crass stupidity. I shudder to think what else she isn't telling me."

"Oh, come on. You don't really believe she's guilty."

"Luckily for Lois, it doesn't matter what I believe. My job, if I keep it, is to provide the best defense I can, no matter how difficult the client makes that for me."

"All right, she's been less than candid, but the entire case against her is only a rap sheet of circumstantial evidence. And you of all people know better than to fall for a trout in the milk."

"Resorting to Thoreau now, are you?" Helen was scornful. "Well, let me tell you something about circumstantial evidence. Corelli has more than enough to get the case brought to trial. All I have is a fishy story that stinks to high heaven, unless you can find me a homily that will make Lois's evasions seem halfway credible."

"Credible to whom?" I asked coolly. "The judge or you?"

On that parting shot, I turned on my heel and left the elegant Helen to put another layer of powder on her aquiline nose. She might claim a lawyer didn't have to believe in a client's innocence to make an adequate defense, but who wanted a mechanical Barbie doll in court who'd just go through the motions? I thought she owed Lois something more than a legal right to counsel, although if attorneys were required to sign an article of faith before taking a case, they'd happily perjure themselves before losing a fee. So Helen was honest. She agreed with the prosecution's allegations that since the accused had motive, opportunity, and the poor judgment to leave her fingerprints at the murder site, she had sufficiently incriminated herself. All that candor should make Lois feel great.

I certainly didn't enjoy Helen's unsparing frankness with me; it was an unprovoked and unnecessary attack on my sense of discretion. Still steaming when I was leaving the office that day, I gathered up coat and purse, real leather if not Gucci, and detoured to the doorway of Mark's office. He was working late, as usual.

"Helen Ramirez," I announced to him, "condones the slaughter of helpless calves for the proliferation of designer labels."

He looked up quizzically from the papers that engrossed him. "What's the problem? I thought Helen was your favorite clotheshorse."

"Not anymore." Coming in, I plopped myself on a chair whose ample dimensions were designed to cradle the ample posteriors of worried but weighty clients. "A member of Fifth and Shoreside was arrested for murder today. I will probably not be in agreement with the findings, even when I learn what they are, but the police think she killed her boss."

"And you would like to imitate her strategy."

"Don't tempt me." I couldn't help a little smile.

"Let me guess what's got your dander up. Helen refuses to act as attorney for the defense."

"No. She's acting, all right, but with great overzealousness. You see, Joe Corelli is the prosecutor." I stared into Mark's green eyes, willing him to make the obvious connection.

As always, he was way ahead of me. Tossing down his pen, he leaned back in the wheelchair and folded his hands like Solomon the Wise. "Small world, isn't it? In fact, a little too tight to be altogether comfortable."

"Can't you see me squirming?"

"What do you want me to say, Ellie? Do the noble thing and stop dating Joe, or tell Helen to blow it out her ear?"

Mark was grinning, so maybe there wasn't anything to worry about after all. "No." I laughed a touch shamefacedly. "But I want you to know that my big mouth will remain shut about this case and all others."

"I never doubted it for an instant." Then he added, "And I don't believe Helen does either."

"Maybe not," I allowed. "But it was the thought that counted."

As if I would weaken the defense with an unmindful word to Joe. Everything I said to the D.A. was prudently thought out, judiciously considered, and edited for publication. Naturally, a theoretical discussion was bound to crop up now and then, but when it did, I was careful to give Joe only my personal interpretation.

Perhaps it was my eagerness to do that very thing that made me accept his invitation to go sailing on Sunday afternoon. Or maybe it was Joe's sly promise of merry maritime maneuvers once we were moored at some secluded cove. Whatever the reason, I forewarned Joe that I'd never developed my sea legs; but he swore that with his expert tutelage, I'd be a first-rate first mate in no time. No time was right. It should have been obvious that a woman who didn't know starboard from port would be all at sea on the briny.

When I arrived at the marina, at least I looked like a sailor. Saturday, I'd gone shopping and come back with white duck pants, a long-sleeved boat-necked sweater in bright crimson, and to match it, a pair of red canvas deck shoes so that when Joe swept me off my color-coordinated feet, I wouldn't fall overboard entirely. He provided the rain slicker and hat in case the weather turned miserable.

But it was an ideal February day, with not a cloud in the sky and enough of a breeze to blow away the smog and keep the sails billowing. The *Paisana* was an impressive twenty-foot cruiser with the added advantage of an inboard motor.

My misgivings about helping Joe buffet the deep soon disappeared as he directed me how to belay the ropes while he ran up the spinnaker. This was great. Why had I been worried about my lack of experience? Joe didn't mind teaching a raw recruit how to hold a steady course, and I relished the idea of sharing his favorite pastime with him. After all, he had taken up double acrostics for me.

However, an hour after we left port, I remembered why I was a dyed-in-the-wool landlubber. Not merely because I disliked Popeye cartoons as a kid, but out of deference to a stomach that had never learned to digest spinach . . . on the water . . . with the boat rocking . . . back and forth.

We were anchored about a mile offshore when my condition developed. Joe broke out the picnic hamper, and I broke out in a cold sweat. No problem, I told myself firmly. I just wouldn't eat. He accepted my lame excuse of not being hungry but insisted I have a glass of wine. That was a mistake. Five minutes later, my stomach was ready to jump overboard. I even thought of joining it. So what if I drowned? At least I wouldn't have to watch the skipper of this ever-moving vessel lunch on truffle pâté while his sole passenger wondered how much longer she could keep her breakfast down.

No. I couldn't spoil Joe's outing. He wanted so much for me to have fun. Mind over matter, Ellie, I echoed my mother's directive whenever we took a car trip, and since there was only one other matter on my mind at the moment, I led with it.

"Joe, have you considered the possibility that the police made a mistake about Lois McCoin?"

"No, but I gather you have." He smeared cheese and pâté on a cracker and plopped it in his mouth.

I looked away. "The notion has occurred to me. Drake Prescott seemed to be an unlikeable character by all reports, and I can't help thinking there were others who might have wanted him out of the way."

"Who, for instance?"

"I don't know, but there were plenty of people at the reception."

"And the myriad possibilities have stirred your Nancy Drew curiosity, huh?" He smiled good-naturedly.

Ignoring the rise and fall of the ocean and the wine sloshing in his glass, I offered my theory about Lois's innocence. Joe's reaction wasn't as harsh as Helen's, but he did say I had a prejudiced attitude. Biased in Lois's favor.

"Maybe so," I conceded, "except she doesn't . . ."

He took more cheese. "Doesn't what?" When I didn't answer, he looked at me closely. "Ellie, are you all right?"

About to tell him I was perfectly fine, I thought better about opening my mouth. Fortunately, Captain Corelli was no novice at recognizing what a green face meant, and he rushed me to the rail where one unendurable glance down at the billowing waves was enough to make me heave ho.

"Why didn't you tell me you were feeling sick?" he asked afterward, tenderly wiping my forehead with a damp napkin.

"Because I was having so much fun," I gasped before diving for the side again.

The trip back to the marina took only twenty endless minutes, thanks to the auxiliary motor, with Joe alternately steering and casting anxious glances over his shoulder to make sure I didn't become shark bait. Not that it wasn't a tempting escape from my misery, but Joe just would have dragged me back aboard, *sans* a leg or two. This way, I was able to wobble up to my front door, needing only his supporting arm to keep me from falling into the hydrangeas.

"You'll be out of sick bay soon," he promised like a true oarsman. "I'll dose you with Alka Seltzer."

When that didn't work, he fed me every stomach disorder remedy I had in the bathroom cabinet. Finally I collapsed into bed from sheer exhaustion, vaguely hearing Joe close the door behind him as he left.

Not until the next morning, when I opened one eye as a tester and realized I was over the worst, did I feel up to suffering some healthy embarrassment. What a captivating companion I turned out to be. Dressed in all my nautical finery, I spent half our romantic voyage hanging over the taffrail. Charming, Ellie, charming. A picture-postcard view of your spreading behind. Joe must have been dazzled. I did warn him of my inexperience as a coxswain, but he was so sure a woman who owned ocean-front property and a man with a boat would be a perfect match. I showed him, all right. "Love the sea? I dote upon it—from the beach."

Well, chalk up one unshared pastime. My handsome gondolier probably would tell me to paddle my own canoe from now on . . . if he hadn't already paddled off in his, I thought with a prickle of unease. Gentleman Joe hadn't exactly offered to spend the night bathing my fevered brow, and that was unusual for him. So what did I expect from my attentive lover, I scoffed, a gift-wrapped bottle of Pepto-Bismol left on the bathroom sink? No, but a phone call this morning to find out if I were still alive. It wasn't like Joe to neglect such courtesies.

When I didn't hear from him by eight, I knew I'd been left in dry dock. And by eight-thirty, I had also come to the conclusion that it wasn't only my unlovely performance of yesterday that prompted his lukewarm departure. If *mal de mer* were no way to kindle the flame of romance, a discussion of murder was certainly no aphrodisiac.

Chapter Seven

When I arrived at work, tardy but tenacious, there was a message on my desk. Reprieve. Joe wasn't casting me adrift after all. But the name on the note was Dan Gordon, whom I wished someone would maroon on a desert island. My pest of an ex-husband was calling on the average of twice a week now, which was twice as often as I wanted to hear from him. It was hard to believe how that man could interpret a direct no as encouragement. Then, to make my droopy spirits sag even more, Helen buzzed for me.

Great. That was just what I needed on a blue Monday when I still looked green around the gills. A comparison test with the beauteous barrister. No doubt Helen would be aglow with Color-Me-Perfect blush and Lovlier-Than-Thou lipgloss. But when I sucked in my sore gut and went to answer her summons, she wasn't exactly oozing with radiance herself.

"Ellie, I'm glad you're here. Would you run over to PSSC and pick up some papers from Lois's secretary?" Intermittently rubbing her wan but wondrous brow, Helen explained that she'd requested the last six months worth of memos from the pr department, hoping they would show that Lois and Drake Prescott had an amiable working relationship.

"Clever thinking."

"Thank you. Oh, and while you're there, find out which way the wind blows with Lois's secretary. I'm probably going to use her to back up all the nice notes, but see what kind of supporting witness she'd make."

"You mean, you value my opinion after all?" I couldn't resist the dig.

"Of course," she answered with a poke of her own. "It's only your pseudo-Freudian theories I fault, not your normal judgment."

"Touché. But as long as the layperson is playing legal beagle, why don't I check out April Evans while I'm at it?"

"Forget Prescott's secretary. She's being called by the prosecution, so all I need is a copy of her police statement."

"You may be missing an opportunity. April is the girl who showed Lois the infamous memo, the one that may outweigh all the others. I think it would be an advantage if the murdered man's own secretary spoke up in behalf of the accused."

"Very well," Helen consented. "Sound her out too, but don't spend all morning over there."

Her phone rang just then, and she covered her eyes before answering it. The call only lasted a moment, but after hanging up the receiver, she laid her head on her arms. "God, I feel rotten."

"A touch of the flu?"

"Hangover."

So that was why she looked almost as bad as I did. "I thought your hot date was for Friday night. Don't tell me you spent the whole weekend carousing."

"Only part of it. The rest of the time I was trying to drown my sorrows," she admitted wearily.

"Some fun. Who drove you to the bottle, anyway, a two-timer in a three-piece suit?" I figured it had to be another lawyer.

"You don't know him." Helen managed a halfhearted smile, and pushed back an errant lock of hair.

After suggesting that she take two aspirin, though even Extra-strength Tylenol won't remedy heartache, I left to carry out my assignment.

Too bad Helen was having personal problems, but professionally she had done the right thing by employing my investigative skills. Previewing witnesses was no simple task. It called for tact, discretion, and an ability to make character analyses. Being sent to pick up the memos was a clever way to get me inside the door, but once there, it would be up to me to separate the chaff from the wheat.

Feeling only slightly compensated for not getting a call from Joe this morning, I circled the power company for ten minutes in search of an empty parking meter. Finally I gave up and drove to the municipal garage three blocks away. It wasn't the walk I minded, but the dark gloomy cavern of a building that was unguarded and unprotecting of lone females who couldn't find a space lower than the fourth level. Waiting for the creaky elevator to inch its way up always made me jittery, and I always imagined being accosted where no one was around to hear my cries. After all, who knew what evil lurked in the shadow of a blue Chevy? Fortunately, none today, and I made it downstairs without being mugged or raped or held for ransom by Guatamalan terrorists.

In sharp contrast with the decor and ambience of Casa Grande's drive-in haunt, PSSC's headquarters was a modern high-rise with velvet ropes at the entrance and two uniformed doormen whose mission in life was to accord visitors the VIP treatment. I got it all the way up to the Public Relations Department where Lois's secretary was waiting for me. Surprisingly, Jane Chestnut was a young, plumpish woman rather than the matronly type I had pictured.

"Ms. Gordon, how nice to meet you at last." She smiled and handed me a manila envelope. "It took some doing to get this together for you, but nothing's too much trouble if it will help Mrs. McCoin. Isn't this whole thing just too, too awful?"

"We all appreciate your cooperation in such trying circumstances," I told her.

She rolled her prominent blue eyes expressively. " 'Trying circumstances' is an understatement. It's been a madhouse around here. Nobody knows what to do, though they did send someone down from the sixth floor to handle things for now. But with Mr. Prescott and Mrs. McCoin gone . . . excuse me a minute, please, while I take this call."

Leaving her on the phone, I peeked into Lois's office and was reassured to find her nameplate was still on the desk. A few plants and a bright cushion on the swivel chair were the only dash of individuality in the rather cramped quarters, but two-room suites and walnut bookshelves were undoubtedly reserved for the upper echelons of management. Lois had to make do with metal-trimmed formica.

"That was Records on the phone." Jane Chestnut came up behind me. "They want to know when we can expect the file back from Ms. Ramirez."

"Not for quite awhile. The courts prefer originals as evidence, but if you need the information, I can have everything Xeroxed and send you the copies tomorrow."

"Would you? Not that I think we'll need all that old stuff, but Mr. Jamsheedi might want to take a look to familiarize himself with procedure. He's the one from the sixth floor." She lowered her voice. "An Iranian gentleman. Quite an expert with statistics," she added, as though that special skill compensated for his unfortunate choice of nationality. "I've offered to help him, but he seems to prefer April."

Sensing an office rivalry and banking on the theory that people who speak in hushed tones generally have plenty to say, I decided it might be a good idea to plumb Mrs. Chestnut's loquacious depths. Mentally tightening the belt of my imaginary trench coat, I deviously suggested we adjourn for a danish, my treat.

Her chubby cheeks flushed with the hungry glow of a sweetaholic. "There's an employee coffee shop right on this floor," she said, taking her purse and double-checking to be sure that she'd locked her desk securely.

"Are you always so cautious when you're just going down the hall?" I asked, thinking of the trusting way we operated over at Abbotts, Devlin, and Devlin.

"We've been asked to keep tight security ever since the picketing began a few months ago." Again she dropped her tone to a barely audible murmur. "One of them actually got inside the building before the doorman tackled him at the elevator. Who knows what those kooks might steal."

"Well, they're certainly not after nuclear secrets, though your purse might be tempting. But I wouldn't worry. There were only two of them out there just now, and one was a young, pregnant girl. Very easy to tackle."

Jane sniffed. "They get on my nerves. Some of them heckle us when we come to work in the morning. It shouldn't be allowed."

Rather than stir her ire further with a patriotic remark about freedom of speech and the right of assembly, even outside the doors of the all-powerful power company, I responded with a non-committal grunt.

We had been threading our way through a maze of dividers which sectioned off the floor into a series of cubbyholes masquerading as real offices. It was the modern concept so beloved by commercial architects and so hated by the junior executives who have to cope with the noise, interruptions, and lack of privacy. The coffee shop, however, occupied a space blessed by walls that went all the way to the ceiling and an actual door instead of a doorway. Jane pushed it open and strode purposefully over to the counter where there were two or three people ahead of us.

"I suppose everyone is pretty upset about Drake Prescott's death," was my opening gambit.

Jane looked around, then said out of the side of her mouth, "Some people are more upset than others."

I contained my curiosity until we placed our orders and found a secluded table in the corner. Then, over a very large cinnamon roll, Jane Chestnut unburdened her resentful little heart.

"I'm not one to speak ill of the dead," she murmured before doing exactly that, "but Mr. Prescott won't be mourned by many around here. Mrs. McCoin isn't the only person he hurt, one way or another. When he didn't like someone, he undercut them."

"Guess he wasn't the most popular guy in the company," I said with deceptive disinterest, inwardly delighted at this confirmation of my earlier deduction.

"You can say that again. But he also had some close friends . . . or should I say, one especially intimate friend." This was announced *sotto voce* and punctuated by a quiet snicker.

All it took was another giant cinnamon roll to get the rest of the whispered story from her. It was amazing how gossip traveled around this rabbit warren of a building, especially when the spicy stuff was passed mouth to mouth in undertones. By the time Jane completed her tale of love, lust, jealousy, and revenge, she had bent my ear, all right.

However, the rest of my senses were able to appreciate that what I'd learned could be put to good use. All the defense needed was a reasonable doubt, and Jane Chestnut had provided enough reasons to doubt practically everyone connected with Drake Prescott. I couldn't wait to inform Helen what her personally handpicked supersleuth had discovered, but when I presented her with an account of my cleverly garnered information, she was unimpressed, to say the least.

"What's the matter with you? I asked for some papers, not another batch of harebrained ideas."

"You also told me to speak to Jane Chestnut, which I did. And just look what I found out."

"Nothing."

"What do you mean, nothing? Don't you think it could be significant that Drake Prescott was having an affair with his secretary?"

"I don't know whether it's significant or not, or even if it's true, unless you verified with April Evans that she was sleeping with her boss."

"The point is," I said patiently, "that Carole Prescott thought it was true. She had come to PSSC only three days before her husband was killed and had made a real stink about his being out to lunch with the gorgeous April. Then at the reception on Saturday at Canyon Escondido, after another public set-to with hubby, Carole spilled champagne accidentally on purpose all over the voluptuous secretary's low-cut dress."

"And that's what took you an hour and a half, collecting all this ridiculous gossip? I don't believe it. I send you to check on two character witnesses and you come back with two characters torn to shreds."

"Three," I corrected. "The women in his life may have been less than wonderful, but Drake Prescott was no living doll, either. There are evidently a lot of people glad to see him gone, though I still think a jealous wife is a more likely murder suspect than a disgruntled co-worker."

"Even one who lied on her police statement?" Helen reminded me.

"Carole Prescott could have lied too," I argued. "Maybe she just hasn't been found out yet. What if she neglected to mention that after her champagne glass was empty, she wandered over to the testing facility where her husband ran to escape her wrath?"

Helen waved me away. "Why don't you write thrillers, Ellie? Put that vivid imagination to use, but not on company time, please. Right now, I'd appreciate having these letters typed. Thank you."

Anyone else would have been smart enough to leave, letters in hand, tail between legs, but I had to stick my neck out one more inch. "There may be no proof at the moment, but I'm positive there's a damn good murder motive in that love triangle somewhere. I know Carole Prescott from the country club. Why don't I go talk to her after work?"

"Don't you dare. Not after work, not during work, or any other time." Helen tossed down her pen impatiently. "I don't think you quite understand, but my job is to see if I can get the charges against my client dropped, not get myself charged with malpractice. You don't know what you're looking for; you don't even have a right to look."

"Certainly, the defense has a right to build a case."

"Against someone else?"

"But Lois may be innocent," I protested.

"Of course she may be innocent, and that's exactly what I hope to show, in my own limited way. But I am not Perry Mason. In the world of non-fiction, lawyers do not get their clients off by providing the D.A. with the 'real murderer.' " Do I make myself clear?"

Here I was, selflessly offering to extend my services as a private eye, free of charge, fully in the interest of justice, but Helen wanted no part of it. Because she preferred going by *corpus juris* rather than Erle Stanley Gardner or because she thought Lois was guilty? That still bothered me, although Helen had stopped making noises about dropping the case, which was some improvement. And in all fairness, I'd never known her to shortchange a client because her professional opinion didn't coincide with her professional obligations. Maybe the hangover just hadn't worn off yet.

"I gather you never got around to asking the notorious April Evans if she'd put in a good word for Lois," Helen said dryly.

"And I gather you never got around to taking the two

aspirin," was my retort. "But as it happens, I did see April, and she'll do anything she can to help Lois."

"Thank goodness for small favors."

"You're welcome."

Back at my desk, I pawed listlessly through a pile of messages. Betsy wanted to meet me at Barney's after work for a drink. Good. Dennis wanted to know what had happened to the default judgments he needed to have typed. Hadn't Barbara taken care of that yet? Damn. And then I struck gold. Two phone calls from the D.A.'s office, an hour apart. Would Ms. Gordon ring back you know who, ASAP, Kimberly had written.

"May I speak to Mr. Corelli, please?" My voice was subdued, totally businesslike, and as anonymously impersonal as a long-distance telephone operator. Joe's secretary recognized it immediately.

"Oh, Ms. Gordon." Dina's tones dripped with soothing syrup. "Mr. Corelli's been trying to reach you all morning. He's going to be so disappointed."

"He's out now?" I asked redundantly.

"Yes, but he left a note . . . wait . . . here it is. He'll meet you for lunch at the tamale stand on the south side of the Civic Plaza at twelve sharp. But it's too late, isn't it? Oh, dear."

"Well, thanks anyway. Just tell him I returned his call."

I stared at the clock. 11:58. Might as well forget catching Joe. Anyway, this was my day for a workout at the spa. Then I stood up, grabbed my purse and ran for the elevator.

It was 12:15 when I found him sitting on a bench by the fountain. He looked very attractive to my prejudiced eyes in his blue three-piece suit, his dark hair slightly mussed by the wind. "Sorry I'm late." I flopped down beside him. "Only got your message at noon."

He didn't seem at all perturbed. In fact, he was solicitous. "I would have called you this morning, but I thought you might want to sleep late."

Was that considerate or was that considerate? "I'm fine. Completely cured. Dry land does it every time."

"Yes, you look terrific." His brown eyes approved me.

Either Joe was less discerning than my mirror, or detecting had worked magic on my appearance. At least my stomach was back to normal, which was lucky, because we lunched on tamales, *alfresco*.

"I'm sorry about yesterday," I said as we fed the pigeons our leftovers.

"You don't have to apologize for getting seasick."

"No, I mean for talking shop when we're really in competing businesses. It's your job to build the best possible case you can against Lois, and I had no right trying to influence the prosecution."

"You're not exactly the defending attorney, so I wouldn't worry."

"Still, it was a breach of ethics," I insisted.

"Fine. You can put on some sackcloth and ashes and model it for me."

"Okay. When?"

"Next Tuesday," he laughed. "But I have a better idea. Why not sentence yourself to doing a community service instead?"

"Like what? Volunteer for weed and litter patrol?"

"Hardly. With my ingenious plan, you could use your bloodhound instincts to ethical and humanitarian advantage. Join Crimewatchers. My personal invitation."

"I thought we weren't going to mix business and pleasure ever again."

"Just consider it another shared interest." He squeezed my hand confidently, as if the one we shared yesterday had been so wonderfully unifying. "You'll get your very own beeper," he coaxed.

"I want a Dick Tracy watch or nothing."

The truth was, I felt above his grown-up Eagle Scout group. The idea of reducing my role to mere voyeur held little appeal to someone who had been an active participant in crime-solving once upon a time. Even this morning, I had been close to making some real discoveries. But then, close only counts in horseshoes.

"I hate to eat and run, Ellie, but I've an appointment in a few minutes. Think you can live without me until tomorrow night?"

"It'll be tough, but I'll do my best. Wait, Joe. One question." I tagged behind him as he hurried to the corner before the WALK signal changed. "Do lawyers for the defense ever get a client off by finding the real culprit?"

"Sure," he called over his shoulder. "Perry Mason does it all the time."

Chapter Eight

Barney's was conveniently located catty-corner from the office, but when I slid into the black Naugahyde booth where Betsy was waiting, it was well past five and she was definitely annoyed.

"I've had to send three different men packing in the last ten minutes," she complained. "And one of them was really quite personable. I don't know why I didn't let him join me."

"Because you love sitting in bars alone like an ice princess while men drool from afar and wonder what it would take to melt those big blue eyes."

"One double martini usually does the trick." She indicated her half-empty glass. "But I paid for this one out of my own pocket."

As if someone had spread the news over a loudspeaker, a double martini was delivered to our table, compliments of the gentleman in the back booth, the waitress told us.

"Is he the one you liked?" I asked Betsy, glancing over my shoulder at the fellow in the gray suit.

"If you will look in the opposite direction," she informed

me, "you will see the donor. It's Dennis Devlin, and I'm fairly certain the drink's for you."

Sure enough, when I turned my head the other way, there was Dennis waving at me. "Oh, this is my reward for being wonderful," I explained.

"How wonderful?" she asked skeptically.

"Rather than bore you with my accomplishments, let me just say I earned a lunch too. My third this month."

"My, my, you do drive a hard bargain."

"Not all my efforts are so appreciated."

Perhaps because I was still smarting from Helen's evaluation of my morning's work, I told Betsy about my discoveries at PSSC. My deductions didn't seem so much far-fetched to her as impossible to prove.

"First of all," she said, "this reputed affair between Prescott and his secretary is unverifiable, unless you find a motel receipt or something. And secondly, even if Carole Prescott believed her husband was cheating on her, killing him seems an effort in futility. Knocking off the appetizing April would have been more to the point."

"Not necessarily. If Drake planned to leave his wife, getting rid of the future Mrs. Prescott would have been, at best, a temporary solution. Obviously, the man was looking for greener pastures, and he would have found a replacement for April eventually. Maybe not as *zaftig*, but Carole couldn't very well spend the rest of her life eliminating all bosomy competition. It would be too big a drain on the world's secretarial skills."

"You really think she coolly chose to be widowed rather than divorced?" Betsy's tone implied grave doubt.

"Who said anything about 'cool'? Carole was madder than hell at the guy to make those scenes in public. Still, look what she had to lose. A ten-room house in Brentwood, country club membership, bottomless charge accounts, plus the status that goes with those trappings. A widow receiving double indemnity can afford all that and heaven too. But a divorced housewife is lucky to get her alimony check on time, especially if ex-hubby has to support a second family as well. Remember Dr. Willoughby's wife? She tried to commit suicide after he ran off with his nurse. Said her ritzy friends dropped her when she couldn't keep up with them anymore."

"That's because she hung around with plastic people."

"I know. But Carole Prescott runs in those same circles, so she could be just as brittle."

"Possibly, but not all birds kill to stay in the gilded cage. Some survive being set free from captivity. You didn't crack under the strain."

"I most certainly did. Don't you remember your rescue operation?"

"A minor resuscitation. Yours was strictly a bush-league breakdown. No attempted suicide or murder."

"And because I didn't bludgeon Dan to death with a frozen brisket, Carole couldn't have killed her husband either?" I scoffed. "Well, allow me to disillusion you. Given the opportunity, I might have been tempted to flip a switch and scramble Dan's blood cells, but not for his insurance money. I'm not that practical. But I think I understand Carole. We suffered similar blows to the ego, if nothing else."

"Nothing else is right," Betsy agreed.

"You're entitled to your opinion," I acknowledged, "but the one I really don't understand is April Evans. Why would a girl with her bait go after an already hooked fish when she could net a nice, eligible bachelor?"

"Who could be more eligible than a man getting a divorce so he can marry you?"

"Aha," I pounced. "Your sapient observation has brought us right back to Carole Prescott."

"Not us. You," Betsy said, picking up the menu. "Don't gape. You heard me correctly. Your theory sounds valid, but it needs a bit more research."

"You're actually suggesting that I pursue the question?

No tricks?" I prodded. "No bean sprout surprise if I take your advice?"

"You can start with a triple-decker pastrami sandwich this very minute," Betsy assured me as the waitress came to take our orders.

"Then as an appetizer," I said, jumping at the chance, "let me send this note to Dennis."

"A thank-you for the drink?"

"Not really." I pointed him out to the waitress who was too new at her job to be able to tell one three-piece suit from another, and while she went scurrying off with my message, no doubt imagining a romantic intrigue, I leaned across the table. "Dennis happens to be April Evans' attorney."

"So I get to watch an undercover agent in action. How fascinating. Shall I take notes?"

"Shut up. Here he comes."

As usual, Dennis had a girl at his table, but he left her there when he joined us. "See?" he grinned. "I always keep my promises. Want another one?" He nodded toward my empty glass.

"That was just a one-martini brief, thanks, and it will be sitting on your desk very shortly."

"You're a jewel, Ellie, a regular jewel. Isn't she?" Dennis looked at Betsy for confirmation.

"A diamond of the first water," my friend answered obligingly.

Dennis tilted his chair backward and beamed at her. "So, how are things going with you, Bets?"

"Just ginger-peachy."

I shot her a withering glance. "What Betsy means is that her work at Canyon Escondido has slowed to a snail's pace since Prescott's death. The murder left the company with egg on its face. Sadly, they lost their media expert just when they needed him most."

"What's that got to do with Betsy?" Dennis asked. "I

thought she worked for the construction firm that's building the plant."

"She does, but some investors are thinking of scrubbing Phase Two. The adverse publicity has them biting their nails," I explained before Betsy could tell him I didn't know what I was talking about. "You don't walk in and turn on a second nuclear reactor just like that." I snapped my fingers. "It takes great preparation as well as millions of dollars. Some people are wondering if the game is worth the candle."

Having paved the way, albeit with a few potholes, I poked the olive in my glass and said almost indifferently, "Do you suppose the new public relations director will keep April on as his private secretary, or will he bring in someone else?"

Thus urged, Dennis began to discuss the very topic I found most interesting. "He better keep her. April really depends on that salary. Her ex-husband is holding back on child support payments until the custody suit goes to court."

"What's he trying to do, prove he's an unfit father?"

"No, show that April isn't capable of giving the kids what he can. The guy's got money, but it's not the children he wants to deprive. It's his ex-wife."

"Poor April. What's she going to do?" I asked with casual concern.

"Not pay my fee for starters," Dennis shrugged.

"Can't you take it out in trade?" Betsy offered slyly.

I was about to kick her under the table when Dennis answered quite seriously. "Believe me, I tried. That girl has everything I ever wanted in a woman."

"Beauty, boobs, and a behind," I specified.

"Maybe," he admitted with a sheepish smile. "But all that anatomy is going to waste. She's off men."

"Says who?"

"Says April. I didn't exactly ask her to spend the weekend with me in Tijuana," he qualified, "but she won't even go to the movies unless her kids come along."

"The lady could be committed to someone else," I suggested.

"Could be, but she never said so."

"Then maybe it's the kind of relationship a girl doesn't brag about," I said offhandedly.

"You mean an involvement with a married man?" Dennis shook his head. "The last thing she needs is one more complication in her life. Besides, April couldn't be that dumb. If her ex found out, he'd nail her with corrupting the morals of his children."

"People sometimes do foolish things, Dennis. 'The heart has its reasons that reason knows not of.' "

"Yeah?"

"Yeah."

"So maybe she is that dumb. Waitress, another round of drinks for these charming ladies. I hate to leave"—he stood up—"but it just so happens that I have a date who's getting restless for my company." He winked. "Thanks for the fast work on the brief, Ellie. See you around, Bets."

"Interesting," she remarked as Dennis picked his way through the crowded room, "but you didn't learn a thing."

"Oh, yes, I did."

"Really? And what was that?" Betsy raised her brows.

"That Lois McCoin isn't the only one who doesn't tell her lawyer everything."

Actually I'd gotten zilch on my fishing expedition, an apt bit of legal linguistics that meant angling for an angle. I was just hoping all the sines and cosines in Prescott's trinomial geometric configuration would prove the basic mathematical equation that two is company, three is a crowd. Too simple a formula perhaps, but as Shakespeare said, "There is divinity in odd numbers." Maybe what I needed was a mystical Napier's rod.

What I didn't need was a triple-decker pastrami sandwich. My artful sleuthing had earned me nothing to merit so delightful a reward, and certainly my figure couldn't stand the strain of so much unbridled joy. A Western omelet was my compromise, hold the hash browns and toast.

"What are you going to do now?" Betsy asked.

"Eat my supper."

"Don't tell me you're giving up."

"There's nothing to give up. You heard Dennis. April Evans is a poor working girl who doesn't want to cash in on her assets."

"No more jealous wife theory?"

"Theories are the easy part. As you pointed out yourself, where's the evidence? Why should I believe the torrid tale Jane Chestnut mumbled in my ear this morning? Just because April Evans looks like Miss February doesn't mean she was Prescott's personal centerfold."

"Can you check his bank account?"

"What for? To see if he paid for his *Playboy* subscription?"

"No, you idiot," Betsy said with the triumphal air of one pulling a bunny out of a hat. "To see if he withdrew large sums of money for no apparent reason. If you had a sweet little lover burdened with financial problems, wouldn't you feel obliged to line her empty pockets with a suitably generous gift now and then?"

"You wily conniver." I grinned in admiration. "That's fantastic. But it would take a court order to check his private finances. I can't gain access to that kind of information."

"How about a search warrant?"

"You mean print one up at the office tomorrow in my spare time? That's a good idea. Then all I have to do is steal a uniform and impersonate a policewoman."

"Warrants are reserved for those who wear the blue, huh?" Betsy mused. "Well, you know an officer of the law very personally, and I think he might check something out if you asked him nicely."

"Joe? Not on your life."

"Why not?"

"A jurisdictional conflict," was all I said, not mentioning my pledge of permanent nonintervention.

Still, Betsy's about-face was pretty amusing. The bearer of bean sprouts had suddenly sprouted a reconnoitering eye herself. The idea that Prescott's bank account might reveal the truth was the scientific thinking of a real investigator, I praised my friend, but Betsy modestly disclaimed any such talent. Crime detection was my area of expertise, she said with conviction.

"But why are you encouraging me? Come on, fess up. I don't trust skinny blondes bearing pastrami on rye."

"I was going to tell you anyway," she admitted. "I saw Lois today."

"You went to her house?"

"No. She came to Canyon Escondido while I was there."

"What in hell for?"

"I don't know." Betsy shrugged helplessly. "But it wasn't very pleasant. The men on construction didn't know who she was, but one of the bosses spotted her and asked her to leave."

"You're joking."

"That's what Lois said, and I'm sure he was quite serious."

"So, did she leave?"

"Yes. I took her to a quiet coffee shop not far from there and we talked." Betsy paused a moment. "She swears she didn't kill Prescott."

"I know."

"She even thinks she's being framed."

"By whom?"

Betsy raised her hands, then let them fall listlessly. "She has no idea, but when I heard her at the plant, I thought she was going to accuse all of them of being in a conspiracy against her. The way she carried on . . ."

"Oh, crap," I said quietly.

"It took two cups of Sanka to calm her," Betsy sighed, "but nothing will convince her that once this is over, she'll get her job back."

"She's still worried about her damn nameplate at PSSC when there's a good chance it'll be converted to a number at the state pen? What's wrong with the woman?"

"Is the case against her that strong?" Betsy asked, then after a look at my face, retracted the question. "I realize you can't answer that, but Lois did tell me she lied on her police statement."

"Wonderful." I closed my eyes. "Why doesn't she take an ad out in the paper? Oh, I don't mean that your knowing will do any harm"—I waved my hand in apology—"but Lois certainly picked the wrong time to make a full disclosure. What she failed to tell the police, they got from everyone else."

"She's frightened, Ellie."

"That's understandable."

"She thinks no one is on her side, including Helen."

"That might be understandable too," I said, not elaborating.

"Well, you know the details," Betsy granted, "but I think it's crummy of Helen not to hire a private investigator."

"Does Lois want one? Interesting. But I'm afraid her attorney has an aversion to Perry Mason tactics."

"And an aversion, it seems, to doing what her client requests."

Betsy was full of surprises tonight, and for none of them did I have a ready answer. Aside from any other consideration, since Lois had talked to an outsider, I didn't know how much still was deemed privileged information between attorney and client or if the client had waived confidentiality for the privilege of friendship.

"I'm probably not supposed to know all this," Betsy said perceptively, "but I thought if you weren't aware of the ramifications, you should be."

"Why me? There's nothing I can do. Helen already posted a KEEP OFF sign for my benefit."

"Too bad." Betsy grabbed the check from the waitress and got to her feet. "Then you'll have to tell that to Lois when she calls you tonight. Oh, and by the way, dinner's on me."

And so it should have been, though a free omelet was hardly adequate recompense for being made the next recipient of Lois's complaints. Not that I didn't want to help her, but my hands were tied thanks to Helen Ramirez. Even if they weren't, there was no reason to think I could accomplish a storybook ending to Lois's problems. She, however, had more faith in my abilities.

I expected a phone call, but it was my doorbell that rang at nine that night. "I want to hire you as a private investigator," were Lois's opening words.

Instead of rejecting her rash offer immediately, I shoved a drink into her hand. She took a gulp of scotch and repeated her request. "Will you do it?"

What a question. Naturally I'd like to, if only for the sake of proving myself right. But personal conceit wasn't the only issue here. Lois's future might depend on my answer, and according to the attorney for the defense, the best strategy was to observe the rules.

"Lois, since you're already paying for legal advice, why not take it?"

"Because Helen has a very narrow view of proper procedure," she said tartly, "and I don't want to be ground under the wheels of justice."

"You won't be. Helen is a good lawyer, and if she doesn't recommend a detective at this stage, we should trust her. After all, a preliminary hearing only determines if there's enough evidence to warrant a trial. It doesn't decide guilt or innocence."

"Oh, no? What do you think people will presume after the hearing? I've worked in pr for twenty-five years, and I know about selling an idea. With all the publicity this case is getting, if I'm charged with a crime I didn't commit, I could just as easily be convicted of a crime I didn't commit. You find me twelve people in this county who haven't read about Prescott's murder, and I'll show you a jury from outer space."

"That doesn't mean you won't get a fair trial. Impaneling a jury is a very selective process that weeds out those with preconceived opinions."

"So you agree Helen is unlikely to win a dismissal next week."

"I didn't say that."

"Then why are you touting the benefits of being judged by my peers if you don't believe it will go that far?"

"What I believe has nothing to do with it, Lois," I echoed Helen's words. "The law is designed to move one step at a time. An arrest is not a verdict, which is why police findings are taken to court for evaluation. That's the preliminary hearing. One judge, no jury. Afterward, and only if the prosecution's case is found to have merit, does the defense get a chance to counter the charges at a trial."

"The truth is, you're guilty until you can prove yourself innocent."

"Forget what I said. I'm explaining this poorly. Each side just takes turns, that's all."

"I think you're explaining things very well," Lois said in a quiet voice. "Much better than Helen did."

"Please, don't listen to me. I only know what I read in a brief." No laugh from Lois. "Ellie Gordon, amateur advocate," I jeered. "Everybody else has to go to law school for years to understand statutes and doctrines. I just graduated a six-month course in managing a law office, and already I'm hanging out a shingle." Still no answering titter. "Just promise me one thing, Lois," I said in a last frantic attempt at humor. "Don't tell Helen I infringed on her territory or she'll sue me for impersonating a shyster."

"I'll pay you a hundred dollars a day."

"What?"

"And if you find the person who really murdered Prescott, I'll send you on a two-week Caribbean cruise as a bonus."

"Lois, hold on a minute," I said hastily. "If you're serious about this, you need a real private eye. I'm not qualified."

"You solved Katherine Busch's murder, not the police."

"Yes . . . well . . ." I searched my dithering mind for an excuse. "She was practically a stranger to me."

"And you wouldn't do as much for a friend?"

"Lois, please, don't push me into a corner. At least check with Helen first. If I go around asking a lot of uninvited questions, it might antagonize people on your side."

"What people? Everyone already thinks I'm guilty." Morosely she took another sip of her neglected drink.

"Nonsense," I said briskly. "No one would condemn you out of hand."

She gave a little snort. "Then you obviously don't know what happened to me today. I went out to Canyon Escondido to do some checking on my own. Mainly to look at the electrical testing lab where Drake was killed and talk to the janitor who saw me there. His testimony can explain my fingerprints on the wall. Anyway, my ID got me inside the gate, but the minute Red Johnson saw me, he ordered me to leave, then confiscated my clearance badge."

"Does he have that kind of authority?"

"Not really, but I shouldn't have blown up at him. It's only that I've known Red for years, yet he treated me as if I'd just crawled out from under a rock. He said that since I was on leave of absence, I had no right to be on the premises. Can you imagine?" Her voice shook with remembered humiliation. "Retirees come back to visit all the time, and everyone welcomes them with open arms. No reception like that for me. And do you know why, Ellie? Because even though I haven't even been indicted yet, they've tried and convicted me. Lois McCoin, murderess."

"Take it easy. They'll all come round when you're cleared."

"But even if Helen manages to win a dismissal, it will only mean the charges were dropped for lack of evidence. Everyone will just think I'm another criminal let free on a technicality. Who'll believe I'm innocent? Not my employers, not unless someone else is arrested and brought to trial. That's why I need you to find the real killer."

"So the company won't put you on permanent leave of absence?" There was a touch of exasperation in my voice which I regretted instantly. As Betsy said, Lois's job was her life. She had nothing else. I had no right to belittle the one thing that kept her going.

She swallowed the rest of her drink, lit a cigarette with shaking fingers, then paced to the window. With her back to me, she said, "If you don't help me, I'll be on permanent leave all right, in prison. Do you hear me? Prison! With all those animals, those monsters. As God is my witness, Ellie, I'll die first." She took a deep breath as if to hang on to her precarious self-possession. "Those few hours in the detention center were unbearable."

"I can imagine."

"No, you can't," Lois cut off my easy sympathy. "You can't possibly imagine the horrors in that place. I certainly had no idea what to expect." She smashed out her half-smoked cigarette, then walked back to the couch and reached into her purse for another one.

I watched her light it, wondering if her long fingernails were painted the same shade of fire-engine red when she was in jail. "Did someone . . . bother you?" I asked, my imagination running riot.

"Someone? Everyone, but not the way you mean." Lois looked at me, the smoke curling out of her nostrils, then she stubbed out the second cigarette too. "There was a fight in the rec room. Two women shouting filth like I'd never heard before, literally scratching at each other's eyes."

"Didn't anyone try to stop it?"

"Sure, the guards stepped in. They even called for help, and the whole episode didn't last very long. But one of the women got hurt, a kick to the crotch while the fight was in full swing, but she still wanted to stay and kick back rather than be taken to the infirmary. When the guards carted her off, she was screaming she'd get even when they got to the state pen."

Having no adequate response, I remained silent.

"Now will you help me?"

It would have taken a harder heart than I possessed to tell her no. Still, I temporized. "Lois, I'm not even sure where to begin."

"Start at PSSC. You've met some of the people there. They'll talk to you."

"Some of them, perhaps," I said, thinking of Jane Chestnut. "But why should I go to the power company? Do you suspect anyone in particular?" She shook her head. "Come on, Lois. You had to have a reason to mention it. Who might have hated Drake Prescott enough to want him out of the way permanently?"

"Besides me?" she said without irony. "It's hard to tell. He was moving up fast, and any number of people resented the way he did it. I guess that gives half the department a motive to despise him."

"Did he have any personal enemies?"

"He could have had the Mafia after him for all I know, but whoever killed him was at the reception and had enough technical knowledge of transformers to understand what switch to pull and when."

"An engineer, you think?"

"Why not? The place was filled with engineers that day."

"But no one you can pinpoint as having a grudge against Prescott."

"Are you kidding?" she snorted. "I could pinpoint most of them."

Rather than remind her that most of them had probably accounted for their movements while Prescott was getting his goose cooked, I went back a few steps. "Let's take it from the personal angle again."

"I can't, Ellie. If you want to find out who Drake screwed during his off hours, you'll have to ask his wife."

Without telling Lois what an apt figure of speech she just used, I smiled. "That's an excellent suggestion."

"You're serious?" she asked anxiously. "You'll do it?"

"Yes. But not for a hundred dollars a day."

Lois stood very straight. "Just name your price."

"It's on the house."

Chapter Nine

Miss Marple move over. Ellie Gordon was once again joining the ranks of amateur buttinskies. What else could you call an unpaid, unofficial, and definitely unauthorized meddler? "Dumbo" was certainly another term for it, and that's the one I chose after an hour or so of painful introspection.

Why had I agreed to go tiger stalking? For the thrill of the hunt or out of sympathy for the prey caught in the mantrap? Probably both. Maybe I should have been afraid to go looking for a killer, but I was more scared that Helen would find out. She had told me plainly that I was to ask no questions, peer into no keyholes, search for no clues. Now I was about to disregard her orders and risk being drummed out of the service for conduct unbecoming an office manager.

The ethics of the situation were a bit sticky. As an employee of Abbotts, Devlin, and Devlin, I was gagged legally by the laws of confidentiality between lawyer and client. As for Joe Corelli, I was bound by the rules of common discretion to stay out of his cases. And if all that left me a toe or two free to wriggle, as Lois's friend I was not necessarily acting in her best interests by doing what she wanted. If I had refused to help, she might have gone out and hired someone better qualified for the job, say a genuine, certified P.I. with a .38, a knockout punch, and nerves of steel.

Though possessing none of the above qualifications, I soothed my tender conscience with the thought that I only said I'd try. After swearing Lois to secrecy, I'd carefully reiterated that there was no promise of success implied in our deal, just an attempt at it. But her tear-streaked, hopeful face when she kissed me goodbye showed she was counting on me for a miracle.

It might take a miracle to get me inside the Prescott home and make Carole babble intimacies to a mere acquaintance. Once in bed, I cudgeled my brain with farfetched schemes. Would she open both door and heart to a sympathetic Avon lady? No, the product wasn't glamorous enough. Then, in that creative instant between wake and sleep, inspiration arrived. It was farfetched, but it might work. After all, a woman who valued her status would cooperate with any project to enhance it.

The next morning, I prepared for my covert operation by taking an extended coffee break. There was a light drizzle falling when I left our beige stucco building with its red-tiled roof, but with coat buttoned and head covered I hurried around the corner to the phone booth in front of Duran's Pharmacy. All special agents use pay phones. And with good reason. No taps, no eavesdroppers, no Helen Ramirez. My call successfully completed, I went into Duran's for the large, economy-sized bottle of aspirin. This was the ingenious excuse for my errand. Then later, moaning realistically about a headache, I could leave work early and have time to sleuth first, then meet Joe for our seven-thirty date.

At four that afternoon I stood on the front porch of the Prescott house, my finger poised to push the bell, and asked myself what I was doing there. I looked the part I was about to play, in navy blue suit, white macintosh, carrying a briefcase stashed with pens and paper I'd filched from the office. But would anyone really believe Ellie Gordon had taken up freelance writing in her spare time and was doing an article for a national magazine on how women deal with the sudden loss of their mates?

As it turned out, Carole's ego more than compensated for any lack of credibility in my cover. She opened the door almost eagerly, no doubt spurred by visions of herself revealed in print as a heroine facing tragedy with uncommon grace. That's what I'd promised over the phone, and that's what she expected now. It was too late to turn tail and run, so I plunged on.

Though I had my suspicions of her, I didn't think Carole would solve Lois's problems by confessing immediately. And I was so right. The newly bereaved Mrs. Prescott, wearing a simple black dress that screamed money as loudly as grief, ushered me into an opulently furnished sun room, all chintz and ferns, then offered me a glass of sherry. She hadn't changed much in the year since my membership in the country club had expired, along with my marriage. Long and lanky, her light hair styled in a Princess Di backsweep, Carole as always looked chic. Though none of her artifices could disguise the plain Jane reality, the trappings of affluence embellished the ordinary. My goal was to see how deep the ormulu went, and after the appropriate murmurs of condolence were delivered, the first coat of mournful veneer began to peel away.

"Exactly what sort of story are you planning to write?" she asked warily.

"Uplifting," I said with a pious expression. "A factual account of courageous women confronting the aftermath of violence."

Her brow creased in thought. "What's this for, one of those magazines that pays by the word?"

"How well you know the publishing business."

"Yes, I do read a lot. I just want to be sure you're not writing for something like the *National Enquirer*."

So that's what she kept on her nightstand. "Oh, no," I reassured her, groping for a mainstream magazine that would please her. "The article is for *Family Circle*," I improvised hastily.

Carole nodded. "That would be all right. But you have to promise that there wouldn't be anything critical of Drake in your story. Or me."

"You needn't worry. My whole focus will be on your stamina in such terrible circumstances."

"It's just that people talk." She twisted the heavy gold wedding band on her finger. "You know how it is here in Casa Grande. What they don't know, they invent."

"An accurate reporter never listens to rumors." I only meant to utter a soothing platitude, but Carole picked up on something else.

"Then you have heard the gossip." She got to her feet abruptly. "Is that why you want to interview me? To find out if it's true? Well, it's not. Drake and I had a wonderful marriage. We were perfectly compatible in every way, no matter what anyone else has told you. That's what you should write."

"Good copy," I agreed, flicking my Bic and starting to take notes. "Husband . . . wife . . . relationship . . . excellent." Then I paused and looked up at her. "You were quite fortunate, Carole. Most couples can never claim to have reached that degree of happiness. You and Drake were one of the exceptional few."

Feeling more assured by that commendation, she relaxed a fraction. "Well, we had our ups and downs like anyone else."

"The best marriages have room for discussion, even disagreements. Have you been able to resolve the downs yet?"

"What?" She stiffened again.

"That's what this article is about," I explained, trying to

sound plausible, at least. "There are several stages of bereavement after a loved one's death, and one of the primary phases is guilt. We regret a hasty word spoken, an argument never quite resolved. When there's no opportunity to straighten these things out, say in the case of an accident or . . . uhm . . . unexpected death, we carry around a sense of failure, as if we should atone, but we don't know how."

"That's really deep."

I bent my head modestly.

"Actually," Carole admitted, "we did have a slight problem. But nothing we couldn't have taken care of if this awful thing hadn't happened," she added defensively.

"Yet you're coping quite well with the shock, I can tell. That's why I want to write about you as one of the courageous women in my story."

"Courageous?" She inspected a yellowing leaf of philodendron and picked it off. "I don't think so. One minute I'm crying my eyes out, and the next, I'm so mad that if he were still here, I'd be throwing the china at him." She flushed. "That's not for publication, you understand."

"Naturally. But anger is a legitimate part of the grief process. Losing someone makes us feel abandoned, resentful. Believe me, I understand. After my divorce, anger was the only thing that kept me going."

"I remember. Dan left you for his secretary, didn't he?" she said, slowly drawing the connection.

Dropping pen, notebook, and professional pose, I leaned forward confidentially. "You wouldn't believe what that man did."

"Oh, yes, I would," Carole grimaced.

"Not you too?" I asked in feigned surprise. "His secretary?"

"His private pussycat," she nodded.

And there went the seventh veil. Once Carole was promised that neither one of our stories was for public consumption, she opened up like a floodgate. If I had known that exposing my own sores would make her reciprocate, I wouldn't have spent so much time pretending to be Barbara Walters. Carole trusted my discretion now that I was a victim of the same betrayal, a sister in suffering, and therefore a safely sympathetic audience. After all, we were old friends of a sort. Hadn't we once played mixed doubles in the country club tennis tournament? Apparently that gave me credit enough to share her darkest secrets.

"It had been going on for months. I knew it. I could always tell when he was fooling around, and he did it plenty. But every time I caught him, he'd say it was just sex, the floozies meant nothing to him so I shouldn't worry. To be honest, I didn't. Not much anyway. Then I discovered that April was different from the rest. Drake wasn't getting his kicks free this time. The whore was charging him for her favors, and he was paying . . . out of our joint bank account."

So Betsy had been on the right track—*cherchez le* money. "How did you find out?" I asked.

"It was just luck. He certainly didn't confess. I should have known something was up when Drake claimed we couldn't afford to go skiing in Aspen this year. I argued with him for weeks, but he wouldn't give in. Then, the Tuesday before he was . . . before he died, I found out why we were so strapped for cash. I was emptying out the pockets of his camel hair sportcoat so I could take it to the cleaners, and I found a receipt. 'What's this for?' I asked him. He turned bright red and grabbed it out of my hand, shouting that it was none of my business. I got suspicious immediately and told him five thousand dollars is very much my business. Who did he pay it to? The money was for a private investment he said, a deal he couldn't discuss. But that money belonged to me too, and I had a right to know what happened to it." Carole threw out her hands as if asking for my agreement. "Except I already had a pretty good idea. Paying with a money order is so conveniently anonymous. A nice way to keep his 'investment' a secret from me, don't you think?"

"How do you know it was for April? Did you see her name on the receipt?"

"I didn't have to." Furious tears sprang into Carole's eyes. "When I accused him of giving her our money, feathering a new nest so when the time came, my half of the community property would be down to a fourth, he said I could believe whatever I wanted. An open admission practically," she sniffled.

It was hard to muster up much sympathy for a woman who was more wounded by a betrayal of the savings account than any treason to the marriage bed. "Was the money order purchased at your bank?"

"He took it away too fast. I didn't see."

"But he didn't actually admit the money was for April or ask you for a divorce?"

"No, but there really wasn't time. Four days later he was gone." She groped for a Kleenex and blew her nose.

Was Carole crying for a semilamented husband or the missing five thousand dollars? It was hard to tell. "Maybe it was a business deal," I comforted. "You should look for that receipt just to put your mind at ease."

"I did. I looked everywhere." A venomous expression flickered across her face. "But that Evans woman probably has it, if it's not destroyed already. She's the one who went through Drake's desk at the office and sent home all his personal effects. Come to think of it, his gold pen and pencil set is missing too. The little thief," Carole said bitterly. "Who knows what else she stole from me?"

Besides a husband's affection, I wondered cynically. Listening patiently to the widow's complaints, I waited for more revelations, but none were forthcoming. The tale of the money order seemed to prop up my theory, but I still had plenty of doubts. Carole Prescott had been angry with her husband before his death, but she admitted it much too readily. Wouldn't a guilty woman have played it smarter, claimed undying devotion to her dear departed spouse so my article could read like a certificate of innocence? Perhaps I was underestimating her, but I found it hard to believe she had the cunning to run a double bluff. But then, if she were clever enough to get away with murder, who knew what else she could maneuver?

Good question. Who knew? Certainly not me. My first real case as a private eye and all I had dug up was the festering carcass of a marriage gone rotten. Still, I couldn't rule out Carole as a murder suspect, especially since I didn't have a replacement. So maybe I should just continue as I had started, prove she killed her husband. Find the money order receipt, and pin it on her black dress.

Chapter Ten

"Where have you been?" Joe fussed at me. "I called the office, but Mark said you left work early."

"I did."

Joe hung my coat on the back of the chair, then scooted me up to our quiet corner table. "What happened? Did you have car trouble?"

"No, you worrywart. I just had to run a little errand for Lois."

Joe sat down and scanned the menu, obviously not for the first time. "Do you realize there's nothing to eat in this place but raw fish?"

"That's why I suggested it. Sushi is very low-calorie, which I need for a change, and iodine perks up the metabolism."

"I still think lasagna does it better, but for your sake I'll force myself."

"You don't have to be so noble. Fish is supposed to be brain food, or don't you think yours needs any improvement?"

"Not after what I dreamed up for dessert. You're going to applaud my genius."

"Really? What did the master chef cook up?" After Joe leaned over and whispered the details in my ear, I grinned. "You want to do what with chocolate mousse?"

"I can't think of a better way to get the taste of fish out of my mouth."

Between us we came up with a few other remedies, all equally exotic, then got back to selecting an appropriate entrée. After we placed our orders with the waitress, Joe asked what I'd done for Lois. His question was just idle chitchat, although the answer wouldn't be. He probably thought I dropped off a dress at the cleaners for her. But as long as he was the one who raised the subject, I decided to sound him out.

"Joe, let me ask you something. Do you need positive proof that someone else is guilty before dropping charges against the original suspect?"

He laughed. "In Lois McCoin's case, you mean. I knew you wouldn't be able to stay away from the topic despite all your talk of penitence."

"Hey, you asked me about it first."

"So I did," he acknowledged fairly. "Very well. We don't need positive proof, but the evidence has to have merit before we'd reevaluate the situation." Then he looked at me uncertainly. "You're not running around looking for some mythical clue to clear your friend, are you?"

"Who, me?" I stared at him in wide-eyed innocence.

"Yes, you. Now listen to me, Ellie. It's one thing to theorize that someone else killed Drake Prescott, but trying to find that someone is not a very good idea."

"I think Lois might disagree with you."

"I'm sure she would, but Lois has an attorney, and if either of them wants to locate another suspect, they'll hire an investigator."

"You're absolutely right," I said as the waitress brought our dinner. "A professional is the only way to go."

That appeased him, though I wasn't quite sure why I didn't want to tell him I'd already been snooping into the Prescott case. Infringing on his territory again, or to avoid a lecture? Both maybe. Joe did have a tendency to drape his cloak across the mud before escorting me across the street, and since I hated to make him worry about me unduly, I just didn't mention my plan to see April Evans the next day.

I even called her from my desk at the office. No covert operation this time, although I did wait until the titty-tats were on a lunch break, leaving me in sole charge of the switchboard. And it was surprisingly easy. April agreed to meet and invited me over to her house that evening, all without asking why I wanted to see her. This was just as well since I hadn't settled on an approach yet, except that I had decided not to adopt an elaborate disguise the way I had last night. Of course, I couldn't come right out and inquire politely if she'd been having an affair with her boss and if he'd paid for the privilege. In fact, I wasn't sure how to get her to talk about anything. From my brief conversation with April at PSSC, I judged her as having a certain reserve. This was an admirable trait in an executive secretary, but for my purposes, it would have been better if she were a motormouth like Jane Chestnut.

I left home early to allow time for getting lost on the way to an unfamiliar section of Casa Grande, but by eight fifteen I was creeping down a dreary little street lined with shoe-box-sized houses set about three feet apart. The landscaping was minimal. The few trees looked starved for water, while the standard adornment in the front yards was a torn-down junker.

In the dark, April's house wasn't any more impressive than its neighbors, but at least the '77 Ford parked in the driveway was in one piece. On my way up the concrete path to the door, I had to dodge a tricycle, and when I knocked, I did it cautiously. The screen was hanging loose near the handle, and though the frame had been painted recently in a forlorn effort to hide the cracks in the wood, the whole thing seemed flimsy in the extreme. This was certainly a marked contrast to the Prescotts' sprawling tri-level, overdecorated in California nouveau riche.

But the shabby exterior had misled me. When April opened the door with a welcoming smile, I stepped across the threshold into a nine-foot-square living room that managed to be both bright and cozy. A homemade book-case, just some two-by-six boards painted white and stacked on bricks, stretched along one wall. It was crammed with paperback romances and topped by well-tended houseplants. Though the couch had a noticeable sag at one end, any other deficiencies were covered by a colorful Mexican blanket. But most surprisingly, crowded into the minuscule dining alcove was a baby grand piano, polished to a sheen, with a stack of sheet music piled neatly on the bench.

As for April herself, I had to admit that in her own setting, she was even more attractive than at the office. Wearing jeans and a tight pink tee-shirt, her long, black hair pulled back with a matching pink ribbon, her bare feet stuck into thongs, she was completely natural and perfectly stunning. The pajama-clad child clinging to her leg simply added the finishing touch to an already appeal-ing picture. Poor Carole's expensive Junior League ele-gance couldn't compete with this vital beauty.

My hostess seemed genuinely pleased to see me. "Sorry, but I still have to put Jason to bed. Jennifer's already asleep. Want to come with me and take a peek?"

"I'd love to," I said truthfully, following April down the short hall and trying without luck for a smile from Jason as he stared at me from over his mother's shoulder, owl-eyed, with two fingers stuck in his mouth.

The children's room was faintly illuminated by a night light that cast a golden glow on an array of stuffed animals on the dresser. In one corner was a low bed with a side rail for Jason and across from it, Jennifer's crib. April looked lovingly down on her daughter.

"How old is she?" I whispered, caught as always by the vulnerable sweetness of a healthy baby, the fan of eyelashes on rose-petal cheeks and the dimpled, little hands.

"Twenty-one months last week." April smoothed the blanket over Jennifer, then tucked Jason into his bed, raising the rail into place. "Say goodnight to Ms. Gordon," she instructed.

"Wanna story, Mommy."

"You had your story," she protested with a soft laugh. "Two of them and your glass of water. Say goodnight, darling."

"Goodnight," he answered obediently, smiling at me at last.

"Goodnight, Jason." I tiptoed out as mother and son hugged each other one more time. It had been such a long time since Michael was a baby, I'd almost forgotten how dear those bedtime rituals were.

A few minutes later, sitting at an antique golden oak table in the kitchen and dunking homebaked chocolate chip cookies into freshly brewed coffee, I was ashamed that I'd pigeon-holed April as some stereotypical sexpot. Not that her husband-borrowing ways were commendable, but it did seem possible there was a side to the story I hadn't heard yet.

"You have two very beautiful children."

Evidently that spontaneous tribute won her heart, because she confided the details of her long custody battle, fully expecting and getting my complete sympathy. April's ex-husband, a poverty-stricken medical student during their marriage, was now in private practice and had decided he could provide a better environment for his children than their mother could furnish.

"Max has tried everything to take them away. Accused me of dating too much, said this house was a firetrap, that my daycare arrangements are inadequate. I should never have divorced him when I did. There was nothing to divide then except the debts, student loans mostly. So all I asked for was child support, never suspecting that when he started earning real money he'd spend it dragging me into court. God bless Dennis Devlin. I owe him the earth, and some months I can't pay a penny on that bill. And then there are the court costs . . ." She looked at me with a half-humorous, half-despairing smile. "Sometimes I wonder if I'm going to make it."

"You certainly are sacrificing a lot to keep those children."

April looked fierce for an instant, a tigress prepared to defend her cubs. "I'd do anything to keep them. Anything. They're my life."

"Then I presume joint custody is out of the question."

"Children shouldn't be shunted from pillar to post," she said with feeling. "They need one home, not a place to lay their heads on alternate Tuesdays, Thursdays, and Saturdays. Living like that, they'd never feel secure anywhere."

Her sentiments were admirable, though she paid a high cost for them. Working full time, caring for two children, with financial worries on top of everything else had to be an incredible strain. Wishing I knew if April's desperate straits were partly due to the loss of a sugar daddy in Drake Prescott, I asked her if at least her job at PSSC were secure.

"It better be!" Then she checked herself on a sigh. "I mean, without that paycheck every month, I'd be in real trouble."

I used the mention of the power company to bridge smoothly into my pitch. "You've been very patient waiting for me to explain why I'm here, and basically, it's because of your position at PSSC. You see, I've been asked by Lois McCoin to try and find some new evidence before the hearing next week."

April wrinkled her pretty forehead and said she'd like to help Lois, but how?

"You know more about Prescott's business affairs than anyone else. Did something unusual happen at the office that last week? Was he worried about anything? Had he antagonized anyone lately?"

"Not that I know of," April replied thoughtfully. "In fact, I told the police everything was normal, even with the turmoil of publicizing the Canyon Escondido plant opening. We were extra-busy arranging media coverage and responding to ANSWER."

"But he still found time to criticize his executive assistant in writing," I said dryly. "Why did you show that memo to Lois? Aren't things like that supposed to be confidential?"

"Sometimes they are and sometimes they aren't," she answered with seeming sincerity. "I just wanted to clue her in, warn her that Mr. Prescott was axing her promotion. She'd been walking around on cloud nine, thinking it was in the bag. I never dreamed she'd do anything worse than yell at him about it."

"You really think she killed him?" I asked with a sinking feeling in my stomach. If April implied as much at the hearing, it would be tough to convince the judge that the prosecution's case was only a collection of unfortunate coincidences.

"I don't know what to think. But Mr. Prescott could be very sarcastic, and maybe he pushed her too far the day of the reception."

"What do you mean?" Fascinated, I stared as April's slender fingers picked apart a cookie and assembled the chocolate chips in a neat row in front of her.

"Lois was really furious with him, and for good reason. What if she went into the testing facility to ask him to reconsider, give her a chance to prove she could handle the job, and he gave her a hard time? He might have said she'd never be promoted because she was too old, too incompetent." April firmed her soft lips. "He did pick on her like that, but maybe Lois just wanted to wipe the smirk off his face, give him a little jolt. Isn't it possible she didn't mean to kill him at all?"

A prickle of unease went down my spine. While I didn't think Lois would kill cold-bloodedly, she could have done it the way April described, on an impulse, without fully thinking through the consequences. Of course, he could have driven someone else to murder as well.

"Sounds like Drake Prescott was the kind of man who could be pretty cruel," I said slowly. "How did you get along with him?"

"Fine. He was nice enough to me. You know, let me take off early if one of the kids was sick, didn't give me a hard time when I had to make another court appearance in the middle of the day. But he and Lois were another story. The truth is, she resented him right from the beginning when he was hired over her head. That's why I think maybe the two of them got carried away arguing. If she really flipped out, couldn't she plead temporary insanity?"

"She says she didn't do it."

"I'd like to believe that. But who else could have?" April looked worried.

To tell or not to tell? What flowed between Drake's wife and his secretary wasn't precisely the milk of human kindness. It was champagne, to be exact, and at today's dry cleaning prices April might not be willing to forgive and forget. Should I chance it? Yes, but diplomatically.

"All right." I pretended to change the subject. "Let's take a look at Drake Prescott the man. I really don't know very much about him or his associates, although I did hear he and his wife were having problems. Any truth to that rumor?"

Apparently I was a bit more heavy-handed than I intended, because April gave me a sharp glance. "You're looking for another motive for murder, another suspect, not just an alibi for Lois, aren't you?"

"That's the idea," I admitted. "What do you think of Carole Prescott as a possibility? Maybe she's the one he pushed too far."

"But that's crazy! Carole wouldn't have ... " April paused, reconsidering. "What am I saying? Anything's possible. Only don't people get a divorce when they've had it with each other?"

"Well, you saw Prescott every day. You talked to him. Was he planning on leaving his wife?"

"He never mentioned it."

"Which doesn't necessarily mean he wasn't considering that option. After all, Carole created an extremely embarrassing scene at PSSC. He might have been fed up with her. They do say she was the jealous type." I held my breath and looked innocent.

April frowned. "You've been talking to Jane Chestnut, who's a certifiable idiot. Take it from me, you should discount half of everything she says on any topic."

Clearly I was treading on touchy territory, so I backed way off into what I hoped was a neutral zone. "Did you see Carole Prescott leave the reception area after her husband? Do you know if she followed him down the hall toward the electrical testing lab?"

"No, I'm afraid I wasn't paying any attention." April sounded tired of my questions.

It was understandable. I was tired of going in circles myself. Feeling as if I were panning for gold in a pot of mud, I embarked on a new tack and asked what papers the police took from the office.

"I really couldn't say. They ransacked the place for a week while they were getting everyone's statements. It was a mess."

"Well, in the mess, did you notice if they removed any of his personal effects? Private business records, his calendar, unidentified papers?" I prodded as if April would actually tell me what happened to the infamous receipt.

"Why don't you ask the police what they found," she

suggested sensibly, sweeping up the row of chocolate chips on the table and popping them into her mouth.

Because I didn't have to ask the police, I realized, feeling immensely stupid. A list of all those items was sitting in Helen's file right now, along with copies of several dozen statements, the medical examiner's report, and God knew what else. There might even be a record of the mysterious money order. But I'd certainly never find out if I stayed here pumping April for information she didn't have or just didn't want to reveal.

I looked at my watch. "My goodness, it's ten already. I've got to get home, but thanks so much for your time. Lois is going to be grateful."

April was apologetic. "Gee, I don't think I was any help, Ms. Gordon. I wish there was something I could do. I feel bad for her, you know?"

"Listen, you tried. That's all any of us can do. But if you could be as kind to her as possible next week at the hearing . . . "

"No problem. I'll say all the nice things I can."

That was one plus for Lois anyway, I thought, taking my leave. But in the main, the results of my evening's work were disappointing. I really never expected April to admit a romantic liaison with her boss, but I'd hoped for some confirmation of my jealous wife theory. I got none. Still, April was the first person I'd talked to who had offered even one word of praise for Drake Prescott. Maybe that wasn't evidence, but at least it didn't contradict what everyone else was saying about the two of them.

Not that proof was necessary; Carole Prescott believed her husband had been on the verge of leaving her for his secretary, and one woman's opinion was all that mattered here. What I needed to learn was whether or not she had an airtight alibi for the time of his death, and the information should be where I was going to look anyway. However, when I drove to the office, there was a light in the fourth floor window. Someone was burning the midnight oil and I couldn't sneak into Helen's private files with a witness on the scene to report my reconnaissance mission. I'd just have to wait until tomorrow night and hope no one else would decide to work late.

Chapter Eleven

"Well, there is one advantage to dating married men. What you never expect can't disappoint you when you don't get it."

"That's a nice excuse for not making a commitment. Did you hear that, Ellie?" Rhoda grabbed my arm as I was threading my way through the crowd, trying not to spill the drink in my hand. "She likes to pick draft choices from the ineligible list."

"Since when did you become an armchair quarterback?" Claudette Washington flashed at her. "Hello, Ellie." She smiled briefly at me before volleying a shot at her supposed sister in solidarity. "Seems to me you had a fling with your boss prior to his divorce. Then you changed jobs."

"That was different," Rhoda defended herself. "I was still in school at the time."

"Are you pleading youthful ignorance or statutory rape?" Claudette asked sweetly.

"Pardon me," I interrupted, "but Rhoda, would you please give me your napkin?"

"I'm sorry," she apologized with a little laugh. "I didn't realize you were carrying a drink when I pulled you into this conversation."

"That's all right. It sounds as though you two need a referee. But why the scrimmage on tonight of all nights? Isn't Fifth and Shoreside's cocktail party providing enough excitement with the added attraction of fresh shrimp on the buffet table?"

"You're joking!" Rhoda squealed. "I didn't see any shrimp. Where?"

"Next to the crab claws."

As she tore off, Claudette murmured, "Watch her. She'll take one bite, then have an orgasm."

"I know the feeling. Hot fudge does that for me. Would you mind holding this glass for a minute while I dry my hand? Thanks. Oops. Now your fingers are sticky. Here, take this napkin."

Claudette held it away from her. "This reminds me of my mother's handkerchief when she used to spit on it and wipe my face."

"My mother did the same thing." I gave a shudder of remembered distaste. "Did yours line the seat of public toilets with paper before she let you sit down?"

"Of course, but that was only after asking me, in the middle of a crowded department store, and in her loudest voice, if I had to make peepee."

"My mother called it 'pishy.' "

Claudette grinned. "In sympathy for someone who suffered the same childhood torments, I'll be glad to forge an opening through this crowd so you can get wherever you're going with that drink."

"No place special. How about you?"

"Just away from Rhoda." She looked around. "I don't want another lecture on homewreckers."

There are two things a person can do when someone makes a leading remark. One is to pretend you didn't hear it, and the other is to pretend you think it's a joke. Since this was the second time the subject had been brought up, I could hardly do either without sounding like the village idiot, so I tackled it head-on.

"You don't have to explain your actions to me, but if you want rabbinical approval, I'll see what I can do."

"It's going to take a papal dispensation to get rid of the guilts on this one. Rhoda assumed I was talking about myself when she got all hot under the collar, but I was just repeating some logic a friend gave me."

"A friend who went to parochial school, apparently, and sees shades of scandalized nuns in her dreams."

"You got it."

"Such are the perils of modern-day mores." I shrugged. "You trade ideals for idylls."

"It's called 'sexcess,' " Claudette grinned. "Or do you have hang-ups about it too?"

"Not any more. I grin and bear it quite nicely, thank you, but so far I've managed to steer clear of married men with a wandering eye."

"But you do go for D.A.s with a hankering for petite brunettes," she teased. "I hear you and Joe are a real item these days."

"It's affecting his work, I hope?"

"Not that I can tell, but he's smiling a lot more than he used to. Is that good enough?"

I invited Claudette to join me in the lobby where we could find a couple of empty chairs. After a little more lighthearted conversation about my stirring the D.A. to unprecedented transports of joy, I asked if she were going to assist Joe at the McCoin hearing.

"Yes. I prepared most of the case myself, so he's keeping me around as a valuable resource."

"And how does it look for Lois?" I queried, taking a sip of gin and tonic.

"Not good. We have a lot of heavy artillery."

"Yes. I saw the lineup of witnesses for the prosecution. Very formidable indeed, and you've probably added more names by now. On the list I read, Carole Prescott's name was missing."

"We have enough people who can testify when Drake left the reception. There's no need to bother his widow."

"How thoughtful of you to spare Carole that ordeal." I smiled. "As long as you already know what time she left the party, I guess she doesn't have to repeat it under oath."

Claudette's expressive brown eyes were suddenly alert. "Does that have some special significance?"

"I don't know. Does it?"

"Come clean, Ellie. I can tell you're leading up to something. Why does Carole Prescott have you bugged?"

Now that I'd brought the conversation to this point, I had second thoughts about continuing it in the same vein. If Claudette had been in charge of preparing this case, she must have stumbled over the same discrepancy I had. Of course, she wasn't looking for a loophole that would benefit Lois, so what seemed important to me might have meant nothing to Claudette. In that event, maybe it was my duty as a citizen to alert her. Then again, maybe trying to influence the opposition was as much a crime as jury tampering.

"How much of what I say will be held against me?" I asked cautiously.

"Nothing. This is strictly off the record."

"Okay. Then why didn't you investigate Carole's movements on the day her husband died?"

"The police investigate. We prosecute."

"Well, you must have made a comparison of all the statements taken. Didn't you notice an empty spot on hers?"

"Not really."

Claudette might have been playing it cagey, but on the off-chance that she really had missed the not so obvious, I called it to her attention. "Everyone, including Carole, admits she took impromptu leave of the party by herself.

But she and her husband arrived in one car, which means she left him stranded. Why?" I leaned forward. "Because she knew he had another ride, or because she knew he wasn't in any condition to need one?"

Prudently, Claudette remained silent.

"If answer number one is your choice," I continued anyway, "what happened to the person who was giving him a lift? When Prescott didn't reappear, no one questioned where he might have gone. No one said, 'Gee, I've been waiting in the parking lot for fifteen minutes.' Wouldn't you ask around if your rider never showed up? I'd bitch like mad. And I'd certainly think it was important enough to mention on a police statement. Yet nobody did. If nothing else, it would help pinpoint the time of death."

"Most people don't think in those terms."

"Most people don't get electrocuted either."

Claudette pressed her lips together and swirled the drink around in her glass before answering. "Have you told any of this to Joe?"

"No. I only discovered these things tonight." Prying into Helen's files, I didn't add. "But what about you? Don't you think it's worth checking into? Joe would certainly listen to any recommendation from his assistant."

"I already gave him one," Claudette informed me dryly. "It was my suggestion we prosecute."

"Then apparently you didn't consider the police report all circumstantial evidence."

"Ellie, circumstantial evidence is not a dirty word," Claudette remarked testily. "It carries weight when it puts a suspect with a motive at the scene of the crime, and at the moment, we don't have a motive for Carole Prescott. Unless you want to contend that any wife is likely to murder her husband these days."

Feeling a trifle testy myself, I raised my eyebrows. "Oh, Carole had a reason, all right. The classic one—jealousy. Drake Prescott was having an affair with his secretary.

Not only that, but it's possible he was giving her money as well."

Claudette looked pained. "So what? The unhappy wife was seen eating dip and drinking champagne about the time we think the unfaithful husband bought it. Really, Ellie . . ."

Before she could tell me I was out of line, I made one more try. "You know you don't have an exact fix on that. The coroner said Prescott died after four-fifteen and before seven P.M. And Carole left . . ."

This time I was the one interrupted. "I don't think we should be discussing this." Claudette stood up and put her unfinished drink on an end table. "It's been interesting, but I have to get home."

Thanks but no thanks, I thought as she walked away. Was it my selling technique or my sense of timing? No doubt, it had been a mistake to talk murder suspects with the assistant D.A., especially during a chance encounter at a mixed social. But my impulsiveness aside, wherever I cornered Claudette would be the wrong place if she didn't want to hear what I had to say . . . or what Carole Prescott neglected to mention.

Chapter Twelve

The only one who noticed my sagging spirits the next day was Mark, and only then because I made three typos on a brief for him and didn't defend myself when he teased me about losing my touch.

"You're not kidding." I fell into my favorite chair across from his desk.

"What's the matter, this month's supply of males at Fifth and Shoreside didn't laugh at your witty one-liners last night? Or is your heart still reserved for Joe and he hasn't responded accordingly?"

"You know you're my best audience, but don't talk about wit. The major part of my evening was spent with Claudette Washington, and she made me feel like a very dim one."

Mark doubted anyone could take the shine out of my superior intelligence, but when I told him what I was doing for Lois, even my kindly boss eyed me askance.

"She hired you as a *what*?"

"Thanks for the vote of confidence. But hire isn't exactly the right terminology since I've refused all remuneration."

"Don't want to lose your amateur status, huh?"

"Or my job here." I hesitated. "Do me a favor, Mark. Don't tell Helen, will you? Not that I'm interfering in her case," I rushed to explain, "but I want to surprise her with a Perry Mason coup. A private eye joke." My voice faded into a mumble. "Or rather a 'private I' joke."

"Yes, I get the pun," he nodded, "although I'm not sure Helen will think it's funny. Wouldn't it be better to get her blessing first?"

"You're probably right," I agreed glumly. "But until my encounter with Claudette, I was positive I'd have the last laugh. Now I can see why she and Helen are friends. Neither one of them has the least bit of imagination."

"You make up for both of them." He smiled to himself. "But what exactly was the creative concept Claudette rejected? You didn't just claim Lois is innocent, I gather."

"No, I offered her an alternate suspect. Tell me what you think of it." My presentation was objective and unemotional. Actually, I did a pretty good imitation of Mark Devlin himself addressing the court. I was concise, succinct, but unfortunately a little weak on corroborating evidence. When Mark pointed that out to me, I gave him a catalogue of all the presumptive facts I'd put together.

"Just take a look at the statements. Carole Prescott claims she was at the reception the entire time, but Jane Chestnut saw her in the ladies' room a little before five o'clock."

He laughed. "I can understand Carole not mentioning a call of nature. Do you tell everyone when you go powder your nose?"

"All I'm saying is that her movements are not completely accounted for, and it might be important."

"But since you don't know how long she was in the bathroom, there's no way to know if she had time to go potty and kill her husband all in one trip."

"You have such a positive attitude," I sighed lugubriously.

"Look, Ellie," Mark said, serious now, "I'm not going to encourage you to do something Helen expressly forbade. It would be bad office policy. But"—he held up his hand to forestall my protest—"I can give you a little off-the-record advice. If you are dead-set on continuing this project, get some proof to back up your ideas. It will take solid evidence to convince the police to reopen their investigation. Without it, you're wasting your time." Then he winked conspiratorially. "And if you won't tell Helen what I said, I won't tell her what you said."

"Don't worry, your secret is safe with me." I got to my feet. "Everybody's secrets are safe with me, especially the murderer's. As you say, I've got no real evidence."

"You're a smart cookie. You'll find some."

"Think so? Well, Darwin was a lot smarter than I am, and they still call his *Origin of the Species* a theory."

"But he didn't have your perseverance. I have no doubt you'll unearth your missing link. Just keep digging."

No wonder Mark was my favorite boss. He was the only one who believed there was method in my madness, unless he was just dosing me with Unguent of Indulgence. But despite his professed faith in my abilities, finding a two-million-year-old fossil seemed easier than locating the missing money order receipt. If someone had mistakenly packed it away in PSSC's files, nobody would notice until the year-end audit when the books wouldn't balance. Then there was the possibility the receipt no longer existed. Drake Prescott might have used belated sense and burned the thing before his suspicious wife could get around to ransacking his entire wardrobe. But the main point was, without that piece of paper, I couldn't even prove a motive for murder, let alone the mechanics of it.

Then I had a divine inspiration. There must be other carbon copies in this world of data processing and reprocessing. Places that issue money orders have to keep a duplicate for their own records, and by now even the original probably had been cashed, canceled, and entered into a ledger. All I needed was a peek at some microfilm, but gaining access to bank records might take a court order. Or something resembling it, I thought shrewdly. And I knew just where to get an open sesame. Joe Corelli wasn't the only one with a "valuable resource." I might have been detecting for free, but I had ways and means.

"I'd like to help you, Ellie, but you read the papers. I got my hands full trying to find out who's flying cocaine in here." The chief of police rubbed his grizzled-gray head. "We got two kilos of the stuff from a downed Piper Cub, but the pilot killed in the crash didn't have one damn piece of identification on him. I don't know where in hell to look for his drop-off."

Though I had skipped lunch to come ask for Matt Steunkle's advice about my case, I felt obliged to offer some advice about his. "Why don't you have the state crime commission work on it?" I suggested.

"Hell, they don't wanna waste their time on anything that isn't a mob operation. Some piker was cutting his eye-teeth running this contraband."

"So you have one informant anyway," I said knowingly, which impressed the chief no end, but not enough to give me carte blanche for my quest.

"You want me to get a search warrant?" he protested after I explained. "How? You don't even know what you're looking for."

"I just told you. Carole Prescott said the receipt was for a money order, but I called the bank this morning and there's a five hundred upper limit on them. Two hundred some places, and the one thing Carole assured me of was the amount. Five thousand dollars, which means the receipt had to be a carbon copy of a cashier's check."

"Trust me, Ellie, if she thought you'd be able to incriminate her with it, she wouldn't have told you a damn thing about the money."

"I wormed the information out of her."

"Good for you. But why? What's this McCoin woman to you that you're trying to get her off the hook?"

Intending to sound professional, I just got myself in hot water. "She hired me to find out who really killed Drake Prescott."

"Yeah? You opened a detective agency or something?"

"No. I happen to believe Lois is innocent."

"Then you best high-tail it down to City Hall before the Better Business Bureau gets you for operating without a license."

"Hey, you wouldn't fink on Nancy Drew, would you?" I joked weakly, hoping to remind him that he used to like me.

"Not unless somebody files a complaint," he relented. "But I'll never get a judge to sign a search warrant for every damn bank and savings and loan in town just so you can see a name on some cashier's check. Even if there was any point to it, I can't spare the manpower to do all that leg work. It could take weeks."

"Not weeks," I contradicted. "I need to find out in days. The preliminary hearing is next Wednesday. Look, we'll start at Prescott's bank, try all the branches, then if we don't have any luck, we go farther afield, try some others near his office, a few in Brentwood where he lived."

"No way." The chief dismissed my suggestion with a wave of his hairy paw.

I moderated my request. "Okay. I've got another idea. This one won't take much time at all. Get me a look at April Evans's bank account. We could find the money that way."

"Ellie, kiddo. You aren't listening to me. The Prescott case is closed as far as the police are concerned. And it's gonna stay that way unless the McCoin woman's cleared. Got it?"

Feeling as if I'd just bruised myself on a brick wall, I pleaded. "Matt, I'll bring you new evidence. Just cut through some red tape for me and we'll have something the D.A.'s office can't ignore."

"Oh yeah? And what if the cashier's check only shows Prescott was paying off his bookie? Come on, Ellie, you ain't got a case; you got a prejudice. Your pal couldn't be guilty, so it had to be somebody else."

"Seems reasonable to me."

"Well, it's not. We didn't pick on Lois McCoin because nobody better showed up. We double-check pretty careful before arresting anyone on suspicion of murder, and we looked into Carole Prescott, believe me. Detective Peters did a damn good job, and I'm not going to undercut him. If we got the wrong person, it'll be fixed at the prelim."

"Was Peters the investigator on the case?"

"Why do you wanna know?" the chief asked suspiciously.

"No special reason," I shrugged. "But he should be made aware of what he missed so he won't make the same mistake next time."

"Damned if you ain't got nerve." Matt smiled grudgingly.

"Let me see all the evidence he collected," I pushed while he was in a softened mood. "I want to go through everything that was taken out of Prescott's desk, whatever you got from his house, so I can make my own analysis, not just rely on neatly typed reports filtered through Peters' eyes."

"Hey, we haven't put you on payroll yet. You're still a civilian, and you got no right to tamper with police property. Like she was somebody from internal affairs," he said at large, shaking his head.

"Why are you being so stubborn?" I stuck out my jaw.

"Me stubborn?" He reared up, no longer amused by my *chutspah.* "Look here, Ellie. The police department don't operate like the Lone Ranger. Every bit of material Lieutenant Peters had was gone over by the D.A.'s office, and they recommended prosecution. That's the bottom line as far as I'm concerned, and if you think some crazy idea about a missing cashier's check is gonna change their minds, you're nuts. Even if we found it for you, it wouldn't prove a thing."

"It'll prove Carole Prescott had as much a motive as Lois did."

"Okay, okay. You wanna go on a wild goose chase, you do it. But I don't have time to help. My men are up to their asses in this cocaine thing, and I can barely spare Peters for an hour so he can go testify at the hearing. Tell you what, you're so all-fired sure you're right? Go to McCoin's lawyer. Ask her if she can get you a search warrant. It's her client you're trying to get off anyway."

"Thanks for the suggestion," I muttered, getting to my feet.

"See? Aren't you glad you came to me?" He grinned, probably in relief that I was going. "I know how the system works better than you do. Go see her," he encouraged, walking me to the door and ushering me out of his office. "She ought to be real happy to hear your ideas."

Happy? If I admitted to Helen I'd been sleuthing despite her strict orders to keep a respectful distance, she'd cheerfully wring my neck. And there'd be no running to Mark Devlin for protection. He wouldn't interfere. Bad office policy.

So why had I expected the chief of police to go out on a limb for me? Because we both belonged to the same mystery of the month book club? Some sentimental attachment. Steunkle had done his job already, gotten the D.A.'s go-ahead. Who needed Ellie Gordon's stamp of approval? Maybe I should just be grateful that the chief hadn't thrown me in jail for imitating a private eye.

Actually, I didn't have to worry about prying without a permit anymore. There was nowhere I could turn, unless I wanted to commit a few more infractions of the law in the name of justice. But if ex-officio sleuths were unsanctioned in crime-fighting circles, think what would happen to one who was caught conducting an unconstitutional search and seizure. How long a sentence could I get for breaking into April's bank and checking her current balance? Lois would be out before I made it to the parole board.

Damn. It was going to be miserable telling her I hadn't achieved a thing. She had been depending on my overrated talents as a nosy parker. Of course, I had suggested she hire a pro. I warned her that I might not be the right bloodhound to sniff out the truth. But I never imagined I'd get this far in the chase only to be tripped up by the hidden snare of bureaucratic inertia. It wasn't fair. It wasn't even giving Lois a sporting chance.

Be realistic, I told myself. The police had their priorities to consider, and opening a new cocaine investigation took precedence over a presumably closed murder case. There was no sense in their backtracking now. Lois McCoin looked guilty enough. The D.A. agreed. Let a judge decide if she had been arrested without probable cause. And if he found for the prosecution, poor, overworked Lieutenant Peters could continue his hot pursuit of the local drug dealer without interruption.

That was the real bottom line. The police department didn't have time to mete out justice for all. As far as they were concerned, Lois would receive due rights by having her day in court. What more could an accused felon ask?

Chapter Thirteen

Helen thought my presence would be unnecessary at the preliminary hearing, but if I insisted on coming, I had to take care of a few jobs at the office first. Feeling more than a little like Cinderella, I began bright and early Wednesday morning by calling all the witnesses for the defense and reminding them to be on hand when needed. Personally, I doubted if there were many people stupid enough to ignore a subpoena, but Helen was compulsive about details. I took care of a bunch more, then shoved the rest on the titty-tats and made my escape.

It was eleven-twenty by the time I found an empty space in the municipal complex parking lot. City offices took up half the quadrangle and across the tree-lined path was the county courthouse. A new wing had been added recently to accommodate the rising need for more judges to preside over more appellate actions, a sign of our lawless times, no doubt. But the newer part of the building was almost too functional to be imposing; not that the older section was anything more than 1950s modern. Casa Grande didn't even exist in the days of marble floors and real oak paneling. The room where Lois's fate was to be decided had all the banal splendor of green painted walls, sturdy teak benches, and carpet the shade of intense neutral. No windows brightened the atmosphere either, but why bother when fluorescent lighting and climate control made nature superfluous? Besides, the drama being enacted within more than made up for the nondescript setting.

When I slipped into a front-row seat, Lois turned around and asked anxiously, "What kept you?"

"Work," I mouthed, patting her shoulder and sitting back to watch the leading man in action.

From center stage, Joe had noted my tardy arrival, but he certainly couldn't stop the show to wave at someone in the audience. Anyway, he knew I wasn't here to applaud his performance. Neither was I intending to throw rotten tomatoes. We had discussed the whole thing the night before and sensibly concurred that although we were on opposite sides of this case, we would not let it interfere with our personal relationship. But now that the curtain was up, I wondered if I could keep a cool perspective on the proceedings. With only the prologue over, I already wasn't crazy about the dialogue.

Joe had made his opening remarks, none of which were very flattering to Lois, questioned the two night watchmen who discovered Prescott's body, and started with his expert witnesses before I arrived. The on-the-scene medical investigator, the pathologist who did the autopsy, and Lieutenant Peters from Casa Grande's finest were agreed that Drake Prescott died when someone turned on the power while he was leaning against the defective transformer. The as-yet-unnamed someone had then shut off the ten thousand volts of current and wiped the blade switch clean of prints with a Kleenex, leaving only a telltale bit of tissue in the handle's cracks and a body on the floor. When these details were added to the fact that Lois's fingerprints were on the wall nearby, it began to look like an open-and-shut case. That synopsis of testimony was hissed rapidly into my ear by a very nervous defendant, while Joe conferred quietly with Claudette Washington before calling his next witness to the stand.

Roy Walker, a field engineer for Public Service of Southern California, had enough credentials to make everything he said seem irrefutable. He boasted a B.S.E.E. from Iowa State University and was a registered professional engineer, licensed in Iowa, Texas, and California. While conducting a routine check on the new, oil-cooled, step-up transformer, he discovered the recently delivered machine had a short between the high-voltage windings and the metal casing. That was on Friday, the day before the open house.

"The crew and I closed down the lab by the book. Every safety procedure was followed, and the work order with the test results was taped up on that transformer. It was under warranty, so we planned to ship it back to the manufacturer on Monday. There shouldn't have been any problem, but we didn't expect anyone from the party to come wandering into the electrical testing facility, either. It's a restricted area and clearly labeled as such on the entrance from the administrative building. Even so, it was safe enough. The way we left it, Prescott could have climbed all over that transformer without hurting himself. I wired the switch in the off position myself before I left for the day."

"Wired it with what?" Joe asked.

"A red tag that says HIGH VOLTAGE. DO NOT CONNECT. It's standard procedure."

"And what about the work order taped on the transformer? What did it say?" Joe pursued. "Anything a non-engineer could understand?"

"Besides the technical stuff, I stamped DANGER-SHORT on the bottom. A lot of people might have understood what that meant."

Joe handed him an 8″ by 11″ piece of paper with some masking tape around it. "Is this the work order you're talking about?"

"Yes. That's it."

"Your Honor, I'd like to enter this as evidence that the transformer was clearly marked as a potentially lethal piece of equipment."

Then from a stack of documents on the table where Claudette was sitting, Joe pulled out a manila envelope. Inside was a rectangle of red cardboard with two pieces of wire dangling unevenly from a reinforced hole on one end. "Police found this tag on the floor of the testing facility under the blade switch. Is this the warning label you used?"

Mr. Walker examined the tag. "Looks just like it, but I can't say for sure. We have boxfuls of these in the lab."

Joe concluded that there were certainly ample warnings posted and that it seemed extremely unlikely that Drake Prescott could have electrocuted himself accidentally. Then he waved to Helen, acknowledging that the witness was all hers, if she could get anything helpful out of him.

I felt sure she would hit the right anode. After all, how could an electrical engineer be immune to the dazzling Helen's feminine wattage? He couldn't. Roy Walker's smile when he saw her approach was fatuous.

"Mr. Walker," Helen smiled back, "can you describe the testing facility for us?"

"Sure. It's about four thousand square feet with a large dome roof, sort of like an airplane hangar, with a concrete floor and twenty-foot-high double doors for moving in heavy machinery. On the opposite end is a regular door that connects it to the administrative building. All along the walls, there are work stations with benches and tables, each with their own electrical outlets so teams can test or repair equipment before it's put into operation."

"And where was this particular transformer?"

"Near the door that leads back into the administration building. Within fifteen feet of it, I'd say."

"And the light switch for the lab is near that door, as

well as the blade switch that controls electrical power to the work station where the transformer was plugged."

"That's right. The whole circuit board is on the wall there."

"So someone entering the room in the dark, someone unfamiliar with the testing lab, could easily turn on a blade switch by mistake, thinking it controlled the lights."

Roy Walker looked doubtful. "Maybe, but a blade switch is a handle, not a button or anything. You just can't flick it with a finger."

"Perhaps not. But a layperson might not know the difference in terms of its function," she reiterated, "especially in the dark where any warning label wouldn't be visible. Isn't that correct?"

"Yes."

"One last question, Mr. Walker. Where exactly on the transformer did you post the work order?"

"On the side."

"In plain sight to anyone entering the room?"

"No, ma'am. You'd have to come in a ways."

"Provided the lights were turned on so you could see 'a ways,'" Helen finished. "Thank you, Mr. Walker. You've been most helpful."

That was the last time Helen could say such a thing for quite a while. The prosecution's next two witnesses not only showed that Lois lied on her sworn affidavit given during the initial police investigation, they identified her as the last person known to have been with Prescott. All Helen could do was attempt to minimize the importance of what had been seen and heard.

First came Mr. Jamsheedi, the Iranian gentleman who had been sent down from the sixth floor to take over the public relations department after Lois was arrested. Tall, thin, and well dressed, he was distinctly urbane and spoke with a charming accent.

"Did you observe Ms. McCoin and Mr. Prescott in conversation at all during the reception?" Joe inquired.

"Yes. I am not sure of the time, but it was during the party. She approached him and they talked for a few minutes. I think it was about something important because Mrs. McCoin seemed rather agitated. Then they went out of the room together and I didn't see her again until some time later." Ominously, he added, "Mr. Prescott I never saw again."

In cross-examination, Helen tried to get the witness to modify the word 'agitated,' and she succeeded to a degree. However, the next person to take the stand was a precise, gray little man, identified as an account executive at PSSC, who more than picked up where Mr. Jamsheedi left off. This was the trivia expert, one of those people who remembered every movie Lorraine Day ever made, how many times Babe Ruth came up to bat on June 4, 1936, and what he had to eat the day before . . . Babe Ruth, that is. According to Mr. Heron, the target of this hearing had more than ample time to commit murder before she returned to the reception area and her duties as *ex officio* hostess. The same time lapse I noticed in Carole Prescott's movements now was being applied to Lois by this human stopwatch.

"When did you see Ms. McCoin talking to Mr. Prescott?" Joe asked.

Without a moment's hesitation, the man answered. "It was four-thirty."

"And how long before they left together?"

"Certainly no more than two minutes."

"And where did they go?"

"Down the hallway and around the corner. I couldn't see them after that."

"In the direction of the testing facility?"

Mr. Heron confirmed that was where the hallway led.

"Did you see them return to the reception?" Joe inquired.

"I did not see Mr. Prescott again, but I noted Mrs. McCoin's reappearance at four-fifty."

"Twenty minutes later?"

"That's correct."

Getting this master of memorabilia to impeach his own powers of retention was tantamount to rocking the Rock of Gibraltar. Helen gave it the old heave-ho, but he wouldn't budge.

"Do you know how many people attended the reception?" she pushed.

"The guest list was two hundred and fifty including the press, so I imagine the actual attendance figure was close."

"But even without a head count, the room was crowded," Helen stated.

"Yes." Mr. Heron adjusted his horn-rimmed glasses.

"And in that throng of people, you were able to keep track of Ms. McCoin's whereabouts?" Helen was gently skeptical.

"There was a reason for my interest," Mr. Heron bristled. "Mrs McCoin was in charge of refreshments, and I told her I was afraid the food wouldn't hold out until six o'clock. She then confided that the caterer was short a tray of hors d'oeuvres, and when I saw her talking to Mr. Prescott a little later, I assumed she was telling him about the problem and that when they left the room together, it was to use the phone. When Lois . . . er . . . Mrs. McCoin came back by herself, a delivery man arrived with the missing tray. I looked at my watch, thinking the caterer had been quite prompt to bring it from town in only twenty minutes. And their truck had to get past that mob of demonstrators, too."

Helen paused thoughtfully. "Did you see the truck drive through the gates? The entire front wall of the lobby is plate glass, so the entrance is clearly visible from the reception area."

"I'm afraid I wasn't watching when the truck pulled up."

"But you did observe the demonstrators at some point, didn't you?"

"It was difficult not to, since they were in full view and doing their best to be noticed."

Helen's smile reminded me of the Cheshire cat's. "Then perhaps, with so much else to capture your attention, your eyes were not on the hallway for the entire twenty minutes."

"Well, no, not for twenty minutes continuously." Mr. Heron smoothed back his gray hair with a nervous hand.

"It is possible that Ms. McCoin was not absent as long as you thought. Though you observed her presence at four-fifty, she might have reentered the room earlier."

"I know when I saw her in the doorway," he said stiffly.

"But not if she just arrived there," Helen concluded.

"No, I guess not."

Joe whispered something to Claudette, then got up and approached the bench. "Your Honor, the prosecution has three more witnesses who can attest to the fact that the accused left the reception with Drake Prescott and came back alone approximately twenty minutes later. For the sake of brevity, I would like to hold them in abeyance for now and get on with another line of questioning."

Judge Marion Lovell, a majestic figure in her black gown, seemed happy to do so. "The defense has no objection? Fine. Let's move on, Mr. Corelli."

Lois leaned over to her attorney. "Is April next?"

Helen nodded expressionlessly, moving Prescott's secretary's statement to the top of the pile of papers in front of her.

Chapter Fourteen

The courtroom had been gradually filling up during the last hour. There were plenty of spectators who had come out of sheer curiosity, but most were members of the press. The notoriety of the case had brought reporters all the way from Los Angeles and San Diego. What a feature story they could do on April Evans. A ripple of appreciative comments broke out as she was ushered to the stand and the oath administered. In a bright red sweater and gray skirt, she already looked newsworthy, but when she sat down and crossed her shapely legs, headlines were made.

"Order, please." The judge glared over her half-frame glasses. "I will not tolerate whistling in my courtroom. Any more noisy outbreaks and I'll have the bailiff clear the area. Is that understood?"

Affirmation was a chorus of silence.

Joe began by introducing the infamous memo. After Helen viewed it and April attested that this was the self-same interoffice communication she typed for Drake Prescott, Joe asked that it be read into the record. At a nod from the judge, Claudette Washington rose to her feet and did so.

"It's dated February second and reads, 'Dear Ted, re Lois McCoin and job as communications development director at Canyon Escondido. Sorry, but cannot recommend her transfer to plant operations area. All the supervisory personnel are men and I suggest we keep it that way. You know how the hard hats react to skirts. No point in stirring agitation from the inside when we have so much to deal with on the outside. Let's just say McCoin would not interface effectively with productions crew.' It's signed, 'Drake,' and then 'P.S. Our racquetball game still on for Monday?' "

"When did Mr. Prescott dictate this memo to you?" Joe began.

"On Friday morning, the day before he was . . . he was killed," April said in such a quiet voice it couldn't have been heard in the back of the room.

"But you didn't send it off to Mr. Ted Osoff right away."

"No." Her answer was barely audible.

"Why not?" When April did not reply, his tone sharpened. "Please speak up. Why did you delay sending the memo as directed?"

"Because I wanted Ms. McCoin to see it first."

"As his executive assistant, didn't she automatically receive a copy of Mr. Prescott's memos unless he gave specific instructions to the contrary?" Joe prodded.

"He said to keep it confidential," she admitted finally, "but I thought if Ms. McCoin knew he hadn't recommended her, she might be able to get him to change his mind."

"Does that mean you think his decision was unfair?"

"Sort of." Her tone was self-defensive.

"Did you also believe that Ms. McCoin would think it unfair?"

"I . . . well . . . yes."

"Then why didn't you take the memo to her as soon as you finished typing it?"

April stared down at her hands.

"Ms. Evans," Joe said a bit irritably, "in the police report, you stated that you delayed until noon before showing the memo to Ms. McCoin. I would like you to tell the court why you waited two hours when you were so anxious for her to read it."

"The witness's reason is immaterial," Helen objected.

"Not at all," Joe countered. "It has a direct bearing, as the defense will see if the court permits Ms. Evans to answer."

When the court did permit, April licked her lips nervously and glanced at Lois. "I waited because I knew Mr. Prescott would be leaving at noon for the day."

"Thank you," Joe acknowledged ironically. "Now would you please explain why it was preferable that he be absent?"

"I didn't want him to know abut it," she stalled.

"Why?" Joe was relentless. "Were you worried about losing your job if he discovered you passed on his confidential correspondence to Ms. McCoin?"

April flushed. "No! Not at all."

"Then why did you wait until he left?"

Joe was understandably annoyed by his witness's uncooperative attitude. No doubt they had gone all over this in conference, but for some reason April didn't want to speak up in court. Nothing I read in her statement was incredibly damaging to Lois, so I couldn't imagine why she had qualms about giving the information now. A minute later it became obvious why. Helpful April Evans had been much more expansive with the D.A. than she had been with the police originally. All Joe wanted was for her to repeat her words under oath, and all she wanted to do was forget she ever said a thing.

After a remorseful glance at Lois, she came clean, as they say in police circles. "I didn't want Mr. Prescott around when Lois read the memo. She was sure to be angry, and I thought they might get into another argument."

Lois tugged at her attorney's sleeve. "Why don't you object again?"

"On what grounds?" Helen whispered back. "That her answer doesn't suit the defense? Sit still and be quiet."

"Listen to me," Lois insisted, "you've got to stop her, or you know what's going to come out."

I had a funny feeling I knew too, but there was no way to stop Joe. "You say, 'another argument,' " he pressed the point home. "Does this mean Ms. McCoin and Mr. Prescott argued frequently?"

"No, I didn't mean to give that impression," April recanted.

"And I am not asking for your impression," Joe said, forestalling a protest from Helen, "merely for facts that will demonstrate how well Ms. McCoin and her supervisor got along. "Did you ever hear them quarrel?"

"Yes," April murmured reluctantly.

As Joe probed into what caused the flare-ups between the former public relations director of PSSC and his executive assistant, what emerged was a description of a bigoted male at constant odds with a frustrated, suffering suffragette. Drake Prescott seemed to have taken great joy in needling Lois about her secondary status in the office, making slighting reference to where a woman's rightful place should be. It certainly established a pretty clear picture of their working relationship, which Joe emphasized in his next question.

"Then you were aware that Ms. McCoin would resent the sexist overtones in Mr. Prescott's memo, correct?"

"I . . . yes."

"And how did she react when she read it?"

"She was upset, naturally. Mr. Prescott said he'd give her a good recommendation, but he put her down just because she's a woman."

"I understand your related sense of indignation, Ms. Evans, but what did Ms. McCoin say after reading it? Her exact words, please."

April looked at Lois, then at the judge. "Honestly, she spouted off a little, that's all. She didn't mean it. We all make threats we don't . . ."

Judge Lovell interrupted as my heart sank. Lois was hunched over, her head bent to receive the coming blow. "Ms. Evans, you have been asked a direct question and I must insist you answer. What were Ms. McCoin's words when she read the memo from Mr. Prescott to Mr. Osoff?"

April bit her lip then blurted, "She said, 'I'll kill the son of a bitch. He won't get away with this.' "

Several thoughts popped into my head as a collective murmur of surprise erupted through the courtroom. One, Betsy and I weren't the only people who could attest to Lois's state of mind prior to the murder. Two, Joe must have made April fall in love with him to worm such incriminating information from her. And three, if this were April's idea of helping Lois, what would happen if she tried to hurt her?

To give the devil her due, April really was struggling to balance truth and loyalty, but she couldn't make them come out even. Still, if she continued in this vein, resisting Joe, he might just ask to be allowed to treat her as a hostile witness. Then he'd be able to cross-examine her as though she'd been called by the defense, a position that would give him quite a bit more leeway. But apparently April decided to dance with the escort who brought her. When Joe focused on the events at Canyon Escondido the following day, she hardly protested at all.

"Did you see Ms. McCoin and Mr. Prescott together at the open house on that Saturday afternoon, February third?"

"Yes."

"And where was this?'

"They were around the corner in the hallway."

Joe handed April a piece of paper. "This is a diagram of PSSC's plant at Canyon Escondido. I've marked the electrical testing facility with an *E*, and the main lobby where the reception was held with an *R*. Would you please put a check-mark in the connecting corridor where you saw Ms. McCoin and Mr. Prescott?"

April studied the outline for a moment, marked the spot, then silently handed the paper and red pencil back to Joe.

"If it please the court, I would like it noted in the record that Ms. Evans saw the deceased and Ms. McCoin standing only twenty feet from the door to the testing facility. I think this clarifies where they went after leaving the lobby," he added with a glance at Helen.

She remained tight-lipped, but Lois was visibly shaken.

"And where were you at this time?" Joe continued with his witness.

"At the top of the corridor, on my way to the ladies' room."

"And when you observed them, what were they doing?"

"Just talking."

"According to the diagram, the ladies' room isn't a great distance away. Could you hear any of their conversation?"

April sighed. "A little."

"Were their voices raised?"

April clenched her hands. "Yes."

"Then you overheard them quarreling. Is that right?"

"Objection." Helen raised her hand. "Prosecution is leading the witness."

Joe turned around. "Computing that a conversation plus raised voices equals a quarrel is merely elementary addition."

"I think we should let the witness calculate that for herself," was the judge's liberal evaluation. "Ms. Evans, why don't you describe exactly what you heard," she directed.

April wasn't about to disobey another court order, as it were, and her words came out in a rush. "I only stood there for a moment, so I didn't hear very much, but Ms. McCoin accused Mr. Prescott of stabbing her in the back. He called her an hysterical old fool with an inflated sense of her own worth, and then I went into the ladies' room, and that's all. They were gone when I came back out."

And I wondered what April could do to harm? Good Lord, her dagger thrust was a hundred times deadlier than Prescott's. Admittedly she didn't want the role of villainess that Joe had assigned her, but she sure turned a cameo appearance into a show stopper. It even made Judge Lovell call for a timely intermission. She adjourned the hearing for a lunch recess, which gave Helen a sorely needed hour and a half to regroup before cross-examining the last and best of Joe's *dramatis personnae*.

It was going to take quite a production number to upstage April's performance, though Lois thought the girl had held the spotlight much too long. She was furious that her attorney allowed the prosecution to twist April's testimony into a defamatory noose of distortions, while Helen curtly accused her client of not understanding legal procedure. That only inflamed Lois more, and I suggested we leave the emptying courtroom to discuss the matter somewhere else.

"Good idea." Helen stuffed a mass of papers in her briefcase and shut it with an angry snap. "Then maybe you can explain to your friend why I couldn't object to every word April uttered."

"Right, Ellie. Do that. Explain to me why my lawyer sat on her hands and did nothing." Lois's eyes were too bright, her tongue too sarcastic.

"Actually, your lawyer did an outstanding job," I soothed. "Didn't you notice how she modified the testimony of every single witness for the prosecution? Just you wait. By the time she's through, all the evidence against you will look like nothing but a few coincidences."

"Only if Lois gets her story straight this time," Helen said tartly, leading the way out of the room. "Remember,

Joe Corelli is going to tear it to bits. That's what we should discuss over lunch, Lois's testimony, not April's."

"But she made it sound as if Drake and I fought all the time," Lois protested. "It wasn't like that. I was sweet and charming and controlled and polite and took his crap day in and day out."

"Don't worry, you'll get to tell your side of the story," I said, giving her hand what I hoped was a comforting squeeze.

"Just don't tell it now," Helen directed as we stepped outside the building and into the glare of popping flashbulbs.

A reporter from one of the local TV stations stuck a microphone in Lois's face while a minicam recorded the event for the six o'clock news. "Ms. McCoin, do you think corporate discrimination against women will figure prominently in this case?"

From the back of the crowd, another man shouted, "How do you stand on PSSC's plan to check into the feasibility of using a breeder reactor for Unit Three at Canyon Escondido?"

Stepping in front of her flinching client, Helen Ramirez smiled sweetly and told the press Ms. McCoin had no statement to make on any subject at this time.

"How about an interview with her after the hearing?" one reporter asked brashly.

Helen kept walking while Lois and I trailed behind. "When the charges are dropped, Ms. McCoin will gladly hold a press conference to answer all your questions on nuclear energy."

That got us as far as the parking lot where I had left my car. As I jumped into the driver's seat, Helen pushed Lois in next to me, then dove into the back and ordered us to lock the doors.

"Don't duck," she told Lois sharply. "Hiding always makes you look guilty. Keep your chin up. That's the way.

For crying out loud, Ellie, what are you waiting for? Start the goddamn car and let's get out of here."

Chapter Fifteen

Lunch was a dismal affair. Barney's offered a dark corner where no one but the waitress paid the slightest attention to us, but Helen wouldn't let Lois have one of his noted double-olive martinis. Her client needed a clear head for the coming ordeal. So instead, Lois fidgeted nervously, picked at her salad, and drank two cups of coffee, none of which had a very therapeutic effect on her. By the time we got back to the courthouse, she was not only displeased with Helen; Lois wasn't too happy with me, either. I'd made the mistake of trying to defend April. After all, the girl hadn't promised to commit perjury on Lois's behalf, and Joe hadn't left his witness much choice when it came to telling the tale. Helen would just have to elicit another slant on things during cross-examination.

That noble effort began as soon as the hearing reconvened at one-thirty. Looking distinctly apprehensive, April Evans was recalled to the stand and reminded she was still under oath.

"Ms. Evans," Helen began with a reassuring smile, "there are a few details in your testimony that I'd like to clarify, but first"—Helen picked up a brochure from the table in front of her and showed it to April "—did you work on this pamphlet?"

"Yes. It's PSSC's publicity packet on Canyon Escondido and it was mailed out to all our customers on January twenty-eighth."

"Who wrote and designed it?"

"The art department did the layout, but Ms. McCoin wrote the copy and Mr. Prescott did the final editing."

"Then it was a joint effort?"

"That's right."

"How long did this project take to complete?"

"Gee," April paused thoughtfully. "Most of January. No, longer. Some of the research was done in December."

"Did it require conferences between Mr. Prescott and Ms. McCoin?"

"Oh, yes," April nodded wisely, having just figured what Helen wanted to bring out. "They spent a lot of time putting it together."

"And putting their heads together," Helen said lightly. "Was Mr. Prescott satisfied with Ms. McCoin's contribution?"

"Sure. He never had any complaints about her work."

"Then despite any philosophical differences of opinion they had, it did not interfere with their ability to function as a team?"

"Not at all," April said eagerly. "And it was really due to Ms. McCoin. She's just not the type to make trouble. Even when Mr. Prescott said the most outlandish things, she never went off the deep end answering him back."

Helen probably didn't appreciate that addend, but with professional aplomb, she made use of it. "And did she go off the 'deep end' when you showed her the memo? For instance, did she cry?"

"Oh, no."

"Or raise her voice?"

"Not really. It was more like a snarl. You know, the way

you sound when you're aggravated. That's why when she threatened to kill him, I didn't take her seriously." April sat back in a more relaxed pose as if she had just said something helpful.

However, Helen was none too pleased to have the court reminded that Lois had been in a murderous mood the day before Drake's death. "So you were sure that Ms. McCoin's words were only a figure of speech?"

Joe rose to his feet with an objection. "What Ms. Evans thought about it is irrelevant."

"Your Honor," Helen answered, "Ms. Evans has spent the last two years working in the same office as my client. In that time, the witness must have learned a lot about how Lois McCoin responds to stress, even her speech habits. Therefore, I think Ms. Evans' opinion in this matter is very relevant."

"I agree. The witness will please answer the question," Judge Lovell ruled.

"Of course, I thought she was talking through her hat."

"But you did expect her to approach Mr. Prescott about the problem? And you believed, based on your knowledge of Ms. McCoin, this would be done in a calm, rational manner?"

"Yes."

"Then to capsulize your testimony, you state that Drake Prescott and Lois McCoin had a working relationship that was both effective and amicable. And when you showed Ms. McCoin the memo, her reaction was neither hysterical nor excessive, an attitude you were confident she'd maintain."

It was amazing how lawyers could get to the meat of the matter by slicing through the bone and gristle as though they didn't exist. Helen's summary was a little short on flavor, but what she served up had a nice, bland texture that cut the aftertaste of Joe's pungent remarks. April was a little staggered to hear her own words boiled down to a *soupçon,* but she concurred with Helen's condensed version. It wasn't wrong, merely abridged.

"Now let's get on with the open house on Saturday afternoon at Canyon Escondido," Helen continued. "You testified that when you went to the ladies' room at approximately twenty to five, you observed Mr. Prescott and Ms. McCoin in the corridor, some distance from the door to the testing lab . . . about twenty feet. Is that correct?"

"Yes."

"I'd like to draw the court's attention to the fact that if my client and the deceased were having their conversation in the hallway, they certainly weren't having it in the testing facility. And since this discussion was seen taking place only ten minutes before Ms. McCoin was seen returning to the reception, I propose that the intervening ten minutes gave Ms. McCoin insufficient time to go into the testing lab with Mr. Prescott, discover that there was a short in the transformer, and with no arrow posted on the wall, know what switch controlled which piece of machinery."

She turned back to April. "One last thing, Ms. Evans. "According to your own earlier testimony, you expected Ms. McCoin to try and change Mr. Prescott's mind about her qualifications for the job. Wouldn't that suggest she would be persuasive rather than argumentative?"

"I guess so," April agreed.

"Thank you, Ms. Evans. No further questions."

Prudently, Helen left off before April reminded the court that Lois called her boss a backstabber, hardly the way to win friends and influence people. Still, Helen's strategy in narrowing the incriminating twenty minutes that Lois spent out of sight with Prescott to an inadequate ten did create a reasonable doubt of how much she could have accomplished in that short a time. Reading a circuit board was no quick feat, especially if she had to con Prescott into holding onto the transformer until she found the right switch, though the warning tag would have helped.

Joe, wisely enough, didn't debate this hypothetical scenario. When he got up to redirect, his questions were aimed at discrediting April's judgments without actually impeaching her credibility as a witness for the prosecution.

"Ms. Evans, you made some rather scientific observations in your previous testimony concerning Ms. McCoin's emotional state on the Friday before the murder. Do you have any special training in psychology? Have you taken any college courses in it?"

"No."

"Then what qualifies you to recognize whether or not a person is capable of a violent action?"

April squirmed uncomfortably. "Just common sense. If someone has never done anything terrible, it isn't likely she'll suddenly change into a monster, is it?"

"I don't know. I'm not a psychiatrist either. But as a layman, I believe that there is such a thing as a breaking point. Pushed too far, ordinary people do extraordinary things. But since your opinion has been included in the record, I would like to clarify that it *is* a layperson's. You do not hold a degree in psychiatry, and as you described, it was your common sense that led you to believe Ms. McCoin would not carry out her threat to kill."

April's answer marked the conclusion of the prosecution's case. Joe made a brief summary, reiterated the pertinent facts, then turned the floor over to Helen. She opened the defense by calling the janitor, the only person who could verify that Lois had been in the testing facility early on Saturday afternoon. Helen quickly established this as the time Lois left her fingerprints on the wall.

She and I exchanged triumphant glances as Helen resumed her seat, but alas, we rejoiced too soon. Five minutes later, our witness recanted under the D.A.'s cross-examination. Mr. Brown had only seen Lois in the doorway of the lab and could not swear she was coming out. It was possible she hadn't yet gone in when she heard him coming down the hall.

I think we were all discouraged at that moment, but Helen didn't let it show. From her manner, anyone might have supposed we had the opposition on the run. Calmly she called Jane Chestnut to the stand.

The beginning was routine: getting the basics on record, who Jane was and that she had been Lois's personal secretary for the last four and a half years. Helen then asked the witness how Ms. McCoin interacted with Mr. Prescott on a professional basis.

"She bent over backward to help him," Jane said positively. "And she saved him from some embarrassing mistakes a few times. He wasn't a good detail man." Jane smiled to herself as though enjoying the memory of his discomfort. "But Ms. McCoin is just the nicest, most considerate person anyone could want to work with. And not just to Mr. Prescott. When my Tony was sick with the measles and I came to the office anyway, she sent me home to take care of him. And she drives herself hard too. I can't tell you how many times Ms. McCoin came early and stayed late. I'm no clock watcher myself, but she's really dedicated to her job, not like some people in the office I could mention."

When this flow of excess finally ceased, Helen picked up a large manila envelope. "Your Honor, I have here the interdepartment correspondence between Mr. Prescott and Ms. McCoin for the last six months. Without exception, the tone is courteous and informally chatty. They show incontrovertibly that the working relationship between my client and the deceased was friendly and that the two routinely cooperated to the fullest in the running of the public relations department at PSSC. I would like Mrs. Chestnut, who collected this data, to attest to its completeness."

I sat back and let my mind wander as the tedious business of the memos was taken care of and the file

entered as evidence. Of course, Prescott had been satisfied
with his assistant's work. Why not when she took care of
the nitty-gritty running of the department while he reaped
the credit? As long as she remained in a secondary role
and tolerated his highhanded attitudes, he had no reason
to complain. But let her aspire to a position equal to his
and everything changed. Drake would have been a Samson
shorn of his hair if Lois were to move on to Canyon
Escondido. He knew she was his greatest strength, and not
recommending her for a promotion was such a simple way
to keep the ox plowing his own fertile field. That was one
way the memos could be read, along with the postscript
that the poor, dumb animal was finally provoked into
throwing off her yoke and goring the unfair taskmaster.

But if Jane Chestnut had unconsciously drawn that
illustration, she also painted a picture of a woman who was
just too nice, too sweet, too kind to be a killer, and of
course, much too busy.

"On the afternoon of Friday, February second," Helen
continued with her witness, "did Ms. McCoin seem unusu-
ally distressed in any way?"

"No, though she was worried about the printers."

"Did she say anything about the promotion she had
applied for? Tell you Mr. Prescott didn't recommend her
for it, or indicate she was angry with him?"

"No. As I started to say, she was concerned about the
insert for the next billing. Mr. Prescott promised to call the
printer that morning with some important changes, but he
forgot. I told Ms. McCoin she'd better take care of it
herself, because April said Mr. Prescott was gone for the
day. He had to see some man about the demonstrators who
were planning a big confrontation out at Canyon Escondido during the open house. He had a real bee in his bonnet
about them."

Helen had waited patiently through this cascade of
irrelevancies. Now she picked up on the essentials. "Then

you would characterize her behavior, her mood, on that Friday afternoon as perfectly normal?"

"Certainly."

When Helen said she had no more questions at the moment, Jane Chestnut got to her feet and had to be instructed that Mr. Corelli still needed to cross-examine her. What the D.A. was going to dig out of this too-talkative, too-loyal secretary scared the holy crap out of me.

Casually, he strolled over to the witness stand. "Mrs. Chestnut, did Lois McCoin ever tell you she felt unappreciated by her boss?"

Jane wriggled unhappily. "Well, everyone feels that way sometimes. I do. Some people have a kind of flashy style that attracts attention, while the ones who just come in every day and get the work done are taken for granted. That's life."

"It may be life, Mrs. Chestnut, but did Ms. McCoin ever complain about that aspect of reality? Tell you she was overworked, exploited, taken advantage of by Drake Prescott?"

"She might have. Once or twice."

"Think carefully, Mrs. Chestnut. Didn't Ms. McCoin criticize Drake Prescott's opinions, work habits, and attitudes more than once or twice in the past year since he'd been put in charge of the department?"

I could see that Lois expected her lawyer to object, but there were no grounds. Leading the witness was perfectly permissible during cross-examination, and Joe knew exactly where he wanted to take Jane Chestnut.

Her doughy face stiffened with resentment, but she came through for him just the way he hoped.

"Well, he did exploit her. He came in late, took long lunch hours, went on all the cushy business trips. Ms. McCoin made him look good, so he got all the commendations."

"Are you saying Lois McCoin had every reason to dislike her boss?" Joe's tone was calmly inquisitive.

Helen half-rose from her seat. "Mr. Corelli is asking the witness to draw a conclusion."

"Objection overruled."

Jane spoke up smartly. "I really couldn't say how Ms. McCoin felt."

Joe shifted his ground a little. "Would you resent a boss who treated you the way Mr. Prescott treated Ms. McCoin?"

"Objection. Irrelevant and immaterial. What Mrs. Chestnut would feel in a hypothetical situation has no bearing on this case."

This time the judge agreed with Helen, but Joe's getting our star witness to make an impassioned declaration on why Lois had reason to dislike her supervisor was a real coup for the prosecution. And supposedly this was our inning, though the stats looked pretty bad. The first two batters Helen sent to the plate had struck out, thanks to Joe Corelli's curve balls. The game wasn't over yet, but I had a funny feeling our last slugger was not going to hit a home run either.

Chapter Sixteen

Helen asked for a five-minute recess to confer with her client. Judge Lovell extended it to fifteen and rustled out, as did most of the audience, which had dwindled down to a few diehards anyway. Most people probably thought the dramatic climax had come and gone when the prosecution rested its case. Even the bulk of the fourth estate had decided to skip the afternoon session. Too bad. If they'd been able to see the dress rehearsal, there wouldn't have been an empty seat in the house for the matinée performance.

"Come over here, Ellie." Helen jerked her head at me. "We need your opinion. I'm going to make a radical suggestion. What say I make a speech and then we call it a day? The judge will either go for a dismissal or she won't. We're not going to change anything now, I'm afraid."

Lois was surprised. "What? You mean, just give up, not tell my side of it at all?"

"No, not give up. Concede this round." Helen was tired and impatient, and it showed in her voice. "As I explained before, the prosecution doesn't have to prove its contentions today, only present enough evidence to justify a trial. And Lois, he's done it. Corelli's shown motive, opportunity, plus state of mind. I won't say it's absolutely positive Judge Lovell will rule against us, but I wouldn't bet any money on it going our way now. The bottom line is, why put you on the stand when it really won't make any difference?"

"But I want to tell my side," Lois argued with stubborn persistence. "If I can explain what happened in my own words, the judge will understand. She's a woman and my age too."

Helen looked ready to strangle her intractable client, so I butted in with my two cents worth. "The D.A.'s going to use every one of Jane Chestnut's hyperboles to build up your motive for killing Prescott. Then he'll fit that right into the holes in your police statement."

"Listen to me, Lois," Helen said with an edge to her voice. "The D.A. knows exactly how to pry the worm from the apple. Under cross-examination, you might say something better left unsaid."

Lois stuck out her jaw. "Like what? That I hated Drake Prescott? That his job should have been mine, so I had a double reason to get rid of him?"

"Will you be quiet?" Helen admonished. "People are starting to come back into the courtroom."

"And you're afraid they're going to get a preview of my full confession under Corelli's attack? Thanks for the vote of confidence," Lois said snidely. "Maybe I should just plead guilty right now and save you the bother of going through the motions."

"Of course, it's your decision." Helen was stiff, formal. "However, as your attorney, I advise you not to take the stand today."

But Lois wasn't open to persuasion from any source. We both tried to reason with her, but when the bailiff announced Judge Lovell's return to the bench and the three of us moved hastily back to our places, Lois hissed, "Put me up there."

And so she went. But even Helen's carefully worded questions weren't able to bolster the weakness of her client's answers. Maybe I was hypersensitive, but when Lois admitted forgetting a few details on her police statement, I winced. Oh, yes, she'd been in the testing facility earlier on Saturday afternoon. It had simply slipped her mind when Lieutenant Peters asked her originally.

And then there was the other little error on her police statement, Lois added with an apologetic smile. She *had* spoken to Drake Prescott at the reception. "It was stupid not to say so at the time, but I was shaken by the news of his death," she excused herself. "Actually, I didn't intend to raise the issue of the memo to Drake during the open house. I wanted to be calm and businesslike when I confronted him," Lois explained, her voice low and steady, her eyes pinned on Helen. "But when I found myself standing next to him, I couldn't not speak, if you see what I mean."

Whether or not Helen did see, she skipped over whatever compelling force drove Lois to approach Prescott at that moment and asked instead for the gist of the conversation. Lois should have had her answer down pat, but for some reason she chose to offer a bunch of editorial additions, nuances included.

She described how she questioned Prescott, with a pretense of casualness, on her chances for being named communications coordinator at the new power plant. Naturally, he tried to bluff her, claiming he'd done a masterful job of selling her to the board of directors, but the scuttlebutt was that they wanted a hotshot from the East Coast. Dropping a good bit of her pose, Lois accused him of lying through his teeth, and after a hasty look around the room, Prescott suggested they have this discussion in more private surroundings. Lois followed him down the hallway and around the corner where they both assumed no one could hear them. Then she gave him what-for.

Poor Helen. She'd had bad luck with all her witnesses today. One recanted, and two were entirely too talkative. Lois, at least, should have known better. She was supposed to describe a rather colorless encounter, not take a leaf from Jane Chestnut's book and fill in all the missing adjectives. Now Helen had to tone down the scenic effects before Lois painted them too black.

"Allowing for your annoyance with Drake Prescott, you did not need the privacy of a soundproof room, did you?"

"No," Lois said. "We were not shouting at each other. Our conversation was low-key, considering."

Helen shot her client a warning look. "What was Mr. Prescott's response when you told him you'd seen his memo to Mr. Osoff?"

"I guess you could call it an apology of sorts. He said he had nothing against me personally, but he didn't think any woman could handle the job. I told him I wasn't buying his evenhanded bigotry, but after a few more minutes, I realized that nothing I could say would change his mind, so I gave up and left."

Lois stole a quick glance at Judge Lovell, who didn't show any particular sign of approval at the defendant's professed restraint in such a trying situation. Her Honor's face remained placidly inscrutable.

"Then you accepted his apology."

"Well . . . yes," Lois finally said without elaborating, as if the judge needed to hear a supplementary clause on Lois's acute frustration.

"And did you then return directly to the reception?" Helen asked.

"No, I needed a moment by myself, so I decided to wait in the ladies' room until I felt more like facing the crowd again. But when I opened the door to go in, April Evans was at the sink cleaning her dress. So instead, I ducked into one of the empty offices across the hall and smoked a cigarette. After that, I went back to the reception."

"Which would have been at approximately a quarter to five, a little before Mr. Heron noticed you in the doorway."

"I believe so."

"And Drake Prescott was fine when you left him?"

"He was alive." Lois's tone was dry.

Helen's last two questions wrapped it up. "Did you enter the testing facility with Drake Prescott?"

"No, I did not." Lois was emphatic.

"Did you kill Drake Prescott by turning on the blade switch that activated the transformer while he was touching the machine?"

"I did not."

"No further questions, Your Honor." Helen seated herself gracefully while Joe took the spot directly in front of the witness stand.

"You forgot to mention quite a few important details about that day at Canyon Escondido on your police statement," Joe said, his hands clasped behind his back. "Are you sure you're still not 'forgetting' something? Like going into the testing lab with Drake Prescott because the hall wasn't really private enough for all the ugly things you were saying to each other."

Lois's eyes darted to Helen. "I didn't go into the testing lab."

"Your fingerprints were found there."

"I explained. That happened earlier."

"Why don't you think about it again? With everything else you forgot, perhaps you might have also forgotten that your fingerprints got there when you were quarreling with Mr. Prescott after all."

"It wasn't a quarrel. It was just a disagreement. And we were in the corridor."

"Very well. Tell me about this disagreement in the corridor. Ms. Evans overheard you accuse Prescott of stabbing you in the back, and by your own testimony, you admit calling him a liar. How did Mr. Prescott . . . uh . . . disagree with these charges?"

Lois twisted in her seat. "I already said. He apologized."

"Did he also apologize for being a male chauvinist pig?"

"Objection, Your Honor," Helen interrupted. "Nowhere in Ms. McCoin's testimony is there a record of her using that phrase."

"Sustained. Mr. Corelli," Judge Lovell directed. "Please refrain from figurative references and be more precise when you recall testimony."

"Certainly, Your Honor." He nodded and referred to the legal pad of notes he was holding. "Ms. McCoin, to be precise, when you stated that Mr. Prescott wouldn't have recommended any woman for the post of communications coordinator, were you implying that his remarks were sexist?"

"Yes." This time she didn't glance at Helen.

"According to Ms. Evans"—Joe looked at his notes again—"this was a frequent topic of dissension between you and your supervisor at PSSC."

"It came up a few times."

"And you always took exception to his attitude?"

"When I could."

"Meaning you usually let it slide rather than debate the issue in the office."

"That's right." Lois was very erect, very tense in the witness chair.

"But on Saturday afternoon when you were both standing in relative privacy by the door to the testing facility, there were no curious ears to prevent you from raising the subject. Did you take advantage of the opportunity then?"

"Yes. I did say something about it."

"But not nearly as much as you could have."

"Not nearly as much," she agreed, raising her chin. "I was polite. Sarcastic but polite."

"Do you consider yourself a feminist, Ms. McCoin?" Joe laid a subtle stress on the "Ms."

"If you mean, am I in favor of equal opportunity for women, yes."

"And how do you stand on sexual discrimination?"

Lois looked at Joe with some suspicion. "The EEOC has been of great benefit to women," she acknowledged carefully.

"Then why didn't you appeal to them?"

"I beg your pardon?" Lois was puzzled.

"You said a moment ago that Prescott's attitude was sexist. I want to know why you never reported his conduct to the EEOC?"

"I . . . it wasn't important enough," she faltered.

"Yet you complained to your secretary, to Drake's secretary . . ."

"Your Honor," Lois twisted around in her seat, "he's badgering me. Helen, why don't you stop him?"

Judge Lovell rapped her gavel. "Ms. McCoin, you are out of order. And you, Mr. Corelli, if you're trying to determine to what extent Ms. McCoin resented Mr. Prescott's attitude, ask once and be done with it."

"Very well. How much did you resent Mr. Prescott?" Joe snapped out before Lois could regain her composure.

"Not enough to kill him."

"Are you sure? Can you remember exactly how you felt when he called you an hysterical old fool, or is your memory faulty about that too?"

Lois glared at him. "I remember."

"And do you also remember stepping past the double doors where you were standing, into a big, quiet room where no one could see or hear you?"

"No."

"No, what?" Joe's voice was a whiplash. "No, you didn't go in? Or, no, you don't remember going into the testing facility because you were too infuriated to realize where you followed Drake Prescott?"

Lois shook her head. "You want me to say I killed him. But I won't. We didn't go into the testing lab. I never even saw the transformer, and if I had, I still wouldn't have known how to electrocute someone with it."

Joe raised his eyebrows. "Then your memory is worse than you thought, Ms. McCoin." He held up the same pamphlet Helen had shown April Evans. "Didn't you write this?"

"Yes." Lois stared at him, transfixed.

"Then aren't these your words that describe the physical setup of Canyon Escondido and how a nuclear power plant functions?"

"Yes." She gripped the arms of her chair.

"And your words that explain all the safety features, including the purpose of a red DO NOT TOUCH tag when it's attached to a power switch?"

"Yes."

"Then how can you honestly say you knew nothing about how the transformer worked, or how it could have electrocuted someone? You, Ms. McCoin, wrote a manual on it."

"No!" She jumped to her feet, ignoring the judge's pounding gavel and Helen's frantic signals. "You're twisting everything. That information was straight from the engineer's report. I only copied it. You're just trying to make me sound guilty because I had a reason to kill Prescott. Yes, he made nasty little jokes about women, and yes, I resented it like hell. But he was right about us. We can't handle high-powered jobs. That's the proof right there." She pointed at Helen and started to laugh. "Can you imagine Drake Prescott making the mistake of hiring a woman lawyer?"

It was horrible. The silence in the court and that laughter.

Helen stepped forward. "Your Honor, I request a recess. My client is too upset to continue."

Judge Lovell looked disapprovingly over her glasses at the defense attorney. "I can see that. Take her into my chambers. The hearing will reconvene in half an hour." The gavel rapped once.

By now Lois had subsided into a pathetic heap slumped

back in her chair. When the bailiff took her arm, she got to her feet without a murmur and let him lead her away. Just as Helen motioned for me to follow, Joe raised his hand and signaled me to wait. I turned my back on him and walked out of the room.

Chapter Seventeen

It wasn't exactly a surprise to anyone when Judge Lovell ruled that Lois be bound over for trial. If the outcome had ever been in question, Lois had settled the issue herself with a live demonstration of her turbulent reaction to stress. An explosion of anger followed by hysteria was hardly a reassuring display of emotional stability. But then, Joe Corelli's tactics might have shaken the nerves of anyone in that situation. Certainly I hadn't felt particularly calm, and it wasn't even my future at stake.

In the judge's chambers, Lois had accused Helen and me of being a fine pair of Job's comforters. "You're fast talkers," she railed bitterly, "but when it comes down to the wire, you both do a quick fade."

Helen, exhibiting her usual sensitivity, responded by offering her client a Valium. I couldn't even come up with anything half that good.

No thanks to either of us, Lois pulled herself together and completed her moments on the stand with some semblance of control. But of course, Joe Corelli collected the honors for doing his homework and making Helen's gingerly conducted redirect sound lame by comparison. But even if she came off a poor second in court, Helen at least earned her fee with hours of examination and research, whereas I turned out to be worth exactly what Lois paid me.

No matter how I argued with myself, reasoned, analyzed, and excused, the end result was that I had botched the job. Cocksure Ellie Gordon with all her delusions of being a supersleuth had accomplished zilch, nothing, *nada*. What made me think I had a Sherlock Holmes mentality when even Doctor Watson knew better than to dream up theories without getting any basis in fact? Suppositions were fine and dandy if I wanted to be an armchair detective, but I was hired, and I used the term loosely, to conduct an investigation. Some investigation. I had had coffee with a maternally minded adultress, a notebook of scribbles for a mythical magazine article, and a time schedule that showed Carole Prescott and Lois McCoin both unaccounted for while Drake Prescott was being murdered.

In all fairness, of which I deserved little, I did take a swing at deciphering who-really-dunnit, but I had no follow-through. It wasn't enough to question people, imagine the worst, then expect Matt Steunkle to prove me right. When he refused to aid and abet my quest, I should have continued the probe by myself, using other resources. Mark Devlin could have pulled a few strings for me; Fifth and Shoreside boasted a judge who might have been amenable to issuing a search warrant. Hell, I could have hired my own private eye. Instead, I gave up when the going got rough and thought that was the way the pros did it. Bull! A pro wouldn't have let a few bureaucratic rules stop her. And a pro wouldn't have hidden her perfectly legitimate efforts from Helen Ramirez like some chicken-hearted amateur.

Why hadn't I just told her the truth and then insisted she get a postponement of the hearing until my investigation was completed? Maybe if I'd behaved like a *mensch* instead of a mouse, Lois wouldn't be facing a murder trial now. And then again, maybe it wouldn't have changed a thing.

In any event, I wanted to clear the air. It was a little late for a confession, but I owed the ethical, if unbending attorney an explanation. Besides, a slap on the wrist might make me feel better. I certainly deserved a few harsh words for my useless interference, and who would be happier to supply them than Helen?

Bright and early Thursday morning, after deciding I didn't quite deserve to be tied to the whipping post, I screwed my courage to the sticking point and went into her office. "I'm here to make a full disclosure," was my forth-right opening.

"If you're referring to your detective work on Lois's behalf, don't bother," Helen said in a tired voice. "She told me all about it."

"So Lois snitched, huh?" I watched Helen for signs of imminent pouncing in case I had to race for the door, but she didn't move from behind her desk. "I went to see Matt Steunkle."

Still, she didn't move. "Doesn't surprise me."

"I even spoke to Claudette Washington."

"Good for you."

Something was very wrong here. Instead of flaying me with the tongue-lashing of my life, Helen was having a tough time getting more than two consecutive syllables out of her mouth, and none of them especially cutting. Even her eyes seemed lackluster. I looked closer. Well, no wonder; she forgot to put on mascara this morning.

"Aren't you going to yell at me?" I prompted, starting to worry about her. "I did everything you told me not to do. I questioned Carole Prescott and April Evans. I even read your files."

The hint of a smile crossed her lips. "You're a smarter sleuth than I credited."

"Oh, no I'm not. Nothing I did was any good."

"So, you didn't do any harm either."

"Do you feel all right?" I asked, coming farther into the room.

"No, as a matter of fact. I feel like shit."

When she stood up and walked to the window, I could see that she also had neglected to put on blusher. For the pristine-perfect Helen to overlook such an important detail, she must have felt rotten. Not even a hangover last week had reduced her to such a state.

"Want to tell me your troubles?" I coaxed, fully anticipating another "you don't know him anyway."

"I spent the better part of last evening with Lois," she said with her back to me. "It was a rude awakening. But I've been going around with my eyes shut for so long, the glare of reality was bound to be upsetting."

"What reality?"

"The inescapable fact," she turned around, "that even your fruitless investigation showed more care and attention than I've been giving her case." She rubbed her forehead. "I let my personal problems affect my work, and that was the whole point of . . . never mind. Just don't make the same mistake I did. Human relationships can't be filed away in tidy cubbyholes. They're too sloppy not to run over onto each other. It's like pouring syrup on your pancakes and expecting it to stay in one neat . . . oh shit." She covered her face. "I'm babbling like an idiot."

"Sit down, Helen. Come on. Now tell me what this is all about. I came in here to atone for my sins, and you're reversing our roles. Why, I can't imagine. It was very considerate of you to stay with Lois last night. I called over there myself, but the line was busy for so long, I figured she had taken it off the hook."

"I did. Reporters kept pestering her for a comment."

"Typical. So both of you sat and talked with each other instead."

Helen sipped the glass of water I poured for her. "We had a lot to discuss."

"Fine. Start at the beginning."

"Basically, I wanted to explain that she wasn't convicted of anything yesterday. After a while, I got through to her, but not before she got through to me. Do you know, Ellie, I finally realized why Lois asked me to defend her. Not because I'm such a great lawyer . . . or a woman," Helen added caustically. "She wanted a friend on her side, someone who would see her as more than just another case. Except I didn't give her that advantage," Helen said with a catch in her voice. "I took her on as a client, and turned my back on the person."

"What did Lois say that brought you to this conclusion?"

"It wasn't any one thing. We were talking about a line of strategy for the trial. I suggested using some members of Fifth and Shoreside as character witnesses, and she said they couldn't testify with as much knowledge of her as Jane Chestnut could. When I asked if she were particularly close to any of the women, Lois gave me a funny look. 'How close am I with you?' At first, I thought she was being facetious, but then she began talking about her life, revealing things I never bothered to find out for myself. They were important too. Here I was, ready to parade a string of loving friends who could swear to her integrity, when there aren't any such animals. Lois told me she never had the time to make many personal contacts. When her kids were small, they took up all her after-work hours, though you'd think she'd ask for a few back in return, but Lois won't even call them now. She says they live too far away and can't afford to make the trip here . . . as if the publicity on this case won't reach Chicago or Des Moines. Anyway," Helen sighed, "the extent of her activities these days is visiting her mother on the weekends."

"Didn't you know any of this before?"

"Not enough, and that's why I'm so furious with myself.

I should have made it my business to know. In fact," Helen said in a tight voice, "it was my business to know. Presumably, I'm defending the woman, except I was so busy pretending that my personal life had no bearing on my professional life that I wouldn't admit they could overlap. Claudette warned me." Helen gave a little laugh. "She said the head doesn't rule the heart, but I was so sure I could control both. I couldn't, of course."

"Man problems?" I asked, having a fairly good idea what knocked Helen off her marble pedestal.

She nodded. "It spoiled quite a few cherished illusions I had about myself. I was the career-first girl who didn't want to be distracted, so I logically picked someone who was off-limits. No possible strings meant no chance of an attachment, and that added up to no messy emotional entanglement. I could enjoy the pleasure of a romantic relationship without risking my freedom." She reached for the glass of water, then pushed it away. "Except I couldn't stop there. I began to want the unattainable. It's almost consumed me and my precious career. Too bad Lois had to pay for my sins."

Claudette had been right about her unhappy friend. Helen did need absolution, though she picked a rather unprepared mother confessor. Not that I didn't sympathize; I just felt surprised that a woman with better-than-common sense had gotten caught in such a foolish game of blind man's bluff. Believing that dating a married man was protection against Cupid's arrow was like closing your eyes and thinking nobody could see you. One good thing came out of that mistake though. A clear look at herself had changed Helen's view of Lois, and at long last the counsel for the defense was totally committed to her client.

That was exoneration enough, I told Helen. There was no point wallowing in useless regrets. Just put on some war paint and go get 'em. She seemed cheered by my vindication, and even went to her purse for a makeup kit.

But Jewish guilt couldn't be dismissed so easily. I had failed Lois too, and admitting it didn't stop my hair shirt from itching. I had to make amends by restitution, and if Helen could promise a rededicated effort, I could pledge a new and ceaseless attempt to dig up the truth. However, when I said as much to her, she shook her head decisively.

"Lois and I agreed that it might be practical to hire a professional investigator. I'm not sure we need one, but I hope you understand."

Certainly, I did. They wanted someone who'd do the job properly on the first go-round. No second chances in this business. Only lawyers get a motion for continuance. I accepted my walking papers gracefully and wished Helen well, but making my peace with Joe was another matter.

He called that evening, primarily to find out if I still thought the only thing missing from his interrogation of Lois was the rack and thumbscrews. What he referred to was our brief conversation in the corridor after the hearing when he stopped me to confirm our dinner date. Bad timing on his part. I was hardly in any mood to celebrate his victory. In fact, I was scarcely able to acknowledge that he had only been doing his duty, an excuse Adolph Eichmann made too. However, I kept that comparison to myself and merely told the district attorney that his cruel and insensitive third degree was a reenactment of the Spanish Inquisition. Joe just rubbed the dent in his chin and said he'd call me tomorrow.

Well, tomorrow was here and so was I—stuck with breaking my vow of staying emotionally uninvolved. Ha ha. But why blame Joe for doing the same thing? I even paid taxes so he could. Feeling justifiably contrite and mopey about life in general, I apologized to him. Joe said my reaction was understandable and he expected me to feel bad about Lois. I was warm, sweet, human, and vulnerable. He almost brought a tear to my eye, but that's when he suggested an un-Joe-like way to cheer me up.

"What do you say? You want to go on a police Ride-Along tomorrow night?"

"No thanks. I don't need that much cheering."

"Sure, you do. Come on, Friday is payday and Casa Grande jumps."

"Even more reason why I don't want to go cruising around in a marked car."

"I thought you had a passing interest in law enforcement," he cajoled.

"Enforcement? When did you ever hear me say I have the slightest desire to patrol the streets with a pair of trusty six-shooters swinging from my hips?"

"Good grief, Ellie, we won't be going into combat. The Ride-Along is an educational tour de force."

"Is that supposed to be a pun?"

"Is that supposed to be a put-down? Never mind. I can tell that nothing I say appeals to you at the moment."

"Untrue. Your invitation appeals to my sense of the ridiculous. Most men would have sent candy."

"Next time," he promised.

Joe said that I had to go by the police station in the morning to sign a release. Then, if I were killed or maimed during our peaceful outing, the city wouldn't be held accountable. Of course, he went on to advise, that this in no way precluded me or my heirs from suing whoever did the damage.

Thank you, Mr. District Attorney. I wanted a guarantee of safe passage, not a quitclaim deed on my life. But, I swallowed my misgivings and discharged the city from liability. That didn't mean my ghost wouldn't come back to haunt them, and Joe too, if something happened to me. But at eleven o'clock on Friday night, the ever-fearful Ellie Gordon was ready for her perilous voyage, traveling tourist class in the back seat of a police car as it began the graveyard shift. Even the name boded ill.

Chapter Eighteen

"Why are you sitting all the way over there?" Joe asked as we pulled away from the precinct station. "Scoot closer and I'll hold your trembling hand."

"Uh-uh. I want to be next to the door in case I have to use it in a hurry."

That was how I began, timorous, cautious, and sorry I came. But it didn't take more than a half an hour for me to realize that Casa Grande hardly offered the same thrills and chills as Fort Apache, the Bronx. Our most dangerous call in that time was to check out a suspicious-looking character lurking in the park. When we arrived, he was relieving himself in the drinking fountain. An intriguing misdemeanor, I told Joe, but an evening spent on defecation detail wasn't the learning experience he promised, unless the police wanted to illustrate the city's crying need for more public toilets.

"Don't worry. Things will pick up," the D.A. assured me.

I would have been perfectly happy if they didn't. While cruising the local low spots wasn't my idea of a Friday night on the town, I did find it comforting that our mini-metropolis couldn't be classed as a festering inferno of evil. Actually, as my fear for life and limb wore off, I could appreciate why Joe and Matt Steunkle supported this program. The Ride-Along was an excellent way to promote rapport between average citizens and their ever-vigilant home guard. Traveling with a cop on his beat gave people a chance to see what law enforcement was all about, though not too many jumped at the opportunity. According to the driver of Car 57, a nice young man and recent graduate of the police academy, the few volunteer passengers he got were journalism students and employees of the D.A.'s office. Did I work for Mr. Corelli, Officer Jensen asked?

"No, she's an aspiring criminologist," Joe answered for me, once again reaching across the seat to take my hand.

"Not in front of the *kinder*," I murmured.

He kept his distance while Jensen issued a speeding ticket, but when the officer got out to direct traffic until a crew arrived to repair the broken stoplight, Joe took advantage of our privacy. "Have you recovered from the hearing yet?" He clasped my fingers.

"Oh, sure."

"And you're not going to buy me an iron maiden for my birthday?"

"Not this year."

Joe didn't answer for a moment. "Ellie, I hope you understand that I didn't persecute your friend. I prosecuted her. With good reason. Every bit of evidence points to Lois McCoin. I couldn't change the facts."

I could have told Joe that he might not have all the facts, but since I wasn't going to find them, why bother? Then, why did I bother? "Don't you think it's a little far-fetched that a woman would murder a man over a job?"

"Ellie, this is a new world. Men and women don't just kill each other over infidelity anymore. A crime of passion can be a corporate affair these days."

"You stole that line, didn't you?"

"No. I just made it up myself."

"Liar." I pretended to kick him in the shins. He grabbed my ankle. "Let go. I want to ask you another question."

"Can't you ask while I'm holding on?"

"Okay. Why did you bring up feminism in court? It's a dirty word to a lot of people, and Lois isn't exactly a die-hard bra burner."

"That was my point. She never even went upstairs to make an informal complaint, and chances are she wasn't going to make an issue of the memo either. But that doesn't mean Prescott hadn't pushed her to the brink."

"I can just see your next campaign slogan. Joe Corelli Prosecutes Women Who Don't Fight Discrimination."

"What's that patronizing remark supposed to mean?" He laughed and pinched my ankle. "You should be saying I'm a man for all seasons."

He was a man for not wasting an opportunity anyway. With the dim light from the lamp post casting us in shadows, he slid across the seat and took me in his arms. The feel of his thigh as it pressed against mine had its usual effect, and so did his tongue moving sensuously over my lips.

I hadn't done this in the back seat of a car since 1959. But Billy Snodgrass never got to first base. Joe, a more experienced hitter, opened the top button of my blouse and made a slide to second while I cheered from the grandstand. But before he could steal third, he was tagged out because Officer Jensen had made a quiet return. Hastily, I pushed Joe away and pretended a great curiosity in the two-way radio.

Our police escort was delighted to translate the messages coming in. He explained that the ten-code was an international system of communication where every number represented a particular set of circumstances. For local use and specific messages, they also used a twenty-seven code.

"Is all that complex cryptography to maintain secrecy?" I asked, no longer faking an interest.

"Partly, but it's a real timesaver too. We have to report our location when a call comes in, register where we're going, why, and for how long. Then there's another form to fill out for the National Crime Information Center. See this hook up? It taps directly into their computer bank so we can get an instant dispatch on a suspect's past and current status. You'd be surprised how many people stopped for a routine traffic offense are identified as wanted in other states."

"So Big Brother has finally arrived via a data processor."

Joe and I got to see the machinery in action when we were summoned to check out a three-car accident on the freeway. Fortunately no injuries were sustained except to the vehicles. One was going to need extensive plastic surgery, though the other two only would require some minor first aid. The driver of the Mercedes didn't seem to think such a piddly collision called for a police report. Let the insurance companies do the paperwork, he suggested affably. But Chris Jensen assured him it was no trouble to write it up . . . on two forms. When he radioed the gentleman's license number to NCIC, it became quite clear why Harry Blumenthal, traveling salesman, wished to remain anonymous. He had eighteen outstanding parking violations in total, from California, Nevada, Arizona, and New Mexico. His was the biggest territory in the company, he explained.

"One more fugitive from justice brought to his knees by computer programing," I remarked.

After that, things did pick up, as Joe predicted. We cruised the bar district where our chauffeur alit three times to squelch budding romances, though two of the women denied being in the line of business Officer Jensen suggested. The third spotted me in the patrol car and accused the fuzz of harassing poor working girls.

I gave her a thumbs-up sign as we drove away and commented on the young policeman's open-minded attitude in not arresting her.

"First I issue a warning," he informed me. "I told all those hookers that I'd be back in an hour, and if they weren't off the streets by then, I would run them in."

As he entered that in his log and recorded our present location, Joe gave me the practical reason for such apparent leniency. It wasn't that the police encouraged sidewalk soliciting, but there was a certain give and take between cops and courtesans. No one had ever been able to eliminate the world's oldest profession, so rather than go through the motions as a daily exercise in futility, police closed a myopic eye to the less conspicuous Circes.

That was a very sensible approach, I told Joe. After all, striking up a casual conversation with a man was an acceptable social convention these days. The police couldn't very well go around arresting every unaccompanied female they saw on suspicion of hanky-panky. Besides, love was legal provided a gentleman exchanged goods for services. The fine line between pandering and permissiveness depended on the honorarium involved. Dinner and a movie were perfectly legitimate recompense for a trip to the moon on gossamer wings. Just don't ask for cash.

Joe took exception to my comparison by saying that lend/lease love didn't have the value of an honest relationship where affection was given freely.

"What could be more honest than a girl who tells you right up front she's worth fifty dollars an hour? You can't accuse her of leading a man on under false pretenses. The worst she may be guilty of is overcharging."

"Okay," he laughed. "You win. Name your price."

"Excuse me, folks," our driver coughed delicately, pulling over to the curb. "I've got to go check on a suspected robbery, so if you both want to get out of here, I'll send another patrol car to take you home."

"My goodness, did a call just come in?" I grabbed my pocketbook and the door handle in one move. "I believe we will disembark here, thank you."

Joe pulled me back. "Come on, Ellie. Don't be silly. Nothing's going to happen, and this will be a real treat for you."

"No," I squealed as the car shot off. "I don't want to be treated to a nine-sixteen or seventy-two-fourteen or whatever the heck it's numbered. Joe, you gave me your word this would just be a sightseeing tour."

"Calm down." He put his arm around my shoulder. "We're not going to the St. Valentine's Day Massacre. Most likely the store's burglar alarm went off by mistake, that's all."

"What store?"

"The All-Nite Grocery on South Williams."

Simultaneously, the red light on top of the police car started flashing and the rhythmic beep of the siren began. My threat to charge the D.A. with kidnapping was lost in the deafening blast of two more police sirens. I put my hands over my ears and tried to feel reassured that there was safety in numbers, if not any silence. How could Chris Jensen hear the directions coming through his radio? But apparently he did make contact with his colleagues, because when all four police cars converged on the parking lot of the store, each one screeched to a halt at a different location. We were the farthest from the building, back by the gas pumps. I liked the spot, and I especially liked it when the sirens were turned off.

"Keep low, ma'am," our stalwart protector motioned to me. "I'm going to see what's happening." Cautiously he got out of the car, waited a moment, then darted behind a gas pump.

"The place looks deserted," I whispered in the eerie quiet.

"Where are you going?" Joe put a restraining hand on my shoulder as I leaned over the back of the seat.

"Just to get a better view."

"I thought you wanted to watch from afar, like as far away as you could get."

"Well, I asked you to leave me on the street corner with the hookers, but you wouldn't."

"So you're only making the best of a bad situation," he said dryly.

"Look, Joe. One of the policemen is going into the store. Oh, no. He's coming right back out. Maybe the crooks have gone already," I said in disappointment.

"You're really enjoying this, aren't you?"

"It's not without a certain fascination, but you wanted me to have fun, so stop complaining. Nothing's happening anyway. You were probably right about the false alarm."

"For crying out loud. Now she's sorry this isn't a gangland war."

"What's the matter with you?" I glanced at his scowling face. "Change your mind about introducing me to the world of practical crime-fighting?"

"Crime-watching," he corrected me, "and I'm not at all happy with the vantage point. Come on, duck down behind the seat."

"Why? I like it up here."

"I can see this was a mistake," he muttered. "You're much too impetuous. Now get down before I drag you down."

At that moment, a man in faded jeans and a flannel shirt came around the side of the building and took a leap toward the fence in the alleyway. He must have been hiding behind a big garbage dumpster all this time, hoping the police would come and go. But since we didn't leave, the robber had two choices: surrender or run. With one leg straddling the fence, his decision was obvious, even after Jensen rapped out a halt order. The man paused but only until a second figure charged from the same corner with a gun in his hand.

My sole thought was for the two policemen who were

open targets as they stood by the entrance of the store. Chris Jensen, at least, had the dubious protection of an explodable gasoline pump, while the fourth officer was crouched on the far side of his patrol car.

"Freeze!"

As if that shout from the police were a signal to the man with the gun, he shoved his accomplice over the fence, then latched onto it himself. Like Quick-Draw McGraw, one of the standing targets pulled his own weapon from his belt and fired a warning shot in the air. I didn't even flinch at the thunderclap of noise, but then, neither did the robber. Calculating how to hold off an attack until he and his friend could make a last-ditch attempt at an escape, he scanned the parking lot, found the spot of least resistance, and took aim . . . at me.

Then everything broke loose at once. As I prudently took a nose dive to the floor of the police car, Joe flung himself on top of me, a volley of gunshots rang out, and the windshield cracked into a giant jigsaw puzzle. Shatter-proof glass.

I could hear the pounding of footsteps, the clamor of shouting voices, the cry of "All Safe," but I didn't budge. And not by choice.

"Ellie, Ellie, are you all right?" Joe demanded, pressing my face further into the plastic floor mat.

"No. I'm smothering. Will you please get off me?"

"Don't move yet," he ordered unnecessarily.

Since Joe wouldn't take his elbow off my nose, and the rest of me was pinned under his entire one-hundred-and-sixty-five-pound weight, my oxygen intake wasn't restored to normal until Chris Jensen rushed over and opened the back door to see how we fared. He was visibly shaken.

Joe wasn't in much better shape. "Ellie, are you sure you're not hurt?" he asked anxiously, helping me to a sitting position.

"Honestly, I'm fine . . . now. So what's the story? Was anyone shot? Did we catch the dirty crooks?"

"I'll find out." Joe climbed over me to follow the police officer. "You stay here and relax."

"How about if you stay here and relax while I find out?"

But even though I was the calmest of the lot, the men banded together to prevent my leaving the protective custody of the police car. I insisted my feminine nerves weren't all aflutter from such a harrowing experience, but chivalry triumphed. I had to learn third-hand that one of the armed robbers was seriously wounded, while the other got as far as the next block before he was apprehended. Several times Joe came back to the car to make sure I hadn't lapsed into a swoon from the aftershock of missing a gunman's bullet by a hairsbreadth. He looked so distressed, I almost hated telling him I had survived the ordeal quite nicely.

Actually, the cowardly lioness was feeling rather proud of herself. After all my timorous mews about being a scaredy-cat, I never dreamt I'd react with such composure under fire. Bravery and coolness weren't exactly two of my predominant personality traits... at least, not until tonight. And it was rather exhilarating to discover that if "I am not splentive and rash, yet I have something in me dangerous."

But bloodthirsty I wasn't. The gruesome held no appeal at all, which was why I didn't get out of the car and join the crowd who arrived with the ambulance. They were mostly people from the neighborhood who simply wanted to be sure their corner convenience store was convenient for shopping again. One woman watched the robber being lifted onto the stretcher, nodded her head in approval, then came over and peered in the window at me, no doubt disappointed to see I wasn't in handcuffs. I understood her concern. If I weren't under arrest, why else would I be sitting in the back seat of a police car? Not for a joyride, certainly.

Chapter Nineteen

"That is the craziest thing I ever heard." Betsy dabbed at the tears of laughter threatening to wreck her mascara. "Joe Corelli drags you protesting to the scene of a robbery where you're shot at, and you claim he unwittingly gave you the most stimulating evening of your life. Ellie, my sweet, I do believe you've added a new dimension to kinky sex."

"You're probably right," I agreed glumly, "especially since the most exciting part had nothing to do with Joe."

"Are you saying he wasn't around when you spent the night at his place?" she teased with all the indelicacy that twenty years of friendship entitles.

"Hey, I'm not that kinky. Certainly Joe had something to do with thrilling me during the latter part of the evening. He just didn't like the way I enjoyed myself during the earlier segment."

"Well, your idea of foreplay is somewhat unusual."

Betsy had taken me to the fanciest restaurant in town in celebration of a birthday most women of my coming age would rather ignore. Then, to add insult to injury, she accused me of having a midlife crisis merely because I said Joe was beginning to show annoying signs of protective proprietorship.

"Two weeks ago you called it chivalry," she reminded me.

"I still do, but Joe is carrying it to an extreme."

"Why, because he put a run in your pantyhose with his flying fortress technique of lifesaving?"

"No, Madame Snide. I'm not such an ungrateful Jewish Princess. I can accept Joe's heavy heroism as a knightly gesture. But he's getting ridiculous. One little Ride-Along and no more Crimewatchers."

"I can understand why."

"Traitor."

"Not at all. I just know you."

"Unfortunately, Joe doesn't. But being a broad-minded person, I overlooked his concern and enlisted in his pet project this morning as a birthday present to myself. They even gave me gifts. Look here." I dug them out of my purse. "An identification card with my very own number, and this pager. You push a button, punch in a coded message and voilà, the police are on their way."

"Now you've got carte blanche to go out looking for trouble," Betsy observed. "Couldn't you be satisfied with more ordinary daredevil pursuits like sky diving or bullfighting or investing on the Commodities Exchange?"

"Hey, old Blood and Guts Gordon may have discovered a certain derring-do in her nature, but I'm not suicidal enough to try and corner the soybean market. Don't worry, Bets," I soothed, putting my prized possessions away. "Even if I mounted a twenty-four-hour surveillance, the chances are slim this Crimewatcher will ever see another crime."

"My condolences. Now will you please wipe the wistful tear from your eye and finish eating?"

"What's the rush?"

"Didn't I tell you? I've got to be home by nine. A late date."

"Sure, go party with someone else on my birthday. Dump me now that I'm over the hill."

Betsy was undisturbed by my lachrymose complaint. "You won't be lonely. Just turn on your new toy and beep into a crime somewhere. That should keep you sufficiently enraptured for the rest of the evening."

On that note, I finished my baked potato, asparagus vinaigrette, and truly delicious pepper steak, then told Betsy she could return me to my empty house on the beach. She reminded me that I was getting another celebration tomorrow night when Joe fêted me with his home-made baked Alaska, but I said it would be better if he catered to my less fattening interests.

Ten minutes later, as we pulled into my driveway which was almost blocked by all the cars parked in the cul de sac, Betsy suggested that if I got too bored with my own company, I could jog next door and crash the Talbots' party. They'd never notice me in the crowd.

"That's odd. They don't usually entertain on such a large scale, but maybe it's their housewarming." I started up my flagstone path with Betsy following behind me, but as I reached for my house key, I saw that the front door was partly open. "Stop! Don't go in there." I threw myself at Betsy. "Either my neighbors came to borrow a bottle of scotch and forgot to lock up or it's time for me to inaugurate my pager." While I fumbled in my purse to get the blasted thing from under a wad of Kleenex, my brave friend pushed past me into the foyer and switched on the light.

"Surprise!" A dozen smiling faces crowded around as I was hauled inside. "Happy Birthday, Ellie. Welcome to the prime of life."

"Oh my God, you sneaks . . . I was scared to death . . . Betsy, you liar," I laughed.

Rhoda shoved a Margarita in my hand. "We helped

ourselves to your liquor cabinet. You are now out of Triple Sec."

"And she was worried about the scotch," Betsy said, grinning.

"There isn't much of that left either."

It wasn't hard to see why. As I got kissed and hugged and congratulated for surviving so long past my majority, I could tell that my buddies from Fifth and Shoreside had been toasting my endurance for quite some time.

"This shindig is for women only"—Jessica raised her glass with a flourish—"because we hold our liquor better."

"That's not why, you drunken boob," Rhoda hooted at her. "It's because we have a better appreciation for art."

"Right on," came a cry from the other corner of the room. "So where is the work of art?"

Then Betsy stepped forward and directed everyone to sit down and shut up. "To prove that women have an innate esteem for the value of the human body and an unblushingly prurient interest in viewing these values, we have pooled our resources to give Ellie a private showing." She pointed her glass at me. "Be sure you take special note of the well-developed pectorals and undersized gluteus maximus. Maestro," she look around, "if you're ready."

Someone turned on a tape, and from out of the kitchen emerged a living, breathing, California-style Adonis. This one was blond, blue-eyed, five-eleven, and every bit as esthetically pleasing as a sex objet d'art should be. First he posed à la *Gentleman's Quarterly* in white slacks, open-necked shirt, and sports jacket, while everyone applauded in a spontaneous tribute. Then after being pointed in my direction, he gyrated over in time to the music, flung his majestic head back with the drum roll, then tossed his silk scarf in my lap as the cymbals crashed.

"My name is Steve"—he flashed a dazzling smile—"and I'm going to make sure you have sweet dreams tonight."

"What about me?" Rhoda tugged at his arm. "I'm an insomniac."

Betsy turned off the overhead light, leaving only one table lamp to cast a muted glow over the room, while Steve shed his jacket and draped it around Rhoda's shoulders. Then he began unbuttoning his shirt with such sensuous grace that no one could tear an eye away from his compelling performance.

"God, he's gorgeous," Helen sighed. In response, Steve moved over to her and, with a ceremonial gesture of obeisance, offered her his shirt. She whistled at what it had been covering.

Hands toying with the buckle of his belt, he pivoted slowly to the disco beat from the tape, then began undulating his pelvis. Raucous shouts of "Take if off!" and "Come on, big boy, show us what you've got!" inspired him to do just that, and he let his trousers slip to the floor, then stepped out of them. Clad only in a G-string and English Leather, Steve danced over to me, pretended he was lowering the boom, but then just repeatedly stuck his covered manhood in my face while the music throbbed to a climax, then absurdly swung into the strains of "Happy Birthday To You."

He didn't have the voice to match his physique, but what his vocalization lacked in finesse, he counterbalanced with fortissimo. It earned him a standing ovation, though if the truth be told, I stood up to get my face out of his crotch. Then he blew kisses to the roomful of laughing women and bowed his way out of the room to get dressed.

"Do you believe in lust at first sight?" Marilyn Banes asked with a hand pressed to her heart.

"Sure," Rhoda answered, "but I thought you only lusted after mink."

This jibe was in reference to Marilyn's latest purchase. She was a successful pediatric dentist who had just bought herself a full-length fur coat thanks to so many rotten teeth in so many rotten kids, as she explained her good fortune.

Betsy led me away to the couch where a pile of beribboned gifts awaited me. I had a strong suspicion none of the boxes contained anything as ordinary as talcum power, and did I know this crew of cutups. From crotchless panties to topless nightgowns, their presents ran the gamut from ribald to obscene. But the biggest hit below the belt, aside from Steve, was the large blue package Jessica handed me. I read the card aloud.

" 'Now that you've reached those watershed years when you've past the peak and are sliding down the other side of life's mountain, don't give in gracefully. Fight back! These are your weapons, Ellie, and I encourage you to use them unsparingly.' "

"I have a feeling I'm not going to like this," was my comment at large as I tore off the wrapping and rummaged through the excelsior. "Thank you, Jess," I held up the first insult. "A jar of Porcelana to bleach my age-spots."

"It may be early days yet," she replied with a straight face, "but an ounce of prevention is worth a pound of cure."

"More preventative maintenance." I displayed the next bottle. "A blue rinse from Clairol. And here's my very own tube of Preparation H. And ... oh, Jess, you shouldn't have ... Prunes too? I'm overwhelmed by your concern for my geriatric complaints, although I was hoping to enjoy advanced maturity before senility sets in."

"Start wearing a chin strap too," called Vivian Wheeler, one of the women who had already passed the threshold of two score. "I'll give you one of mine."

Amid the shouts of laughter, Betsy came through with a fitting homily. "Just remember, Ellie: 'Forty is the old age of youth, but fifty is the youth of old age.' In ten years you'll be a mere child again."

"Hey, who's side are you on anyway?" I protested. "I'm only thirty-nine now."

"You and Jack Benny," Rhoda jeered.

"Just wait until you hit that much-maligned number," I warned. "Then you won't be so amused that its credibility has been destroyed forever." I thanked them for Steve and the array of gifts, and as they toasted my good taste in having such wonderful friends, the doorbell rang.

"Lois." I pulled her inside. "I'm so glad you came. How are you?"

She seemed a bit hesitant when she saw all the people in the living room, but then she gave me a peck on the cheek, handed me a package, and apologized for being late. "I'm fine really."

She looked a little drained, but the blond curls were in place, the makeup applied perfectly, even her bright yellow dress attested she was trying for some semblance of normalcy. And Fifth and Shoreside came through. With no mention of her ordeal past and coming, they gave her a warm welcome, poured her a glass of my birthday bottle of champagne, and provided a colorful description of the art exhibit she missed.

I whisked Helen aside. "How did you manage to get Lois here?"

"By twisting her arm. I told her she had to make an appearance for your sake. Left to her own devices, she'd just hide in her house until the trial. And that might be as long as six months away."

"No problem now," I said with confidence, watching how the sisterhood was rallying around her. "They'll make sure she doesn't hole up all alone and lick her wounds."

When Betsy brought out the birthday cake, a veritable dancing sea of flames, everyone converged around the dining-room table and sang to me again. "Make a wish," they chorused. So I closed my misty eyes, invoked a silent plea for peace to near and far, unoriginal but heartfelt, then blew out the candles. Of course, there were too many to extinguish on one breath, which probably was why my wish didn't come true. War erupted not ten minutes later, right in the middle of my Oriental rug.

I was in the kitchen at the time sneaking another slice of cake, so I missed the opening of hostilities. Apparently Jessica fired the first shot when she assertively pledged the eventual shutdown of the Canyon Escondido plant. When I finally realized the sound of raised voices wasn't another toast to me and went into the living room, full combat raged.

Lois's cheeks were burning with two red patches that owed nothing to Merle Norman. "You're nuts," she rasped at Jessica. "If you want to save humanity, worry about nuclear disarmament. We're using atoms for peace. Do you know how far ahead of us France, Italy, Germany, and Japan are? They've built nuclear power plants all over the place, and it's working. Their cities have cheap, almost unlimited supplies of energy, and meanwhile they're cutting pollution and acid rain. But because of impractical reactionaries like you, our country is bogged down in daily changing regulations that hamper the industry with fantastic costs. How many people have died from the long-term effects of mining and burning coal? Thousands. Millions. And how many have perished from radiation exposure? I can't even name one in the last ten years. The risks are minimal."

Jessica tossed back her long hair. "The reason you can't name one is because companies don't release that kind of information. But I'm not just talking about a few deaths from radiation. I'm talking the potential death of the ecosphere. If one of those nuke plants has an accident, it's not only people who can cash in their chips, but the entire earth."

"Bull," Lois nearly spat. "We have safety precautions."

"Tell me about the precautions at Three Mile Island," Jessica charged. "Tell me about the contractors who cut corners by using inferior products and only admit it when they're caught. Tell me about the storage containers for nuclear waste that are already leaking underground." She pointed an accusing finger at her adversary. "Your problem is you've been brainwashed by PSSC into believing that what's good for the utilities is good for the people. Hell," Jessica snorted in contempt, "you even write their fucking propaganda."

"Keep screaming like that and you're the best propaganda we have," Lois said with disdain. "Extremists like you quickly render themselves ineffective when the public realizes how you exaggerate."

"I'm exaggerating?" Jessica raised one well-shaped eyebrow. "You're the one defending the system when, by your own experience, you should know better than anybody how unsafe it is to be anywhere near Canyon Escondido."

If looks could have killed, Jessica would have been dead on the spot. "Are you referring to Drake Prescott?" Lois asked in a shrill voice. "That has nothing to do with the issue at hand."

"Oh, really?" Jess snapped back angrily. "I thought the issue was extremism."

In the silence that followed, everyone was trying not to make some sort of unpleasant sense out of Jessica's words, but the very mention of the taboo subject was more than Lois could take. Her face crumpled, and she ran out of the room with a choked cry. Helen went after her while the rest of us stared at each other in discomfort. Jess looked away first, then muttered an oath and stalked into the kitchen.

Well, so much for my party. With no one in any mood for further merrymaking, my guests expressed subdued joy at celebrating my birthday with me and said goodnight. As Marilyn slipped into her mink, Helen inched past us with a murmured, "Don't worry about Lois. She'll be fine in the morning." Betsy patted me on the back and said I would be too.

Finally there was just me and Jessica, who elected to

stay behind and help me clean the mess my departed party-givers had left.

"I'm sorry if I broke things up a little ahead of schedule," she apologized. "I shouldn't have been so hard on Lois."

I stopped stuffing torn wrapping paper into the waste basket and turned on her. "Did you want to make her cry?"

"Of course not."

"Then why did you mention Drake Prescott's death? The woman's hanging by a thread now."

"I know, I know. It just slipped out."

"Here." I gave her the full trash can. "Go get me a plastic garbage bag from under the sink."

"Don't you want to hear why it slipped out?"

"After you bring me the garbage bag," I said absently, then realizing she wasn't moving, "Are you waiting for me to say please? Okay, please get me a bag."

"I really didn't stay to help you clean this pigsty," she confessed.

"You have to state the obvious?"

"Actually, I was going to ask if you'd mind taking a look at some evidence that might be connected to Prescott's murder."

"Prescott's . . . ?" I shoved her down on the couch and parked myself next to her. "Explain. Where do you come to have any involvement at all in his murder? Or is finding evidence ANSWER's latest subversive activity?"

"Might be, but I won't know for sure until tomorrow, and provided the information is delivered as promised, that's when I'll need your expert opinion. Tell you what," she said with an impish grin, "come over to my house in the morning. You bring the bagels; I'll supply the lox and cream cheese—and the clue."

"You're a clever little witch, tempting me with a meal and mystery." I eyed her suspiciously. "But what is this clue you're using as smoked salmon bait?"

"Well," she leaned forward, too eager to wait after all, "it might mean that Prescott and the power company . . ." She broke off and stared over my shoulder.

Following her startled gaze, I turned around to see Lois standing in the doorway. I thought she'd left when the others made their grand exodus, but apparently she'd been in the bathroom all this time.

She glared coldly at Jessica, then eked out the trace of a smile for me. "I just want to say goodnight, Ellie, and wish you many happy returns again. Is my coat in the hall closet?"

Jess came into the foyer with us. "Get mine too, please. If I'm going to keep that early appointment in the morning, I'd better hit the sack. Say, Lois," she extended her hand, "I'm sorry. Let's swear off mixing politics and parties."

Lois touched her fingers briefly. "Ordinarily a debate like that wouldn't have bothered me in the least, but I'm a bit nervy these days."

Jessica merely nodded and shrugged into her jacket. "See you tomorrow, Ellie. About ten?"

"Wait, Jess." But she just waved and sailed out the door. I lifted my hands helplessly. "Forgive her, Lois. Sometimes Jess can be too much of a good thing, but she doesn't mean any harm."

"That is exactly what she means, which is why I felt it my duty to respond to her wild statements."

I sighed. "Can't you ignore her?"

Lois looked at me reproachfully. "I may be on leave of absence, Ellie, but exposing ANSWER's line of misinformation is part of my job. I only regret that Jess's impetuous behavior chased everyone away," she sniffed, taking no responsibility for that on herself.

"Forget it. I think the party ended on time."

"You really don't mind that I came? Perhaps my presence did put a damper on things," she reconsidered.

"Don't be silly. Everyone was delighted to see you."

"I'm not so sure about that, but for your sake they put on a good show."

"Lois," I said sternly, "that was no show. Fifth and Shoreside sticks together. We're buddies, pals, the female fraternity, loyal to the core. We don't desert each other in bad times. We hang in there."

My pep talk sounded inspiring, even to me. It had that locker-room spirit of "We might have lost the first half, troops, but get out there and win one for the old Gipper." How could I guess that tomorrow I'd be kicking Lois off the team?

Chapter Twenty

Some say one advantage of getting older is not needing an alarm clock to wake up. I say that ranks with claiming baldness saves you the time-consuming trouble of having to comb your hair. I suppose it's all in the fine distinction between gray skies and silver linings, but on this particular Sunday morning, just when I would have preferred a total blackout, my eyes popped open at six-forty-five.

Habit, of course, though most weekends I could fall back asleep, then rise and shine at a more civilized hour. But all the excitement last night must have rejuvenated my moldering metabolism. I didn't even try to recapture the arms of Morpheus, but got up, donned my cuddly terrycloth robe, and stepped out on the redwood deck. It was a typical, bright, glad-to-be-alive morning that California serves up more often than most other places. The sky was cerulean; the sea, calm and green with just a few white curls of foam rolling in on the rock-ribbed beach. There was even a brown pelican down there among the usual clutter of noisy gulls. No gripes about living in a high-rent district now. I sucked in a gulp of moderately unsmoggy air, stretched and touched my toes, then realized I wasn't the only person communing with nature.

A mere fifteen yards away, Tom Grabowski was sitting on the open edge of an uncompleted townhouse, his feet dangling over emptiness as he smoked a cigarette and stared out at the sea. His precarious perch eventually would be a sundeck too, once this as-yet-ugly stepsister to my condo was graced with walls and a roof. Right now it was still a maze of raw orange steel girders that supported its dramatic hang over the cliffs, a sight I automatically edited out of my view which was probably why I didn't notice Tom at first.

"Good morning," I caroled. "How about some coffee?"

Tom flicked his cigarette into the breakers below and stood up. "I'd love a cup, but in a half-hour or so. There's a little wiring I have to finish."

"I'll be ready when you are."

That gave me time to jump into jeans and a T-shirt, run the vacuum, and clean up a few other remains from last night's bash. When he knocked at the door forty minutes later, the kitchen was spotless, and Tom cheerfully accepted my offer to dirty it again.

"Eggs and toast? Thanks, I'm starving."

While I fussed at the stove, Tom announced that he had buyers for units three and four. "With the profits, I'll be able to finish Five and Six, which means the eyesore next to you will soon be another gorgeous duplex."

"So that's what you were doing out there, visualizing a spread in *House Beautiful*."

"Not quite," he smiled. "I was really seeing the light at the end of the tunnel."

"That's terrific." I set a plate of scrambled eggs, toast and fried tomatoes in front of him. "When construction slowed to a halt, I wondered if you were having a cash-flow problem."

"Cash stoppage was the problem. In fact, for a while I was on the verge of bankruptcy." He dug into his breakfast with a hungry gusto while I spilled coffee on my lap.

"Are you serious? Bankrupt like in my having to pack up and leave?"

"No, it wouldn't have affected your place, just left you neighborless until some other builder took over." He reached for toast.

"So what happened?" I asked, wiping off my pants and wondering how Tom could be so calm about it. "A friendly banker come to your aid?"

"Not so friendly, but he saved the day. Hey"—Tom finally looked up from his plate—"aren't you going to eat anything?"

"I'm having brunch with Jessica in a little while."

His mouth turned down in wry amusement. "Didn't you get enough of her last night?" When I asked how Tom knew about the party, he explained that Jess had gotten his passkey so everyone could get in without my being any the wiser. "Did you have a good time?"

"It had its moments," I smiled reminiscently. "That is until the monster of nuclear energy crept into the conversation."

"Jess, naturally." He buttered another piece of toast. "What a fanatic."

"Wait a second, my boy. I remember a time you were just as rabid. Or did the hot lights of the television cameras cool your ardor completely?" I teased.

Tom was so taken aback at my accusation that he almost swallowed a lump of food without chewing it first. "Hell, no, nothing's changed . . ." Then he paused, finally noticing I was laughing at him. "Very funny. For a minute there, I thought you'd taken Jess's side."

"Come on, you know I wouldn't take sides. Anyway, I consider you and Jess both renegade reformers. It's only that she wants to nuke the nukes, while you'd be happy talking them to death."

"To a purpose," he argued. "I want to educate the public, develop voter awareness." When I merely leaned my chin on my hand in a dutiful listening pose, Tom gave a sheepish grin. "Sorry. I'm sure you got an earful last night. What did Jess do, bore everyone with statistics?"

"Quite the contrary. Her performance was electrifying, if you'll pardon the expression. In fact, when Lois McCoin added a spark of her own by defending PSSC, the two of them were almost as explosive as the male stripper."

"Sounds like some party," he shrugged, going back to his food. "Even your guest list must have kept everyone on the edge of their seats. Isn't Lois McCoin the woman who killed Drake Prescott?"

"Allegedly killed him," I corrected. "People are innocent until proven guilty, if you remember."

"And you're going to prove she's not, right?"

"If I can" was my modest reply.

"Yeah? How you going to do that?" he asked, the last mouthful of egg making mush of his words.

"With new evidence, I hope. Want some more?"

"Uh-uh." Tom wiped his lips. "What new evidence?"

I got up to put the dirty skillet in the dishwasher and clean the grease spatters off the range. "When I find out, I'll tell you."

"You don't even know what it is yet?"

"In a general way," I bluffed, not wanting to lose credibility after Tom's flattering assumption that investigating crimes was all in a day's work for me. "But I'll be able to make a firm analysis after seeing the information."

He stacked cup, saucer, and silverware on his plate and carried them over to the sink. "Don't tell me you're getting this information from Jess."

"Hey, I didn't mention Jess's name."

"No, but you said you're going there for brunch, and you said . . ."

"Enough." I waved away the rest of his appraisal. "The next time I do an undercover job, I'll be sure not to invite you for breakfast."

"Say, you're not mad at me, are you?"

"Because you're a very astute detective? Heck, no. I don't

indulge in professional jealousy. But now that I've talked out of school, just be sure you don't. This is highly confidential."

"What could Jess possibly tell you that's confidential?" he scoffed.

"I'll discover that when I go see her," I admitted frankly. "She didn't say too much last night, except that she had a clue about the murder."

"I'll bet she's got nothing. You know how Jess exaggerates." He gave a perfunctory glance at his watch. "Anyway, I wish you luck, Ellie, and thanks for the meal. It was great as usual."

"No strudel?" I asked in surprise.

"Not today. I'll take a rain check, although you could have saved me a piece of birthday cake."

"Next year," I promised, following him to the door. "And Tom"—I touched him on the arm—"I'm glad your financial problems are over."

The second he left, I raced into the bathroom, took a quick shower, dressed in a more Sunday brunchy outfit than my old jeans, and tore off for the Bagel Factory to pick up a dozen assorted as my contribution to the feast. Pushing my aging Datsun over the speed limit and zooming around curves along the shore road, I made it to town in record time. Good thing too. There was a long line for fresh-baked bagels. I took a number and waited impatiently with all the other drooling customers as the aroma wafting from the ovens tantalized our appetites to a fever pitch. But while this incited some people to purchase indiscriminately, I merely increased my order to three dozen bagels, a chocolate chip coffee cake for dessert, and one small cheese danish to eat in the car. Even with all that restraint, I arrived at Jessica's ten minutes late, although for her that was practically early. My friend the absent-minded professor probably had her nose buried in a book and didn't realize the time. As long as she didn't forget about the mysterious clue, I'd forgive her, even if I were beginning to doubt such a clue existed. Jess was too excitable not to have called me the minute she got her hot little hands on anything. Oh, well. At least we could console ourselves with a king-sized breakfast.

Appropriately, Jessica Tobler lived in a tree-lined neighborhood near her campus where every street was named after a college. The dean's residence was on Harvard no less, while the rest of the faculty spread from Yale to Pepperdine. Of course, once you left the Ivy League for lesser environs, the size of the homes decreased in proportion. Jess's house was on Drake, a quiet avenue of modest bungalows with attached one-car garages, most of which had been converted to dens. This meant the two-to-three-car homeowners had to park at the curb, leaving no space for visitors.

I finally found a miniscule spot around the corner between an Audi and a Winnebago. Gathering together my bags of baked goodies minus one cheese danish, I decided it was Joe Corelli's influence that caused me to buy enough food for my hostess to feed the twelve other people she didn't invite. As I trudged up the pavement, I looked for someone else to ask, but everybody was either at church or sleeping off a Saturday-night Saturnalia. The entire block lay under a spell of profound Sabbath peace with not even a weekend gardener in sight. Whether it was the result of vice or virtue, the silence was so intimidating that I just about whispered as I called through Jess's screen door.

"Yoo hoo. Miss Piggy is here with poppyseed bagels and a half-dozen bialies. Is the lox and cream cheese ready?"

In answer there was a strange thump and the sound of breaking china.

"Jess, what's the matter? Are you all right?"

When there still was no response, I elbowed open the screen door and went in. To my utter amazement, Lois was standing in the living room, hanging onto the top of a bookcase. A small weed pot lay smashed on the floor at her feet.

"Oh my God, Ellie, help me." She pressed a hand to her chest.

I dropped the bagels and made a grab for her as she bent over in apparent agony. "Lois, what is it? Answer me. Where's Jess?"

Lois's eyes were rolling up in her head and her lips looked blue. It scared the hell out of me, but I manhandled her over to the couch and put her feet up. Then I made her tell me what was the matter.

"My heart," she panted, clutching at me. "I can't breathe." She seemed even more frightened than I was.

"Do you have a heart condition?" She could barely nod. "Then where's your medicine?"

"In my purse. I took it already. Nitroglycerin. But I don't think it's helping."

"Don't move. I'm calling an ambulance."

"No! Just stay with me."

She held onto my hand as if it were a lifeline, then tried to sit up and fell back gasping. I didn't know much about heart attacks, but this sure looked like the real thing. So where the hell was Jess? Why wasn't she here to deal with this crisis? I gazed around wildly, pulled free from Lois's grip, and made a dash for the phone. Wonder of wonders, 911 answered on the second ring. Not only that, I remembered Jessica's house number without having to go outside and look next to the door.

Rushing back to the sofa, I knelt beside Lois and took both her hands in mine. They felt clammy and limp. She whimpered in pain, but her fluttering eyelids wouldn't open. Finally, they stopped moving altogether. Dear God, she wasn't going to die on me, was she?

"Lois?" I touched her cheek gently. "Lois? Can you hear me? The rescue squad is on the way."

Her head jerked. "Ellie . . . they . . . Jessica . . ."

"Don't talk. Just keep breathing, nice and easy." I brushed the curls from her sweaty forehead.

What was Lois doing here anyway? After their quarrel

last night, it seemed odd that she and Jess would want to break bread together. I certainly brought enough, but I couldn't imagine Jess's phoning this morning to invite her for brunch and a peek at whatever information was supposed to be delivered and probably wasn't. Maybe Lois just dropped by unexpectedly to make an unexpected apology, and Jess asked her to wait while she went shopping. That's where my unpunctual pal had to be, out buying lox and cream cheese because she was too busy reading to do it earlier. So where did she go for food? All the way up to L.A.? She should have been back by now. How long since I arrived? The grandfather clock on the other side of the room showed 10:25, but who knew if that was the right time. My antique clock was always off by five minutes at least. Even ten when it rained. So where was the rescue squad, for that matter? As if in answer, the sound of the siren, faint but coming nearer, promised help.

"The police?" Lois asked in a weak voice before gripping my hand tightly again as another spasm of pain wracked her body.

"An ambulance for you," I comforted.

Her eyes opened for a moment, then closed again. "Too late," she whispered, her fingers slipping off mine as her head fell to the side.

"Lois!" I said sharply. "Lois, wake up!"

But she had stopped breathing.

Panic would have engulfed me if I hadn't heard the siren getting louder. But the paramedics would know what to do. They had all kinds of lifesaving equipment . . . provided they got here soon enough to use it, I thought in rising fear. Hoping my unpracticed eye was wrong, I forced myself to put an ear to her chest. But there was no heartbeat. Then I leaped up and raced to the door in pure dread. What if they didn't get here in time to revive her? Damn my stupidity. Why hadn't I ever taken a CPR course?

I watched as the second hand on the grandfather clock went all the way around twice, the pendulum swinging ponderously back and forth. It was easier than looking at Lois. Technically she was dead, although nowadays it didn't mean she'd have to stay that way. Not if someone did something soon. All I could do was pray.

The rescue squad arrived a half a minute later. They double-parked in the street, which was now filled with people, while I held open the door and shouted for them to hurry. Two young men in reassuringly white uniforms dashed into the house carrying oxygen and trauma and drug kits. They checked Lois's nonexistent pulse, then one of them began pushing rhythmically on her chest. The other spoke into a walkie-talkie, relaying the answers to the questions he was asking me.

"Name of patient?"

"Lois McCoin."

"Her physician?"

"I don't know."

Then I remembered Lois's purse was on the coffee table, its contents half-spilled-out from when she frantically went looking for her medicine. The plastic vial lay on top, and printed under the prescription number was dosage information and the name of her doctor. While I hastily stuffed billfold, glasses, and a miscellany of papers back inside her purse, then dropped it in my tote bag to take to the hospital, the medic continued peppering me with questions. Who was I? When had her pain started? Did Mrs. McCoin have health insurance? That one they always get in.

Finally I got a turn. "Is she going to be okay?"

"It's too early to tell, but if you'll just wait over there"— he pointed toward the kitchen—"I'll let you know how she's doing in a little while."

That was fine with me. I didn't want to watch the paramedic pummeling Lois's poor inert body, although a mass of bruises was a small price to pay for having the rest of your life to recover from them. I turned my head away, walked across the room, and stared down at my shaking hands. At least I'd waited until now before letting my nerves get the best of me, because for a moment, I thought I was hallucinating.

Was that blood on my fingers?

Behind me, one of the men shouted triumphantly. "I've got a pulse! Oxygen, quick!"

People don't bleed when they have a heart attack, do they? With a sick feeling in my stomach, I looked past the archway into the kitchen. The table was set for two with blue placemats, matching linen napkins, and Jessica's new earthenware dishes. Would she go to all that trouble and forget the food? But she had served someone this morning. Three steps closer and I could see both coffee cups had faint traces of lipstick on the rims.

In a fog I heard the stretcher being brought into the house, but I didn't pause. My leaden legs carried me past the table and around the corner to where an alcove in the wall held a few shelves and a telephone table. There was the answer to what brought Lois here.

At my feet, Jessica lay sprawled face down on the floor, her glorious auburn hair making a splash of color on the pale linoleum. Next to her head was a brass bookend, its base stained with the same red on my hands.

"Hey, lady." One of the paramedics strode through the doorway. "We're taking her to the city hospital. You coming?" Then his eyes widened in disbelief. "Holy Jesus! Another one?"

Rushing past me, he knelt beside Jessica's body and with a supporting hand under her neck, gently turned her over. On her temple was a wide gash where the skin had been split open, and from the corner of her mouth, a thin trickle of blood had dried to a powdery brown.

Automatically the young medic felt for a pulse at the carotid, then met my gaze with a shake of his head.

"Too late for her, I'm afraid."

Chapter Twenty-one

"Ellie, I never knew you could be so cruel. I thought Lois was your friend."

"So was Jessica." I didn't look up from the typewriter.

"One has nothing to do with the other," Helen insisted. "Lois has been asking for you for five days, and you won't even spare her five minutes."

"I have no interest in Lois McCoin." My fingers fairly flew over the keys. "Just because you've developed a belated sense of kinship with her doesn't mean I have to share it."

"The woman had a heart attack, Ellie. She's in the Coronary Care Unit, hooked to oxygen twenty-four hours a day, monitored by a vital-sign machine in case something goes wrong. Have you no compassion at all?"

"I used up the last of it yesterday when Jessica's body was flown back to Detroit for burial." I made a typo but kept going. "Now I'm sitting *shivah*, so would you please let me mourn in peace?"

"Damn it!" Helen reached across my desk and turned off the machine with an angry snap. "You're not the only one grieving over Jessica's death. The rest of us are not heartless monsters, but we do have a sense of responsibility to Lois too. You're being unfair and unreasonable by condemning her without a hearing."

"She's already had one, remember?"

"Just listen to yourself, Ellie. You're making a presumption of Lois's guilt when she hasn't even been accused of anything yet."

"Funny how obvious some things are." I pulled the paper out of the typewriter, then rolled it right back under the carriage. "When you see someone at the scene of a crime, discover bloodstains on that person, then find a body on the floor, it's amazing what you'll believe."

Helen wasn't crazy about my attitude, but instead of hitting my hand when I flipped on the Selectric again, she merely unplugged the machine from the floor socket. "Lois says the door was open when she arrived and Jessica was already dead."

"What do you expect her to say, that she overheard Jess claim to have new evidence on Prescott's murder so it seemed wisest to prevent her from telling anyone?"

"How can you be so sure Lois heard anything Jess said to you? Honestly, Ellie, the two of you were sitting in the living room while Lois was in the bathroom. You don't know when she came out or how long she'd been standing in the doorway. Besides, Jess never told what this evidence was supposed to be."

"No, but she apparently told Lois."

"You're presuming again."

"Don't worry. I'm presuming to myself."

"You mean you haven't shared your suspicions with Joe Corelli yet?" Helen sounded bitter.

"No, as a matter of fact." I lowered my voice and checked around the office for eavesdroppers, but none of the titty-tats were close enough to hear our exchange. "The D.A. didn't ask, and I didn't volunteer. As far as he knows, my projected brunch with Jess was strictly social.

No mysterious clues. No hint that Lois might care if there were."

"So you're withholding information," Helen accused, but lightly. Evidently I'd moved back into her good graces by refusing to aid the opposition.

"I don't have any information to withhold, as you pointed out. Jess was dead when I arrived, according to the medical report, and all I know is that I wasn't busy tending to her murderer while her own life leaked quietly away. Small consolation, but some."

"I just don't understand you." Helen leaned over the desk. "For a bright woman you sure have a way of not thinking with your head. First you're positive Lois is innocent, no facts, just insight; then you use the same kind of whimsical yardstick to decide she's guilty."

"What do you want me to do?" I asked sarcastically. "Go out and find proof your client is a double murderer before I condemn her?"

"No. I just wish you'd admit your reversal is emotional and not intellectual."

"Don't worry, Helen. If Lois goes to court for Jessica's death and I'm called to the stand, you'll have a great opportunity to make my testimony sound like *fatuum judicium*."

"I don't think I'll be disproving your poor judgment anywhere," Helen said seriously. "With the condition Lois is in now, her heart probably won't survive the strain of the Prescott trial, much less get her to a second one."

So the attorney for the damned was resorting to sentimental strategy. Make Ellie feel guilty for refusing a dying woman's last request. Better if Lois had asked for a cigarette and a blindfold. Those I'd have given willingly. But to hide my aversion and pretend an interest in her welfare I didn't feel seemed hypocritical. Of course, I agreed to see her anyway.

Paradoxically, Joe thought I'd be doing the right thing. And this from a man who had arrived at the scene of the crime only moments after the police, having heard the call on the two-way radio in his car. I appreciated that perk for Crimewatcher executives because never was I so glad to see my knight in shining armor. After bursting into tears of relief and soaking half a box of Kleenex as well as the shoulder of his jacket, I felt more up to giving my statement. Then Joe took me home and fed me chicken soup.

"Are you going to charge Lois?" I asked between spoonfuls.

"Not now. I don't know what she was doing there besides having a heart attack. First the police have to question her, and that won't be until she recovers enough to talk. At Helen's request, we are stationing a guard outside the hospital room for Lois's protection. The press will be mounting a siege, and I wouldn't be surprised if ANSWER tries to cause a ruckus."

"For Lois's protection," I repeated, pushing the bowl away. "Now I realize what the complainers mean when they say the law leans to the side of criminals' rights."

Joe carried my bowl to the sink. "You want her to be lynched?"

"Not really, but I could cheerfully choke myself for claiming she didn't have a killer mentality."

When Joe rinsed off the dirty dishes in the sink and then sat back down with nary a word, I squeezed his hand gratefully. Not just for his housekeeping either. Who wouldn't treasure a man who had the grace not to say "I told you so"?

Nevertheless, heading reluctantly for my meeting with Lois on Saturday morning, I was fully prepared for an avowal of innocence which I would not believe, or an admission of guilt which I would prefer not to hear. Maybe if I kept my visit short and limited the conversation to "How do you feel?" and "Isn't the food terrible here?", I could stave off all talk of murders or motives. Thank goodness the occasion didn't call for gushing effusion anyway. Only yesterday had Lois been removed from the critical list, so I should be able to get by with grave solemnity and sympathetic platitudes.

The atmosphere at Casa Grande City Hospital made it difficult to maintain a somber deference for the ill. Every employee wore a smile button that matched the sunny cheerfulness of orange carpeting and a chromatic dispersion of painted arrows on the walls. Green and red markers pointed to such happy places as Intensive Care and the Emergency Room, while the purple stripe was an unveering line to X-ray. Obviously, this colorful concept in modern medical care was to foster the illusion that the path to recovery is a yellow brick road. But even in the old days, doctors talked through their spectroscopes. "A dose of ultraviolet will get rid of that green around the gills and you'll be in the pink of health in no time." Apparently, the medical dictionary just says it in black and white.

After gaining admittance to the proper floor, I was escorted by a nurse down the hall to where a policeman was on guard duty outside Lois's room. I handed him my note from Helen.

"Mrs. Gordon?" He looked at me more closely. "Didn't I meet you last week? At the Day and Nite Grocery Store?" he prompted.

"Of course. Officer Tillborough, isn't it?" I shook his hand, then turned to the nurse and explained. "We both attended the same robbery."

The apple-cheeked angel of mercy seemed unimpressed by my claim-dropping. After casually nodding her head, she still asked for official permission before telling me to follow her.

Lois had been transferred from CCU to a private room only this morning, the nurse informed me, but some of the same rules applied here too. No smoking, no moving the patient, and all visits limited to ten minutes. Then she left, closing the door behind her.

I approached the bed, not knowing what to say but finding I wasn't as unmoved as I expected to be. Lois was tied to oxygen by a tube inserted into her nostrils, while her arm was taped to an IV of glucose. On top of that, she looked terrible. Minus the usual covering of makeup, plus the new lines etched on either side of her mouth, Lois McCoin could have passed for a young seventy-five rather than a strained fifty-two.

"I'm glad you came," she whispered.

"Is it all right for you to talk?"

"Yes. I'm just so weak."

"Well, you take it easy. I can carry the conversational ball myself. You know me, motormouth."

"No, Ellie . . . I need to tell you . . ."

"By the way," I interrupted, hoping to forestall an unburdening of her conscience, "I brought your purse with me. It's been safe at my house all week, and I figured you weren't in any rush for your car keys." I pulled her pocket-book from my giant carryall and started to put it in the night-stand drawer when Lois began to choke.

"Ellie! That's it . . . you . . ."

"Wait. Let me get the nurse," I said in a panic. "Don't move."

Before I could rush out of the room for help, forgetting there was an emergency call-button on the bed, Lois clutched at my suit jacket.

"Please. Don't get anyone. I'm fine." But even that small exertion sent her head falling back on the pillow. "I just didn't realize you had . . . my purse. I thought the police took it."

"What would they want with hand-tooled leather?" I soothed. "Now you relax while I put this in the drawer for you."

"No, not yet." Lois strained forward.

"Look here, lady." I tried to sound authoritarian. "You are in no condition to be jumping around so much. Will you lie still? Maybe I should go and let you sleep for a while."

"Ellie, please . . . don't leave." Lois begged. "I want . . ."

"All right, all right," I cut her off again, if just to keep her from attempting to sit up. "I'll stay two more minutes, but then it's nap time for you. The nurse will be here soon to kick me out anyway."

"Hurry . . . before she comes," Lois implored. "Open my purse."

"What's the matter, you don't trust me?" I said a trifle impatiently. "You think I purloined your Diner's Club card?"

"I'm serious, Ellie . . . you've got to . . ."

"Stop talking," I ordered. "If you feel it's so important to check the contents, here," I humored her, emptying the purse and laying each item on the bed. "Wallet, keys, handkerchief, pen, a receipt of some kind . . . my goodness, you're a neat person. You should see what I keep . . ."

"There," she pointed in excitement. "I wasn't sure . . ."

"Lois, calm down," I pleaded with her. "Do you want to land back on the critical list?"

Under my stern eye, she lowered her blue-veined arm to the bed, but her voice was insistent. "Look at the receipt."

Hiding my impatience, I smoothed the crumpled carbon copy, gave it a perfunctory glance, then did a double take at the signature. "Good Lord! This is Drake Prescott's cashier's check."

"That's what I wanted to show you," she said with a tired smile.

"Lois, do you know what this is?" I demanded.

"Yes, but I don't think you do. Read the whole thing, Ellie."

So I did. But the recipient of Prescott's largesse wasn't a luscious secretary out to feather her own nest. Carole Prescott's diatribe against April had been as far from the mark as my jealous wife theory, which since last week I had given up anyway. Still, for a moment, the spark of being right for a change did flicker in my heart before being snuffed out again.

"Why are you making such a big deal over this?" I chided Lois. "It's no crime for my contractor to moonlight by doing home improvements for PSSC executives. Tom's membership in ANSWER isn't that restrictive. He can take money from the enemy."

"Even hush money?"

"What are you talking about?"

"Listen to me." Lois sounded animated now, eager to make her case. "I happen to know the Prescotts didn't have any work done to their house. And you remember how Jessica claimed her associate suddenly went from Supermenace to being the mild-mannered Clark Kent. Well, something changed Tom Grabowski's methods, softened his stand. And I'm sure it wasn't because he became a born-again believer in the blessings wrought by nuclear power plants."

"Are you seriously suggesting this five thousand dollars was the conversion fee?"

"Isn't it obvious?" she asked, her brief spurt of vitality beginning to ebb.

"That's a heavy accusation, Lois," I reproved mildly. "Aside from slandering Tom's ethics, you're saying that PSSC made an illegal capital investment in a fraudulent joint venture."

"Not the company." Lois shook her head weakly. "I think this was Prescott's private enterprise."

"Meaning, he would have ensured himself a promotion if it seemed his brilliant pr were responsible for quieting ANSWER," I said skeptically. True, the man had been aiming for a room at the top, but would he have paid out of his own pocket for the privilege of an office on the sixth floor? And would Tom have accepted a bribe?

"Lois, I find all of this very unlikely, but if the cashier's check was issued because of a secret deal, how did you get hold of this copy?"

"That's the important part," she said, her voice fading fast. "I found it beside Jessica's body."

"What?"

She closed her eyes as if against a too-vivid memory. "It's true, Ellie. After I saw . . . saw that she was dead . . . I noticed the paper. All I really remember is picking it up, reading the names . . . realizing the implications . . . but when the pain started . . . I just ran for my purse, took the pills . . . then you came."

Several hundred questions popped into my mind, but even Mike Hammer would have hesitated to ask any one of them. The patient was at the end of her strength, though as I reached across the bed to ring for the nurse, Lois covered my hand with hers.

"Ellis, please," she murmured. "I need your help. . . . Don't give up on me." Her voice broke. "Use that receipt as evidence. Prove I didn't kill anyone . . . not Drake . . . not Jessica . . . please."

That was some deathbed plea, if Lois really were on the verge of breathing her last. But somehow I doubted she'd be so concerned about a posthumous vindication. My suspicion that Helen's mournful plaint had been a ruse was verified when the nurse came in to give me my marching orders. Mrs. McCoin was much improved and nearly out of danger.

Medical danger maybe, but the rest of her well-being seemed on shaky ground. My dilemma was, did I want to help her to terra firma? Or more to the point, did I believe her farfetched claim that the connection between Tom Grabowski and Drake Prescott was the link to two murders?

Chapter Twenty-two

I didn't need a search warrant anymore now that I had the receipt, but the bloody thing raised more questions than it answered. Was this Jess's mysterious clue, the one she'd wanted me to see? She had said only that information was being delivered on Sunday morning, but not whether it would arrive in written or oral form. "He dies and leaves no sign," I thought in frustration. Had someone come by her house earlier and dropped off the receipt? Or was Lois just using what she had overheard to make me think so?

Her tale of finding such convenient evidence next to Jessica's body seemed a little too pat. How did I know the copy of the cashier's check hadn't been in Lois's pocketbook when she arrived? Maybe Drake Prescott hadn't given her the receipt as a memento, but she could have taken it from his files for some insurance of her own. I still wondered if the money came from Prescott's personal bank account. Contributing to the moderation of a reckless radical seemed more like a company policy, and who was to say Lois hadn't been in on the arrangements herself? It was a public relations ploy in the broadest sense of the term, but even calling the scheme a way to peddle undue influence, she might not have balked if the package deal included a letter of recommendation for herself. And when Drake reneged on his end of the bargain, perhaps she had decided that eliminating him would give his deserving executive assistant a chance to collect the credit for defusing ANSWER. At the very least, she could have angled for that job she wanted at Canyon Escondido. Or was the very least wriggling out of two murder charges by incriminating someone else?

I didn't know what to believe. But presuming her story wasn't an elaborate deception, I still found Tom Grabowski's guilt hard to accept. Of course, the morning Jess was killed, I had invited him for breakfast and idly chattered about her having new information on the Prescott case and that I'd be using it to exonerate Lois. Tom had made an abrupt departure immediately after that revelation, which would have given him plenty of time to drive over to Jessica's, discover she knew all about his payoff from Prescott, then knock her on the head with the bookend and leave before either Lois or I arrived.

Wait. It was a bit premature to blame myself for directing the murderer to his next victim, although I couldn't help feeling that on some occasions I should be bound and gagged. But if Tom had killed Jessica to keep his association with Prescott a secret, how could he be careless enough to leave the telltale receipt behind? And if he had goofed royally, did that still mean he had murdered twice? I suppose the mere fact of Tom's presence at Canyon Escondido on the day of the reception could be considered as opportunity. After all, he was inside the building, although he claimed to have been caught and dragged out before he could get very far . . . before he had been able to reach the reactor core room or the testing facility. But even assuming he had been the person Drake Prescott had gone to meet in the lab, why would Tom want to cut off the source of his income? He had admitted to me that he'd been in financial straits until recently, and if Prescott were the philanthropist who had saved an almost-bankrupt builder from total ruin, why close the account? My next question was, had he ever opened one? The receipt did appear to be evidence that Tom had accepted an honorarium for altering his politics. And it wouldn't be the first time someone had been bribed out of his high ideals. But that only made him a faithless fraud, not a murderer.

Driving home, I decided the most sensible course to follow would be for me to do my civic duty and simply turn over the receipt to the authorities. Removing anything from the scene of a crime was illegal anyway, though Matt Steunkle wasn't going to charge Lois for absentmindedly putting a little piece of paper in her purse. And if he knew about the receipt, would it prompt him to reopen his investigation into Prescott's death? The copy of this particular cashier's check merely hinted at graft, and it implicated Lois McCoin as much as it cast the shadow of a doubt on Tom Grabowski. Naturally she wanted me to blacken that shadow, but it wasn't as if I were a real detective and could actually untangle this confusion of clues. On top of everything else, I didn't want Tom to be a murderer. Hell, I liked the shnook. The trouble was, I still liked Lois too.

It wasn't quite four o'clock when I pulled into Vista del Mar, and Mr. Talbot was in front, planting baby rosebushes.

"Hello there, Mrs. Gordon," he waved as I climbed out of the car. "What do you think of my landscaping?"

"You're going to have the best-looking garden on the block," I praised. "How's your wife doing? Is she over her cold yet?"

"No." He leaned on his spade. "In fact, I'm going to take her down to Mexico next week so she can get some sun. The air here's been a little nippy."

"Cliff dwellers are open targets for the sea breeze, I'm afraid."

"Guess so. Would you mind keeping a look-see on my roses while we're gone?"

"Sure. I'd be glad to water them for you. But I'll sure miss having a neighbor around."

"I don't reckon you'll be too lonesome," he said, grinning.

Since the Talbots had met Joe, I assumed that remark referred to him; but after I parked the car in the garage and went into the house through the utility room, the unmistakable aroma of charred cheese told me otherwise.

"Michael?" I called.

"Right here, Mom." He came out of the kitchen with a smoking frying pan in his hands. "You hungry?"

"For your burnt offering? No thanks. I'll make my own omelet when I finish smothering you in kisses."

"Will you smother my egg in onions too while you're at it?" he asked, giving me a one-armed hug.

My son looked marvelous. One would hardly know by the glow in his brown eyes that he'd just suffered the rigors of another physics exam. Even his curly hair seemed to have an extra spring to it.

"How's the grade point average?" I followed him to the stove.

"On an upward spiral."

"Just like inflation, huh?"

"Sort of. You got any chili around here? Good. Mix the sauce with the onions."

After hearing a few more instructions on how much garlic to add and what flavor jelly to smear on his peanut butter sandwich, I was once more making maternal noises about Michael's zest for the unpalatable.

"How can you like such a revolting conglomeration?" I shuddered, setting the plate in front of him.

"Didn't you ever hear of sweet and sour?"

"Not quite the way you combine them, but *esse mein kind*. Eat. I'll give you Alka Seltzer for dessert."

Actually, it was a pleasure feeding my son again, no

matter what the menu. I did very little cooking for myself, especially since Joe was always experimenting with fattening dishes and encouraging me to make all gone. When he wasn't around to quadruple my normal intake, I dined on Lean Cuisines. Nice for me, but a lithe nineteen-year-old like Michael would perish on three hundred calories a meal.

"Hey, Mom. Don't fool with the dishes now. Sit down a minute and talk to me."

"Okay," I agreed, obeying him.

"Aren't you even going to ask me why I'm here this weekend?"

"Because you love me and couldn't bear for us to be separated another minute."

"That too," he humored me, "but I want to know what happened to Jessica. You didn't say much on the phone, and the papers stopped carrying the story. Why was she murdered?"

"Michael, I can't answer that question."

"Oh, yes you can," he insisted. "I'm not a kid anymore. And Jess was my friend too, you know."

"No, sweetie. I didn't mean it that way. I just haven't got the answer. Neither do the police."

"After a whole week, nobody knows anything?"

"Nothing more than I already told you."

"But you said you found Jess with that woman. Hasn't she confessed yet?"

"The opposite," I sighed, going to the sink and running water into my abused frying pan. "Lois claims she didn't kill anyone, not Prescott either."

"Baloney! Her fingerprints were all over the place."

"Wrong. They weren't on the blade switch at the nuke plant or the fatal bookend at Jessica's."

"So she wiped them off."

"Maybe, but I'm not speculating. Neither case has anything to do with me."

"That's not true. You're involved in Jess's murder."

"Only as a very peripheral witness after the fact."

"Yeah, but you'll still have to testify about what you saw," he argued.

"Which was nothing."

"You might think it's nothing." He leaned against the counter on one elbow and watched me load the dishwasher without his help. "But have you ever seen the way prosecuting attorneys badger people on the stand into admitting all kinds of things? Who knows what the D.A. would wring from your testimony."

"You're jumping the gun, Michael. Lois hasn't been charged, so there isn't any trial scheduled. Besides, the D.A. is a friend of mine. If he tried wringing anything from me that doesn't come out of its own accord, I'd wring his neck."

"That's real friendly all right." Michael grinned. "In fact, it sounds like true love."

"Wrong again." I waved my finger at him.

"Just sleeping with the guy, huh?"

"Get out of here, you precocious brat. Go unpack or something. Surely, you've brought home a bundle of laundry for me to wash."

With typical teen-age perseverance, he followed me to his bedroom. "Come on, fess up. You're having a sleezy back-street affair and you don't want your loving son to find out."

"How would you like me to stick a dirty sock in your mouth? My God, look at this mess." I stepped over the pile of clothes Michael had dumped on the floor.

"I'll change my semantics," he continued doggedly. "You're enjoying an adult relationship, right?"

I started to gather up an assortment of jeans and sweaters. "If you want a full exposé of my sordid sex life, take this garbage into the utility room."

"Then will you tell me?" he asked eagerly.

"Maybe."

Once Michael had carried out every errand I assigned

him, separating dark clothes from light, turning on the washing machine, and stowing his knapsack in the closet, I did nothing of the kind. Telling any kid my private affairs would be in poor taste, and admitting to my own son that his mother was any less chaste than the Virgin Mary was unthinkable.

"We just date," I informed him with maternal dignity after Michael and I had settled comfortably in the living room. "And if you make one more remark about it, I will not feed you for the remainder of this weekend or all of next summer when you're home for three months. Get the threat?"

"Right in the stomach, although I don't see why you should be embarrassed about your life-style. Okay, okay," he caught the decorator pillow I threw at him. "Just tell me one thing. Does dating the D.A. give you an inside track with the law?"

"What are you leading up to?" I asked suspiciously.

"Well, I had this idea." He clasped his hands behind his head. "If you could get the cops to lay off tomorrow . . ."

"Hold it. What's tomorrow?"

"We're gonna have a demonstration at the nuke plant."

I sat bolt upright. "Since when? I didn't hear anything about a protest on Sunday."

"I know. We planned it only the other night, but a media release went out today. You'll read about it in this evening's paper."

"Slow down. First of all, who is 'we'?"

"Everybody in ANSWER." The expression on my face must have indicated that not "everybody" would be taking part, because Michael dropped his nonchalant pose and leaned forward earnestly. "We want to do it for Jess. In her memory."

"I'm sure that's a very fitting tribute," I granted, "but at the moment, it's also very impractical. Ever since Prescott's murder, there's been a twenty-four-hour guard around Canyon Escondido. You'd be courting confrontation to stage a protest there."

"There won't be any trouble. All we want to do is make a public show of strength, to prove ANSWER hasn't disintegrated. Don't you think we owe that much to Jess? When Vickie called me at school, she said it was a unanimous decision."

"Then Tom Grabowski probably didn't attend the meeting," I murmured dryly.

Michael was quite impressed with his mother's perspicacity. "How did you know he wasn't there?"

"Tom has told me on numerous occasions he thinks keeping a low profile and working behind the scenes pays off better for ANSWER in the long run," I explained glibly. Not that I didn't trust Michael's discretion, but it seemed wiser to remain mum about the latest developments, at least until I'd figured out things a bit more clearly.

"What's that supposed to mean?" my son asked, instantly on the defensive. "Are you criticizing Tom? You don't like him anymore?"

"I like him fine. I was merely commenting on his methodology."

"Oh, yeah? Since when did you become a supporter of civil disobedience? The last time I went out with ANSWER, you brought down the roof."

"And if you participate in this demonstration, I'll cut you out of my will without a penny. Forget it, Michael. I think it's a dumb idea."

"I don't understand you, Ma," he said with good reason. "If Jess's approach was too strong for you, why are you complaining because Tom's is too soft?"

"I'm not complaining. I approve of a nice middle-of-the-road concept in anarchy."

"Be serious."

"Do you see me laughing?"

"Anyway," Michael said with adult superiority, "I don't need your permission to go. I'm over eighteen."

"Which means nothing," I reminded him. "You can't drink, support yourself, or clean your room without my help."

"I can vote."

"No, you can't. It's not an election year."

"What's the matter with you, Mom? Don't you care about Jessica? Don't you care that she gave her all to preventing a nuclear accident that would wipe your precious condominium off the map?"

Sometimes he sounded just like his father, I thought in exasperation. "Keep things in perspective, Michael. She did not die for the cause."

"How do you know?" he demanded belligerently. "Her murderer worked for the power company. It could have been a corporate conspiracy to destroy ANSWER."

Now he sounded like me. "No theories, please." I rubbed my head. "I have so many now, I can't think straight." But Michael might have hit on part of the truth. I even had a piece of evidence in my pocket that screamed of conspiracy, though not the kind he meant.

"Why, don't you think that woman killed Jess?" he asked perceptively. "Have you been working on this case?"

Instead of feeling justifiably proud that Michael, like Tom, assumed I had a professional interest in solving any and all crimes, I denied even a remote curiosity. "Your mother is simply a passive participant who happens to know some of the circumstances."

"Okay. Maybe you're not sleuthing actively, but I bet you've come up with a few ideas. How about if I play Dr. Watson and you tell me your brilliant conclusions?"

"Being snide, are you?"

"Snide?" Michael was incredulous. "I just compared you to the inimitable Holmes. That's a compliment."

"Well, you can hold the accolade. The little I found out was mistaken, and since then I haven't analyzed a thing."

"But if you had," he said with a crafty gleam in his eye, "what would you analyze?"

"The obvious, my dear Watson: who would benefit from Jessica's death."

"The power company," he replied promptly.

"That's too obvious," I enlightened him, drawn into a discussion of crime-detection despite my claim of nonintervention. "First of all, they wouldn't send an accused murderess to kill again, employee or not. A gold watch at the end of her thirty-year prison term is hardly an incentive. Secondly, Jess had a divisive factor right inside her own organization. PSSC was the common enemy, not her personal nemesis."

"Are you saying someone in ANSWER killed her?"

"No. I am merely elucidating some facts for your education, so you can grow up to think exactly like your mother."

Michael frowned in a good imitation of me in a deep study, then copied my habit of jumping to conclusions, albeit with provocation. "You think Tom Grabowski murdered Jess because he disagreed with her tactics."

Damn! Why didn't I wear a muzzle at all times? To even skirt around my suspicions in front of an impressionable and partisan member of ANSWER's coalition was stupid. I guess Michael's thought process was close enough to mine already; though I wasn't convinced of Tom's guilt in anything yet, even if convincing my son that I harbored no doubts was heavy going.

"Well, it sure sounded like you were accusing him," Michael said as he finally came around. "But I can tell one thing about Tom. He's incapable of hurting anyone. His biggest fault is being too much of a pacifist."

"My, my. Now you don't seem very enamored of his tactics, or were they Jessica's you questioned?" I couldn't resist the dig that if Mother isn't always right, she's never totally wrong either.

"Are you trying to discredit him?"

"Not at all. It just appears he must have done that to himself by now, if ANSWER doesn't care about getting his approval for tomorrow's demonstration."

"That's not true. They respect his opinions. You ask anyone if they believe Tom is a traitor to the cause."

Funny Michael should use that expression. Those very words might well be the clue "too early seen unknown and known too late." Despite myself, I found I was going over the same ground again, this time with a slightly different emphasis. The date on the cashier's check was mid-January, when the Talbot place finally got carpeting and light fixtures. Yet according to Tom, money to complete units three and four hadn't come through until last week. Did that mean he was still on PSSC's payroll?

"Mom! You aren't listening."

Michael's call for attention pulled me out of my reverie. "I'm sorry, hon. What did you say?"

"I said, Tom wouldn't undermine ANSWER. You can ask anybody."

Anybody, I mused to myself? Well, my son was a very bad influence on me, because I was going to do just that.

Chapter Twenty-three

My Old-World-wise immigrant grandmother used to say that dreaming of rain meant good luck. Why a dream of snow prompted her to place a sizable bet on the third horse in the third race at Santa Anita had us all perplexed until we asked how she figured such an unlikely longshot would win. "Rain, snow. What's the difference? They both come out of the sky. And since snow starts with *C*, the third letter of the alphabet, how could I miss?"

My mistake was not taking off for the afternoon and going to the racetrack too. How I ended up at Canyon Escondido only proved my *bubbe* understood English better than I did. Michael said, "Ask anybody," and I interpreted that to "Ask everybody."

Well, here was everybody, milling across the access road, sitting cross-legged on the weedy grass and leaning against the ten-foot-high chain-link fence with its triple strands of barbed wire on top. Some people were pushing strollers, though the children were just balloon-carrying members of ANSWER. Printed on their helium-filled globes was the symbol of the atom, stamped with a barred circle, meaning "not permitted." In case the message was unclear, the grown-ups toted signs that spelled it out. Across the closed gates to the plant hung a banner that said "MAN IS THE NEXT ENDANGERED SPECIES." Under it, a neatly dressed young chap with a guitar was plucking out the strains of "Toot Toot Tootsie, Goodbye."

That might have seemed flippant in view of the fact that today's demonstration was supposed to be a memorial to Jessica, but she would have loved it. Her people were keeping the faith instead of getting bogged down in the maudlin. Even so, I was a bit taken aback by the carnival atmosphere. Of course, any public gathering was bound to be a merchandiser's delight, and several independent captains of industry, uninvited I'm sure, had set up pushcarts to cater to the hungry. At inflated prices, one could enjoy an international smorgasbord ranging from tamales to egg rolls. Michael told me on the QT that, in addition, the hot dog vendor peddled pot on the side. If you asked for the works, you got it.

This was my first protest, so I expected to be surprised. What I didn't expect was the upper-middle-class activists this event had attracted. In contrast to the barefoot, bearded, and beaded hippies of the sixties, these civil insurgents were upwardly mobile professionals. Their jeans were designer, their sunglasses monogrammed, and their median age thirty-five. Sprinkled through the well-washed masses was a contingent of passionate youth, but they were balanced by almost as many golden-agers, just as willing and able to carry signs and sing protest songs. In fact, it was someone else's granny who raised my *bubbe*'s convoluted reasoning to sheer genius. But that came later. First I was given a guided tour of the environs.

"Satisfied?" Michael asked smugly. "These aren't a bunch of kooks. This is a lawful gathering of concerned citizens. You worry too much."

My son was under the harmless delusion that I came here to see for myself that he hadn't fallen in with bad company. After all, a mother couldn't be too careful these days, and this mother wanted to be particularly careful that her idealistic offspring didn't find out what really had brought her to ANSWER's rally. If Michael had known I'd come to learn something more about Tom Grabowski, he'd make sure I discovered nothing even modestly critical of his hero. This way, I had an unimpeachable excuse to pry. Beneath the cloak of parental precaution, I could easily satisfy my own curiosity without arousing anyone else's. Provided the kid at my side would detach himself for about a half-hour.

"Just point out Vickie to me, then you can go get a hot dog. Relish only on top," I admonished.

"You know I'm not into that stuff, but I don't like relish either."

"Fine. Have onions. Then meet me at the car at two o'clock."

"Two? I don't want to leave that early."

"So bum a ride home. I'm not staying all afternoon."

"You ought to. Jess was your friend."

"Don't start up, Michael."

Recognizing the tone of voice, he shrugged good-naturedly. "Okay, do what you want, but when you talk to Vickie, don't make it sound like I needed your permission to come here today."

"Rest assured. I won't even mention your name. Now where is she?"

He directed my gaze to a frizzy-haired girl in khaki slacks and a rugby shirt who was sitting on a blanket and twining daisies into a long chain. No, she wasn't trying to relive her years at Vassar, I soon learned, or even to hark back to the days of flower power. She was stringing a wreath in Jess's memory to decorate the speaker's stand for the eulogy service later.

"That's a lovely tribute," I said after she outlined the schedule of events. "Is Tom Grabowski slated to say a few words too?"

"Oh sure. He'll be here as soon as he fixes a leaky pipe or something."

Since I hadn't seen Tom's pickup truck at Vista del Mar, my devious mind wondered if his tale of plumbing woes wasn't merely an excuse not to show. "If I know Tom," I offered casually, "he probably had to be persuaded to take part today."

"Surprisingly, no. He's the one who suggested some kind of memorial for Jess, though I got the idea of having it out here. Tom just warned everybody not to block the road."

"How typical." I smiled benignly. "He prefers the path of least resistance, while Jessica . . ." My words drifted into an expressive silence.

Vickie sighed, her fingers still busily lacing the flowers together. "I know what you mean. But Tom wasn't always that way. When he joined ANSWER, he was gung-ho for Jess's craziest schemes."

"Really? I wonder what changed him."

"Who knows? But Jess sure wasn't happy about it. She had depended on his support at the January meeting when we voted on having the demonstration here at the grand-opening reception."

"In January, you say. Goodness, I didn't realize their differences started that long ago." This was my carefully controlled reaction to discovering that the date of Tom's reversal and the check coincided. "Were you at that meeting too?" I probed further.

"You bet. I couldn't believe it when Tom said we shouldn't bother coming to Canyon Escondido in force."

"Then why did he agree on having the memorial here? Do you think he's altered his thinking again?"

"I doubt it. He probably realized he'd be outvoted. Even the moderates, of which there's a growing number, were convinced a public tribute to Jessica would be more effective at the nuke plant. She created our organization, and if nothing else, we want to show that basic concept didn't die with her." Vickie got to her feet and brushed some bits of daisy leaves from her pants. "Want to help me hang this on the fence?"

"My pleasure." I lifted one end of the garland and traipsed behind her around the makeshift dais. "So what direction will the group take now?"

She handed me several green twisters to attach the flowers to the crisscross of wire. "Well, we're going to have an election, and the way things are shaping up, it looks as though the choice will be between me and Tom. As far as who might win, I'd say he stands a better chance."

"Why?"

"I guess because ANSWER has come to an ideological intersection, and Tom's ideas are getting more popular. I don't have Jess's charisma, even though I share her views. She's the one who taught me that a polite request for publicity earned us coverage in Section Four of the newspaper, page sixteen, under Meeting Announcements. But when I stand up and argue that moving a hundred antinukes from a church social to a street corner makes us a media event, it doesn't sound the same."

"It will," I encouraged her. "Just keep practicing."

"Yes, but I'll never have Jess's dynamics. And Tom makes sense when he says demonstrations can get out of hand and antagonize the very people we're trying to reach."

"True," I granted, "but there must be alternative strategies, somewhere between civil disobedience and quietly biting your nails in frustration."

"Not many, except becoming a protest-by-post-office organization. But that puts our message in the junk mail category, and it's expensive to boot."

"What does Tom suggest?" I asked offhandedly. "He must have ideas."

"Well, the other night we talked about bringing a class action suit against PSSC. He might go for that."

Not if he were still on the company's profit-sharing plan, I thought cynically. Naturally, I didn't voice my suspicion to Vickie. I just wished her luck in the upcoming election, then went off to take a random survey of her chances.

This wasn't so I could report any good findings to her. Learning that Tom wanted to take over the leadership of ANSWER was an important new angle in my investigation. His political aspirations could have been a motive for eliminating the incumbent president, and if he had control of the organization, it also would make PSSC so happy. A shaky premise but worth further scrutiny.

The results of my straw poll gave a wide edge to the power company. Tom was chosen two to one over Vickie as the next ruler of the roost. I may not have taken a truly representative sampling, but most of the people I questioned thought he was the logical, even inevitable successor to Jessica. After all, don't vice-presidents automatically move up when the chief executive dies in office?

"Tom did so much of the work," one bespectacled man informed me. "He deserves the recognition."

"What about Vickie?" I asked. "I hear she's been a real asset to the cause."

"We'll make her recording secretary."

Deciding not to get sidetracked on the issue of sexual stereotyping, I swallowed my arguments and continued on. The next person I approached for the one-minute interview was a woman in her thirties with a young infant strapped snugly to her bosom. Professing admiration for the little darling was a wonderful icebreaker, and in minutes his mother and I were chatting like old buddies . . . or was that biddies? It certainly didn't take her long to reveal she had abandoned a lucrative career as a stockbroker for the responsibilities of motherhood. With all the enthusiasm of the convert, she confided she loved staying at home and taking care of her precious Jeremy. This had to be one of Vickie's supporters, right? Wrong. My new friend, the happy housekeeper, thought Tom Grabowski had stronger leadership qualities.

"Remember how he sneaked into the plant during our

last protest here? Showed them all up," she recounted, eyes alight. "Well, I saw him do it, and you know how he got in? He just flashed a yellow credit card that looked like a press pass, then walked straight through those gates with a TV crew. Tagged along as if he had every right in the world."

Interesting. Tom never had revealed how he penetrated the building, and I had assumed he'd climbed over the fence, though my seeing all the barbed wire should have dispelled that notion. "Too bad he was caught right away," I pretended to commiserate.

"But he wasn't." As the baby started to whimper, she patted him gently. "Tom went in at four-fifteen, and they didn't bring him out in handcuffs until ten after five."

"Are you sure?"

"Absolutely. I timed the whole thing so we could use it for publicity. Do you realize that if he'd been a terrorist, he would have had plenty of chance to set explosives?"

Or if he were a murderer, he'd have had more than ample opportunity to kill.

"Hey, Ellie. Come here and give me a hand." It was Marilyn Banes, the dentist, sans her mink coat for once, and kneeling in the grass beside a large piece of poster board.

"Painting propaganda?" I asked, walking over to scan her artistic efforts.

"I meant to finish this last night. Do you think it'll pass muster?"

The sign, written in Magic Marker, wasn't exactly a glowing example of caligraphy, but the words were perfectly legible: NUCLEAR SAFETY IS THE BEST PREVENTIVE MEDICINE.

"It's the sentiment that counts," was my appraisal, "and Jess would have appreciated how hard you tried."

Marilyn stapled the poster to a dowel. "I can't tell you how often she asked me to come to one of her demonstrations, but I was always too busy. Today, I made it." Her eyes filled with tears. "God, Ellie. I can't believe she's gone. What a waste."

"I know."

She blew her nose then managed a lopsided smile. "I've got some more poster board. What shall we put on it?"

"How about DON'T WAIT TO TREAT THE SYMPTOMS—FIGHT THE DISEASE NOW?" I suggested.

"Great. You do the lettering though. My printing is atrocious."

And so, regardless of my cream linen slacks, I got down on the ground and made my first antinuke protest. Not so much because my artistic ability was greater than Marilyn's—I just wanted to do something for Jess too.

When Michael wandered by and saw that I had embraced his favorite cause, he was delighted. "Let me call Gary over to take a picture of you."

"Who's Gary?"

"A photographer from the newspaper."

"Keep him away from me," I ordered. "I would prefer my involvement in this to go as unnoticed as possible."

"No chance," Marilyn said. "The police have had their eye on you for the past ten minutes."

"What police?"

She pointed with a purple Magic Marker. "Look down the road. They're parked by that row of oleanders."

The hedge was a good six feet high and loaded with pink blooms, but it didn't hide the black and white. "Maybe it's a radar trap," I said, squinting into the sun.

"You hope. But I say they're here to make sure we don't break down the fence and level the nuke plant."

"Stop pushing the panic button," I scoffed, "unless you're planning to raze the place. But as soon as the police see this is more like a picnic than a demonstration, they'll leave."

"Hey, they're starting the speeches. Let's get up close so we can hear."

I handed her the completed sign. "You go. Eulogies make me cry."

Presently encumbered with one poster, she gave me back my masterpiece and said I should keep it. Then she hurried after Michael who was loping toward the speaker's stand. I lingered at the back of the crowd and used the sign to block the sun from my eyes as I scanned the crowd. If Tom had fixed his leaky pipe in time to be number one on the agenda, I sure didn't spot him. But neither did I intend waiting around to see for myself that he'd probably never show up. The afternoon had been revealing enough already.

Chapter Twenty-four

Too bad I didn't leave right then to do some evaluating, but it must have been someone else in the family who inherited my grandmother's powers of prediction. I didn't even get a chill of foreboding when the little old lady with the shopping bag came over to apprise me that I had a grass stain on the seat of my trousers.

"I do? Heck." I tried vainly to inspect the damage.

"Make a paste of Tide and let it sit on your pants overnight," was her advice. "That's a nice poster. Want me to carry it for you?"

"Why, thank you. But it might be awfully heavy for you to manage alone."

She shook her gray head definitely. "I exercise with Jack LaLanne every day." Then she leaned close and whispered in a confidential tone, "Besides, I want to be armed when the time comes."

"Armed?" Obviously, the old lady had had a bit too much sun.

"Those four men over there." She nodded toward the hot dog stand. "They're going to make trouble."

I could have told why four strange-looking characters chose to hang around that particular pushcart, but instead I smiled comfortingly. "You don't have to worry about them."

At that moment, ANSWER's treasurer introduced himself from the raised platform and asked for everyone's attention. Behind him and grouped against the chain-link fence, was the lineup of scheduled speakers; no Tom, but there was Vickie, two men I didn't recognize, and Michael.

"Michael!"

"Who?" Granny asked.

"My son," I said through gritted teeth.

"The balding gentleman?" she inquired sweetly.

True, the speaker with the prematurely receding hairline couldn't have been past his mid-twenties, but only last week Betsy assured me I didn't look a day over thirty. Either she was a dirty liar or Granny assumed I had been your typical five-year-old bride.

"No, my son is the kid wearing the blue shirt," I corrected her. "He didn't tell me he was making a speech this afternoon. I would have gotten a lot closer."

"You must be very proud of him," she beamed. "So many youngsters don't understand the importance of protecting the environment. I only regret that when the voting age was lowered, political awareness wasn't raised. You notice how few young people are here today."

In the interest of family solidarity, I didn't reveal the fact that I wasn't exactly thrilled with the idea of Michael's being featured by the media again. For one thing, his father would be on the phone tomorrow, blaming me because our son was an antinuke nut-case.

A timely burst of applause put an end to this conversation, and I stood on my tiptoes to get a better view as Vickie stepped forward. Grandma, who was several inches taller than I, didn't have to stretch herself to see, though she couldn't seem to take her eyes off the hot dog stand.

"Ladies and gentlemen," Vickie began, "we are here to

pay tribute to a woman and her legacy. Jessica Tobler cherished an idea, a commitment to the quality of life . . ."

"She was a goofball," someone shouted.

For a moment there was a stunned silence, then Vickie raised her hand to still the murmur of surprise that followed. "This is a memorial service," she reproved sternly. "Anyone who does not wish to participate is requested to leave." When there was no response, she continued. "As with every cause for right and justice, there are opposing forces. We cannot let them prevail."

"Stick it, sister."

Once the source of that raspy voice was located, all eyes were on the hot dog stand and the same four men Granny had pointed out to me. "Yeah," another of them jeered. "Why don't you 'fraidy cats go home and crawl under the bed? We don't want your kind around here. Commie sellouts!"

Vickie had the advantage of a microphone. "May I remind you that this is a solemn occasion?" she said angrily, lifting her chin in defiance.

"Solemn, my ass. Bleeding-heart liberals is what you are. You gonna stop progress with a few balloons?" This was from the fourth member of the group, a man with a day's growth of stubble on his face and a seedy yet menacing air.

Some nightclub performers can deal effectively with hecklers, but sweet, earnest Vickie was unequal to the task. She tried answering their charges and got drawn into a shouting match.

"You don't have the right to disrupt a private meeting," a pro-ANSWER voice came from the crowd.

"This ain't private," the first loudmouth argued. "You're on public land. What's private is on the other side of that fence, and we ain't gonna let you mess with it like you want."

Now that I didn't need second sight to see what was coming, I deemed it prudent to make a hasty departure.

But Michael was on the dais, and I was on the edge of the road. I did consider leaving him there to face the consequences of his idealism, but I had my own quixotic standards. Child abandonment might have deprived me of the satisfaction of child abuse, and I was going to give it to that kid once he was safe at home.

"I told you those men were up to no good." Granny poked me in the ribs with my sign.

Were all *bubbes* clairvoyant? Before I could ask this one for a tip on the horses, I had an intuition of my own. Somebody must have arranged this discordant note in an otherwise mild gathering. The fearsome foursome hadn't just happened to congregate by the notorious hot dog stand. Their act was too practiced, too coordinated. They came together, ate together, hurled insults together, and together were about to turn ANSWER's peaceful demonstration into a militant uprising. And just in time to make the evening news. Naturally, the name Tom Grabowski popped into my head. Had he sent these *agents provocateurs* to prove his claim that public protests can get out of hand? Based on my most recent findings, that did not seem unlikely, and it would explain why he wasn't here. But if Tom were responsible, he couldn't have afforded to hire mercenaries, at least not without additional financial backing. Another cashier's check or C.O.D. this time?

Grandma jabbed me in the ribs again. "Watch that heavyset man on the left. I don't trust him."

"I don't trust any of them."

For once, my vibes were semiprophetic. I saw the man on the left pick up a rock, but I never predicted that a little old lady would cast the first stone. Obviously she noticed the same thing I had, except that her reaction wasn't a sensible duck behind her neighbor. She bent to the ground, seized a good-sized chunk of basalt, then slung it at the man while he was still warming up for the pitch. Thanks to Jack LaLanne, our side drew first blood.

Unlike a duel of old, that didn't settle the issue. With

howls of rage, all four rowdies sent a hail of missiles into the crowd. The result was an instant free-for-all around the hot dog cart, with those who had the misfortune of not being in the immediate vicinity pushing to get there. The rest of us formed a circle on the sidelines, women and children to the rear and me in the middle.

While I was doing my best to avoid any active participation in the melée, not even cheering for ANSWER's victory, the forgotten police car down the lane made its own noisy entrance on the scene. The two officers posted at the access road to watch for trouble had seen it erupt and came to put a damper on things . . . but not before they radioed for reinforcements just in case the bullhorn didn't work.

"Break it up! Come on. Break it up!"

Their voices blared loudly over the yells of "Hit 'im again" and "Show the bastards," but to no avail. The not-so-innocent bystanders stayed rooted to their spots as if they'd paid good money to get a view from the forty-yard line. The two officers tried prodding a few people toward their cars, though they did not attempt to referee the fight. That privilege went to the state troopers who answered the call for backups with commendable speed. From four miles away we could hear the sirens, an intimidating mob demobilizer in itself. It got the mothers with strollers off the premises anyway. However, to many of the demonstrators, the sound was a call to arms. Husbands kissed wives goodbye; college students threw down their books; even some of the pugilists responded accordingly. They dropped where they were, lay spread-eagled on the ground, and showed what passive resistance was all about.

Jessica would have burst her buttons with pride. So many prone bodies were impossible for the police to overcome. When the four scapegraces who began the disturbance saw the direction things were going, they made a quick exit along with the people who decided to take official advice and leave before they were carried off.

I would have obeyed as well if I hadn't given in to a natural parental concern to be sure that my son wasn't among the peaceniks on the ground. With people rushing to their cars under uniformed supervision over the sea of bodies, it was pure and simple bedlam. I called out Michael's name first, an exercise in futility, then skirted around the cordon of policemen in hopes of spotting a blue shirt and a mop of dark curls.

"Lady, you better get out of here," a state trooper warned me.

I should have listened to him, because sometime between the intervention of the first two policemen and the arrival of ten more officers of the law, an additional 10-32 went out on the radio waves. As usual, the authorities overreacted. The fight itself was no longer in progress, and it seemed unfair to label inert guerrilla warfare as combat action. Most of ANSWER's protesters had followed instructions to depart, and even if that did cause a massive traffic jam, surely a dozen armed troopers could have handled fifty or so recumbent rebels.

Apparently not. With another kind of siren cutting through the air this time, a fire truck came tearing down the highway. Like an avenging red dragon, it bypassed the access road and squealed onto the soft shoulder, skidding to a stop about thirty feet from me. Stupidly, I looked around for a fire, not learning until later that water is used to disperse an unruly mob more effectively and less dangerously than tear gas. The courtesy was lost on me.

First of all, I had just located Michael. Smart kid that he was, he'd been behind the dais with Vickie, safely watching the proceedings. I saw him grab her hand and make a run for it, but when I tried to follow him, pushing against the press of humanity who knew what was coming, firemen turned the water cannon on me.

The pressure knocked me right on my fanny, and all I could think was, this is no way to remove grass stains from good slacks. I scrambled to my knees only to be blasted by another gush. A portable tank with an adjustable valve did the job of a sedentary hydrant. But damned if I'd ever donate to the volunteer fire brigade again. Didn't they know California had a water shortage? More H_2O was being expended on one defenseless woman than was needed to irrigate the entire Napa Valley for a month. I was soaked, in danger of having my contact lenses washed away, and unable to escape the stinging shower raining on my head. Eyes closed, I tried to crawl out of the line of spray when some klutz tripped over me.

"Watch it!" I sputtered.

Powerful hands raised me to my feet and began propelling me out of this mayhem.

"Michael?" I clutched a fistful of sleeve to make sure he didn't lose me, but when we finally emerged to dry air and I could open my eyes again, the first thing I saw was his badge.

"No, ma'am. My name is Officer Grimes. Now move along peaceably."

Next to us, someone who chose not to move along peaceably was being dragged to the paddy wagon that had just arrived. "It's going to take two of you guys to lift me," he shouted. Three tossed him into the van.

I thought it only fair to explain that I did not deserve like treatment. "Thank goodness you saved me." I pushed a dripping curl off my forehead. "But as you can see, I'm not a demonstrator."

"Then what were you doing on the ground?"

"Trying to stand up," was my terse reply.

"Okay, you're up. Now beat it."

"Certainly. As soon as I find my son."

Officer Grimes gave me a pained look. "Do yourself a favor, lady. Go home now before I escort you somewhere else."

"There's no need for you to threaten me. I merely wish to see that my son is safe. Then I'll be glad to go, I assure you."

He pulled a pair of handcuffs out of his pocket. "I'm giving you one more chance, lady."

My forty-five-dollar pants were ruined; my shoes were filled with mud; and this overzealous strong arm of the law was definitely irritating me. "Read my lips," I said with a bit too much sarcasm. "You are under a misapprehension. I am not a member of ANSWER, but merely a spectator here today. In fact, though I don't like throwing my weight around, I'm a registered Crimewatcher."

"Good. Then you'll enjoy the view from the window of the paddy wagon." He clamped the handcuffs on my wrists.

"I'm warning you, Officer, if you take me into custody, it will be a grave miscarriage of justice." That was certainly an understatement. He hadn't even read my rights. "Now I insist you release me from this modern-day iron maiden so I can find Michael and leave, exactly as you wish." With a sigh of exasperation, he let go of my arm, ostensibly to get his key, when my unreliable ESP sounded another alarm. "Oh, for heaven's sake! They haven't arrested Michael! He's not in there, I hope."

All I wanted to do was take a peek inside the Black Maria, but Officer Grimes obviously misinterpreted my dash away from him as an attempted escape. At least, that's what he wrote on the citation, along with disturbing the peace, disorderly conduct, and resisting arrest. Personally, I thought he went overboard. Only the last charge was legitimate.

Chapter Twenty-five

The last time I flouted authority, I had been hauled to the principal's office for cutting algebra class. This time, for not cutting out when I should have, I was sent to jail.

"Some people have all the luck," a familiar voice called as I was shoved inside the police van. It was Michael, giving me a two-fingered *V*-for-victory sign.

That he could still walk the earth a free man was small consolation as I cowered in the corner next to a welter-weight with a bloody nose who also considered his defeat a win for the good guys. Not me. I was thoroughly unhappy with my triumph and not at all proud that I had no one to thank for it but myself.

While I brooded, my fellow malefactors could hardly contain their joy at being arrested. In deference to Tom Grabowski, this rambunctious group had agreed to a peaceful demonstration, but Providence had intervened. Outside agitators had caused a riot, and now ANSWER could apply the kind of tactics that attracted the most attention.

They started by hassling the armed guard whose sole

duty was to see that these advocates of passive resistance didn't destroy the truck before it arrived at the detention center. I had no ambition to pull out the nonmovable benches from the wall of the van and lie on the floor. The home-grown Ché Guevera in the army camouflage jacket, however, took exception to being denied that fun. He was identified as an air traffic controller in his saner moments, but now was definitely not one of them.

"Do you realize you're a tool of the Military-Industrial Complex?" he accused the annoyed guard. "Or maybe you get a kick out of pointing your gun at an unarmed citizen."

"Shut up, bub."

"The Constitution guarantees my right of free speech."

"Not when you're in my custody, it don't."

"So what are you going to do? Shoot me?"

Given my mood and the policeman's .38, I might have obliged, but only after plugging dear, sweet Granny. Yes, she had managed to get herself arrested too and predictably was delighted by the adventure.

"We showed them, didn't we?" she said gleefully, exhibiting the cuffs on her veiny wrists while I wondered why they didn't shackle her mouth instead.

Needless to add, my second Ride-Along as a guest of the police department was not as enjoyable as my first; though once we got downtown, I wasn't anxious to disembark. But neither did I wish to emulate the protesters who chose to be carried out of the truck for the benefit of reporters who showed up in droves to snap our pictures. So I used my purse to shield my face and tried to hide behind Ché's camouflage with the hope that its concealing powers were transferable.

Inside the jail, we were herded down a long corridor to R and D, or as the policeman translated, Receiving and Discharge. There were about thirty of us, twenty-nine eager to make life difficult for the sergeant at the desk, and one ready to drop through the floor at the sight of Matt Steunkle. He must have forfeited his Sunday off to oversee this debacle. The demonstrators' past strategy had been not merely to resist arrest, but to make the entire process as slow and disorderly as possible. Matt probably wanted to prevent more of the same.

First in the order of events, the sergeant explained to the few who didn't know by now, was to get the booking card filled out. Then we'd be fingerprinted, have our pictures taken, and be released on our own recognizance until the arraignment tomorrow.

That brought a storm of protest. If they weren't going to keep us in jail overnight, how could we bog down the system and fill all the cells so there'd be no room for deserving criminals? How could we claim our civil rights had been violated?

Earlier today, I had distrustfully questioned Tom's position on the value, or lack thereof, of demonstrations. And while I still wondered about his motives, a bit of time spent with ANSWER's radical wing made me think he wasn't so wrong after all. I wanted out of this place as quickly as possible, but these glory-seekers were trying to win me a prison term. Gritting my teeth in agony, I listened as Granny did her best to keep us here for the next year.

"Name," the sergeant rapped out.

"Greta Garbo."

"I'll mark that as your alias. Now tell me what your parents called you."

"Their little girl," she giggled.

Everyone quieted to hear this exchange.

"Lady," he sighed impatiently, "are you going to cooperate or do you want to get in more trouble?"

"That would be nice." She adjusted her dentures.

"Okay, but if I'm going to book you on extra charges, I got to know your name."

"Martha Washington," she said promptly.

The poor sergeant looked at Chief Steunkle for help. "How should I handle this?"

"Let her go."

"You can't do that," she argued. "I was arrested fair and square. It's your duty to lock me up."

This provoked another group discussion, with everyone defending the elderly woman's right to incarceration. "I thought America was supposed to be a democracy," piped one astute debater. "Yeah," came a second creative orator, "her tax money helped build this place, so why can't she sleep here?"

Matt Steunkle roared for silence. "All of you, shut up! Now listen to me, this ain't the Hilton. If you people got in mind bunking with some paint-sniffer upstairs, that's just too bad. I ain't renting out no cells tonight. Now get this line moving. Out, Greta. We don't cater to senior citizens."

Nothing could abash Granny, and she called Matt a rotten fuzz with no sensitivity to a person's political preference. He said he ran a police state and ordered two uniformed escorts to lead her to the door. I could just hear her complaining to reporters outside that the autocratic chief had forcibly freed her when she wished to be detained behind bars. People certainly had no respect for age these days.

Now Matt was riled. He demanded that everyone follow procedure in an orderly manner or nobody was going to get charged with any crime. Naturally, his reverse psychology worked. ANSWER also had a routine they performed in court, and rather than be deprived of that opportunity, they obeyed the irate chief. He started to walk away, satisfied his threat had done the trick, while I breathed a sigh of relief. At least, Matt wouldn't be standing over my shoulder when I got to the front of the line. This entire ordeal was humiliating enough without the chief of police witness to it. Let him read my name on the arrest sheet tomorrow when I wouldn't be around to cringe in embarrassment.

But then he turned around to scan the crowd for any hold-out dissenters. Thinking I needed a better disguise than the water hoses had provided, I raised the purse dangling from my handcuffed wrists to cover my face again. Stupid move. It attracted the very attention I was trying to avoid. Matt's keen eyes instantly recognized the drowned rat behind the tote bag.

"Ellie . . . ? What the hell . . . ?"

I peeked over the strap. "Hi there, Chief. Read any good mysteries lately?"

He walked over and pulled me out of line. "I don't believe it. You were protesting at Canyon Escondido?"

"Only my arrest," I told him truthfully.

Matt scratched his grizzled head in a familiar gesture of perplexity, then took me by the elbow. "Come on."

Ché Guevera saw me being led away. "Hey, you're not releasing her too, are you?" he called, obviously concerned that I might be denied the pleasure of being fingerprinted.

"Hell, no!" Matt growled realistically. "I'm taking this one for interrogation. Move it, sister."

A rousing cheer of acclaim that I'd been singled out for persecution followed as Matt shuffled me around a corner and into a room marked Records. Once the door was closed, he removed my handcuffs.

"How in the goddamn hell did you get into this mess?"

"Honestly, Matt"—I rummaged in my purse for a comb and lipstick—"I was just minding my own business when the police arrested me by mistake."

"You never mind your own business."

Unable to argue the truth of that, I merely tried to get my hair in some semblance of order. Putting on lipstick was even a more slapdash affair.

"You didn't improve anything," the chief informed me when I finished my toilette.

"Well, at least I feel more human. By the way, thanks for saving me just now. I didn't really want you to see me out there, but sometimes it pays to have friends in high places."

"You're welcome. Now tell me what you were doing at the nuke plant. Privately eyeing the scene of the crime?"

"You always suspect the worst," I evaded, perching on the edge of a desk and probably looking as ridiculous as I felt. My once crisp shirt was plastered to my back, while water dripped steadily off the toes of my canvas espadrilles. Assuming a pose of insouciance seemed the only way to carry it off. "My son is a member of ANSWER, and I went to the rally to please him."

"Then you're not still working on the McCoin case?" he asked skeptically.

This was the third time in a week someone credited me with being an instrumental influence and the third time I demurely deflected the compliment. "Why, Matt, you make me sound so professional."

"No, just persistent."

Was he being droll or disapproving, I wondered uncomfortably? It might be a good idea to tell him everything now, but I wasn't quite sure how the chief of police would react to my committing two infractions of the law. Getting myself arrested for rioting could be considered a laughable offense. But, by all that was serious and sanctioned, I should have given him the cashier's check receipt as soon as Lois turned it over to me. I probably compounded a double felony by keeping it. Maybe a gentle lead-in would help pave the way.

"Well, you know how I am, Chief, always trying to stumble onto new evidence, though today was more of a pratfall, I guess."

"Yeah, you got a funny technique," he agreed, "but if there is anything new around, you'll probably be the one to trip over it."

"You really think so? And you wouldn't mind?"

"Why should I mind? You never hide anything from me, and sometimes your theories make sense," was his teasing qualification. "Just don't fall for a pig in a poke," he warned, "and don't run in front of anymore squirt guns. You're ruining the top of that desk."

"Sorry." I slid off. "But Matt, suppose I found something that might or might not be important information . . . a document for instance? Would my actions be acceptable if . . . ?"

Just as I began my mitigating explanation about the receipt, someone knocked on the door. "Chief? Are you in there? The D.A.'s looking for you."

"Tell him I'll be right out. You coming, Ellie?"

"No. I can't let Joe see me until I do something with my hair," I begged, all thought of making a full disclosure about my evidence replaced by more pressing considerations.

"There's nothing you can do. Let's go."

"But what about those people in Booking?"

"They seen your hair already."

"No, I mean what if they expect me to show some visible signs of being interrogated, like bruise marks or a fat lip? You realize, Matt, they want me to become a martyr for ANSWER, and if they think you won't oblige, they'll tie me to the stake themselves."

"You look like a pretty good victim of police brutality right now, but it might be smart if you stayed out of sight until that crowd leaves. I'll send Corelli in here." He paused at the door. "Now don't go poking through any files. Unauthorized personnel aren't supposed to be in Records."

"I won't touch a thing except my hair," I promised, though that proved to be a waste of time. My curls were drying into stubborn knots, and combing them out only resulted in a wild frizz. Oh, well, Joe wouldn't care about my unlovely tresses. He'd just carry on about how they got that way. I added a drop more lipstick for cajoling purposes, although I really planned to appease him by revealing what I never got around to telling Matt Steunkle. When the D.A. heard how successful my fishing expedition was, how could he fuss about a little water hazard?

The door opened and I swung around. "Joe, my sweet,

I'm in disguise. But if you can guess who I am in less than five seconds, you get a big wet hug."

"I don't believe it," he said in a quiet echo of Matt Steunkle's initial reaction.

"I'm that unrecognizable, huh?" I tugged at the frizz. "But you're forgiven. The police made a worse identification. They took me for an antinuke protester. Can you imagine?"

"Yes, if you were at the demonstration today," was his unsmiling response.

"But I went because . . ."

"It hardly matters what sent you," Joe interrupted, finally coming into the room, though not to give me a hug. "You had no business going there at all."

Allowing for the fact that the unruly mob down the hall had stretched his endurance to the breaking point, I coaxed nicely, "Hey, don't let it get to you. Nothing bad happened to me. I'm fine. I survived. See?" I raised my arms to show him only my clothes had suffered, but Joe was not placated.

He tightened his lips. "The only reason nothing worse happened to you was because Matt intervened. And he isn't usually so accommodating."

"Wait a minute. Before you get too carried away"—I held up my hand as if that would stop him—"the chief and I have a special understanding. He permits me to pry for information, and I give him the results of my fact-finding missions."

"What are you talking about? Matt didn't ask you to report on ANSWER's activities."

"No, but he knows I'm interested in the Prescott case, and he encourages my sleuthing. In fact," I said with more than a little pride, "he gave me professional approval."

"I doubt that," Joe scowled, "but I should have guessed what took you to Canyon Escondido was some crazy investigation. Just look at what you've done to yourself." He pointed at my hair. "And if that isn't bad enough, you were arrested for breaking the law."

I leaned against the desk, regardless of the damage to the wood, and crossed my arms. "Aren't you overreacting, Joe? I may be a little worse for wear, but going to a demonstration is legal, or it was the last time I heard. So is finding new evidence."

If I had expected praise or even a show of curiosity, I was doomed to disappointment. Joe turned away with a gesture of impatience. "You are not on special assignment with the police. They don't need or want your help. And in the event you've forgotten, the Prescott case is closed. Even you decided the McCoin woman is guilty."

"Now I'm not so sure."

"Damn it, Ellie. You're not starting that up again," he charged, as if I changed my mind every hour and a half on a whim.

I should have reminded the D.A. that just a couple of weeks ago he told me himself if new information were discovered, he'd evaluate it fairly even if that information came from fickle little me. But when there was a commotion in the hall, I suggested Joe go out and cow them into submission.

"I'd better see who's charged with what so I can schedule enough time for the arraignment tomorrow. You wait here," he directed with a glance at his watch. "I'll be back in a few minutes to take you home."

"You don't have to bother. Michael should be here soon. He probably went by the house first to get me bail money." My tone was a bit dry but perfectly civil. Joe's was not.

"You think this is funny, don't you? You think it's a big joke to have your name smeared in the newspapers. For crying out loud, Ellie, don't you understand that if you'd been booked, it would have gone on your permanent record?"

"Oh, dear, a nonerasable blot on the family escutcheon."

Joe's face turned red. "Obviously," he bit out in a tight voice, "you don't care if your good name is dragged through the mud."

"Why this preoccupation with my respectability? Worried it will become public knowledge that the district attorney sleeps with a would-be felon?"

"Don't try to make me the bad guy, Ellie. I don't like what you're doing to yourself. This business about finding clues and discovering new leads is pure nonsense. You're playing a foolish game. Life isn't a mystery novel where you can indulge in unsolicited snooping. One of these days it's going to land you in serious trouble, and neither Matt Steunkle nor I might be around to save you."

That sanctimonious speech almost did me in. Arms akimbo, I glared at my self-appointed savior. "I don't recall your coming to my aid this afternoon, unless insulting my intelligence is supposed to be beneficial. But what concerns you, my safety or my reputation? I can't figure out if you're ashamed of me or afraid for me, and to be quite honest, I don't like either choice."

Then he really got mad. His nostrils flared. "I'm certainly not worried that some imaginary murderer is going to kill you for being in hot pursuit. What I am is disappointed that a woman of your supposed good sense could behave so irresponsibly."

"By chasing phantoms?" I asked in a dangerously soft voice.

"No, for thinking you can catch them."

So the truth is revealed at last, I fumed. Joe Corelli thought I was an incompetent Doña Quixote who charged at windmills backward with my beribboned lance pointed in the wrong direction. He had never taken my involvement in the Prescott case seriously. For all his professed concern, his championship of my delicate person, the only reason my knight errant felt protective was to save me from myself.

"Please leave, Joe. Go prosecute some demonstrators before you say anything else I'll regret."

"We'll both go." He took my arm. "And don't badger Matt about the Prescott case anymore. He likes you, so he's a good sport about listening to your ideas. But enough is enough."

"Is it ever!" I pulled out of his grasp. "And evidently you've had enough of me as well. After all, bearing a fool company, 'though it make the unskillful laugh, cannot but make the judicious grieve.' And I certainly wouldn't want you to suffer more than necessary."

"I won't unless you keep waxing poetic. Whenever you're angry, you quote Shakespeare."

"And that annoys you too, does it? Well, 'though familiarity may not breed contempt, it takes the edge off admiration.' Hazlitt," I cited.

"What do you want from me, a pat on the head because you think you have some claim to fame as an amateur busybody? Okay. I recognize your rare talents. Does that suit you?"

"Not really, my 'courageous captain of compliments,' but 'those only deserve a monument who do not need one.' Shakespeare and Hazlitt," I informed him sweetly.

"Don't do that, Ellie."

"Fine. I won't tell you my sources so 'cudgel thy brains no more about it.'"

"Goddamn, you're impossible," he accused somewhat fairly. "Can't you ever admit when you're wrong?"

"Certainly. I was very wrong about you, and I admit it freely."

"What's that supposed to mean?"

"Simple translation. I was under the mistaken impression that you were a cut above the average man, when you're really excessively ordinary. But even 'the devil hath power to assume a pleasing shape.' Guess who?" I finished nastily.

"For crying out loud, Ellie. You've got an obsession about this case, and it's making you totally irrational."

"Well, let me tell you something, Mr. Clear-Thinking D.A., the police chief does not find me irrational, nor does he indulge my idiosyncrasies by pretending to listen to me. He believes it when I say I have evidence. You didn't even ask what it is."

"Forgive me." Joe bowed his dark head. "What amazing fact did you uncover that proves Lois McCoin's innocence?"

"There's no point in my telling you."

"Then even you must have doubts about it."

"None at all," I said with a superior smile.

That brought him up short. "What have you got, Ellie? Come on. Don't play games." When I didn't answer, he pulled rank on me. "Withholding evidence is a crime, you know."

"As bad as bribery, corruption, and multiple murder, all instigated by our local, lovable power company?"

"No Communist conspiracy too?"

"That's it, Joe! Get out of here before I clobber you with my wet shoe."

"Come on, Ellie, be reasonable. You can't announce the whole world is part . . . all right, all right. Put your shoe down. I'm leaving. But when you come to your senses, call me."

"No chance," I said to his retreating back. " 'Our revels now are ended.' That's Shakespeare and Ellie Gordon."

Chapter Twenty-six

The white-hot rage that sustained during my war of words with Joe finally burned out, leaving an enduring resentment which I nursed along with the sniffles. Naturally, I caught a cold hanging around the detention center in wet clothes, and naturally, I blamed Joe for it. If he had been as concerned as he professed, he would have dosed me with Contac instead of criticism.

It only increased my acrimony that he was right about the inglorious results of my escapade. Sunday's saturation at Canyon Escondido had turned into a media event, so everyone not only knew what happened to me, but felt obliged to offer cutesy comments about it. Sure, Matt Steunkle had saved me from an obligatory court appearance, but the notoriety of having my half-hidden face make Monday morning's paper brought me more attention than if my mug shot had been plastered on the Post Office's ten-most-wanted list. It was especially galling that anyone even recognized me from the picture.

As if unfunny jokes about my hair and unwanted advice on what to do for split ends didn't rankle enough, there were also the phone calls. I finally took the receiver off the hook at home and notified the receptionist at the office as to just which *nudniks* I categorically refused to speak. At the top of my shit list were two men: one ex-husband and one ex-lover. Oh yes, Dan had reacted to seeing that unlovely photo in the paper. He was appalled, annoyed, yet rather intrigued by my brush with the law. Evidently, this new, daring, unkempt Ellie Gordon, the one who kept embarrassing him with her forays into the limelight, was much more appealing than the dependable, neat, little wife he had discarded so easily. The ex-lover was Joe Corelli, who decided he had been too hasty in his condemnation on Sunday afternoon. He was prepared to overlook my quarrelsome conduct after all. Too bad, because I wasn't about to overlook his. But hope springs eternal, and he sent roses to the office on Tuesday after I hung up on him Monday night, and chocolates on Wednesday after I instructed Kimberly to inform him I'd be "out" no matter when he called.

Of course, this intense melodrama enthralled the titty-tats who considered themselves experts in matters of romance and reprisal. Diane relied heavily on the lessons learned through watching soap operas in the days before she abandoned television to go to work. Kimbie-baby came through with first-hand recommendations on how she and her newlywed hubby always resolved their arguments in bed. But Barbara Beauchamp, after tasting one of my ignored orange creams, was the most pragmatic of the lot.

"Single, professional, heterosexual men under sixty are hard to find," she cautioned. "Let Joe say he's sorry, then take him back. It's obvious you've got him by the balls already."

"Which is precisely the spot I don't want."

"Why? It works, doesn't it?"

I raised a lofty brow. What was the point of arguing with a woman who believed good sex was a justifiable reason to encourage a bad relationship? Barbara simply didn't subscribe to the theory that a meeting of the minds is preferable before an attachment of the genitals.

She shook her mane of dark hair at me. "I think the guy truly cares about you. These are Godiva chocolates, you know."

"Anyone who equates candy with love deserves the sugar coating. Dig in," I waved my hand at her. "I don't want any."

"You don't? Gee, you must really be mad."

She hovered over the heart-shaped box, no doubt looking for a truffle. I could have disclosed the disappointing truth—that Dennis Devlin had eaten the last one—but I kept my mouth shut in the interests of continuing detente between labor and management.

Another source heard from was Mark Devlin. He thought the least I could do was listen to Joe's apology. "So he got sore at you and said a little more than he meant. You're not the only one who can get carried away in an argument."

If I hadn't been in the middle of a sneeze, I would have walked out of his office on a wave of offended dignity. Instead, I wiped my nose. "This time, I did not go overboard, as you just intimated. I held onto my cool, even joked while the man cut me to pieces."

"Quoted from the immortal Bard, did you?" Mark started to smile, then thought better of it.

I contented myself by waving the Kleenex at him. "Sure, you think it's funny now, but you wouldn't be snickering if you'd been the recipient of Joe's slander. Never mind that after he laid himself wide open for a defamation of character suit, he expected gratitude for not charging me with obstructing justice."

"I'm sure Matt Steunkle would have stepped in again if he tried anything so unhandsome," Mark said mildly. "But can't you consider Joe's offense only a misdemeanor? After all, he didn't draw *much* blood. So how about a month's probation? That's not overly lenient, and imposing a stiffer sentence would be cruel and unusual punishment. What say, Your Honor?"

What say, he asked me? The D.A. had shown contempt for this court by sneering at my abilities as a legitimate investigator, and only one verdict would do. Call me the hanging judge, but I wanted total vindication for my impugned intelligence with a little quid pro quo thrown in. Measure for measure. An eye for an eye.

"You're an eloquent jurist, Mark"—I got to my feet—"but request denied. A simple apology will not suffice in this case."

"Which can only mean," he said thoughtfully, "that Joe's going to have to eat his words before you exonerate him."

As usual, the High Mullah of perceptive analysis struck the hidden depths of my psyche. Certainly I intended to make Joe eat his words. The trick was finding the right spice for his humble pie, and at the moment all I had was a bland copy of a cashier's check. Even bolstered by my fancy suppositions, the receipt merely hinted at corporate skullduggery. Trying to use it as evidence in a murder at this point was like putting the chicken before the egg, or vice versa, without even getting inside the henhouse yet. If I expected to prove Tom Grabowski guilty of killing two people, first I had to prove he and PSSC were guilty of an illegal power-play. And the receipt by itself wasn't enough. Paper just can't hold all that water. What I needed was backing, unporous corroboration.

Feeling quite professional about having a sensible campaign strategy, this "amateur busybody" went right to the source of information. But when I called Lois and asked where at PSSC I could find some confirmation that Drake Prescott's payment to Tom had been from power company funds, she told me to forget that angle.

"You won't be able to trace anything through bookkeeping. Not even an internal audit would show redirected funds, and I can assure you the money didn't come from petty cash. But hasn't Joe Corelli already opened a probe into it?"

When I had to admit that Joe knew nothing about the receipt, Lois was definitely displeased, especially after I voiced my original suspicion by applying it to the D.A. "Let's be realistic. There's no proof you found the receipt at Jessica's. How could he be sure you didn't have it all along, or at least since Drake's death?"

"What are you saying, Ellie, that you don't believe me? I made up this whole story? Oh, God, you think I lied to you."

I calmed her down eventually, but of course, I couldn't help wondering if she really weren't using me to muddy the waters. Injured innocence was such a convenient dodge. On the other hand, maybe I was getting paranoid. Everyone couldn't be guilty.

Determined to follow through no matter what the results, I dialed the Public Relations Department at PSSC. I was in luck. April Evans would be glad to meet me at The Garden Spot for lunch. Could I make it over there in ten minutes? You bet. Ignoring the dirty looks from the titty-tats who normally took a lunch break before me, and promising miracles of productivity this afternoon to a disapproving Helen Ramirez who had expected them this morning, I dashed off.

This was the stuff of which espionage tales were made, although showing secret documents to would-be snitches usually occurred in dark alleys or a secluded niche under the Tower of London while rain dripped gloomily off a parapet. My covert encounter took place in a flower bower. The Garden Spot was just too bright and sunny for words, especially for the exchange of dialogue going on in our latticed and leafy booth. Above my head was a skylight; at my back was a growth of lush vegetation in every conceivable color; while across from me, April Evans leaned closer to hear what I was mumbling.

"This is extremely confidential," I whispered à la Jane

Chestnut. "But you did say you wanted to help Lois so I'm giving you the opportunity. Just promise you won't say anything to anyone, because I can't reveal where I got the information."

"Oh, I promise," she swore faithfully.

"Very well, you're now on the A Team." I reached into my purse for the wadded-up clue, but kept it hidden in my palm until extracting one more vow of silence from her. Then I slipped her the paper under the table.

To be honest, I didn't expect April to drop her fork on the flowered carpeting in utter incredulity that I'd uncovered the awful truth about the power company. But neither did I expect her to look at the receipt with a totally blank expression on her lovely face and say, "What's this?"

"Don't you know?"

"I've never seen it before."

"Think carefully," I prompted. "Does a cashier's check for five thousand dollars seem at all familiar? Did Mr. Prescott ever mention buying one, or paying that amount to anybody?"

"What for?"

"A business arrangement."

"Gee, I wouldn't know anything about his private affairs."

"Would you know anything about a company affair? Could your former boss have been PSSC's fiscal agent, their emissary? You see, April, I think the money came from a higher source than Prescott, because it was paid to someone in ANSWER."

"Why would the company do that?" she asked in apparent ignorance.

Protecting an old lover or a current employer, I wondered? In the event of both, I redirected my slant. "Actually what concerns me aren't PSSC's doings via Drake Prescott or without him, but the machinations of Tom Grabowski. Remember, this is not to be repeated, but from one of ANSWER's chief radicals, he strangely metamorphosed into a Neville Chamberlain. Peace at any cost."

The allusion was lost on April. Evidently, she'd never heard of Britain's umbrella-wielding prime minister. She probably barely heard of World War II. But what she did get was my point.

Her lustrous eyes widened. "Are you trying to connect this fellow in ANSWER with Mr. Prescott's murder?"

"Not just yet," I said truthfully. "First I want to connect him with Mr. Prescott, and I was hoping you could supply the umbilical cord."

"Golly, I wish I could, but this is news to me."

I didn't dispute her claim, figuring April could be taking refuge in that old employee defense system, CYA. Cover Your Ass. Corporately speaking, PSSC wouldn't appreciate her spilling the beans. And in legal language, she'd be an accessory after the fact if her knowledge of criminal wrongdoing went unreported. So why should she tell me anything? For the joy of it?

Still, I had provoked her curiosity. "What are you going to do with this receipt now?" she asked, handing it back to me.

"Continue my uphill battle to clear Lois. I can't imagine how at the present, but if this clue fits my theory, and I believe it does, tracing its meandering path might get me to the finish line before she goes to trial."

April pondered that for a moment. "Do the police agree with you?"

"They will when they find out."

"You mean, nobody knows about this but you?" she asked in amazement. "You're investigating it all by yourself?"

Well used to the idea of my being considered a legitimate operator by everyone except Joe Corelli, I shrugged. "For now I'm working alone, but if I can't find anyone to make the verification I need, maybe I will turn the whole thing over to the police."

"Don't they already think Lois is guilty?" she asked sensibly.

Touché. Of course they thought Lois was guilty, and so did April by the sound of it. "Does that mean you believe I'm fighting a lost cause?"

"Maybe not," she consoled. "And it wouldn't hurt to keep trying, would it? After all, Lois has nothing to lose. But personally," she added, watching me tuck the receipt back inside my wallet, "I can't see how that's going to help her."

While I poked dispiritedly at my salad, April attempted to cheer me up with a late-developing report on her two little darlings. Jason was into fingerpaints; Jennifer had a new tooth; and they went to a friend's birthday party last week where they played pin the tail on the donkey for the first time. Her beautiful face positively glowed as she rattled off the achievements of her two children, while I marveled how this ravishing creature could be both tenderly maternal and a tempestuous mistress. What it evoked was a picture of Drake Prescott clutching her boobs passionately as she whispered nursery rhymes in his ear. Interestingly erotic, but not necessarily even close to the truth. There was only Carole Prescott's accusation and office grapevine to attest that April had been having an affair with her married boss. Neither were very convincing against the girl's madonna-like image as a mother, and neither did I care since my suspicions had gone in an entirely different direction.

But suspicions they remained, no thanks to April and the addition of two useless lunches on my Visa charge which I could ill-afford. This month's bill was going to be in the three-digit category, what with getting my white pants steam-cleaned and blocked to no avail, buying new espadrilles to replace the pair also ruined at Canyon Escondido, and putting gas in the car so I could drive hither and yon questioning people. Private detection was an expensive hobby for someone on a straight salary.

The rest of the afternoon cost me too, since I had to pay the price of getting nothing done all morning. And as I headed home along the coast road, I wasn't one inch closer to proving Tom Grabowski had been or still was on the take. Maybe my approach was wrong, I thought in irritation. Maybe I should start at the end and work backward. Solve Jessica's murder first, then retreat to Drake Prescott's death and the receipt. Who knew? I might discover Tom was a killer all right, but perfectly innocent of accepting a bribe. Very funny. Or was it not so funny? It might be a good idea to question Jessica's neighbors and find out if anyone had noticed a white Chevy pickup parked there two Sundays ago. Parked where, I reminded myself? If he finally found a space as far away from her house as I did, it would take me forever to canvas a three block radius.

Probably a real detective . . . no, make that one on a per diem . . . would have driven directly over and spent a fruitless evening getting doors slammed in her face. I just went home to face a clutter of dirty dishes in the sink. There was no earthly reason I couldn't have left them there to rot, especially as the residue from last night's Lean Cuisine was already halfway putrified, but I had to choose this very minute to play happy homemaker. Scraping off the plates and silverware, I ran them under water, then loaded everything in the dishwasher. Then I sponged the sink and stuffed all the yuck down the drain, turning on the garbage disposal to dispose of the mess for good. A second later, my favorite suit, the counter, and the window were all splashed with a stinking spray of beef tips, coffee grinds, and shredded broccoli with dietetic hollandaise sauce.

"Damn and blast this contraption!" I shut off the vomiting monster and grabbed a dish towel, but even as I dabbed ineffectually at the stains on my jacket and moaned about another fifteen dollar cleaning bill, I wondered if this were a sign. Not necessarily from heaven, but more like a slug on the subconscious from my *bubbe*.

Without giving myself time to think that maybe the omen meant don't do it, I ran to the phone, dialed Tom Grabowski's number, and begged him to come over immediately and fix my recalcitrant garbage grinder. It was on the blink again.

"What have you been throwing down it?" he asked in exasperation.

"Nothing that doesn't belong in the sewer," I answered aggrievedly. "And if you can't solve the problem once and for all, I think you'd better install a new unit. Really, Tom, complain to the company or something. It's ridiculous to have the thing spit back at me every time I'm in the mood to clean."

Unhappy but completely unsuspecting, my contractor promised he'd get there at six-thirty or thereabouts. Racing madly I changed into a housecoat, wiped up a little, then dithered about where I should hide the tape recorder. Good sleuths always keep one on hand, though good sleuths probably don't let the batteries die either. Since this model was too big to stick in my bra, which had no electrical outlet anyway, I had to find an unobtrusive place to plug it in. First I tried behind the Boston fern hanging over the sink, but the cord didn't match the fronds. Inside the cabinets wouldn't work. The sound would be too muffled. Finally, I just opted for simplicity. Setting the tape deck on the counter, I covered it with a dish towel, then put a plastic colander on top, upside down. A trifle intricate perhaps, but the arrangement had that homey touch. Now all I had to do was decide how in the world I could get Tom to confess.

Chapter Twenty-seven

Fifteen minutes later, with the tape recorder running silently and Tom Grabowski fiddling around under the sink, I sat at the kitchen table and chewed on my thumbnail. I still hadn't received a divine inspiration from my grandmother on how to bring up the subject of the power company. I considered trying it from a consumer angle, but a discussion of utility rates could last forever. I could open with a comment on ANSWER's upcoming election and get on Tom's good side by griping about my arrest, except that didn't seem very promising either.

But while I dawdled and brooded and came up empty-handed, Tom had finished his chore and came over to show what he'd come up with. "Ellie, there's not a disposal on the market that can chew these buggers." He flashed an olive pit under my nose.

"Sorry," I smiled weakly.

"If you had just thrown this in the trash can where it belongs, I wouldn't have had to take apart the drain pipe and unstick the blades." Tom was reproachful.

He looked around for something to wipe off his hands

and spotted the dish towel on the counter. Before he could grab the cover of my artlessly hidden bug, I jumped up and threw myself in front of it.

"Tom...I...here." Using my body as a shield, I reached behind me and tore off a piece of paper toweling from the roller on the wall.

"What's the matter? You don't like doing laundry any better than cleaning house?"

"Well," I shrugged awkwardly, leaning back even further to block his view, "there are more exciting pastimes than soaking dishrags in Biz."

Obviously, my pose, arms back and breasts thrust forward, connoted something more suggestive than preferring a trip to Disneyland over household drudgery, because Tom certainly got the wrong impression.

"Want to do something exciting right now?"

"Actually, yes," I replied, thinking this was as good a lead-in as any and not realizing what a dirty little mind he had. "Listen, ah...Tom. There's something I'd like to ask you."

He grinned and tossed the paper towel on the counter. "Bet I can guess what it is."

"You can?"

"Sure. And the answer is yes. I'd love to go to bed with you."

"I beg your pardon?"

"That's okay, Ellie." The grin widened. "You don't have to beg. And you didn't have to put all that junk in the disposal as an excuse to get me over here. I find you very attractive. You're a terrific-looking woman for your age."

I didn't know whether to laugh or slap the young whippersnapper. Even if my ruse had been rather weak, surely he didn't think my cordial, almost motherly interest in him all this time had been a come-on, merely climaxed by an olive pit. Thank you, *bubbe*. That was not the inspiration I had in mind. The Mata Hari approach to worming confessions from men might be more successful with Tom than it had been with the D.A., but I wasn't prepared to make that big a sacrifice.

Checking to be sure the top button of my housecoat was securely fastened, I attempted to clear up Tom's misunderstanding. "No, it's nothing like that . . . though I'm very flattered . . . but my question was really about business."

Only my vanity suffered when he showed just moderate disappointment. "Yeah? What kind of question? Like is Vista del Mar going into receivership after all? Well, the answer is no, so you can stop worrying. I'm set now. The whole project will be completed by August, then I'll be able to put up those tennis courts I promised."

In a spirit compounded of relief that he raised the subject, and bravado because I had to continue it, I took the plunge. "Now that you mention the condo, Tom, where are you getting the money to finish building everything?"

"I told you before. A friendly banker."

"You said he wasn't so friendly, and that's why I'm wondering if you had to give him extra collateral."

His eyes narrowed. "You're not going to lose your investment, so what's it to you?"

"What's it to me?" I repeated, thinking fast. Now that sexual strategy had been ruled out, the other tried-and-true method of getting someone to confess was using shock tactics. Pretend you know everything already and put the suspect on the defensive by making him try to justify his actions. That seemed the only possible plan at the moment, as long as I stuck to the less heinous crime of palm greasing and left murder out of the picture. "My interest in your financial affairs," I said bluntly, "concerns ANSWER."

"What are you talking about?" He took a wary step back.

I folded my arms across my chest and hoped this "springe to catch a woodcock" would net me my quarry. "Don't bother to deny it, Tom. I know PSSC is paying you to sabotage the antinukes."

"Sabotage . . ." His face reddened. "Where did you get such a crazy idea?"

"Is it so crazy?" I asked mildly.

"Damn it, Ellie. I don't know who you've been talking to, but if Vickie's spreading rumors about me . . ."

"Not Vickie. And I happen to know they're not rumors. For one thing, I saw the hooligans you hired to disrupt the demonstration."

"I wasn't even there," he protested.

"Of course not. The power company is paying you to back off, and you need their money to avoid bankruptcy." Then I hit him with my tin-plated uppercut. "You might as well admit it, Tom. I have proof Drake Prescott gave you five thousand dollars for openers."

"There isn't any proof," he sneered. "You're bluffing."

"Would I go to all this trouble on a bluff?" That was the biggest bluster of all, but it worked.

Tom turned around and smacked his fist into the refrigerator. "Fuck that arrogant bastard! He had to play games with me. He had to hold back on the money then fuck up with a stinking cashier's check. That's how you found out, isn't it? Some shit over at PSSC, some secretary blabbed and showed you the record of that first payment." When I merely nodded, thinking he'd just put another dent in the refrigerator, he grabbed my shoulders and started shaking me like a rag doll. "You made a copy of it, didn't you? That's why you got proof. You made a fucking copy." With my head bobbing up and down of its own volition now, Tom let loose with one more foul curse and sent me bouncing off the cupboards.

Well, so far so good. At the cost of a few broken ribs, I got my confession. A surprise assault worked all right, except I didn't quite account for the effects of shell shock. Trying not to show any untoward distress over the multiple contusions on my back, I pulled myself erect and remembered my boast to Betsy about having an appetite for danger. This was certainly feeding it.

"There's one thing you can explain to me," I said, rubbing my bruised elbow and attempting to regain some control of the situation. "Why did Prescott pay you by check? Aren't under the table transactions usually settled with a suitcase full of twenties?"

"Hell, the creep got cash from the company, but he wouldn't fork over until there was a clear change in ANSWER's policies. I guess he got nervous about carrying around a wad that size for two weeks, so he bought a cashier's check with it."

"Yes, he sounds like a creep," I agreed. "But after Prescott paid out, why did you crash the reception at the nuke plant? Seems to me your maneuver was exactly the kind of thing PSSC was spending top dollar to prevent."

"I know, but the jerk expected me to stop the demonstration that day even after I explained a major reversal in ANSWER's policies couldn't be contrived overnight." Tom scowled and kicked the leg of the table. "When he threatened not to give me another cent, I just decided to show him and the whole damn company how bad I could make them look."

"What credit card did you use as an ID to get in the door, Sears or Wards?"

"An expired Visa card. And how do you know?"

"Someone in your fan club bragged."

"Yeah?" That seemed to please him a little. "Anyway, PSSC got the message real quick. One of their lawyers had me sprung from the county jail in about an hour flat. Funny thing," he added, "afterward I knew they were sorry they bothered. It would have been a lot handier and cheaper if one of their boys could have pinned Prescott's murder on me. 'Antinuke activist runs amok and kills public service company executive.' ANSWER never would have survived that one. But neither would PSSC. If they tried a stunt like that, I'd have talked and pulled them right down with me. So they played it smart and kept me on the payroll."

What did that mean? Had the power company been unable to find proof of Tom's guilt, or were they just covering it up to protect themselves from a justice department probe? In case Tom followed my train of thought, I refrained from musing about murder and got back to money. "Now I see why you were so mellow on that TV interview. Pleasing your bosses."

He looked at me sullenly. "I did what I had to, and there's not a damn thing you can do about it."

"I can ask you to stop."

"Why the hell should I?" he flashed. "Nobody's losing out. I make sure ANSWER stays enough of a thorn in the side to keep the power company edgy, and they're glad to pay so it doesn't get worse."

"Then you're cheating on both sides, not that I care if PSSC gets rooked. But ANSWER is trying to do something worthwhile, and I think you should step out of the picture and let them."

Tom started cracking his knuckles one by one as he stared at me. Interestingly, I wasn't intimidated. My suggestion, or rather, my strong request gave the cornered rat a way out of his trap. Turn honest and Ellie Gordon would forgive him his former trespasses. In the meantime, a tape of this conversation, along with the receipt, would convince Steunkle to do a bit more digging into the Prescott case, and I would have proved my point. Unfortunately, while I was smugly patting myself on the back for being so crafty, Tom was busy picking apart my story.

At the pop of the last knuckle, he said pensively, "I can't figure you, Ellie. How come all of a sudden you care about some kind of moral victory for ANSWER?"

"Jess was my friend. I owe a certain allegiance to her ideals."

"Bullshit! You didn't do all this snooping for a beloved memory. What's your angle?" His face darkened. "You're not playing detective to get me into trouble, are you?"

"Why would I do a thing like that?" When Tom took a

step toward me, I retreated into another lie. "Hey, if I wanted to get you in trouble, I would have given the receipt to the D.A.!"

"You still got it?"

"Sure. With all my important papers, in a safe-deposit box."

That's when he pounced. Two murderous hands closed around my throat as he bent me backward over the counter. "Bitch! I know what you're after. A cut. You want to buy in."

Faced with two choices, my immediate strangulation which would not be recorded on tape, or letting Tom discover I was a criminal at heart which could be edited out, I confessed to the awful truth.

"Yes, yes. I want a cut. The receipt in exchange for a piece of the action."

Expecting to be bounced off the ceiling this time, I almost dropped to the floor in a faint when Tom abruptly let go of me. "Okay. It's a deal."

"Just like that? No more dickering?" I rubbed my sore neck.

"Only with the power company," he said, looking at the red marks his fingers had left. "I get a share for arranging the transaction, but when they hear what you've got to sell, their terms ought to be generous enough for both of us."

I always wanted a mink coat to wear in my Ferrari, but mostly I wanted Tom out of here before he changed his mind about being so accommodatingly dishonest. By naturally assuming there was as much larceny in my soul as in his, he'd provided me with a tattered security blanket. After all, partners in crime only snitch at their own expense, don't they?

"Sounds good to me." I compounded our joint felony. "How much will they pay?"

"Plenty," he said in a cool voice. "But before you rush to open a Swiss bank account, you'd better open that safe-deposit box and get me the receipt."

"First thing tomorrow," I promised, knowing that the first thing tomorrow I'd be at the police station.

"Be sure you don't forget," he murmured with silky menace. "And if you try a double cross, you'll be mighty sorry. PSSC plays for keeps."

And so do you, I thought nervously, hearing the faint click of the tape recorder as it shut off. Praying Tom wouldn't identify the sound, I started walking toward the front door, assuring him of my trustworthy depravity every step of the way.

"You realize, Tom," I complained with rueful self-reproach, "my original plan was to blackmail you into doing the decent thing. And instead, here I am on the wrong side of the law with you."

"Depends on how you look at it, Ellie." He smiled the same smile I used to consider boyishly endearing. "This is a perfect chance to rake in some big bucks . . . and just for returning a piece of paper to the original owners. You might even say it's the virtuous thing to do."

"As virtuous as destroying ANSWER?" I sighed in poignant regret.

"Some people think keeping ANSWER from going off the deep end will make the organization more effective in the long run."

"Well," I admitted grudgingly, "I suppose you could see it that way."

"No, just suppose *you* do," he warned, giving me a heavy-handed love pat on the jaw. "Getting a guilty conscience now would be stupid, Ellie. Remember that."

I closed the door behind him and slipped the lock into place. Me, stupid? I was a bloomin' genius. Didn't I have a half-hour of incriminating conversation duly recorded for the authorities? Hadn't I put together motive, opportunity, and corroborating evidence into a perfect package? Now all I needed was a tube of Ben Gay and a telephone.

Chapter Twenty-eight

After double-checking that my cassette player had caught every fascinating detail . . . yes, there was me choking to death . . . I could hardly contain myself. The crack of dawn tomorrow morning would be soon enough to lay the facts before the chief of police, and I had no doubt he'd listen to every damning word out of Tom's mouth, compliment me on the sound quality, and proceed to reopen the Prescott case. Conceivably, I might have to do some fancy talking about the little matter of concealing material evidence until I had it properly validated, but first things first. Tonight was reserved for another kind of triumph, a little matter of serving up a healthy slice of humble pie to a certain skeptical D.A. Joe Corelli, put on your best bib and tucker. We were about to dine out in style . . . Ellie Gordon style.

I'd done it. I proved him wrong about me. And when he heard how, not only would he have to eat his words, but a plateful of crow along with it. Of course, I would be magnanimous in victory. No rubbing the D.A.'s nose in his error of judgment, nor expecting him to grovel at my feet.

A twenty-one gun salute would suffice, though Joe might feel regretful enough to insist on twenty-two.

But with my hand poised over the receiver, ready to lift it and spread glad tidings that I was now prepared to forgive him, I paused. There was something else to resolve before I granted final absolution, and that was if picking up where we left off also meant giving in to Joe's chronic concern. He might be forced to concede that I had a talent for deduction, but he'd still wish it were a knack for knitting instead. My avocation didn't please him. He worried. He yelled at me when he worried. And I yelled back. In fact, when Joe saw my name on the Crimewatchers' new member roster, it was a wonder he didn't revoke my beeper out of panic that I might use it. I realized, with misgivings, that this was a serious conflict of interest. He was conflicting with mine.

I pondered this impasse for at least two minutes before making my decision. True, Joe was irritatingly protective. He wanted to keep me out of harm's way by restricting me in the loving circle of his arms. However, the circle was quite comfortable and not intended to be a punishment, so why banish him forever because of one little character flaw? I wasn't perfect. There must be one or two minor defects in my nature. So maybe I should just turn over a new leaf . . . Joe's. His mistake wasn't irrevocable. The dear man merely confused "caring for Ellie" with "taking care of Ellie," and I could break him of that bad habit in no time.

Satisfied by my rationale, I dialed his number. The moment Joe heard my voice, he'd proffer the apology he'd been trying to deliver all week, and I would accept it graciously, with only a hint of "Don't let it happen again" in my response. But on the third ring, his telephone answering machine clicked on, giving me exactly twenty seconds to leave a message that would be both properly reticent and enticing enough to get him here. Nothing as crass as "I solved two murders so now I'll take you back on my terms." And no quarrelsome quotes either. For a change, I settled on plain speaking.

"Joe, this is Ellie. We have some unfinished business to resolve, personally and professionally. If you're still in the mood to kiss and make up, come over to my place tonight, and I'll expose myself and the evidence."

Could anything be plainer? Humming to myself, I hung up the phone and pictured his reaction when he listened to that bury-the-hatchet invitation. He'd go ten miles over the speed limit getting here.

Now to set the stage. Placing the tape recorder on the coffee table as a centerpiece, I flanked it with two long-stemmed goblets and a bottle of Chenin Blanc. Then to match the glamor, I went to change out of my housecoat, though if clothes made the man, perhaps the absence of any on a woman would do it faster. But I didn't want to rush the festivities. Before my guest of honor got to see anything else, he had to be shown the worth of my intellect and the soundness of my logic. No need to wear a pin-stripe suit and horn-rimmed glasses to this end; just a costume that would make me seem bright enough to have solved any number of crimes, and at the same time make me appear as desirable as a fertile oasis after a long, dry journey in the barren desert.

Black lace nightgown? Too corny. How about the crotchless panties I got for my birthday? I'd never have the nerve. Did I own anything elegantly elastic? Gloria Vanderbilt sweats was all. Wait. I rummaged through the closet and finally found the perfect outfit. My bought-in-Hawaii, never-worn-since-the-divorce evening pajamas.

A superstitious person would have tossed them right back into the garment bag. Wear a reminder of the disastrous second honeymoon on Maui that ended with Dan telling me he found another woman? Irrelevant, I scoffed. It only proved Dan's bad taste. I looked ravishing in this silk-screen print. The decolletage offered a tantalizing glimpse of bosom, and if the viewer wished further sights, the straps could be lowered without undo fuss. Yes, this was ideal. The sea-blue colors flattered my skin tones, which at my age needed flattering, while the culotte pants hid the worst of my hips and offered the swirling gracefulness of a long skirt. Matching sash belt, sling-back sandals, and the ensemble was complete. Damn if I couldn't model this in *Harper's Bazaar*, the short woman's section.

Soaking in a tubful of water liberally laced with perfumed skin softener, I forced my mind off of pleasure and onto business. It would be helpful if Tom made a repeat confession with details when the police questioned him tomorrow. He'd been willing enough to talk in my kitchen, though I did rather force some things out of him. In fact, it was still hard to believe that the young man I'd fed so lavishly was a vicious killer. I only hoped Tom would be securely behind bars when he discovered his would-be partner in extortion had ratted on him. Even the idea of his running loose right now made me jumpy. If Joe didn't arrive within the hour, maybe I should call Matt Steunkle tonight too, just to be on the safe side.

What kind of safe? This wasn't the end by a long shot, and Matt couldn't provide police protection for me until Tom had been tried, convicted, sentenced, and incarcerated for good. I'd have to hire an army of Pinkertons as bodyguards the moment he was released on bail. This was assuming, naturally, he'd try one more murder, this one sheerly for revenge. But who wanted to tempt fate?

There were some definite drawbacks in this line of work, and not the least of them was sleuthing myself out of home and hearth. My beautiful condominium. What would happen to it after my efforts put the contractor out of business? Even before I threw in a monkey wrench, Vista del Mar's future was uncertain, but now the bank would take the entire development into receivership and sell to the highest bidder. No wonder private eyes always lived in anonymous boardinghouses. We were a real liability. My luck, the power company would buy the property as a diversified investment. They owned a hefty share of it anyway, having financed Tom's costly venture already to the tune of several thousand dollars. Might as well salvage their ill-gotten gain and get the rest at a bargain-basement price.

Climbing out of the tub and toweling my scented and soon-to-be homeless body dry, I was lifted by one ray of hope. PSSC might not be able to afford to buy a doghouse after paying for the battery of lawyers they'd need. Naturally, when the state brought suit against them for misuse of stockholders' funds, they'd claim Prescott was solely responsible. How convenient to blame him for succumbing to thriftless ambition with their misappropriated petty cash vouchers. Besides, his name was on the copy of the check, and "it is not the thief who is hanged, but the one who was caught stealing." I gathered from Tom's story that Prescott's successor in bribery was too canny to put his signature to the fact. Frankly, I commended the company's belated good sense. Tom already misplaced one piece of incriminating evidence that showed his relationship with them was more than just rate-payer versus utility. But thanks to his provident oversight, I reaped the best dividend.

Stepping into the brightly hued hostess pajamas, I was struck by the sheer accident of my discovery. If Tom hadn't been careless enough to leave the receipt at Jessica's, I never would have connected him to either murder. In fact, without that one and only clue, I couldn't come close to establishing any kind of case against him, misdemeanor or major malefaction. I guess it had been rather careless of me as well to keep the evidence stuffed inside my pocketbook since Saturday. What if I lost it too? Lois would never forgive me.

As I was about to sit down at the vanity table, my mind snagged on some discrepancy in that quick summary of events, but the thought of Lois sidetracked me. She was the person I should have called right away. When I spoke to her this morning, I practically accused her of lying to me, and the least I could do was put her fears to rest. Poor thing, stuck in a hospital bed with a guard posted at her door. Our conversation might have sent her into a relapse. Well, that could be remedied fast enough. I thumbed through the telephone book for the number of Casa Grande General, feeling guilty because I hadn't done this before. Clever Ellie Gordon might have solved the mystery, but it was Lois's case.

"Yes. Room three-twenty-two, please." I sat on the edge of the bed and tapped my fingers impatiently on the nightstand. "Hell, Lois? This is Ellie, and I have wonderful news . . . excuse me. I'm sorry . . . they must have connected me to the wrong room. Thank you." More tapping of fingernails. "Operator, would you please put me through to Lois McCoin's room . . . what was that? Discharged? When did . . . today? Thank you."

I hung up the phone, more confused than concerned. If Lois had been sent home, she couldn't be ailing too much, but why hadn't anyone told me? Immediately, I dialed her house, except after eleven rings, I guessed she wasn't there. Since a heart patient hardly would be out celebrating her release from the hospital at the corner disco, I presumed Lois had gone somewhere to convalesce. Helen probably drove her to a nice secluded rest home that barred the press.

"Hello," Helen answered promptly.

"Good, you're back. Why didn't you inform me your star client was given a clean bill of health today?" I charged in, no preliminaries.

"If I didn't recognize your voice, Ellie, I'd know the manner," she yawned. "Now tell me what you're talking about."

"I'm sorry if I woke you, although in another few hours it'll be bedtime. And I'm talking about Lois."

Evidently, Helen checked her watch. "Is it just eight o'clock? I must have dozed off, but try me one more time about Lois. Did the doctor have a good report on her test results?"

"Good enough to give her bed to Sidney Garfinkle. She's gone. Out of the hospital. Free as a bird, though I can't imagine what happened to her uniformed watch dog. Didn't you discharge him of his duties?"

"No. Are you sure about this?"

"I'm not sure of anything, but if you didn't take Lois to Shady Willows Rest Home, then he absconded with her."

"That's odd. I know she was feeling great yesterday, but I don't know where she is today."

"Obviously, out to dinner. They're probably at Burger King this very minute, toasting her restored health with a Whopper."

"Don't be facetious. Let me make a few calls and see what I can find out. Hang tight," she directed. "I'll get back to you."

From where, I wondered, hanging up the phone? Could Lois have been remanded to custody and now sat in the detention center, trying to contact her lawyer? Impossible. The police wouldn't arrest her for Jessica's murder without questioning her first in Helen's presence. Of course, Helen had been snoozing on the job, but there was no sense in my imagining the worst until I knew for sure it had happened. There was probably a very simple explanation for Lois's disappearance anyway, like maybe she jumped bond and flew to Argentina with an ex-cop turned fugitive from justice alongside her. Stop, Ellie, I chided myself. Don't create any more obstacles than already exist. The district attorney would resolve any and all problems with the receipt as his Excaliber. I just had to decide whether to wear hoop earrings or turquoise studs.

After opting for the turquoise, I applied a light coat of foundation, a touch of blusher, and the merest dab of blue eye shadow. Then I preened in front of the mirror, rehearsing a suitably modest reaction to Joe's flattery. "No, I didn't go to any trouble. This old dress has been sitting in my closet for over a year."

From one of the bedroom windows, I saw the arc of headlights swing into the complex. He was here. Rushing for a last shpritz of cologne and a final pat to my carefully disarranged curls, I raced into the foyer, unlocked the front door, then dashed over to the couch. When Joe rang the bell, I'd merely strike a pose of languid relaxation and bid him to enter at his own risk.

As the welcoming smile on my lips gradually grew stiff then faded entirely, I waited. Three minutes. Four. Finally, I got up and looked out the window. His car wasn't in front. Could the Talbots have come back early from Mexico? No, their garage door was closed, and the automatic light that flashed on at six every evening still glared from their roof. Then who . . . ?

Across the way, almost directly in front of the half-built townhouse next door, I found the answer. A car was parked there, but it was just beyond the range of the streetlight so I couldn't identify the model. The hood seemed awfully high for Joe's Mercedes. In fact, the shape was more like a small pickup truck.

My silly imagination again. Why would Tom Grabowski come back? He seemed perfectly happy with our arrangements when he left earlier, unless he had second thoughts and began to wonder if I truly were a crook under my honest exterior. Or suppose he suddenly got worried that I knew more about his criminal activities than I let on? Then too, it might just be a novice encyclopedia salesman out there, working up the nerve to make me his first customer. Or some kids who thought this was a great place to neck. But before I could dream up another comforting explanation, the car door opened.

A lone figure emerged, no kid and no sign of books under his arm. I couldn't discern more than a plaid shirt and a stocking cap, but the man's build was similar to Tom's, medium height, lean and lanky. Final identification was the way he skirted the circle of light thrown by the streetlight and cat-footed slowly toward my front door.

Okay, quick wit, do something smart: I could greet Tom with a hug and kiss, and pretend I got all gussied up because I knew he'd be back to enjoy the charms of a well-preserved older woman. Or I could hide under the bed and hope he'd think I wasn't home. Neither idea seemed too sensible, especially with the living room all lit up and the tape recorder in full view. If Tom fell for my seductive line, he might just assume I prepared for our romantic interlude by having a little background music ready. Except one flick of the switch and he'd be listening to himself sing the blues.

Fleeing to the bedroom with the tape player in my arms, I considered sticking it and myself between mattress and boxspring, but Tom was bound to notice the telltale lump. I also toyed with the notion of dashing to the garage, backing my car out of the driveway at sixty miles an hour, and rocketing down the cliffside road, with Tom right behind me in hot pursuit. Damn. What should I do? Since there was only a slim chance Joe would arrive in the next ten seconds, and a very large possibility it would be too late by then anyway, I had to think of some way to save myself other than becoming invisible. The sound of the doorbell seemed the call to get cracking, but where? How? In desperation I ran to the phone. Good old 911 was always a standby. Then I remembered something better.

Thanks to the marvels of modern technology and my timely enlistment, I had the means to send a more effective and more personalized SOS. In one move the tape recorder was stuffed under my pillow and the beeper was in my hand. After punching in my ID number and setting the emergency button, I waited for the red light to flash on. Yahoo! Message received. Within minutes a patrol car would be here to answer my distress signal. Now the only problem remaining was figuring out how to limit my involvement in the proceedings to Crimewatcher rather than victim.

Idiot that I was, I'd forgotten to lock the door again after opening the latch for Joe. Wonderful. Gifted head-work. When I didn't respond to Tom's summons, it wouldn't take him more than ten seconds to discover he didn't have to break down the door to get to me. I was just a turn of the knob away. Now I knew why they called it a dead bolt.

I debated the logistics of climbing out the bedroom window and hanging onto the ledge with my fingernails, but decided a high-speed chase along the shore road offered better odds of survival. I'd chance Tom's hearing the garage open and jumping on the hood to stop me . . . at least, I would if I could find my car keys. When they weren't in my purse, I tried to remember if I left them on the kitchen counter. Still in the ignition? Hell. Vowing to be more organized in the future, I took a deep breath, tiptoed across the room, slid open the patio door, and bolted into the dark night.

As I crouched behind the small storage shed, shivering quietly in my temptingly revealing hostess pajamas and wishing I'd had the foresight to bring a sweater to cover my more enticing points, Tom searched the house. He prowled from room to room, opening doors then slamming them shut in frustration, as if I'd be hiding in a two-by-six linen closet. Then I heard him in my bedroom, methodi-cally going through the dresser drawers where I couldn't possibly fit. Voyeur. He had the same peeping instincts as his namesake, except this Tom wasn't getting a kick from fondling my underwear, and I really wasn't the object of his search . . . not yet anyway. He probably came back because he didn't believe I had a safe-deposit box, and as soon as he found the receipt in my wallet, he'd know I tricked him. Then he'd come looking for me all right, and not to renegotiate our deal.

Only General Custer ever made as many tactical errors

as I had this evening. From come-hither olive pits to leaving vital evidence lying around for Tom to seize and destroy, I played it like a boob. And I wanted Joe to acknowledge my keen eye and cool hand? I should live so long. I probably wouldn't either, once Tom repossessed the matching receipt to his cashier's check. Now he'd have a memento to paste in his scrapbook under the heading "How I Got Away with Murder." He ought to ask me to autograph the damn thing as a reminder of how I had helped him return it to the rightful owner, if he could bear to part with his souvenir for money.

Wait a minute. Backtrack. Something didn't fit.

Then the discrepancy that nagged at me while I was dressing blossomed into a full-blown flaw. My entire theory was based on the supposition that whoever appropriated the carbon copy of the cashier's check from PSSC was the person who left it at Jessica's. But Tom Grabowksi had no access to Prescott's papers or power company files. ANSWER members weren't even allowed to step foot inside the lobby downstairs, though Tom wouldn't have risked exposure by calling on Prescott openly. By the same token, and presuming the receipt was Jessica's mysterious clue, why would he have notified her of its existence or wanted her to see it? To show how smart he'd been?

I recalculated everything in the next ten seconds, but finally understanding where I had taken a divergent fork in the road was small consolation. Oh sure, it was all crystal clear now as I stood rubbing my freezing arms, except "nine tenths of wisdom consists in being wise in time," and I might have delayed a bit too long in correcting my error. To my credit, I did have one suspicion that came close, but not as close as the murderer was to me at this very minute.

She had stepped outside the patio doors and was walking across the sundeck. Even then, she didn't call my name, not that I would have answered. The intensity of her pursuit indicated she hardly had conversation in mind anyway. Besides, it must have been obvious by now that I was hiding, unless she thought I was down on the beach collecting seashells in the dark. Apparently, she didn't. Her outdoor search for my missing person began on the other side of the yard near the trash cans.

Rather than take that as a personal affront, I used the opportunity to escape. Gathering the folds of my divided skirt, I put my best sandaled foot forward and scurried over to the unfinished patio of the unfinished townhouse next door. The rustle of the wind plus the sound of the surf covered my footsteps, but I was bound to be tracked down sooner or later. When she didn't find me inside the toolshed or under the hammock, she'd figure I was hiding behind a girder somewhere. My best chance was to pick the farthest one and hope the police got to me before the killer did.

The picturesque cliffside that looked so inviting during the day was treacherous terrain at night. Of course, I'd never planned to hike these slopes without lug-soled boots, and it might have been smarter to forego the pleasure of rock hopping and take the wooden steps down to the beach instead. But whatever my route, I didn't figure on the betraying moon. While I concentrated on not tripping and falling flat on my face, my pursuer must have turned around and spotted something moving. Without checking to make sure it wasn't an innocent field mouse or a wild rabbit, she attacked as though it were open season on all defenseless creatures.

A shot whizzed by my head and I dived for cover. What good it would do me seemed questionable, because with a boulder on one side and a steel girder on the other, I really was trapped between a rock and a hard place. My choices were great too. I could stay in this cramped position until she came within shooting gallery range, or try running again under the bright light of the moon. Either one made me a clay pigeon. She had a gun, and I had left my bullet-proof vest at home along with my sweater. So only one other option was left to me.

Without budging from my improvised foxhole, I called to her, "Yoo hoo, April. If you agree to a cease-fire, I'll come out for the truce talks."

Chapter Twenty-nine

Now I could see why I'd mistaken her for Tom. April was dressed in jeans and a lumberjack shirt with her long hair tucked inside a knit cap. Even now, only ten feet away, she was an anonymous figure, her blatant femininity completely camouflaged. The gun, however, was quite apparent; a small metallic-gray automatic that fit snugly in her palm.

"Don't get trigger-happy," I said uneasily, emerging from my hiding place with jello knees and a somersaulting stomach. "We have to discuss matters first, remember?"

This was my equivalent to Custer's Last Stand, since we did so much else alike, and I too needed reinforcements. My hope was that any kind of conversation with April, meaningful or not, would delay her until the police arrived, which ought to be momentarily.

"Just shut up and start walking," she ordered.

"Where?"

"That way." She pointed toward the cliff edge, not my favorite direction.

"But it's so windy out here," I rubbed the goosebumps

on my bare arms. "Wouldn't you rather talk in the house while we have a nice hot cup of coffee?"

"Don't pretend to be dumb," she said curtly. "You know why I'm here."

"Yes," I nodded, trying to sound casual. "You came for the cashier's check receipt you mistakenly left at Jessica's, but you're too late." I raised my hands in a gesture of open honesty. "I gave it to the police today. And I also explained that you took it from Drake Prescott's private papers after you killed him."

But instead of throwing down her gun in surrender, April shook her head coolly. "Good try, Ellie, but I checked with Lieutenant Peters this afternoon, right after you and I had lunch in fact. He didn't have any new evidence on the case, so I knew you still were after Tom Grabowski, temporarily of course, until you realized the truth. And just now, when I was searching the house, I found the receipt in your wallet." She patted her shirt pocket. "So you can quit lying."

"Oh dear, did I say I spoke to the police? Silly me. I told the D.A. Same thing really."

"If you did, really. But I think you're still lying. Now go on. Move it."

Discouragingly far away on Shoreside Drive, headlights traced a swift path along the road, but there was no sign of flashing red, no blaring sound of sirens in the distance. I decided it was better not to ask April if she turned off the pager while she rummaged through my purse for the receipt. With any luck, she thought the small black box was a pocket-sized calculator and left it on so my batteries would run down. Murderers are not noted conservationists.

Obeying the motion of her gun, I started walking as slowly as I dared. The rough going made a good excuse for my snail's pace, although the roughest part of the trek was trying to fathom how miracle workers managed bolts from the blue. I needed one right now; but I didn't know how to make magic, and I was lousy at sleight-of-hand tricks.

Oh, well, nothing ventured and all that malarky. Five feet from me the ground dropped off sharply, and thirty feet below that, high tide had brought the surf foaming over the jagged rocks rimming the narrow beach. I turned to face her. "Can we stop here? Heights make me nervous."

"Ellie, don't play games. I don't want to do this, but I have no choice. So let's get it over with. Climb up on that boulder."

I was tempted to ask why it was so important she shoot me in a particular locale, but since no designated site seemed especially inviting for that purpose, I stalled. Aside from the desirability of wasting a few more minutes in idle chitchat, there was my unquenchable curiosity to be slaked. Of course, it might be extinguished for good if help didn't come soon, but what respectable sleuth wants to meet her Maker with only half a mystery solved? It wasn't fair to get this far and still have unanswered questions about the murder motive. As long as I was right about who did it, I deserved to know why.

"One favor first, if you wouldn't mind honoring a condemned woman's last request. What made you kill Drake Prescott?" When April just stared at me, her face white in the moonlight, her eyes huge, no doubt in awe that I could maintain a scientific thirst for knowledge in such trying circumstances, I offered her a multiple choice quiz. "Since I'm fairly sure you weren't driven to avenge Lois, was it because he refused to get a divorce and marry you? Did he lead you down the primrose path then drop you in the thorns? You were lovers, I know." My semieducated guess, based on rumor, supposition, and the old adage about a woman scorned, hit pay dirt but not in the spot I anticipated.

"Lovers?" She let out a peal of laughter, though the sound hardly could be described as merriment. "What a joke. Oh, we slept together, but our relationship had nothing to do with love. He despised me and I hated his guts."

"Then what was the attraction in this 'unlove' affair?"

"There was no attraction," she sneered. "He screwed me because he always screwed his secretaries, and I screwed him in order to keep my job."

So the conversation turned out to be meaningful after all, though learning that April Evans had been a victim of sexual harassment shouldn't have come as any surprise. I just mistakenly assumed Prescott only picked on older women. Young, beautiful ones were generally cajoled, not coerced.

"Why did you submit to his blackmail?" I asked bluntly, wondering if she also went in for leather underwear and whips.

"Because I'm divorced, have two kids to support, an ex-husband who tries to drag me into court every month, lawyer's fees to pay, daycare costs, and a million other expenses I haven't got money for. I couldn't afford to lose my job."

"You could have reported him. Among other things, it's illegal for an employer to demand sexual favors."

Apparently, I hit a sore spot with her. She responded heatedly, "What makes you think Drake wouldn't have fought back and accused me of seducing him? It works both ways, you know, and women don't automatically win discrimination suits. If I brought charges against him and lost, there'd be a custody hearing the next day with Max claiming I'm morally unfit to raise my own children. How could I risk that?"

So the fiercely maternal, sexually abused April Evans decided to risk murder instead. I don't think I raised my brow at her logic, but for some reason she felt driven to explain herself.

"You don't realize, but I was dealing with a selfish egomaniac. A sadist. Drake got off on hurting people . . . people who couldn't hurt him back of course," she spat. "Most of the time, it was a dirty joke, a cutesy nickname, like with Jane Chestnut. You've seen how she's built. He called her Chesty for short, like it was a nickname, not an insult. And then there was Lois. He loved making nasty cracks about women just because it drove her up the wall. With me, he got a different kind of kick . . . a little bondage, a lot of foul language . . ." Her voice trailed off, then came back with a bitter denunciation. "He was vile. Vicious. What I did to him was justified. He brought it on himself. Now do you understand?"

Whether I did or not seemed immaterial, though given April's need to win my approval for electrocuting her boss, I wondered what motive she thought would appeal to me and came to another belatedly correct deduction.

"He was going to fire you anyway. Is that what happened?"

"That's it," she snorted, getting emotionally caught up in her tale of woe. "After humbling myself for months, letting him slobber all over me, he was going to boot me out on my rear, the bastard."

"But not because his wife found out. I can't see Prescott sacrificing you for the sake of marital bliss."

"You're right. He wasn't that noble. What he didn't want to sacrifice was his future with the company. After Carole came to the office and carried on about me being a home-wrecker and a husband snatcher, Drake got the word from upstairs to clean up his act. That meant dump me. So the day before the reception at Canyon Escondido, he broke the news that I'd be getting a pink slip in my next paycheck. Sweet, huh? First it was 'go to bed with me if you want to keep your job,' then 'people are talking so I have to let you go.' "

"What about transferring you to another department? Wouldn't that have satisfied the top brass and quieted the wagging tongues?"

"Maybe. But when I asked him to have me moved, he refused. I even threatened to expose him if he didn't arrange another job for me, but he just laughed. He knew I wouldn't do anything."

"But you did do something," I said simply. "You killed him."

"It was an accident," she protested, the gun wavering in her hand. "I didn't plan it."

"No, you probably didn't," I agreed. "After Lois confronted him about the memo and named her source of information, he came looking for you, I'd guess. And since you were in the ladies' room, he didn't have to look far."

"Are you kidding? He grabbed me as I came out the door and dragged me down the hall to the testing facility. I thought he was going to smash my face in. Instead, he just slapped me around a little and called me a fucking liar when I said Lois swiped the memo off my desk. He accused me of being too chicken to fight my own battles and using her to get to him. It was true. I did hope Lois would have the guts to take him to court when I didn't. Anyway, I kept apologizing, thinking maybe if I groveled enough, he'd change his mind about keeping me on at the power company. But he said he wasn't only going to fire me, but give me such a bad reference I'd never get a decent job again. I'd have to make a living as a hooker. A hooker," she repeated shrilly. "Then he pushed me away and started laughing, saying my best talent was in the bedroom anyway and with all the variations he taught me, I could make a hell of a living on my back. He'd even give me a recommendation, although the favor would cost me, he smirked. But he'd be willing to take it out in trade. I should crawl across the floor to where he was standing by the transformer and give him a blow job. If I was good, he'd make sure I found work . . . in a cathouse."

April's narration broke down for a moment at this point. I could see the shudder of revulsion that went through her, but she struggled to regain her composure and my sympathy. "He was foul. Disgusting. And he made me feel the same way. When he beckoned me with his finger, leaning casually against the transformer like it was a corner lamp post and I was a streetwalker who wasn't worth the price of a two-dollar room in a sleazy flop house, I couldn't stand it another moment. The blade switch was right by me, with the warning tag almost hanging in my face, practically telling me what to do. I just reached up and pulled. Don't you see? He forced me."

I certainly wasn't going to argue the point. What kept April talking all this time was the need to convince me, or herself, that she'd done the only thing possible. But that was the usual excuse. Not many murderers care to claim total responsibility. Death Row is filled with hapless victims of "He made me do it." The trick here was to forestall April's feeling the same compulsion with me until help came speeding to the rescue. The boys in blue, the Green Berets; I didn't care what color. Anybody. Better still, everybody. And soon. If April didn't get around to shooting me first, I stood a good chance of freezing to death.

"Yes, he did force you," I agreed hurriedly. "He provoked you beyond reason, and there's not a jury in the world that wouldn't understand once you explained."

"I notice you're not promising they'd let me off."

"I can promise a good try. Let me help you, April. With a defense attorney . . ."

"No," she interrupted, as if confession had sufficiently expiated her sins and now she could get back to the business at hand. "I'm not telling a lawyer, a jury, or anyone else. And neither are you. It's too late for that. Just consider this your bedtime story, Ellie, because now it's time to say goodnight."

The chill that ran down my spine had nothing to do with the temperature. Those were the words I'd heard her use with Jason, part of a loving ritual that represented tenderness and warmth. It was the flip side of this ugly coin, because for me April intended no sweet dreams, no waking in the morning light. And like a child who tries to delay the inevitable, but with more hope of changing the outcome, I too pleaded for another five minutes.

"Wait. You haven't finished the story. What about Jessica? How did this trail of persecution and revenge lead to her?" Of course, that was why April said it was too late for courtroom vindication in Prescott's death. A second murder is no character reference for acquittal on the first. "I know you planned something with the receipt, but what? Were you looking to implicate Tom Grabowski just in case Lois wasn't convicted?" Then I realized. "It was for money, wasn't it?"

"What kind of detective are you? Don't you ever stop asking questions?" She sighed impatiently. But then, as if the indulgent mother in her were too much in the habit of granting one more nursery rhyme, one more drink of water, she consented to explain.

"Yes, it was for money. I had no intention of hurting Professor Tobler. Believe me, Ellie, her death was an accident," April said predictably. "Honestly, it's true." Her voice rose in excitement. "You were right about me finding the receipt in Drake's desk," she rushed on, as though verifying that another of my guesses was correct would put me in a more forgiving spirit. "I knew about his scheme with Tom. Drake bragged to me how he sold the idea upstairs, the rewards promised him for putting a lid on ANSWER." She took a steadying breath. "I only meant to cash in on a lucky break. I wouldn't have tried anything with the power company and jeopardized my job, but Drake owed me," was her defiant excuse. "All I did was call Professor Tobler and offer to sell her proof that someone close to her had committed a crime."

"Without saying who or what crime," I clarified, finally understanding why Jess thought she'd be getting information on Prescott's murder. That was the only crime she knew about until seeing the receipt.

"I didn't want to say too much over the phone," April affirmed. "But I was sure she'd be glad to discover Tom Grabowski betrayed ANSWER so she could kick him out or something, then use the payoff as publicity against the power company."

"And she *was* glad, until you started haggling over the asking price."

"No, that's not what happened. She agreed to my terms immediately, and I only wanted enough to make a small dent in the amount I owed Dennis Devlin. But she wouldn't let it rest there. When I went to her house, assuming I'd just hand over the copy of the check and collect the cash, your friend acted like it was some sort of hen party. She invited me to sit down, have a cup of coffee. Then she wanted details. Where did I get the receipt? Who else in the company knew about the deal? When she asked if Lois had been part of the conspiracy, I still didn't realize what a can of worms I'd opened, so I said she was completely innocent, not wanting to get her into any more trouble than she was in already."

"Were you sorry Lois took the blame for Prescott's murder?" I sidetracked.

"Sorry but relieved," April replied honestly. "Except when I defended her to Professor Tobler, being sorry backfired. She wanted me to help clear Lois, use the receipt to show Tom Grabowski was a more logical murder suspect. I should tell the police where I got this evidence. When I said my name had to be kept out of it or I'd lose my job, she gave me a speech on civic duty and upholding justice. Funny, huh? Then she offered me another five hundred dollars to tide me over until I found a new job. It was insane."

No more insane than my standing by an open cliffside on the coldest spring night in history and listening to a murderess spill her guts.

April gestured with the gun. "But I couldn't go to the police, not for all the money in the world. As soon as they sniffed around, asked questions, they'd figure out the same thing you did. So I told Professor Tobler no, but she went to the phone anyway, insisting I was going to do the right thing whether I wanted to or not. I grabbed the receiver away from her while she was dialing, then picked up a bookend from the shelf next to me and threatened to hit her with it if she didn't stop. But I'd already given my hand away. She looked at me and said in an accusing voice, 'What are you trying to hide?' I had no choice," April finished simply.

"That's what you call an accident?"

"Yes. She forced me. I didn't want to kill her."

It was amazing how the stong-willed April had been forced to do so many things. Even more amazing was that she'd willingly chronicled her crimes for me. I'd been prepared to use every ploy in my limited repertoire to pry the whole story from her, and not just for the satisfaction of bringing my investigation to a close. Maybe, just maybe, someone at police headquarters would notice that a certain red light had been blinking forever. I couldn't even guess how many minutes had passed. Ten? Twenty? Either the radio dispatcher had fallen asleep at the switchboard or he was trying to reach me this very instant to inquire what crime I wanted to report and there was nobody at my house to answer the phone. Casting a helpless look at the empty highway, I knew it was up to me to save myself. The marines weren't coming.

As if her diminutive weapon had become too heavy to hold, April grasped it in both hands. "I don't want to talk anymore. Turn around and move to the edge. Quick."

Since I wasn't in the same rush, I shot another arrow at one of her many Achilles' heels. "Why the hurry? So you can race home to Jennifer and Jason? Tell them a fairy tale about where Mommy's been and kiss their innocent faces with your hands still dripping blood?" The language was a bit melodramatic, I admit. But then, the blood was mine.

"Don't you understand? Everything I did was for the children, so I could keep them."

"Yes, you have made quite an investment to retain custody." I watched her closely. "But don't you think they'd be better off with a father, rich or poor, than a mother who's a killer?"

"I'm not a killer." April's fingers tightened on the gun. "Nothing I did was on purpose."

"My apologies. But surely, you'll allow a certain premeditation in my case."

"No." Her voice trembled at denying the truth. "You're making me do this. You shouldn't have interfered."

"Even if I accept full blame, you can't keep covering your tracks by arbitrarily murdering people. Eventually, the trail will lead back to you by the process of elimination. Tonight for instance, you must have a babysitter who'll be able to say you weren't at home. And what about a ballistics report?"

April wrangled with that dilemma for a moment, then announced the perfect solution. "Nobody will connect me with you by tracing the weapon," she said confidently, "because I won't be using the gun after all. You're going to fall off the cliff."

Another accident? April was consistent anyway. And she picked a good time for me to stage my suicide. I could just see Joe bent over my casket in grief that I'd taken a swan dive into the Pacific because of him. "If only I'd sent jewelry instead," he'd mourn, regretting the chocolates. And there would be April next to him, wiping a compulsory tear from her lovely eye and remarking what a pretty corpse I was. Thanks to her ingenuity, my body wouldn't be riddled with unsightly bullet holes. Cheered slightly by the cosmetic value of her methods, I wondered how I could get her to change her mind.

"Start walking." She motioned with the gun. "Over there, to that rock."

The crag she indicated was about a yard square and jutted out over the precipice, which would lead me to a very nasty fall indeed. My heart beating madly with dread at the prospect, I gauged the distance between me and April and the rock and decided to stake the few odds in my favor on the longest of long shots. There was no point in continuing this stroll into oblivion, and even though I was scared out of my mind, I had nothing to lose. Why not gamble on a different kind of plunge?

"Circumstances force me to be cruel, April. But I won't take a flying leap into nowhere just to please you. Not that 'I would fain die a dry death' either. But if you want me dead, you'll have to shoot me."

My obstinacy surprised her, though I couldn't imagine why she expected my cooperation. Taking a step back, she lowered the gun a fraction, then girded herself to move closer and raise the automatic until it was aimed at my heart. Still, she hesitated. "If you make me shoot, I will. Then I'll just drag your body to the edge and throw you and the gun into the sea."

"Personally, I think you should do that." It was difficult to manage a nonchalant shrug, but I managed. "Look at it this way, for the sake of argument. What if I obligingly jump, but miss the water and land on the rocks instead, breaking both my legs?"

"What are you saying?" she asked nervously.

"Only that I hope you're enough of a marksman to put me out of my misery. Of course, you could always climb down the cliff and check on my condition in any case. But face it, April, one way or another you have to be sure I don't live to talk, and it's simpler to remedy that from right here. Why take needless chances?"

Persuading the disinclined April to make me her next victim *tout de suite* was not an Ellie Gordon brand of Freudian psychology or a page out of *I'm Okay, You're Okay*. She had to be guaranteed I was silenced once and for all, and to do so now meant firing at point-blank range. From her potshot before, I could tell April was no Annie Oakley, and I wanted her on this boulder with me where she couldn't possibly miss, because then, neither would I.

As she began inching her way toward me, murmuring all the while about having no choice, I wondered if making her face the inevitability of having to shoot me was a mistake I might not live to regret. The other murders had been spontaneous reactions, the spur of the moment reflex of a woman driven to panicked desperation. This one was a necessary execution. I simply knew too much, and no amount of reluctance on her part was going to prevent April from doing what she believed she must. No doubt she'd feel a stab of remorse when my poor, lifeless body was washed up on a sandy shoal somewhere. Her finger might even falter for an instant before she pulled the trigger. But eventually she'd find solace in the conviction that it was my fault after all. Why had I asked so many questions? Why had I trapped her? Why wouldn't I just walk the plank as she instructed? The way she still was begging me to jump now.

So I did.

Not over the edge, naturally. At her. But struggling for the gun was no mean feat. April topped me by several pounds and twice as many inches. On the other hand, I'd been lifting weights for five months.

Since my adversary had possession of the weapon, I mainly tried to keep it pointed away from me. Our battle was curiously silent, aside from grunts and puffs, but we seemed to be evenly matched. Then I wrapped a leg around her shin and pulled us both to the ground. She rolled on top of me but couldn't free her right hand from my desperate grip. I slammed her clenched fist against the hard surface, and with a gasp of pain she let go of the gun.

In relief that my opponent was no longer armed, I relaxed for a foolish instant, and in that instant she had me pinned, her hands on my wrists and her knee pressed agonizingly into my stomach. April's knit cap had come off during our scuffle. The rising wind was now blowing her long, dark hair back from a face that held all the wild beauty of a murderous Medusa. And I was locked in mortal combat with this creature, only three feet from a drop to certain death.

My only hope was to keep clawing at her face and somehow make her get that knee out of my belly. But when she did rear back to escape my gouging fingers, she clung to my arm and began pulling me toward the edge. I dug in my heels, resisting that terrifying progression with every ounce of strength in my body. The idiot! Didn't she realize by dragging me, she was backing into nothingness herself? We'd both go tumbling into space. But April had already gone off the deep end.

Then I heard a shout. "Ellie, hold on. I'm coming."

It was Joe. Not the police. Not the marines. Joe, probably with a bottle of wine tucked under his arm and a reproof on the tip of his tongue that once again I was somewhere I shouldn't be.

So how good was the D.A. at fighting crime outside the courtroom? Because if he didn't get over here instantaneously and peel this madwoman off me, the case would never make it to trial. Staring into April's crazed eyes, I realized that even if she saw Joe scrambling over the rocks toward us, she wasn't about to abandon the struggle. Still, old habits die hard, and I attacked with one last burst of verbosity.

"April, it's all over. Stop."

I really don't think she heard me. She was grim, oblivious, intent on throwing me over the brink. One of my legs was already dangling in thin air. Then I saw the girder. It was just behind me and to the right. Somehow I pulled a hand free and wrapped my arm around the comforting cold steel.

With a howl of rage, April tugged madly on my other arm, but the damp, clammy air had affected her too. Her icy fingers slid over my wrists, and she lost her grip and her footing at the same time. Trying to regain her balance, she took a fateful step to the edge and slipped on the uneven rock. Then, with a look of total surprise on her face, she tumbled very slowly backward off the cliff.

Her scream seemed to go on forever.

Chapter Thirty

It was an accident. That's what Joe said. Matt Steunkle agreed. Lieutenant Peters echoed that expert opinion too. In fact, the official verdict was death by misadventure. April's tragic demise occurred exactly as she would have wished. It wasn't her fault.

However, and simply for the sake of accuracy, it wasn't mine either. Not that a murderer getting her just desserts wasn't an appropriate ending, but I had just been trying to save my own neck. April put hers on the line without any encouragement from me. Quite the opposite. I used every weapon in my well-worn repertoire before abandoning the spoken word. But once again, a well-turned phrase, a timely quote, an apt self-deprecating witticism had done me no good at all. I had a feeling it wouldn't, but I certainly didn't expect to save myself with brawn rather than brain. In fact, what ran through my mind as I tackled April head-on was the absurd irony that I'd been the last one on my block to make friends with a Nautilus machine. Who ever thought it would become such a meaningful relationship? Sharpening my rapier wit to a fine-honed edge had always been my favorite form of exercise. Nevertheless, this 106-pound weakling with too liberal an arts education came through with flying colors. An Amazon I wasn't, but at least my muscles were more coordinated than the Crimewatchers organization.

Their switchboard operator got my SOS all right. She even sent out a patrol car. But when Officer Jensen rang my doorbell and no one answered, he assumed that since I was a novice beeper keeper, I had used the pager from another location and forgotten to tell them.

It was the D.A. who corrected that nearly fatal error. Responding to my come-hither message with commendable speed, Joe was in his car with the two-way radio on when he heard the dispatcher cancel the call from Vista del Mar. When he asked why and got the news I wasn't at home, Joe didn't believe I'd send for him and then disappear of my own free will. Remembering that my recorded *billet doux* hinted at two revelations, Joe had a fairly good idea a strip tease wasn't all I had in mind and suspected immediately that the trouble I reported was my own.

The troops arrived only moments after Joe did, but by the time they were scaling the cliffs, swarming across the beach and lighting up the whole place with their flares and their presence, I was back at home, shaken but unscathed. Predictably, my gallant kept a stalwart arm around me during the walk to the house, but once there, he couldn't decide whether or not to be happy I survived the ordeal or furious that I put myself in danger to begin with. Giving in to both emotions, he ordered me to sit on the couch while he went to put up the kettle, as if this were a crisis that called for boiling water. Since I wasn't about to deliver a baby, nor did I want to soothe his brow with a hot compress, I reached over to the coffee table and poured myself a restorative glass of wine. It worked like knockout drops.

But he was making tea, Joe informed me. Chinese tea laced with extra sugar was the best remedy for shock.

Ungrateful to the end, I told him to give the ginseng

with ginger root to the policemen when they finished their grisly tasks. I was going to bed.

That really annoyed the D.A. It would be a professional courtesy if I explained to them why in hell I'd been rolling around on the edge of a cliff with a madwoman.

"Professional, huh?" But I didn't have the energy to call his attention to the Freudian slip. "Then how about if you explain. I'll fill in the blanks tomorrow after I've had some sleep."

"What about the tea?" he persisted.

"No problem," I yawned. "You pour. My hostess gown is ruined anyway."

I did do one other thing before crawling under the covers and that was dial Tom Grabowski. When he answered groggily on the third ring, my message was curt and to the point. "Our deal's off. I found a better buyer." Then I hung up. At least he wouldn't be here at nine to wake me was my last coherent thought before pulling the pillow over my head.

Ten hours later, when I finally opened my eyes again, Tom was not waiting on the doorstep, thanks to my foresight. The only thing greeting me was a note on the night stand from Joe, saying Matt Steunkle wanted to see me down at the police station as soon as possible. Groaning first at that prospect, then at my poor, abused body, I tottered into the bathroom for a long, hot shower. But its effects were minimal. Though I dried my bruises gingerly, the purple patches that spotted my behind ached no less, and I still lacked a clear, synopsis for the police chief on how my anatomy became so imprinted.

Of course, I could tell him the truth about why I was only now suffering the pains of discovery. Merely because earlier in my investigation, after correctly figuring a love triangle as the murder motive, I never checked any further than Carole Prescott's corner of it. My lame excuse was a real geometric cop-out too: I simply went off on a tangent, calculating other sines and cosines that weren't even listed in the diagram. Lois made an especially diverting equation, arriving at Jessica's just in time to look guilty. Even when I recomputed Tom as the integral factor, I left out the lipstick-smeared coffee cup, knowing full well he never wore fire-engine red. But neither did Lois blithely walk into Jess's house, find a dead body on the floor, then calmly sit down for a pause that refreshes before collapsing from shock. I forgot to include whoever brought the receipt, Jessica's purveyor of incriminating information. And if I had remembered? Would I have considered April? Silly question. The only time I had ever thought of her was to wonder what she saw in a worm like Drake Prescott. After all, they were in the throes of a grand passion, an authentic case of true lust. Never mind that Jane Chestnut whispered he was the company cad; ignore that his wife complained he chased everything in skirts. If April went to bed with such a nogoodnik, obviously she couldn't keep her hands off him.

By her lights, naturally, she couldn't. Afraid of losing her job and in consequence, her children, April chose the passive-aggressive approach for dealing with her boss. First she took his sexual harassment lying down, then she rolled over and made him play dead. Understanding the psychological dynamics of her dilemma, I almost felt sorry for her. But not quite. Though Drake Prescott had used his secretary in the basest manner, not even mother-love excused April's final solution. Not with Jessica. Not with me. Again fear drove her, but there was no reason to make us pay the price for her mistakes when all she had to do was the right thing in the first place.

After getting dressed with far less attention to detail than when I had when getting glamorious the previous night, I drove downtown where Matt and Lieutenant Peters met me in the chief's office. Definitely touchy from the wounds inflicted by self-reproach, I was relieved when they didn't demand to know why I had delayed so long in solving the murders. Instead the two were quite compli-

mentary. Peters was most interested in getting the statement I hadn't made the night before, a summary of April's
confession and her attempt on my life. Matt, just as I
guessed, wanted me to explain how I got so close to the
killer that she felt compelled to throw me over a cliff.

Even though Joe had given the police a sketchy report
after I went to bed, my tale of derring-do elicited some
"oohs" and "ahs" of surprise. Having the D.A. as an
unimpeachable witness to my narrow escape was no small
advantage. Not that Matt Steunkle wouldn't have believed
me anyway, but getting the charges against Lois dropped
was now a mere matter of paperwork. The prosecution no
longer had a case and admitted it.

But before I could gloat in victory, there was my share
of the paperwork to finish. It took time to read through my
statement, make a few minor corrections, then sign several
copies of it. Afterward, Matt shooed Peters out of his
office, then closed the door and told me to relax.

"With you ready to give me the third degree, I should
relax? Besides, I have to get to work."

"You got time," he said, sinking into his chair and
clasping his hands in front of his potbelly. "I called in sick
for you."

"Thanks. Did you also tell Helen her client was going to
be cleared?"

"Yep. I said you were taking care of it right now."

"Me?"

"You deserve the credit. Why not?"

"Why not give me the Medal of Honor while you're at
it?" I said sarcastically.

"Whatsamatter?" Matt squinted at me. "Mad because
you let the killer trap you?"

"Among other things. But mainly because of the way I
backed into the truth. I set out to prove a conspiracy
against ANSWER and almost outsmarted myself."

"Hold on, Ellie. Maybe you led with your behind, but
you came out on top. We didn't even get close to the

middle, but you don't see me kicking myself in the pants."
When I shrugged in semiacknowledgment, he seemed satisfied. "So tell me where we went wrong."

Since he hadn't done so well himself, I didn't feel bad
about confessing how I had stumbled from pillar to post
and back to pillar again. The chief listened with flattering
attention and was especially curious about the issue raised
during the hearing and never researched any further.

"Everybody was so right, and yet so wrong," I wrapped
it up. "The prosecution exposed Prescott's habit of putting
women down, no doubt from some deep-seated and
deserved inferiority complex, but no one translated that
into larger terms. His general all-round nastiness seemed
proof Lois would want to kill him. It became an argument
to strengthen her motive rather than point out that someone else probably had one as well."

"And the clue that led to April was the money order you
wanted me to find for you." Matt scratched his head.
"Sorry, cashier's check. So where's the receipt now?"

"With your on-the-scene investigator, I suppose. April
had it in her shirt pocket."

"Now you got your conspiracy case proved too," the
chief complimented.

"*Your* case," I advised him, "unless it goes to the state's
attorney or a federal investigation."

"That's a lot of people asking a lot of questions."

"I should hope so. PSSC has a lot to answer for."

"So does Ellie Gordon."

"I beg your pardon?"

"The receipt. Didn't Mark Devlin ever tell you it's
illegal to remove anything from the scene of a crime?
After the McCoin woman gave it to you, I should have
been next in line. I thought I could trust you, Nancy Drew.
You were supposed to keep me posted."

Damn. I knew the matter of the pilfered evidence would
come up sooner or later. How did the conquering heroine
squeeze out of this tight spot?

"Oh, dear. Did I break the law?" I asked guilelessly.

"The state's attorney and the Feds might think so."

Great. Just what I needed. A six-month vacation in Altoona. "Could I plead forgetfulness?"

"Like me forgetting to mention it, you mean?"

Now I saw the reassuring hint of amusement in his eye. "Matt Steunkle, for a minute there I thought you were going to bring me up on charges." Than I looked again. "You are teasing, aren't you?"

"Hey, didn't I keep you out of jail once already? What do you think, I'm gonna turn you in now?" He grinned. "I should put you on the force instead."

My step was light as I left police headquarters. And why not? Hadn't the chief praised my efforts, bent the rules in deference to my ultimate success, and cheerfully admitted I'd beaten the pros at their own game, if just by the hair of my chinny chin chin?

There was only one person happier about the end results of my diligence—Lois McCoin. When I arrived at the office amid a fanfare of congratulations and a dozen eager questions all flying at me, she was on the phone with Helen. After Kimberly plugged in my extension so we could have a three-way conversation, Lois's first words to me were a joyous, "Pack you bags, Ellie Gordon. I'm sending you on an all-expense-paid trip to the Caribbean." When I reminded her that I'd been working gratis, she wouldn't hear of not rewarding me in some way. I said a new pair of white pants would be more than sufficient recompense.

Later, Helen informed me that my skeptical quip about where Lois had gone the night before was right on the button. Officer Tillborough did indeed offer to drive her home, and they stopped for dinner on the way, though he'd taken her to somewhere a little ritzier than Burger King. Apparently, a more interesting attachment than guard and guardee had developed in the past week, and now neither one of them wanted to let the other out of sight, Helen said with a matchmaking smirk.

There were a few other odds and ends to be taken care of, but Joe handled the most important. He had contacted Max Evans, and the children were now safe in the custody of their father without the necessity of another hearing either in civil or criminal court. April's innocent family might have to face a few screaming headlines at the moment, but they would be spared the agony of a public trial.

Of course, another matter was not going to be closed so quietly, but my plans for Tom Grabowski were now in the D.A.'s domain. After I provided him with all the particulars, he could build an airtight case against PSSC, and for a change, have my fullest cooperation in a prosecution. I'd be happy to testify, I told Joe Thursday evening.

"It's nice of you to offer, Ellie, but I don't think your recording makes a case."

"Not by itself. But what about with the receipt?"

"Oh, didn't Matt tell you? They couldn't find it. It must have fallen out of April's pocket at some point last night."

We were sitting in my living room. I had just finished playing Tom's confession and was placidly waiting for the D.A. to impound the tape as material evidence when he just as placidly informed me the receipt had been lost.

"How could you be so careless?" I ranted at him. "Why haven't you had people out scouring the cliffside, searching the beach?"

"Because it would be a waste of time," was his tranquil answer.

"Talk about waste," I spluttered. "I let myself be halfway strangled so you could have corroboration, and now there's nothing to corroborate."

"Calm down, Ellie. You solved two murders. Don't get excited because you can't prove a conspiracy too."

"I proved it all right—on Memorex."

"No. All you've got here is a guy confessing to accepting money for lobbying in the power company's interest."

"You call that lobbying?" I almost choked on the word.

"That's what it's called in Sacramento when the state legislature is in session."

"Don't play semantics with me," I warned. "What about PSSC? Aren't they guilty of misusing funds?"

"Not necessarily. If they claim the expense went for advertising, it's perfectly legitimate."

"Then there's no crime here at all?" I asked in disbelief.

"Maybe, if Prescott really had held onto company funds for six weeks and put it in his own account to collect the interest."

"That's not fair."

"I know, but since they guy's dead, what can I do about it?"

When I didn't laugh, Joe conceded that if he'd known about the secret arrangement between Grabowski and Prescott, he would have checked into it for a possible murder motive. But whatever monkey business the two men had been up to was not a criminal offense.

Maybe not in the eyes of the law, I thought resentfully, but there were other forms of justice, higher forms. And with Ellie Gordon's brand of divine retribution, Tom would pay for his sins at the supreme level. As of this moment, my tape was the property of ANSWER, and I'd deliver it to Vickie first thing tomorrow.

"Come on, Ellie." Joe got up and pulled me to my feet. "I brought something to make you feel better."

"A crying towel?"

"For a winner, you sure are trying to sound like an also-ran. Cheer up, my pet. I'm going to feed you."

"Not now," I resisted. "Joe, I'm not hungry."

Naturally my Italian chef wouldn't take no for an answer. I expected as much when he came into the house carrying two bags of groceries. But as Joe announced with a flourish, the finest way he knew to applaud my success was to honor me with a banquet. Yes, the D.A. had recanted, reneged, and recalled every unflattering thing he'd said about my sleuthing abilities. But once again, he had gone to extremes. Now I had the analytical prowess of Nero Wolfe and the psychological insight of Miss Jane Marple. All I wanted was credit for possessing a bit of perception, albeit more than the average Crimewatcher. I did not require Joe to tell Matt Steunkle I was a daredevil who only signaled the police to be polite.

"Why do you always exaggerate everything?" I carped.

This second stage of our reconciliation took place as Joe hovered over the stove with one of my aprons tied around his waist, while I sat at the table and counted the calories he was cooking up.

"Me exaggerate?" He brandished the spatula. "You're the one who did all the cloak-and-dagger sleuthing. Unnecessarily, might I add. If you'd told me what you were doing instead of hiding everything until the curtain almost came down on your head, I could have helped."

"How, by getting a restraining order to keep me out of your case? First of all, you were the competition. And secondly, you didn't approve of what little you knew about."

"Then you admit I knew too little." He turned over a slice of browned eggplant, then tasted the sauce. "It needs more garlic."

"Under the circumstances, no."

"No more garlic?"

"Will you put that down and listen to me. I'm saying your attitude didn't invite confidences. If I even hinted at doing any kind of detective work, you were ready to order a bodyguard for me. Please"—I waved away his explanation—"I realize you're only thinking of me. I know you're not insulting my intelligence. But Joe, you can't wrap me in cotton wool. Sometimes, I can honest to goodness, really and truly take care of myself. You don't have to be my guardian angel."

"Don't give me that, Ellie. You get yourself in impossible situations. All I'm saying is that the next time you're at a loss on how to confront a murderer, call me before trying it on the edge of a cliff."

"I left a message on your answering machine."

"Damn it, Ellie." He reached for the garlic again and shook the jar over the saucepan at random. "You were almost killed right in front of my eyes last night; and while you may have enjoyed the experience, I would prefer it not be repeated."

"How can I promise you anything like that?"

"By saying the words," he snapped.

"Put down that garlic," I pointed at him. "And I will not make you empty promises merely to put your mind at ease."

"I see. You're going to keep that Crimewatcher's beeper turned on twenty-four hours a day as a Geiger counter. Wherever there's trouble brewing, Ellie Gordon will come to the rescue."

"I knew it! I knew you'd throw that up at me. And he wonders why I hide things from him. You're impossible, Joe. You worry about what happened, what almost happened, what could have happened, what might happen, and what will never happen."

"Meaning you'll never hotfoot after another criminal again?"

"How the hell do I know what I'll do in the future? The only thing I'm sure of is that training you to turn over a new leaf ranks right in there with climbing up Mt. Everest backward and blindfolded."

"Why do I have to turn over a new leaf?" he argued. "Why can't you accept the fact that I care about you enough to show some concern for your well-being?"

"Because if you really cared"—I jumped up and turned off all four burners—"you'd quit trying to make me too fat to hotfoot after anybody. Joe, it's nine o'clock at night, and what you call a little snack is eggplant Parmigiana with pasta and an entire loaf of bread on the side."

"I thought you liked Italian food."

"I love it! But this is a meal fit for anorexics. Look at me." I pointed to my hips. "Are those the dimensions of a person wasting away to nothing?"

"It's what you're wearing," he shrugged. "Nobody looks thin in a flowing robe."

"Oh, really? When was the last time you saw an obese ghost? I've gained four pounds since we met, Joe. That may not sound like much to you, but it's 'the baby figure of the giant mass of things to come.' "

The D.A. put down his spatula and wrapped his arms around me. "There, there," he soothed.

"Why are you hugging me?" I mumbled into the depths of his chest. "I just quoted Shakespeare."

"If you forgive me, I forgive you." He kissed the top of my head.

Not budging from his embrace, I debated the wisdom of his easy two-way pardon. "We really are incompatible, you know."

"Oh dear. And I thought we matched like the Bobbsey twins." He rubbed his hands along my back.

"What if I tell you I never want to go sailing again?"

"I'd say it was a wise decision."

"You would?" I began to feel hopeful. "But what would you say if I confessed to hating Wagner?"

"Not that too?"

I nodded. "The cry of the Valkyrie sets my teeth on edge."

"We'll switch to Puccini," he murmured, nibbling on my ear.

"Joe," I gave him one last chance to back out, "you realize we have almost nothing in common."

"Oh, yes, we do." He untied the neck string of my robe.

"But that's just sex," I protested, remaining helpfully pliant as he slipped the silk off my shoulders.

"A definite sharing experience," he insisted.

Overcome by the strength of his logic, I wrapped my arms around his neck as he lifted me off my feet. "What about the eggplant Parmigiana?"

"You wouldn't like it. I put in too much garlic."

116